Heart of the Wilderness

Books by Janette Oke

Another Homecoming*
Janette Oke's Reflections on the Christmas Story
Nana's Gift
The Red Geranium
Return to Harmony*

SEASONS OF THE HEART

Once Upon a Summer	*Winter Is Not Forever*
The Winds of Autumn	*Spring's Gentle Promise*

LOVE COMES SOFTLY

Love Comes Softly	*Love's Unending Legacy*
Love's Enduring Promise	*Love's Unfolding Dream*
Love's Long Journey	*Love Takes Wing*
Love's Abiding Joy	*Love Finds a Home*

A PRAIRIE LEGACY

The Tender Years

CANADIAN WEST

When Calls the Heart	*When Breaks the Dawn*
When Comes the Spring	*When Hope Springs New*

WOMEN OF THE WEST

The Calling of Emily Evans	*A Bride for Donnigan*
Julia's Last Hope	*Heart of the Wilderness*
Roses for Mama	*Too Long a Stranger*
A Woman Named Damaris	*The Bluebird and the Sparrow*
They Called Her Mrs. Doc	*A Gown of Spanish Lace*
The Measure of a Heart	*Drums of Change*

DEVOTIONALS

The Father Who Calls	*Father of My Heart*
The Father of Love	*Faithful Father*

———

Janette Oke: A Heart for the Prairie
Biography of Janette Oke by Laurel Oke Logan

The Oke Family Cookbook
by Barbara Oke and Deborah Oke

*with T. Davis Bunn

JANETTE OKE

HEART OF THE WILDERNESS

BETHANY HOUSE PUBLISHERS
MINNEAPOLIS, MINNESOTA 55438

Heart of the Wilderness
Copyright © 1993
Janette Oke
Cover by Dan Thornberg,
Bethany House Publishers staff artist.

Published by Bethany House Publishers
A ministry of Bethany Fellowship, Inc.
11300 Hampshire Avenue South
Minneapolis, Minnesota 55438

Printed in the United States of America

Library of Congress Catalog Number 93–5338
ISBN 1–55661–362–8 (Trade Paper Edition)
ISBN 1–55661–363–6 (Large Print)
ISBN 0–7642–2016–0 (Mass Market Edition)

To those I lean on
throughout the writing process—

Mrs. Katherine Hamm,
who never ceases to assure me
that she is praying for me

Bethany House Publishers' Staff,
who gently prod me
through each new endeavor

My family members,
who understand and encourage
And especially Edward,
my constant supporter,
companion and friend.

JANETTE OKE was born in Champion, Alberta, during the depression years, to a Canadian prairie farmer and his wife. She is a graduate of Mountain View Bible College in Didsbury, Alberta, where she met her husband, Edward. They were married in May of 1957, and went on to pastor churches in Indiana as well as Calgary and Edmonton, Canada.

The Okes have three sons and one daughter and are enjoying the addition of grandchildren to the family. Edward and Janette have both been active in their local church, serving in various capacities as Sunday school teachers and board members. They make their home near Calgary, Alberta.

Contents

Chapter One

For Love of Family

"Where is she?" The question seemed to pull from the depths of his anguished soul.

The gray-haired woman opening her door to admit the tall, dark-bearded man standing on her step felt tears form beneath her eyelids.

"Come in, George," she said softly, waving her hand at the simple room behind her. "You look worn out."

She sensed his deep impatience and feared for a moment that he would refuse. Then with a sigh, he nodded his head and moved past her into the room.

She closed the door, stopping first to look out on the busy street already bustling with the activities of another day. The world seemed to be going on as usual—yet she knew things would never be the same again for the man who had just come.

She turned to him. She had known him for many years. Had seen him suffer before. Yet she had never seen the strong, manly face so tightly drawn, the broad shoulders so slumped, the clear, dark eyes so filled with pain. Today he who had never shown his years looked much older than the fifty she knew him to be.

He was slumped in a chair across the room from her. Head lowered, he brushed at his beard with a large calloused hand, a habit she recognized. He always brushed at his beard when he was anxious or agitated.

"She's fine." She answered his question as she moved toward him. "She's in that little Home on Park Street."

His head came up, his eyes darkened. Was he angry? With her?

"I tried to get them to let me keep her here, but they wouldn't allow it. Said that with things like—like they are here—and such . . ." She paused, shrugged, then hurried on when she saw his eyes burning intensely, though not with accusation. "They said they could do nothing until—until they had been in touch with kin. I—I got word to you in the quickest way I knew. Isn't a very good way of communicating—"

"How long has it been?" he cut in.

She stopped for a minute and did some mental calculation. "Almost three weeks since—"

"Three weeks? Terribly long time—for a child."

She nodded at the grief and anger and frustration in his voice, feeling his pain.

He stood suddenly, his dark eyes shadowing more deeply. "I've got to get on over there, Maggie," he said brusquely.

"You look worn out," she hastened to repeat, wanting to keep him from doing anything rash. "You'd better take the time to eat some breakfast—rest a bit. They won't open for another couple of hours anyway."

She was afraid she had lost the argument as he took a step toward the door. Then his hand came up and he began to rub his beard in agitation. At last he retreated and slumped back into the chair and nodded his head solemnly.

"I've traveled day and night since I got your message," he admitted. "I must look a sight."

"Well, I will admit if I hadn't known you, I may not have opened my door." The words were spoken lightly. He managed a bit of a smile.

"You clean up and I'll get us some breakfast," she went on. "Henry will be stirring soon and—"

He lifted his head and looked at her, apology replacing the grief and anger in his eyes. "How is Henry?" he asked simply.

The woman shrugged. There was really very little to say. Henry hadn't changed over the months. The days came and went with little difference in his condition. He seemed to get no better—perhaps a little worse, but it was hard to tell.

"About the same—I guess," she said, her shoulders sagging.

"Can I see him?" the man asked softly.

She nodded toward the small room off the sitting area. "Go ahead. He's likely still sleeping. He doesn't usually wake for another half hour or so. Sometimes he wakens earlier—or during the night. But—but if he is awake, you won't know much difference. He may not respond. He—" She stopped, knowing the man needed no explanation about Henry. He paid a visit to the sickroom whenever he was in the city.

They had been good friends for years. Both big strong men who knew what it was to put in a good day of hard, back-breaking labor. As a younger man, Henry had been George's yardstick, as he had been for most of the community where they'd been raised. Anyone who could keep up to Henry was considered to be a good worker and worthy of his hire. And now Henry lay on the same bed that had taken him to its bosom four years earlier. He could not even lift a hand to feed himself or brush the annoying tears from his eyes. Since the accident in the lumber mill, Henry had been paralyzed—totally paralyzed—and Maggie had to do for the big man all those things he had at one time done for himself.

The visitor moved toward the door, his body showing his dread at seeing again his lifelong friend in such a crippled state.

But Henry was still sleeping. George stood for some moments watching the rise and fall of his friend's shallow breathing. Henry had lost even more weight since the last visit. Gaunt and pale, he looked so wasted that George barely recognized him as the same man who had won the log-sawing contest nine years running.

George crossed to the foot of the bed and spoke softly to the unhearing man who slept restlessly. "I'm here, Henry. Been a long time. Should have come oftener—I know that. But I've been so busy—" He stopped. Would Henry want to hear of his busyness? Henry who couldn't even move.

He shut his mouth on the whispered words and studied the thin, useless right hand that lay pale and helpless on the coverlet. The callouses were gone now. The warm, deep tan from the summer sun had long paled. George stepped forward and took the thin hand in his own. The scar was still there. More visible than ever against the tissue-like skin.

In spite of his resistance to tears, George felt them gather now. Were the tears for Henry? For himself? He didn't know. He only knew that suddenly his world seemed filled with so much pain.

Pain he tried desperately to keep within himself.

He looked back again at the hand he held. That hand had been scarred on his behalf. He remembered the day well. Henry had risked his life to save him. And now Henry lay withering away on his bed, and there wasn't one thing George could do about it.

He placed the hand gently back on the patchwork coverlet and quietly left the room.

❧   ❧   ❧

"What do you plan to do?" Maggie asked the question as they lingered over another cup of breakfast coffee.

The sigh seemed to begin somewhere deep inside him and gradually make its way through his whole being, ending with a little shudder.

What did he plan to do? The words echoed in the air between them.

"I must see her—as quickly as possible," he answered Maggie, but both of them knew that his words did not really address the question.

Maggie nodded and waited for him to go on.

He shook his head, his eyes looking deep and troubled. His left hand stole to his beard again.

"It's so—so—so unfair," he almost spit out. "For a child's father and mother to be taken and—and leave her—alone."

Maggie nodded again.

His head jerked up and his eyes filled with anger as he turned to her. "What were they thinking of, Maggie," he demanded, "to leave a child and go off on some—some helter-skelter expedition into the wilds? Had they no—no thought of—?"

Maggie reached out and placed her hand gently on his trembling one. "Now," she said softly, "you know better than to think like that. After all, you're the one who taught Mary to love those wilds. They'd made trips like that over and over in the past and nothing had happened. It was an unexpected accident, George. An unexpected and unexplained accident. Nothing more. It—it does happen. It doesn't mean that they were uncaring or—or irresponsible parents. They loved her. Did everything for her."

"But—but—*both* of them. Why both of them? The two of them could swim. Why both of them? And why—why take on rapids that they couldn't handle? Mary knew—they both knew the danger of—"

He had to vent his feelings. He had been burying them deep inside ever since he had gotten Maggie's message. He had to let those feelings out. And who better than Maggie to share his pain—his confusion.

"The Mountie said there was a snag under the water," Maggie explained softly. "A broken tree—with a jagged break. The canoe caught it and spun out of control. When they went in—well—they figure he swam to shore. He made it. His heavy boots were found there—on the bank—together. He must have placed them there. But—Mary. I know she was a good swimmer. But for some reason—she got into trouble. Maybe got a bump as they were thrown out. Guess we'll never know.

"But he went back for her." She stopped and sighed. "We'll never know," she said again. "They went down together. Found their bodies downstream from the rapids. He was still holding her.

Still had shreds of her clothing clutched in his fingers."

Hearing the story of the death of his daughter—his only daughter—and his son-in-law filled him with such pain and sorrow that some of the anger was pushed from his heart. There was simply no room for him to hold all the feelings. No room. He felt as if his heart would burst with pain. He wanted to bury his head on his arms and sob until the hurt went away, but he knew it was not that easy. It would be a long, long time until his heart began to mend and memories of his precious Mary would bring pleasure—not sorrow.

Maggie wiped at the tears that ran down her cheeks. George wished he were free to express his grief as easily. He swallowed, hiding his eyes, brushing with an angry hand at the beard that shadowed his face.

"Where are they buried?" he managed to ask, his voice shaky with emotion.

"Beside their cabin—just at the base of the stand of spruce to the west."

He nodded. It was the place he felt Mary would have chosen.

He stood up quickly, two conflicting desires drawing him. He longed to visit the grave of his daughter. The grave of the young man she had learned to love. The man who had given his own life in his unsuccessful effort to save her. Stu Marty. The man George felt he had hardly known—and now would never really know, though he had longed to claim the young man for the son he'd never had. But the miles—the miles had kept them apart. He could not leave his own wilderness—nor could he ask them to share it with him.

And he also wanted to rush to his little grandchild. Little Kendra—now an orphan. His daughter Mary's only child. The child he had not seen since she was little more than a baby. How he chided himself for his error. How he wished that he had taken the long journey, visited his daughter, her husband, her baby girl, more frequently. But there was no going back. No reclaiming of the years that had slipped by so quickly.

"I need to go," he said to Maggie. "I need to—" He stopped and licked his lips. He still had not answered her deeper question.

"Sit," she said, nodding her head toward his vacated chair. Only Maggie would have dared to address the big man in that fashion.

He sat down. Silently. Dutifully.

Maggie waited until she sensed he was ready for her to speak.

"Have you made any plans?" she asked again, softly.

He shook his head, his left hand working vigorously on his beard.

"Shouldn't you?" she persisted after a pause.

"I—I don't know. I—I don't know what to do—how to plan. I'll need to work it through. Figure it out."

Maggie nodded, her expression telling him she knew it was hard to make plans. Hard for a man to be able to think when he had traveled so many miles in such a short time. To know how to properly respond to the present situation.

"Where was she when—?" he began, and Maggie guessed his question.

"They had left her with one of Mary's friends. A neighbor. I—I think she might have wanted to keep her, but she is expecting her first baby. Had to come to the city for delivery."

He nodded.

"She may be willing to take her . . . after," Maggie went on.

He brooded over her words. It seemed so—so difficult to think of trying to arrange for his grandchild. To "place" her. To farm her out. Just as though—as though she were some—some animal that needed care. He shook his head.

"You know I would have taken her—would still take her," went on Maggie softly. "But—but Henry—he needs so much care." She hesitated, studying her thin hands as she rubbed them together in helpless agitation. "I—I really don't think that—that this house is—is the right place for a child to grow up," she finished lamely. "You understand?"

She sounded so remorseful. So filled with shame that she couldn't reach out to her friend in time of need. Her words wounded him. It was his turn to reach for her. He took her two hands in one of his own and gently squeezed in understanding. His tears did fall then. Full and unrestrained tears that made soft damp trails down the weathered cheeks and hid quickly in the heavy, dark beard.

"My dear Maggie," he said huskily. "I know that you'd help me if you could. I know that you loved Mary almost as much as I did. As Polly did. You couldn't take the child in—with Henry needing you like he does. I don't know—I'll never know—how you manage to keep going day after day with all the care he needs. I—I—should have been here to help you. To—"

"Nonsense," said Maggie stirring restlessly in

her chair. "I haven't minded the caring for Henry."

She withdrew her hands and blew her nose noisily on a sturdy cotton hankie.

He wiped away his own tears and fought to get himself under control again.

"You still haven't—" began Maggie.

"I'll just have to find a good home—I don't know how—or where. I won't leave her where she is, I know that. I couldn't. Not in a Home."

"They do give them good care," put in Maggie softly. "Mrs. Weatherall is a good woman."

He nodded, glad to hear the words and at the same time rejecting what they implied.

"I can't leave her in a Home. She needs family. A sense of belonging to—someone. It's important to a child."

She nodded her understanding.

"She won't know me," he went on almost absently. "It's been almost two years since I've seen her. She was just a toddler. She won't even know me—her own grandfather."

Maggie said nothing.

"Do you think the beard will frighten her?" he asked, sudden alarm in his voice. Before Maggie could answer, he spoke again. "Perhaps I should shave it off."

"She wouldn't be frightened of a beard," put in Maggie. "There are bearded men all around. Her own papa had one. Not dark and bushy like yours— but a beard nonetheless."

He looked relieved. Then he stirred restlessly, dreading what lay ahead. Seeing little Kendra in the charge of the matron at the Home would be such a final recognition that his Mary was really gone.

Maggie placed a hand on his sleeve, willing him

some of her strength for the ordeal. "Come back," she said, compassion coloring her words. "Come back—whenever—Stay with us for a few days. As many days as you like."

He nodded his head and reached for his coat and hat. The mornings were still chilly in spite of the fact that they were moving into spring.

"I'll be back," he said. "Tell Henry. I'll be back."

He moved through the door and closed it softly behind him. Then he lifted his shoulders and braced himself for what lay before him. He was facing one of the most difficult days he had experienced in all his life.

Chapter Two

Belonging

"I understand you have my granddaughter," he said to the prim young lady who sat behind the wooden desk in the little room that served as reception area and business office.

Her expression did not change. She still wore the smile with which she had greeted him.

"You will want to speak to Matron," she said, the smile tilting her full lips. He did wish she would wipe the silly look from her face. This was not a lighthearted matter.

"Matron?" he repeated.

"Mrs. Weatherall."

"Mrs. Weatherall?"

"Yes. You will need to speak with her. She answers all inquiries concerning our wards."

He nodded and waited, expecting her to summon the Mrs. Weatherall referred to. She sat where she was, still smiling.

He shifted his weight to his other foot, twisted his hat in his big hands, then lifted the left hand to rub at his beard.

"Mrs. Weatherall?" he repeated.

"Yes," said the smiling young lady.

"Does she come to me—or do I go find her?" he asked impatiently.

"Oh—she'll come. When summoned."

"Then summon her," he ordered, a bit too gruffly. Too impatiently.

"Yes, sir," she responded, and for the first time he saw the smile slip. She quickly regained her composure and returned the smile to its rightful place, rose from her desk, gave him a brief nod and an even bigger smile, and left the room.

He paced the small space. Two steps to the window, three back to the door, three to the window, and back again to the door.

A tall, full-figured woman with a kind face entered the room followed by the still-smiling younger woman. *The Matron,* he thought, and felt that she indeed looked the part. She moved directly to him and reached out a hand. For such a small one, he was surprised at the strength in the clasp.

"Won't you come into my office," the woman invited, and nodded her head toward the door that she had just entered. Without a word he followed her.

She indicated a chair and he took it while she proceeded around her desk and sat down facing him. There was no smile pasted on her lips. He thought he read compassion in her eyes.

"Miss Wilson says that you have a grandchild with us." Her voice was full, yet soft with feeling.

He nodded his head, finding it hard to come up with words. She waited, seeming to know that he was fighting hard for control.

"A—a granddaughter," he managed at last. "A little girl."

He didn't stop to think that his few words were redundant.

She nodded patiently, waiting for him to go on.

"They called her—" For one moment he choked, thoughts of his Mary flooding over him. Mary with her head bent over a new baby girl. Mary with laughter in her voice and love in her eyes. Mary, his little girl, as a mother. He pushed away the thoughts and tried to speak again. "Kendra," he managed. "Mary named her Kendra."

"Kendra Marty?" asked the woman softly.

He could only nod.

"You must be George McMannus," she went on easily. "Mrs. Miller told us that we could expect you—once you got the word."

He nodded again and swallowed hard. So Maggie had already prepared the way.

"Let me offer my condolences. I am so sorry about your daughter and her husband," the woman said, and he could sense the deep and honest sympathy in her voice. He wondered if she had lost someone to be able to feel his pain in such a fashion.

He couldn't answer. He toyed with his hat with the fingers of his right hand and reached his left to his beard. He could not look up. He could not face even understanding eyes.

"I will have one of the attendants get little Kendra," she went on as she rose from her chair. "We have a comfortable little room just for such meetings. Or would you rather meet in the garden?"

"The garden," he said quickly. He was pleased he could escape the closeness of the stuffy rooms. He needed air. He needed space.

"You go ahead. Right through the door at the end of the hall. I'll bring Kendra out to you."

She turned to go but he stopped her quickly. "She won't remember me," he blurted. "She—I haven't seen her for almost two years. She'll have forgotten—by now."

The woman nodded. "Perhaps I will stay nearby for your first meeting," she answered, and he knew she was thinking of the little girl and her many exposures to pain and strangeness in such a short time.

"That would be good," he said simply and left the room for the garden.

He paced about, trying to quiet his troubled thoughts and get control of his mixed feelings when the same gentle voice spoke behind him.

"Grandfather McMannus. Kendra is here to see you."

He stiffened. He wished to wheel around and embrace the child now within his reach. At the same time, he longed to flee. It would be so hard to see Mary's baby—alone.

Reason told him that he had to be careful. Cautious. Slow and deliberate and gentle or he would frighten the little one half to death. She had already been through so much. So much, for such a little tyke.

He knew that the title "grandfather" had been for the sake of the child. To perhaps stir some memory. Make her realize that the stranger before her was somehow connected to her. That they belonged together, the big man and the little girl. Inwardly he was grateful to the woman who seemed to understand so much. If only—if only he knew how to approach the small child. How to let her know he loved her. If he could only reach across the span of time—and miles—and be a—a real grandfather. Could let her know what he felt in his heart.

He turned slowly, took a deep breath and looked

first at the woman. She stood silently, seeming to will him her strength. He knew that tears were in his eyes, threatening to spill down his cheeks. Would they alarm the little girl? He mustn't cry. He mustn't. He almost choked on the intensity of his feelings, then let his eyes drop to the little person who clung to the matron's hand.

She was such a tiny thing. So small. So—so vulnerable. One small child, clutching firmly to a worn rag doll. He remembered the doll. Mary had made it. Kendra had toddled about the cabin, dragging the doll behind her when he had visited them the last time. Mary's baby—smiling and gurgling over her own baby. Dollie.

She had grown so much since he had seen her and held her in his arms. Yet she was still so—so small to have lost so much. He shuddered, fearing that he would not be able to move—to speak. And then she lifted large green eyes to his face. Mary's eyes. His Mary in miniature. He felt the pain rend his heart. He wanted to sweep this child into his arms. To hold her and weep and weep for what he had lost. For what they both had lost. But he could not move. He could not speak.

Kendra broke the silence. But she did not speak to him. She spoke to the matron. Her words were clear, but confusion made the little voice tremble. "Is this my grandfather?" she asked simply.

"Yes," the woman replied in a firm, soft voice. "You have not seen him for some time, so you might not remember him well. But he is your grandfather. Your mama's father. He remembers you when you were a baby—and as you grew a little bit bigger."

Her eyes turned back to him again. He still had not moved.

"Hello, Grandfather," she said, and again her voice trembled.

"Hello, Kendra," he managed. He didn't think he ever remembered speaking such difficult words.

They looked silently at each other.

"I've asked Miss Jane to bring milk and cookies to the garden," the woman said. "We can have them together."

For the first time the large green eyes took on a sparkle. It was clear to him she thought milk and cookies a wonderful treat.

"Shall we sit down?" offered the matron, moving toward a small bench. Kendra did not release her hold on the hand she clutched tightly.

Kendra did not sit. She stood, holding Dollie under one arm, leaning up against the knee of the woman. George McMannus could not take his eyes from her little face. She looked so much like his small Mary. Only the shape of her mouth and the color of her hair were like her father's.

He longed to talk to her, but what could he say? *How are you, Kendra?* He knew how she was. At least he felt he knew. *How do you like living here?* That didn't seem like a proper question for a little girl who had been taken from a loving home and thrust in with a group of strangers. *What arrangements would you like to make for your future?* No. The child knew nothing about the difficult decisions that were ahead. The decisions that he, as her grandfather, must make on her behalf.

He raised his eyes to the face of the woman who sat on the small bench. Her hand rested lightly on Kendra's back, pressing the child up against her knee. There was caring in the touch. Caring in the eyes. If Kendra could not be in her own home—then perhaps—perhaps the best place for her was here.

He stirred restlessly, brushing away the thoughts. He couldn't leave her here. He knew he couldn't.

A young woman in a stiff, clean uniform arrived with a tray. There was tea for the man and the woman, milk for Kendra, and cookies for all to share. He was glad for the distraction. Though he had never cared for tea, he was willing to accept the cup offered to him. At least it would busy his hands.

Kendra seemed to relax as well. She settled on the bench with her milk and cookies, her too-short little legs swinging back and forth as she prepared herself to enjoy the refreshment.

George saw her tilt her head and look up into the branches when the song of a bird lifted against the late morning sky.

Just like Mary, he thought, and the pain stabbed him again.

"Is that a robin?" she asked the matron, interest in her voice.

"That was a chickadee," responded the woman. "I have not seen or heard a robin yet this spring. But they should be coming back soon."

Kendra looked pleased at the fact. Then she said merrily, "Mama and I like the chickadees best anyway. Papa likes the crows, he says. But he's just teasing. He doesn't like the crows. They make an awful squawk." She giggled at her own little joke.

Her words surprised her grandfather. *Didn't she know?* Had no one told her? She was speaking of her parents in the present tense. Surely—surely he wasn't expected to be the one to tell this little child that her parents were both gone and that she was alone in the world. That she really had no one—except for one errant, distant trapper grandfather who came to call so seldom that she didn't even know him.

He lifted his eyes to the woman, accusations deepening his gaze.

But the woman looked unperturbed. She was stroking back Kendra's soft curls and repeating the child's words, but in her way. "So your mama used to like the chickadees and your papa used to tease about liking crows," she said, her smile warm and friendly.

Kendra nodded but her eyes became serious. "They used to," she agreed with a solemn nod, her eyes becoming clouded.

"Your mama and papa liked the birds," the woman went on. "They loved everything about the outdoors."

George McMannus looked again to the woman. He wondered how she knew so much about his Mary.

"It's nice to be in God's outdoors," went on the woman. "It's nice to enjoy His creation. Perhaps when you are older, you'll love it and know about it like your mama and papa did."

Kendra nodded. She was quiet again.

The woman stirred and lifted her eyes to the man who sat silently staring at his delicate teacup. He looked up.

"Did you tell your grandfather that you will soon be four?" the matron prompted Kendra.

The little face took on a sparkle again. She carefully raised a little hand and tucked her thumb against the palm. "I will be four—this summer—in August," she informed him.

Yes—it had been August. He remembered it

well. Mary had hoped that Kendra would be born on his birthday, but the infant had arrived eight days later. "Your 'almost' birthday present," Mary had teased as she handed the small Kendra to him on his first visit to see them after the baby had been born. Even at that time he had thought she looked like Mary. He remembered that now.

He nodded to the small child. "August seventeenth," he said, keeping his voice as even as he could.

"How did you know?" she asked, both curiosity and excitement edging her voice.

"I'm—I'm your grandfather," he reminded her. "I—I remember when you were born."

"Were you there?" she asked quickly.

"No. But I came as soon as I could."

"Came from where?"

He hesitated. How could he explain the "where" to the child. There wasn't even a known name for the wilderness he called home, though the locals referred to the small post and settlement as Bent River Crossing.

"From where I live. From the—the mountains and the woods and the—the rivers—where I live."

To his surprise her eyes widened. Something was going on in the small head.

"Are you *that* grandfather?" she asked him, the green eyes widening with puzzlement, then with understanding.

He hardly knew how to answer her question. What grandfather? He knew that she only had one in Canada. Her papa's folks were in England.

Before he could answer she spoke again. "My trapper grandfather?"

His heart leaped. They had some connection.

Bless Mary! She had linked them in the short time she'd had with her daughter. With his granddaughter.

"Yes. Yes," he answered quickly before the moment was lost. "I'm that grandfather."

She smiled at him. The first tentative little smile she had given to him. It stirred his very soul.

Chapter Three

A Difficult Decision

"I'll need some time," he told the matron after Kendra had been taken back inside by one of the uniformed attendants. "I haven't had a chance to make any arrangements. I just got into town."

He did hope she wouldn't push for him to take the child before he had a chance to carefully select a place for her. He couldn't place her just anywhere. She needed love. She needed family. She needed more than just care.

"I understand," said Mrs. Weatherall. "You need time—and Kendra needs time."

His surprise must have shown on his face.

"Kendra has been through a very emotionally devastating time for a child," went on the woman evenly. "She has faced pain and confusion to the fullest measure. She has been brought to a house filled with strangers. Caring strangers—but strangers nonetheless. She has just begun to adjust to this new life here—and we are going to ask her to make another big change. It will not be easy for her—and should be done as slowly and carefully as we can manage."

He nodded, swallowing the lump in his throat.

"You are very important to Kendra," she continued. "You are a link with her past. Even though she does not know you well, she does remember her mother speaking of you. That is important. It not only gives her family—it gives her a living memory of her mother. Something to tie to—to anchor her. She is not totally alone now. Do you understand?"

He nodded again. It was all so hard for him. To see the child—to remember Mary. He was still wishing for a quiet place where he could let the tears flow. Ease some of the pain.

"We all need some time," said Mrs. Weatherall. "I know you are a busy man, but I do hope you can give us some time. Time for you to just spend with Kendra—while she is still here. Then when she is ready—and moved—time to let her become adjusted in her new home—before you leave her. That will make such a difference for her—to have that transition spanned with love."

He silently agreed with the wisdom of the words. He determined in his heart that he would be there—for Kendra. He would make it as easy for her as possible. Already he felt such love for the brave little waif.

"I'll be here—for as long as she needs me," he managed to say.

"Good," said the woman and she seemed relieved. "Take as long as you need to find the right home. In the meantime you can visit Kendra as often as you like. It will be good for her to have her grandfather. I'll tell her that you'll be calling. Tomorrow?"

He was about to agree when he thought of Mary. He had to go to her. He just had to. His heart would find no rest until he had made that final call.

"Not—not tomorrow," he mumbled through stiff

lips and saw the disappointment in the eyes of the woman.

"I have to—have to go see my daughter," he tried to explain. "It's a full day's trip—each way. I—I have to see—I have to," he finished lamely.

"I understand," she replied, her voice low and echoing his pain.

"You can tell Kendra that I'll be here first thing Friday morning," he went on.

"I'll tell her," agreed the woman. "And with your permission I'll also tell her where you have gone."

"Do you think—?" he began to question.

"I think it is important for Kendra to know that you loved her mother and father. That you are sharing in the pain of their death."

"Do you think—?" he began again, then quickly checked himself. "No, I guess not," he answered his own question.

"Think what?" the woman pushed him.

He shuffled uneasily. "Well, I was just wondering—just thinking—but it wouldn't be wise."

"Yes?" she prompted.

"Well, I was wondering if the child—Kendra—if she'd like to—to go with me, but I don't suppose—"

"Could you wait?" asked Mrs. Weatherall frankly.

"Wait?"

"Could you put off your trip for a few days—until you and Kendra have a chance to know each other a bit better—and then decide if it would be wise to take her or not?"

He thought about his answer before he voiced it. It would be hard to wait. He had longed to go to Mary ever since he had heard of the accident. Then he pictured Kendra. Would the trip be right for her?

She was only a child. Would it be right to take her to the grave of her mother and father? To her former home? He didn't know.

He lifted his eyes to the woman. "What do you think?" he asked frankly. "I'm willing to wait—if it would be the right thing."

"Kendra has not been back to the cabin since the accident. Perhaps it would be healing for her to see where her parents have been laid to rest. I don't know. We can only judge that when we—when we see how she learns to feel about you. I think—I think that Kendra herself will be able to tell us. We'll have to let her take the lead."

He nodded, his heart still heavy.

"Then I'll be here tomorrow," he said simply and rose to go.

"I'll tell her," said the woman.

With a nod he left the small office and moved out into the sunshine of the spring day, glad to fill his lungs with clear, fresh air.

❧   ❧   ❧

"I don't seem to be getting anywhere," George McMannus said to Maggie across her kitchen table. George had just fed Henry his supper of broth and custard. Now they sat down together to partake of the meal Maggie had prepared.

"It might take time," Maggie responded. "You'll have to be patient. She has been through so much for such a little tyke. It might take a while until she is ready to warm up to anyone."

"Oh, it's not that. Not Kendra."

Maggie looked at him with puzzlement.

"I mean—she's chatty and friendly. Seems glad

to see me whenever I arrive. It's this—home situation. I've followed every lead I've been given, and I still haven't found a place I would feel right about leaving her."

Maggie stirred the soup before spooning some into their bowls. She knew George had spent most of his days making calls throughout the city trying to find a suitable place for the young child.

Maggie nodded. It was hard to see her old friend carry such a heavy burden.

"Did you check with that pastor Mrs. Leed told me of?"

He nodded.

"He gave me two names," he answered. His hand stole up to his beard, and Maggie's expression mirrored his deeply troubled one.

"Both fine enough folks, I guess," he went on. "One man has no work right now. Finding it hard to feed his own family. 'Course I could pay him for Kendra's keep—but would the money meant for her be used to feed the others? Could hardly ask a man to feed an outsider better than his own offspring. And the other—I think they mean well enough—but, well—she's rather a sour person. Mary was always so—so bright and cheerful that I don't know if Kendra could—could live comfortably with dour sternness."

"Something will work out," Maggie said, trying to console him. "These things take time."

He nodded. But he was impatient. The days were slipping by so quickly. Days spent hunting for the right place for the child. Days spent with the little girl who was so quickly claiming his heart. He felt as if he were being torn asunder.

❧   ❧   ❧

"Do you know what that is, Grandfather?" she quizzed as they took a walk along the riverbank hand in hand, Kendra holding tightly to her rag doll. "That is a boon."

"A boom," he corrected. "A log boom."

"Yes, a boom," she repeated. "Papa told me. A boom."

It was one of the many things her papa had told her and she had repeated in their few days spent together. George McMannus was getting the feeling that the son-in-law he had hardly known had made a good father for Kendra. She spoke of him constantly. Just as she chatted about her mother.

Her grandfather noticed that she still interchanged past tense and present tense as she discussed them. At times she even spoke of the future. It worried him. Did Kendra really know that her folks were gone? That they wouldn't be coming back to pick her up? He hardly knew how to deal with the child. Should he remind her each time that she would not see her parents again? Was that too harsh for a child to bear? He did not have the answer, but the small child's desire to live in the past tore at his already wounded heart.

He turned his attention to her now as she pointed at the log boom that moved slowly down the river.

"Do you know what that man does?" she asked him. "He makes sure they don't jamp."

Jam, he was going to correct her, but he let it go.

"And sometimes he runs all across the logs— jumpin' and jumpin'," she went on. "Papa showed me a jumpin' man once."

"When did you see the jumping man?" he asked her softly.

"Once—when Mama was home with a tummy ache from the fu and Papa took me with him for a walk by the river."

He didn't correct her word for flu either.

"Mama was real sick that day," went on Kendra. Then brightened. "But she got better. She doesn't got any fu now at all."

He winced. Would she never remember? he wondered.

"Kendra," he began slowly, not knowing what to say, not knowing how to say it, but sensing that this might be a good time to feel his way, "I'm goin' to make a little trip—"

He saw the questions darken the large green eyes. Had she heard those words before? Had he chosen his words poorly?

"Where?" she asked quickly.

"Well, just—just—up to where you used to live—with your mama and papa."

The eyes changed dramatically. He saw the light in them.

"Can I go?" she asked before he could even continue.

He stopped walking. He felt his hand tightening its grip on the small one that was slipped in his. She stopped him and looked up into his face, her eyes pleading. He reached down and lifted her and sat her up on one of the posts that lined the river dock.

"Kendra—" He struggled for the right words. "It—it won't be like it was—you know that. Your—your mama and papa are no longer—they no longer live at your old home."

She looked at him solemnly, then nodded her

head in understanding, tears forming in her green eyes.

"They're dead," she said with candid frankness.

It was his turn to blink away tears.

"Yes," he agreed when he could trust his voice to speak. "Yes, they are dead. Do you—do you know about—about what it is like to be dead?"

She nodded slowly.

"Have you seen anything that was—dead?" he pressed further.

She nodded again.

"What?" he asked her.

"When—when Papa shoot things—they be dead," she answered him.

So her father had been a hunter. At least the child had an idea of what death was.

"But nobody shoot my mama and papa," went on Kendra, shaking her head vigorously. "They got dead in the river rapids."

He nodded in agreement.

When he found his voice, he went on. "Do you know what—what happens to people who—who die?" he asked with difficulty.

"They get buried—in the ground. They make a grave and they—they bury them in a special place so that we always know where they are."

He bit his lip to keep it from trembling. He knew that someone had been trying to explain to her what had happened. He was thankful for that "someone."

"I'm going to your old home to see—to see the graves of your mama and papa," he told her. "So that—so that I'll always be able to remember—where they are."

"Can I come?" she asked again without hesitation.

"Do you—do you really think you'd like to do that?" He still wasn't sure if it was the right thing to do.

"I want to," she said simply. "I want to see where they really are, too."

He nodded. "I'll talk to Mrs. Weatherall about it," he promised her. "We'll see what she thinks."

He lifted her back down from the post and they turned their steps toward the Home.

❧   ❧   ❧

He told Mrs. Weatherall about the conversation he'd had with Kendra that afternoon. The woman said very little as she listened. Just nodded her head occasionally.

When he finished his little account he was stroking his dark beard vigorously. "What do you think we should do?" he asked.

She turned the question back to him. "What do *you* think?"

"I don't know. Honestly, I don't know. She—she seems to understand. But I don't know."

"How do *you* feel—about visiting your Mary's grave?" asked the woman.

His head came up quickly. "I have to go. You know that," he responded.

"Why?" she asked softly.

"Well—because—" He stopped, impatience edging his voice. He had felt that she understood him, and now she was asking this—this question to which the answer should have been so obvious.

"I need to see her one last time." He hesitated.

"Oh, not her—I know I won't see *her*. But I mean I have to—to sort of make that last contact. I have to—to know where she is—to say that final goodbye before—before I can have any rest—get on with life."

She did not speak. She just sat silently, letting his words hang in the air between them. Letting them echo back in the big empty space that had been Mary in his own heart and mind.

"And Kendra?" she asked softly. "Do you think she might need that too?"

"She's a child," he argued, but his tone was thoughtful. "She's so young."

"But she's also a person," spoke Mrs. Weatherall. "A person—a very small person—with a great big loss."

"I don't know," he said after the silence between them had lingered long enough.

"I don't know either," said Mrs. Weatherall. "Perhaps we'll have to let Kendra guide us."

He nodded and rose to his feet. Already he knew in his heart that when he visited Mary's grave, Kendra would be at his side.

Chapter Four

An Exciting Adventure

"I 'member that house."

There was excitement in the small girl's voice. The building she pointed out was nothing more than a log shack along the riverbank, but the sight of something familiar seemed to please her.

She released one hand from holding her doll and swatted at the mosquitoes that buzzed about her face, then turned her little face behind her. "Grandfather. Do you 'member it?"

"Can't say that I do," he answered as he took a long stroke on the canoe paddle. "But then I haven't been up this way in a long time."

"I 'member it," she said again. "When we went by it before, there was a red shirt on that line."

He marveled at her memory.

"Grandfather," she said again, "do you 'member the red shirt?"

He smiled and shook his head. "No," he responded, "I don't remember the shirt either."

She swatted another mosquito. "These 'skitoes are a pesky nuisance, aren't they, Grandfather?"

Surprised, he couldn't hide the smile that played about his lips.

"That's what Mama says," she added.

Yes—Mary had said that. And his Mary had borrowed the words from *her* father. His words were now coming back to him through the grandchild who shared his canoe.

"Grandfather—do you know what I think?"

"Well," he said, resting his paddle against the side of the small craft. "I know what I think. I think that grandfather is an awfully big name. Do you think there might be something else you would like to call me?"

She puckered her brow, deep in thought. He studied the seriousness of the green eyes, thinking back to another little girl who had shared his canoe such a long, long time ago—but that only seemed like yesterday.

"I know," she said, her face brightening. "I could call you Papa Mac."

The words caught him so totally off guard that he heard his own soft gasp. "Where'd you—?" he began, but she was bubbling on.

"Mama used to call you Papa Mac—so I will call you Papa Mac. Okay?"

Another link. Another pull at his heart. He couldn't answer her because he was so choked up, so he just nodded his head.

"How much longer?" she asked, seeming totally oblivious to the sweet pain she had just caused him.

"A long way yet," he managed to answer, clearing his throat. "But I think that it's about time to take a break and eat the lunch Mrs. Miller sent, don't you?"

She agreed wholeheartedly. He eased the canoe up against the bank of the river and helped her from the craft. He was surprised at how easily she seemed to adjust to the sway of the small boat. He wondered where she had learned the rhythm of a canoe. Never once on their trip upriver had he needed to caution her to sit still or not to lean over the edge or never to move quickly. Worried about it, he had been prepared to rescue her from the water should they have a spill. But she seemed to know instinctively how to move.

"Have you been in a canoe before?" he asked her as she stood beside him on the riverbank.

"Oh yes," she enthused. "Mama used to take me. And sometimes Papa used to take me. And sometimes we all went together."

So that was the secret. Already Mary and Stu had been raising a little girl who would love the wilderness just as they did.

They ate their simple lunch in silence. It was the first she had stopped chatting since they had left the city behind. He watched her as she tilted her head and listened to the song of a bird.

"What was that, Papa Mac?" she whispered. He couldn't believe how easily she had adapted to the name.

"That was a wild canary," he replied.

"Mama was teaching me the birds," she said sadly.

The bird called again, and Kendra tipped her head to listen. "A wild canary," she said to herself as though to implant the words firmly in her mind. Then she shrugged her shoulders. "Guess I'll never know the birds now." She spoke quietly, but her voice broke with the words, and he saw her chin quiver.

When she lifted her head again there was strength and determination in the little face. "They don't have many birds in the city anyway," she informed her grandfather. "I don't think the birds like all those houses and all that noise and stuff."

He wondered how *she* felt about all the houses

and all the noise—and stuff. He felt his own chin tremble.

"I guess we should be going," he said to her to break free from the pain he saw in her face. The pain that spilled over into his own heart.

She nodded and climbed to her feet, but much of the excitement of the morning seemed to have left her.

※　　※　　※

In the afternoon, she slept, her rag doll, Dollie, held closely to her chest. He worried about the sun shining down upon her and managed to make a shelter of sorts to shade her face. He also worried about the mosquitoes that buzzed endlessly about her, but there was very little he could do about them.

He still wondered if he had done the right thing. Should he be bringing her on this journey of sorrow? Could he hide his own pain enough to be a source of comfort for one lost, bewildered, heartbroken little girl?

Many times during the day of paddling, he felt a strong urge to turn the canoe around and beat a hasty retreat back to the city. He wondered if he could face the pain that lay ahead in seeing Mary's grave. It was too much. Too much to add to the pain of the past. The pain of losing Mary's mother. He had to get away. He had to brace himself against all the anguish he was feeling. He had to get back to the mountainous wilderness where he was sure he could find some measure of calm and serenity and begin to heal again.

But what of Kendra? He looked at the slight body, the pixie face, as she slept. She still clutched her worn rag doll that Mary had made for her. She had called him her trapper grandfather. She had also dubbed him with Mary's pet name. They were linked together as surely as they would be if actual chains bound them. It brought him joy—and deep sorrow. What would he ever do about Kendra?

❦   ❦   ❦

The two stood, heads bowed, hands clasped tightly. Before them were two mounds of scarred earth. At the head of each a small cross stood, carved from the nakedness of a forest tree. No words were on the crosses, just simple initials. On one was carved M.M., on the other, S.M.

The lump in his throat was so intense that he feared he would choke. He did not even dare let his gaze rest on the silent little figure beside him. She was so still—so quiet. Even in his own grief he was thankful that the child did not understand—could not possibly grasp the meaning of the two mounds.

"Which one is Mama, Papa Mac?" a small, trembling voice whispered.

His body gave a start. Perhaps she did understand. He swallowed, trying to gain control of his voice that he was sure wouldn't work properly. "That one," he managed to answer, fighting to keep his voice even.

"Can I hug her?"

"Hug her?" He did not understand.

She pulled her small hand free, moved from him, and with one quick motion fell beside the mound, reaching out with little arms to embrace the dark, bare earth. Tears came then. Not just the tears of the little girl, but the tears of her grandfather as he dropped down beside her and gathered her close. They cried together for the mother, the daughter, they had lost. They cried until they were finally able to whisper a goodbye and move on to the next silent grave to cry and whisper again.

When their tears were spent, he picked her up in his arms and cradled her close. She put her arms around his neck and held him tightly. At last he turned from the two graves and carried her down the hill the short distance to the small cabin that had been her home. They did not speak. He longed to say words of comfort. To ease her pain. But what could he say?

He did not know what the little girl might be thinking. She could not share her thoughts of loneliness and sorrow with him. But he knew what he was thinking. *They belonged together*—the two of them. There was nothing that could change that. He should have known it from the first time he looked into her large green eyes. She was his. He was hers. There was no way he could ever turn his back and walk away from her. Not if he found the best home in the city. No, she would never be alone again if he could help it. She was going with him— back to the wilderness. Back where she could hear the song of the birds. Away from the "many houses and noise—and stuff." He would teach her to identify the bird songs. He had taught her mother Mary.

He held her tightly and wiped the final trace of tears from her cheeks.

"We need to have our supper and get a good sleep," he said softly to her. "We have a big trip to make tomorrow. And then—after that, we have to get ready for an even bigger trip."

Her eyes widened. "Where?" she asked him.

"Home," he said simply. "Home."

She looked at the little cabin they were about to enter.

"A new home," he hurried to tell her. "A new home—with me."

For one moment she looked at him and then her arms tightened about his neck. He couldn't see her face, but he had the feeling that some of the pain had left the large green eyes.

❧   ❧   ❧

"Are you sure you are doing the right thing?" Maggie asked in a hushed tone. Kendra lay sleeping on a makeshift bed nearby. The days since their return from the trip upriver had been busy. There were always supplies that were needed when he visited the city, but now that Kendra was going home with him, there were so many more things he would need.

They had gathered up her few possessions that had been left behind at the small cabin. The remainder of her clothing, her toys, and a few reminders of her mother and her father. It had made a cumbersome load for the little canoe on its return trip, but he would not have denied her anything that she had wished to take. She needed all that was available to keep her parents' memories alive in her mind.

As the mound of articles from his daily shopping trips grew and grew, he knew his trip back home was going to be slow and costly. He would need to hire another boat or two. There was no way the supplies could be contained in his own small craft when he reached the end of the freight line.

But he did not worry about it. There were always trappers or Indians willing to make a little extra money by paddling freight upstream. He'd have no problem finding someone to share the load.

So he continued to pile up supplies, and Kendra continued to chat excitedly about the long trip she would soon be making with her grandfather and the fact that she would be living with him in his wilderness home.

He had feared that he might have to fight it out with Mrs. Weatherall. She did question him.

"Do you think that is a good place to raise a child?" she had asked soberly.

"No. No, likely not," he answered honestly. "But her own folks gave her a good start in the wilderness. And I can't abide the city—besides, my livelihood is out there."

"And Kendra—?"

"I won't leave her behind," he said firmly. "She needs me."

He didn't say what he could have said quite honestly. That he also felt a need for the little girl. He knew he would never be able to stand being separated from her now.

"And her schooling?" asked the woman.

"I bought books," he replied. "I can teach her for the first years—and then—then she can come out to one of them girls' schools."

The woman had not argued further. He was surprised at how easily he had won. "I'll have her ready," was all the matron had said.

And she had kept her word. When the last of the purchases had been added to the collection and arrangements made for them to board the big paddle boat, George McMannus went for his small granddaughter and found her bag packed, ready for the trip ahead.

"Goodbye, Kendra," said Mrs. Weatherall, and she put her arms around the small girl and held her close. She did not say, "I will miss you." She had far too many other small children who needed her love and attention. She did not say, "I hope you will be happy." She seemed to know as she looked at the two of them together that the best way for Kendra to put her past behind and find a measure of security and happiness was with her grandfather. So she just said again, "Goodbye, Kendra. Whenever you return to the city, I would love to have you visit me."

"I will," promised the little girl, then solemnly added, "but we might not come for a long, long time. Papa Mac doesn't come very often to the city."

The good woman smiled. George McMannus held out his hand. He knew that his eyes were about to betray him again.

"Words can't say what I'm feeling," he said. "But I do thank you for taking her in. Easing her pain. Hugging away some of the hurt."

The woman blinked hurriedly, not wishing to show the depth of her feelings.

"That's why we are here," she said, her voice steady and her eyes direct. "I wish—I wish that all of our children had such a—such a happy ending to their days with us."

He gave her hand a slight squeeze and turned to pick up Kendra's little suitcase.

❧   ❧   ❧

The long, long journey began with the paddle-boat trip up the broad river. Kendra's excitement ran high. Her grandfather, more accustomed to the quiet of his wilderness, was chatted at and led about until he felt exhausted. Relieved when it was time for her to be bedded for the night, he tucked the blankets around her and the rag doll she clutched to herself.

After three days of river travel, they docked and hired a wagon to haul their belongings overland. This meant a four-day journey with frequent stops to rest the team, but the pauses only served to agitate the man. He was anxious to get back home. He had been away far too long.

At last they reached their own river and the group of small shelters that had been built close to the stream.

"Is this our city, Papa Mac?" Kendra asked him.

"We don't have a city," he answered. "This is an Indian settlement."

She looked about with candid curiosity. Children ran back and forth on the riverbank, yelling at one another with strange-sounding words. Dogs barked and women peered shyly from behind draped doorways. In the shade a few men lolled and whittled, looking up now and then to study the wagons that had pulled up in front of the small outpost store.

George McMannus reclaimed the canoe he had left behind with the man who ran the post and managed to find two fellows with sturdy canoes who were willing to move his freight upriver to his cabin home.

"You go on ahead," the big man called to the men in the other two loaded canoes. "I'll only be a short while—then we'll catch up."

"Why are we stopping here, Papa Mac?" Kendra asked, but there was no alarm in her voice, only interest.

"We are going to see Nonie," he answered, reaching for her hand.

As they passed the village inhabitants, he called

out greetings. Kendra had never heard the words before and did not understand them. Some of the men rose to their feet and answered him with strange words of their own. They often chatted for a few minutes before the pair moved on, Kendra's hand held firmly in her grandfather's.

They came to a small, ramshackle home at the edge of the little settlement, and George Mc-Mannus called loudly, then stepped up to the door. Without a knock he bent his head and ducked under the tanned moose hide that had been pulled back to let the sun shine in.

A voice from inside answered him softly and Kendra ducked her head just like her grandfather had done, though she was much too short to have necessitated such a move, and followed him into the dark, smoke-smelling room.

A woman sat on the floor. She worked over a large bowl she held within her bent legs. She did not even lift her head but spoke rapidly in her own tongue.

"Speak English, please," George McMannus answered her. "So my granddaughter will understand."

The woman lifted her head slightly and took one brief peek at the small girl before her.

"This is Kendra," George said to the woman.

"Kendra," she repeated, her native tongue making the name sound strange yet appealing.

"Kendra, this is Nonie," the man went on.

Kendra held back shyly. She wished to duck behind her grandfather's long legs, but she wasn't sure if that would be acceptable. Instead, she turned her face against him.

"Say hello," her grandfather bid her.

"Hello," she said shyly, still feeling uncomfortable in the unfamiliar house and in the presence of this person who was a stranger—and strange—to her.

The woman on the floor chuckled softly, lifting her hand to hide the sound. She was no longer young, but her wrinkled face held serenity, her deep eyes soft merriment. Graying hair hung down over her shoulders in two neat braids.

"Nonie, I need help," the man went on without any preamble. "I need to pick up my dogs as quickly as possible, and I can't leave Kendra alone. Can you stay with her?"

Nonie lifted her head fully and looked from the man to the small girl. She shrugged her shoulders and nodded.

"Good," said the man. "I will look for you tomorrow—at first sun."

Nonie nodded again, then turned her eyes back to her bowl.

Kendra felt a tug on her hand and realized that her grandfather was now leaving the cabin again. He said one last word in the strange language and the two made their way back to the canoe that bobbed up and down with each movement of the river.

Though Kendra had not fully comprehended the exchange, the arrangements had been made. Nonie would be the one who would care for the child while her grandfather tended to some other duties.

Chapter Five

Nonie

"Where's Papa Mac?" A sleepy Kendra peeped out from a tangle of blond curls at the woman in deerskins who worked near the cabin fireplace. The woman did not lift her head at Kendra's question.

"Gone," she said.

Gone. The single word brought terror to the child's heart. First her parents—now Papa Mac. *Gone!*

For one moment she stood frozen—then with a cry she leaped forward and ran to the door of the cabin. Tearing at the door, cries lifting to the rafters of the small cabin, Kendra fought to get out. Fought to escape. Fought to run after Papa Mac.

The woman watched her, silently, motionlessly, and then she slowly stood and brushed off the bits of swamp reed she had been weaving. She crossed to the child in silent steps and gently laid her hands on the small shoulders.

"Tush," she said gently. "Tush."

But Kendra paid no heed.

"Tush," the woman said again and gently but forcefully turned the little girl around to look into her face.

"Tush," she said again. "He come back. Tush."

When Kendra still wailed wildly and tried to

turn back to the door, the woman firmly drew the child into her arms and held her tightly. Kendra had no choice but to weep against the smoky-smelling shoulder of deerskin.

The woman's hands gently soothed as they brushed at the head of tangled hair and patted the thin, shaking shoulders, then stroked the arms, now still.

"Tush. Tush," she said over and over, the word calm and soothing. "He come back. Soon. He come back."

When the words finally got through to the little girl, her struggling ceased, her tears lessened. At last she pushed back, brushed her hair away from her face, and took another look at the woman who held her. She remembered her from the day before. Papa Mac had said that she would be cared for by this woman. She remembered now. He had said he was going to get his dogs.

With the memory of Papa Mac's words, Kendra's fears began to be alleviated, though her little body still trembled and her heart pounded within her. She had not really understood Papa Mac's words. She had not expected to wake up to a stranger in the small cabin.

"Hungry?" the woman asked her now.

Kendra nodded her head.

"First—" The woman pointed to the bunk where Kendra had slept. At the bottom of the bunk some of her garments had been laid out carefully. Kendra didn't know if the woman had chosen them or if her grandfather had put them there before he left the cabin, but obediently she followed the pointing finger and slipped out of her flannel nightgown and into her simple garments.

As soon as Kendra had finished, the woman beckoned her over so she could work on the tangled hair. As she combed and plaited, she clicked her tongue in strange sounds and chuckled. Soft, silvery laughter that almost made Kendra wish to join her.

When the woman was finished and had laid the comb aside, she turned the small girl back to face her and looked deeply into her eyes. "Amo-chika," she said softly. "Amo-chika." She drew Kendra close against her and held her for a long time. For a reason that Kendra could not explain, she felt comforted. The strong, dark arms that held her promised such love. Such security. Kendra buried her face against the rough, skin garments and breathed deeply of the strange smell of woodsmoke.

The woman held her back at arm's length again and spoke softly, pointing at herself, "Nonie."

Kendra nodded. She remembered the name now. "Nonie," she repeated, trying hard to give the name the same soft lilt that the woman had.

The woman smiled.

Then she pointed at the wee girl. "Kendra," she said. "Amo-chika."

The name—her own name—sounded strange to the young girl. And the new Indian name sounded even stranger. But she liked the sound of it. She repeated it, trying to make it sound just like Nonie had said it. It was different to be practicing one's own name. But she tried it again and again as Nonie led her to the small table by the room's one window and sat her down, soon bringing her a dish of breakfast porridge.

Kendra did not like the taste of the simple meal and would have refused it, but she was hungry and

Nonie said "Eat," so Kendra ate.

After she was finished, they gathered up the few dishes from the morning's meal and went to the small creek that ran close by. Nonie hiked her skirts, tucked them in, and bent over the fast-flowing water, washing the dishes in the cold stream. Then she set them in the warm morning sun. Kendra ran about on the shoreline, discovering pretty wild flowers hidden among the grasses.

When the dishes were warm and dry, Nonie gathered them together and they returned to the cabin.

"Now—we go," said Nonie and she picked up a basket that was beside the door and reached for Kendra's hand.

They spent the entire morning out of doors. For Kendra it was a delightful day of exploration. For Nonie it was serious gathering. As they walked, her eyes were ever alert to plants that grew about their feet. Often she would stoop and search out hidden leaves with her fingers. She seemed to sense just where to look for them. Sometimes she took the leaves. At other times she cast the leaves aside and dug the roots for her basket.

"Why do you do that? What do you want that for?" Kendra asked on more than one occasion, and she was always given an answer.

"Good medicine," Nonie would say, or "Makes good to eat."

"Can I pick some?" asked the child.

"Yes. I show," said Nonie.

And Kendra began her own search for special plants and wild herbs.

"This one?" she would ask, holding out a plant to Nonie. More often than not Nonie would laugh merrily and shake her head. "No, no," she would say, "not that one. That one p-f-f-t."

It was a strange sound. Almost a cross between a spit and a hiss, but Kendra quickly got the message that those leaves were throw-aways.

It did not discourage her, for Nonie would show her again just what they were looking for. When Kendra did happen to return to the woman with a few of the right leaves, Nonie clapped her hands gleefully and rewarded the girl with clicks of her tongue and a huge smile. Kendra fairly burst with her success.

The sun had climbed high into the sky when Nonie said, "We go home now." Kendra's short legs were weary with all the walking, the scampering here and there in her search for special plants, but she was reluctant to return to the darkness of the cabin. She wished with all her heart that she could protest, but even at her young age, Kendra had been taught to obey orders without argument. She turned slowly to follow the woman back through the woods.

They had not gone as far from the cabin as Kendra might have guessed. Their search had been leisurely paced, with frequent stops. Now on their way home, though unhurried, they walked steadily and soon the cabin came into view. Kendra was almost glad to see it, for she suddenly felt tired. Yet she could not hide the sigh that escaped her lips as they neared the door.

"You like sit?" asked Nonie, pointing to a grassy place in the shade of a tall spruce tree. Kendra nodded.

"You stay," said Nonie softly.

Kendra nodded again and dropped down on the grass. It was so nice and cool. So soft beneath her. Above her head, clouds floated across the sky and birds darted here and there among the branches. She heard one call across the small clearing and another answered from the other side. But Kendra did not know what bird was calling. She clamored quickly to her feet. She would run and ask her mama. And then Kendra remembered. Mama was gone.

Her face puckered and she threw herself back down to the ground and buried her face in her arms. Nonie found her crying when she returned with their simple meal.

"Tush," she said, laying aside the plates. "Tush."

"I don't know the bird," wept Kendra, not able to explain to Nonie the full meaning of her tears.

"Bird?" replied Nonie.

"I don't know which bird—that sang," she sobbed.

"One does not cry—over birds that sing," said Nonie, still sounding bewildered.

"Mama would tell me."

For a long moment Nonie puzzled over it, her brow knit in a frown, her eyes intent upon the small girl's face. Then a sudden light seemed to brighten her eyes. She nodded and reached to draw the little girl into her arms.

"Nonie tell," she said, her hands gentling and soothing. "Nonie tell—everything. Nonie be here. Always. You see."

Gradually the tears stopped and when Kendra had ceased crying and had wiped her eyes on the hem of her skirt, Nonie offered the plate.

The bird called again and Kendra lifted her head, tilting it to one side as she listened.

"That mountain bluebird," said Nonie without being asked. "Someday I show you. Maybe we find his nest."

Kendra smiled.

It wasn't the name of the bird that brought the

smile. Though Kendra already had a deep love for all things of nature—it was the fact of being comforted after the death of her parents. It was the renewed feeling of security after the terrible shattering of the world she knew. And it was especially the sense of being cared for after having lost the people she loved the most.

๑๑ ๑๑ ๑๑

It was almost sunset when Kendra heard dogs barking and ran to the cabin window.

A team of dogs was coming quickly down the trail that led up the creek. They pulled a strange sleigh that ran on small wheels instead of runners. A man ran behind them calling out orders. Kendra wondered if they could even hear above their yapping. But they stopped suddenly and lay down in the harnesses, tongues dripping and sides heaving.

It wasn't until then that Kendra noticed who was driving the team.

"It's Papa Mac," she squealed. Already she had forgotten that he was coming home, back to them. In her little heart she had expected him to be gone just as her parents were gone. Without realizing it, she had accepted the fact that now it was to be she and Nonie in partnership.

For one moment she stood—torn. She loved her Papa Mac. But already she felt drawn to the kind woman who had held her close and comforted her with such understanding. She looked over her shoulder at Nonie. Which one would she choose? Which one could she choose? Confusion filled her heart and showed in her eyes.

She turned again to the window. Papa Mac was

unharnessing the dogs and tethering them about the clearing. The wagon-sleigh stood deserted—empty.

Kendra swung back to Nonie, her green eyes wide with fright. Was her world to be one of constant change?

"Are you—you goin' to go?" she asked the Indian woman, fear making her voice tremble.

Nonie, not understanding the full import of the question, nodded her head matter-of-factly and answered, "I go now."

The terror deepened in Kendra's eyes and with a loud wail she threw herself at the woman and wrapped her small arms around the pungent-smelling skirts. "No," she wailed. "I don't want you to go."

Gently Nonie unwound the arms and lifted the child up against her shoulder. Understanding filled her dark eyes as she stroked the soft blond head and crooned her soft "tush" in the child's ear.

"I go tonight. I come in morning. You see. You see. I come in morning. Didn't Nonie say, 'I here always'? You see. You see. Tush. Tush."

What was Nonie saying? Kendra hushed her crying so she could listen more closely.

"Papa Mac here. Nonie go. Papa Mac go. Nonie here. You see. You see," promised Nonie over and over. "Tush. Tush."

Kendra's tears stopped. Was this really a promise? Would she be able to keep both Papa Mac and Nonie? Dare she hope that Nonie could keep her word?

Kendra pressed more closely against the woman and wrapped her arms tightly around her neck.

The door behind them opened and Kendra knew that Papa Mac had entered the cabin. She felt more than saw the exchange of glances between the trapper and the Indian woman. A message seemed to pass between them without a word. Then Papa Mac spoke, his words sounding loud after the soft voice of the woman.

"Kendra—I've missed you. How about a big hug?"

Kendra eased back slowly, studying the face of the woman before she was lowered to the cabin floor. With one last glance at the dark face she had already claimed for her own, she turned and looked at Papa Mac. He offered outstretched arms and Kendra smiled and ran to them.

"So, did you and Nonie have a good day?" he asked as he settled her on his knee.

Kendra nodded. Then she turned to her grandfather.

"I don't want Nonie to go," she stated simply.

"Nonie has to go," he said, and Kendra saw a look pass between the two again.

"Look," said her grandfather, sweeping the entire cabin with a wave of one long arm. "Where would Nonie fit? There isn't room for three people here. It was all I could do to squeeze in your little bed in the corner. There isn't room for another person."

Kendra frowned. "Nonie can have my bed," she offered generously.

Her grandfather laughed and gave her a hug.

"Nonie has to go home. Back to her own cabin," he explained further. "Nonie likes her home. She wouldn't want to leave it to live with us."

Kendra looked at Nonie, her big eyes questioning the woman, challenging her.

Nonie dropped her eyes to the cabin boards. She moved silently toward the potbellied stove that stood in the corner of the cabin and pushed more sticks of wood into the firebox.

"Nonie will come again tomorrow," promised the grandfather. "Whenever I am not here—Nonie will be here."

That was what Nonie had said. Nonie had promised. One or the other of the new people in her world would always be with her. Dared she believe them?

The strong arms of her grandfather tightened about her. Kendra snuggled down against his chest and studied Nonie who moved a stew pot back over the hidden flames.

This arrangement wasn't what Kendra would have preferred. She would have liked it much better if both her grandfather and Nonie could be with her constantly. But perhaps she could accept them—one at a time. She laid her head against her grandfather's chest. She could hear the gentle rhythmic beating of his heart. It was a comforting sound. Slowly her head began to nod in assent. If that's the way it had to be, then she would accept it. Just as long as they kept their promise. Just as long as she had one or the other. Kendra felt secure.

"I brought the dogs back home," her grandfather was saying. "Would you like to see them?"

Kendra's attention was quickly diverted. She loved dogs.

"Are they yours?" she asked her grandfather.

"Ours," he answered. "Ours."

Kendra grinned as she took his hand and led him from the cabin.

Almost daily, Nonie and Kendra took treks through the woods. Patiently Nonie taught the young child to recognize the plants that were useful and would be placed in the gathering basket. Over and over the lessons were repeated until Kendra began to understand just what it was she was looking for. Always she was rewarded by an enthusiastic Nonie. Kendra tried hard to mimic the soft clicks of the tongue that expressed approval and soon had the little sounds added to her own vocabulary.

"She's a bright little thing," her Papa Mac informed Nonie, and Nonie nodded her agreement, her eyes, though turned to the floor, sparkling with the thoughts of Kendra's quick achievements.

There were many days over the summer when Papa Mac did not go away and Nonie did not come. Kendra never knew when those days were to be. She sometimes wondered how the two people in her life knew. How did they get their message from the one to the other? Would the day ever come when there would be confusion and they would both be there at once? The thought made her little heart skip with anticipation. And then a chill passed through her. What if, in confusion, they both would be gone at the same time and she would be entirely on her own? It was a frightening thought and it made her heart pound within her.

But as the days passed and those fears were never realized, Kendra forgot them. Perhaps—perhaps her world was not about to turn upside down again, after all.

Chapter Six

Wilderness Child

Kendra's fourth birthday was not spent as a child would normally spend a birthday—but it was not forgotten. Papa Mac even made her a cake. A rather lopsided, strange cake with no icing and no candles, but a cake. No four-year-old could ever have been more excited than Kendra as she looked at the simple creation.

Then Kendra was given a birthday gift. Papa Mac told her to close her eyes and not open them until he told her. She felt something soft and furry in her arms. A puppy! Her very own dog. It was from the litter of one of the dogs in the Indian village. Her grandfather had paid the man dearly for the choice of the pups.

Now as Kendra held the squirming puppy in her arms and squealed over the fact that he was really hers, Papa Mac felt the price he had paid was a fair one after all.

Kendra called the small pup Oscar. A strange name for a sled dog. But Papa Mac did not argue with her choice. He named his dogs as he desired. He saw no reason to deny Kendra the same privilege.

"That not good," said Nonie, pointing to one of the berries in Kendra's basket. "Make sick."

"It was right there with the other berries," she argued.

"Not good. Make sick," Nonie insisted. Then spit out her word, "P-f-f-t."

Kendra picked up the berry, studied it for a moment, then let it fall from her fingers into the grasses at her feet.

"Guess a bird can have it," she said, hating to give up the red plumpness.

"Bird know better. Make sick," Nonie said and turned her attention back to her picking.

They had spent many of their days together picking berries. Kendra had already learned to recognize most of the berries that were "good." She had also been taught to recognize many of the berries that were "bad." Now she had added another one to the list. She did not want a berry in her basket that "made sick."

A bird called.

"That's a loon," spoke Kendra without lifting her head.

"Brother loon," said Nonie.

Kendra was becoming used to Nonie's family references to the woodland creatures, but when she told her grandfather he just chuckled.

"Nonie trying to put silly notions in your head? Trying to make a Cree out of you?" he had asked the young girl.

"Uh—uh. Nonie's not Cree," Kendra had said.

"I really have no idea. I wonder if Nonie knows. She was born mixed blood. Mother was Peigan. I don't know what tribe her father was. She was raised by the Blackfoot and then married into the

Stoney tribe. Now she lives with the Cree. She speaks several languages. I'm not sure if Nonie has figured out just what she is."

Kendra was far too young to understand all that her grandfather's words implied. She shrugged her shoulders and said simply, "She's Daughter of the Earth. She told me."

Papa Mac had laughed good-naturedly. Kendra had said the words the same as if she were announcing her own name as Kendra Marty.

Now as the young girl and the Indian woman picked berries together and listened to the mournful cry of the loon from the nearby lake, Kendra was quite willing to accept the bird as Nonie's brother loon. Just as the sleek mountain lion was her brother lion and the marauding grizzly was her brother bear.

But Nonie interrupted Kendra's picking and her listening for another cry from the lake.

"We go," said Nonie. "Storm come."

Kendra lifted her head to the sky. The sun still shone down upon them. Fluffy clouds skittered across the expanse of blue, seeming a bit more in a hurry than normal, but Kendra could see no threatening rain clouds.

"The sun is shining," said Kendra.

"Storm come," said Nonie again. "We go."

Kendra did not argue further. Although she loved to be outside, she was weary of picking berries. She nodded in agreement and stood to her feet. Nonie led the way back through the forest. There was no trail to follow. Kendra followed closely behind her. The growth was heavy, and Kendra did not wish to be left behind.

They were just nearing the cabin when a loud

clap of thunder seemed to rock the very ground they sped over. Kendra lifted startled eyes to the heavens and was surprised to see that dark, menacing clouds had gathered over them. The child felt a moment of fear and hastened her step to catch up to the scurrying woman. She grabbed a handful of buckskin skirt, her eyes turning again to the sky.

They rushed into the cabin just as the first large drops of rain began to fall. Kendra whirled at the entrance and pushed the heavy door soundly shut behind them, glad to be in where they were safe.

Never had she heard it thunder as it did in that storm. Her wide green eyes grew large and intense in the small face. Kendra trembled, her whole being filled with fright.

Nonie had been busy clucking over her berries and had paid little attention to the young girl, but when a small hand again clutched at her skirt, Nonie turned. For one moment quiet dark eyes met troubled green ones and then Nonie began her little comforting noises. "Tush. Tush," she soothed, gathering the small child into her arms. She held her close for a long time while the thunder crashed and rumbled overhead and the lightning ripped through the sky above them, piercing their small clearing with jagged flashes of light.

"Tush. Tush," said Nonie. She carried Kendra to the rocker in the corner of the room and held her close against the cured buckskin with its strange and comforting smell.

"Father Thunder," she said. "Father Thunder."

Kendra's trembling lessened. The storm moved slowly on until the thunder seemed to echo off the mountain ridge across the valley and no longer shook the small cabin with each clap.

"I tell of Father Thunder," said Nonie, and still holding the little girl close, she began her story.

"Once, before there were people, all animals and trees lived and talked with one another.

"Bear think he was biggest and strongest of all animals, but Fox think he was smartest. He keep telling Bear it was better to be smart than to be strong and that make Bear angry.

" 'We'll see,' said Bear. 'We'll have contest.'

" 'What contest?' asked Fox.

" 'There is not Fire on Earth,' said Bear. 'We need Fire to keep us warm, but there is only Fire in Heaven. We must steal Fire from Sun. But first we must go to Sky and find Fire. Sun keep it hidden in wooden box with three leather thongs around it.'

" 'How will we get to Sky?' asked Fox.

" 'That is part of contest. We must find a way,' said Bear.

"So they both sat down to think and think. They think all day and they think all night. They think all next day.

" 'I'm strong,' said Bear. 'I will build myself a road to Sky.'

"So Bear went to Cedar. 'Will you give me your long trunk for poles for building a road to Sky?' he asked.

" 'If I do, I will die,' said Cedar.

" 'What does it matter?' said Bear. 'You are not strong like me.'

"So Bear took Cedar to build road. And all other forest cedars cried.

" 'I need thongs to tie my poles together,' said Bear, so he went to Deer. 'Will you give me your skin to make thongs to tie my poles together?' he asked.

" 'If I do, I will die,' said Deer.

" 'What does it matter?' said Bear. 'You are not strong like me.'

"And Bear took Deer to make thongs to tie poles, and all other deer cried.

"Fox watched Bear build a long road to Sky with strong poles from Cedar and tie them together with thongs of Deer.

" 'This is not right,' thought Fox. 'Bear will destroy our forests and our friends to win his contest.'

"Sun saw what Bear was doing. It made Sun angry. 'What are you doing?' he said to Bear.

" 'I must get to Sky,' replied Bear. 'I am building a long trail.'

" 'Why do you climb to Sky?'

"But Bear would not tell Sun.

"That night when Sun was sleeping, Bear climbed the long, long cedar trail. He climbed all night. Next morning, just as Sun awoke, Bear made a hole in Sky with one long claw. Bear did not know, but Fox was close on his heels ready to sneak past him and into Sky to steal the firebox before Bear could find it.

"But Sun was angry when he saw Bear. He stopped him.

" 'Why do you come here?' asked Sun, but Bear would say nothing.

"Sun did not see Fox, who hid behind Bear in his shadow.

"Bear went along Sky in search of the firebox. But Fox ran ahead and found the box first. He was ready to climb back through hole and run back down the long, long trail made by Cedar when Sun saw him.

" 'Where are you going with my firebox?' asked Sun.

" 'Bear is trying to steal it,' said Fox. 'I am bringing it to you so Bear cannot find it.'

" 'Thank you, small brother,' said Sun.

"Then he turned to Bear who was close behind Fox. Sun was very angry.

" 'You try to steal my firebox? I will give you Fire,' he said and turned his strong medicine on Bear and sent out great fingers of fire that chased Bear back and forth across the heavens."

Kendra's eyes were wide as she listened and imagined all that was happening in the story.

"Bear began to roar in anger and pain," Nonie continued. "And Fox quietly slipped down the long, long trail of poles from Cedar with the firebox under his arm.

"Sun is still searching for his firebox. Now and then he becomes so angry he chases Bear across Sky. Bear roars as the fingers of fire burn his tail and ears. We call it thunder when Bear roars and we see lightning flash as Sun throws his fire at Bear.

"Fox gave Fire from firebox to all animals. The animals shared Fire with man and that is how we keep warm when the nights are cold.

"So it is better to be smart than strong. And it is better not to treat one's brothers in evil ways."

Kendra decided that the thunder seemed so much less frightening with Nonie's soft voice finishing the story.

"So," said Nonie simply. "Father Thunder is only angry with Bear."

Now the thunder was a distant rumble. Kendra could almost enjoy the sound. She no longer felt fear.

Nonie lowered her to the floor and stood to return to her berries. They needed to be picked over and put to dry as soon as the sun would shine on them again. Nonie would have them ready.

❧   ❧   ❧

As they moved into the winter months, Kendra's grandfather was never there when she awoke in the morning. He left on the trapline long before the sun had touched the horizon. Nonie was always there, sitting before the fire, her braiding or weaving or buckskin work in her gnarled fingers. Occasionally Kendra was already in bed and sound asleep before her grandfather returned in the evening, but always he came to her bed, roused her gently and kissed her on the cheek, then stroked her hair until she had fallen to sleep again.

Oscar, playful and teasing, was a constant companion. Kendra spent hours playing with him, and Papa Mac, when he was home, showed the little child how to teach the growing dog to obey simple commands.

Nonie paid little attention to the animal. She seemed to feel that dogs were not her brothers. She treated the puppy with tolerance, not affection, and he accepted her in the same way.

Kendra coaxed to allow the puppy to sleep in a corner of the cabin, though Papa Mac made it clear that it was totally against his principle to pamper an animal in such a fashion. But, he never did open the door and thrust the animal out into the night, even after Kendra had fallen asleep.

She still slept with Dollie tucked tightly against her, but now she often left it behind when on an outing with Nonie.

So the first winter came and went. Papa Mac came and went. Nonie came and went. But Kendra no longer feared that she would be left on her own again, deserted and frightened and without someone to care for her.

❧   ❧   ❧

Not swiftly, but slowly and silently spring's sound gradually swelled to spill over in the rush of the stream that passed by their cabin door, the song of the birds that filled the forest stillness, the rustle of molding leaves as small animals scurried to retrieve berries missed in their fall gathering, and soft breezes that waved the swelling tender buds on the arms of forest trees.

"Mother Earth stirring," said Nonie, pleasure in her voice.

"Who is Mother Earth?" asked Kendra innocently.

"Long ago, before stars, even before Sun and Moon, Old One made Mother Earth. All was dark and no birds sang. No stream ran through the forest. No animal brothers walked in the shadows. There was nothing.

"Old One did not like nothing. He woke Mother Earth. 'Be mother of all people,' he said.

"Mother Earth took some of her flesh and made creatures. Some were like us. Some walked on four feet and were creatures of the forests. Some had wings and flew about the heavens and others swam in the rivers and great waters. All living things come from Mother Earth. When we look around we see part of Mother Earth everywhere. Like us, the animals, birds and fish are made of Mother Earth.

So we are all earth brothers. That is why we care for one another.

"Mother Earth is old, old woman who has seen many moons," Nonie went on with her teaching. "She was before Moon. She lives still, but she has changed much since Old One first made her to be his friend. The soil is her flesh. The rocks are her bones. The wind is her breath. The trees and grasses are her hair.

"Many people do not care for Mother Earth. They tear at her flesh and bones and pull her hair up by roots. But we must love Mother Earth. We must treat her kindly if we do not wish her to be angry. If we love and respect her, she will thank us by giving us food and shelter. She will always be there to care for her children."

Kendra's eyes were wide, her heart full. She loved Nonie's stories. She resolved that she would always be kind to Mother Earth so she might be accepted as a worthy child.

When summer came again, Kendra saw much more of Papa Mac. He even took her with him to the outpost store where he sold his stock of winter furs and purchased the supplies they needed for the months ahead.

He informed Kendra that she could choose a new pair of shoes, but after studying them carefully she shook her head slowly. She wanted shoes like Nonie wore. Soft, supple moccasins. Papa Mac laughed and then nodded his head. He promised he would speak to Nonie about the new "shoes."

Kendra did pick out some yard goods for a new skirt. And some soft flannel for a new nightgown. Papa Mac was sure Nonie would agree to do the sewing.

Kendra enjoyed the excitement of the trip, but she was glad when they climbed from the canoe and she could stretch her cramped legs and take Oscar for a romp along the bank of the stream. And she could hardly wait to show Nonie the new material.

⚜   ⚜   ⚜

George was home a good deal over the summer months, not a time for trapping. All the traps were brought home on the wagon-sleigh and carefully checked and oiled to make sure that they were ready for the next winter's catch. The summer was also spent in other activities. A garden was planted and cultivated. Wood piles were refurnished. Knives were sharpened. Meat and fish were stripped and dried in the sun. Dog harness was repaired with newly tanned moose hides. Never did there seem to be a day when George did not have something with which to busy his hands.

If his work took him away from the cabin, Nonie came. Kendra and Nonie spent many days back in the berry patch or looking for "good" plants to gather in their baskets. Kendra carried her own basket now. Nonie had fashioned it for her from marsh reeds and stained it with a pattern of red, yellow, and brown. Kendra felt proud as she filled her basket with roots and leaves that would be useful.

Whenever she was in error, Nonie showed her the plant and uttered her little sound "p-f-f-t." The next time out, Kendra watched carefully as she gathered. She did not want to pick the offensive plant again.

But when her grandfather's work kept him

around the cabin, Kendra was close beside him. He taught her the bird songs, along with many facts about their habits. Often they searched for nests together, though they never disturbed the tiny warm eggs. If the nestlings had hatched, they sat silently together and watched the parents feed the nosily demanding babies whose beaks never seemed to be silent or their tummies filled.

Another birthday came and went for Kendra. This time her grandfather had made her a harness for the now-grown Oscar. In the days that followed, they spent time teaching the young dog to pull a small training cart. Kendra giggled with delight as Dollie went for her first ride in the small wagon behind Oscar.

As the first snow of another winter whipped around the corners of the snug cabin, Kendra felt her heart stir restlessly. The cold meant that her grandfather would return again to his traps. She hated to see him go. At the same time, it would mean more time with Nonie. Kendra had been missing those long, quiet winter days filled with stories about the Old One and Mother Earth. Kendra was not quite sure whether to be happy or sad to see the snow shut the door on the outside world.

Chapter Seven

The Ugly Side

Another spring was sneaking slowly through the mountain passes, filling the streams and washing away the drifts of snow that had covered the trails and nearly buried the small cabin.

Nonie was anxious to get out to the meadows to catch the early growth of new plants, tender and potent and good medicine for her herbal cures. Kendra was just as anxious to escape the cabin site as well. It had seemed like a long winter of confinement to the five-year-old. She was glad the days were lengthening, the sun stronger in the sky.

"Mother Earth is coming awake," she said to Nonie one morning as they stood in the cabin door drinking in the freshness of the spring air.

Nonie nodded, making no return comment to the child.

"We go," said Nonie after sniffing at the air and studying the sky.

They wrapped themselves in their deerskin jackets. Nonie had made Kendra a long-fringed buckskin of her very own. Then Nonie wrapped their moccasins with strips of leather thongs and rubbed them generously with bear fat to keep the dampness of the trail from penetrating. They collected their baskets, ready to go.

Nonie chose the trail along the banks of the stream. Kendra was fascinated with the tumbling, frothy water that bubbled and splashed its way over the rocks she knew lined the bottom, though they could not be seen now through the foam.

"Sister River is in a hurry," she said to Nonie.

Nonie nodded silently. She never had called the stream "Sister River," but the child seemed to have taken all of nature into her family.

They were nearing the point where the stream made its sharp turn and headed almost back in the direction from which it had come, giving the Indian people the name of Bent River, when a strange moving in the water caught Kendra's eye.

She stopped short, knowing that the movement was unusual but not able to figure out what was different about it.

She turned to Nonie and saw that the woman had also stopped, her dark eyes clouding as she looked toward the same spot. Strange words escaped the woman's lips. Words Kendra had never heard before. Nonie seemed upset.

Then Nonie's chilling cry filled the air and she raised her arms over her head and began to call to the heavens. "Aiyee—aiyee," she wailed, making Kendra's eyes fill with fright, her spine tingle.

She didn't know whether to cling to the woman's skirts or turn and flee toward the cabin.

"Aiyee," called the woman again, entreating the sky in a nameless petition.

Kendra began to cry. In the water the strange thrashing continued, and Nonie kept up the pitiful cries to the skies.

Soon Kendra was frightened into action. She darted to Nonie, yanking on the woman's skirts, her own wails filling the air around them.

Nonie stopped her strange chants and reached her hands down to the child. She still moaned from somewhere deep inside her.

"What is it? What is it?" Kendra cried, shouting her words above the cries of Nonie and the noisy gurgling of the stream.

"Brother Beaver," moaned Nonie. "Brother Beaver."

Kendra's eyes widened. She had seen many beavers. Many times. That had never caused concern before. She liked to watch them. Nonie liked to watch them. They had spent many hours on the banks of the stream watching the beavers fell their trees and build their dams. Nonie had never wailed before.

"Trap," said Nonie. "Trap."

Kendra knew of traps. Her grandfather had traps lining one entire side of the cabin. Traps had never been cause for lamenting either. She was puzzled by Nonie's strange behavior.

Her eyes dropped to Nonie's moccasined feet. Her grandfather had warned her to watch the trails for hidden traps, though he had assured her that no trapper would set a trap on the foot paths used by the people of the area. Still, he had told her of the dangers of traps and had set and sprung some in her presence to show her their strength. They had snapped small sticks as if they had been kindling wood. Kendra had vowed to watch carefully for traps.

But there were no traps attaching themselves to Nonie's feet. Kendra lifted her eyes again.

Nonie was still moaning and swaying, rocking the body of the small girl along with her.

Kendra looked back at the stream.

And then she saw it. A large beaver had managed to pull itself to the bank of the stream. On one front leg dangled a piece of red-wet ugly metal. The beaver thrashed and pulled, its tail whipping the water, its large eyes wide with terror. A strange agonizing sound escaped its throat. Kendra had never seen anything so awful. Never heard anything so pain-filled.

"What happened? What happened, Nonie?" she cried. "How did it get in the trap?"

"Aiyee," wailed Nonie, letting go of the child and lifting her hands again.

"We've got to help it, Nonie," said Kendra, her eyes filling with tears. "We've got to get it out."

But Nonie had turned them both around and was moving down the trail away from the beaver— away from the stream—away from the ugly sight.

"We've got to help it, Nonie," Kendra said again, trying to pull back from the hand that pulled her along.

They had gone some distance before Nonie stopped her wailing and lifting her hands to the sky. The dark eyes were still shadowed, but the woman now hurried Kendra along the trail, and nothing more was said about the trap.

But the fearful event did not leave Kendra's thinking. All day as she played with Oscar or watched Nonie move about the cabin, she kept reflecting on the scene and wondering why Nonie had done nothing to help the entrapped beaver.

When Papa Mac came home, Kendra would be waiting on the doorstep. Nonie talked when Nonie chose to talk. Kendra had the feeling that Nonie would not be discussing with her the incident that had spoiled their day.

But Papa Mac talked. Kendra felt that she could

ask him anything. Tell him anything—anything, that is, except the stories that Nonie shared with her about Mother Earth and the Brothers of the forest. Already Kendra had caught the displeasure of her grandfather regarding Nonie's strange tales.

So Kendra waited patiently for her grandfather while Nonie stirred about the cabin behind her. Oscar lay at her feet, chewing on a piece of well-worn bone. Kendra wondered absently why he continued to chew. All the meat had been removed long ago.

As attentive as Kendra was, it was Oscar who alerted her to the coming of the team. He lifted his head and sniffed at the air, a whine starting somewhere deep inside him and escaping his dark, curled lips.

"They're coming," said Kendra to the dog as though she had been the first to know.

She reached her hand out to Oscar to hold him to his spot. She didn't want the dog to be the first one to greet her grandfather and the approaching team.

In spite of her hand, Oscar rose to his feet, his whine deepening, his ears perked forward.

Soon Kendra could hear the soft yapping of the dogs, the rumbling of the wheels as they stumbled over the rocks of the trail.

She waited. She knew that it wouldn't be long until the team would come into view at the far end of the clearing.

Just as she had expected, the dogs entered the clearing first, her grandfather close at the rear of the sleigh-wagon. She could see the pile of darkness that meant her grandfather had had another good day at the traplines. She was pleased because she knew he would be pleased. He had told her that the final catches of the spring were important. That soon the trapping season would be over for another year.

Normally Kendra ran to greet him, her voice calling out words of excited welcome, her moccasined feet beating a rhythm on the soft ground as she hurried to him to be scooped up into his arms and carried back to the cabin on broad shoulders.

But tonight she sat where she was, her fingers tangled in Oscar's heavy coat, willing him to wait with her.

The sled dogs raced directly to where her grandfather always parked the sleigh.

"Well," he called across to her, "are you too weary to meet me tonight? Has Nonie been dragging you through the woods all day?"

Kendra shook her head quietly. She did not stir from her seat on the step.

With an order to his dog team to lie down on the spot, he moved toward her, sensing that something was wrong.

He lowered his big frame down on the step beside her, pushing back Oscar who wished to get a share of the attention. His arm slipped around the slight body and drew her close.

"You look sad," he said after holding her for a moment. "Did something happen today?"

Kendra nodded her head, her eyes filled with tears.

"Did you and Nonie have a spat?" he continued.

Kendra did not know what a spat was. She had no one to spat with. She looked up at him, her eyes questioning his words.

"Did you and Nonie have a fight?" he asked her again.

Kendra knew what a fight was. She had seen her grandfather separate sled dogs on more than one occasion. But she couldn't imagine getting into such a fuss with Nonie.

She shook her head slowly, the tears spilling over as the picture of the trapped beaver filled her mind again.

"A beaver," she managed, "a beaver got caught in a trap."

There was total silence. The arm about her tightened.

"He got caught," explained Kendra, her eyes large, her lip trembling. "Nonie wouldn't help him."

Her tone was accusing. Kendra had not been able to understand why Nonie hadn't rescued the animal.

Again silence. The arm around her was joined by her grandfather's other arm until Kendra was encircled. She heard him take a deep breath and then he spoke softly, slowly. "Nonie couldn't rescue it," he said, and there was pain in his words. "She would have been in big trouble if she had."

"But why?" sobbed Kendra. "He was caught and he was bleeding and—"

The arms lifted her up onto his lap, where he cradled her against his chest.

"No one can ever interfere with someone else's trap," he explained.

"But the beaver was caught—by its foot. It was crying and—" The small girl was sobbing too much to go on.

"I know. I know," her grandfather tried to soothe her. "But Nonie couldn't let him out. He was already hurt too bad to be—to be set free anyway, and when whoever owned the trap came to get his animal, he would have been very angry with Nonie. He—he needs the money from the pelt. He—"

But Kendra sat bolt upright and pushed away

from him. The word pelt had caught her attention. She had watched her grandfather many times as he had worked with pelts, cleaning them, stretching them, sorting them according to worth. Never once had Kendra thought of the piles of warm, thick furs as animals. Never once had she seen the traps on the walls of the cabin as instruments of horror. Never once had she dreamed that her loving grandfather was capable of causing suffering—to anything.

Now her eyes opened wide as she began to put the words, the images together. Her green eyes grew larger, her sobbing stopped. She stared at him as the truth began to sink in to her childish mind, and then she pushed back from him, her eyes wide with terror and anger, her voice choked with the intensity of discovery.

"I hate you!" she cried, springing from him. She stood in front of him, her green eyes flashing, her small body trembling. "I hate you!" she screamed at him again. "You hurt our brother animals. I hate you."

With a look of pain, anger, and defiance, Kendra lifted her arms heavenward and screamed out the strange and eerie cry, "Aiyee! Aiyee!"

It came from the depths of her troubled spirit—just as it had from Nonie's.

"Aiyee," she wailed again and ran from her grandfather, across the wooden porch, through the door to the cabin, past a startled Nonie, and threw herself upon her moss and pine-bough bunk bed in the corner of the room.

"I think we need to talk."

They had finished the supper that Nonie had left for them before she returned to the village. It had been a silent meal. He had tried to coax conversation from her a time or two, but she had been unresponsive. Now she sat sullenly before him, picking at her food with her fork.

She raised her eyes and nodded. Already she knew that the pain deep within her needed attention. She didn't want to be angry with Papa Mac. It made her hurt all over.

He pushed back his chair from the table and held out his arms. "Come here," he invited.

She went to him, prepared for another good cry in his arms.

When he had soothed her and the sobs had stopped, the tears had been wiped away, he began to talk.

"Trapping is not—not nice for the animals. I know that. But—but people need the furs—the pelts—to make things. Like coats and moccasins. Oh yes, the moccasins that you like to wear, they came from animals, too.

"Animals get killed. We don't like that. But they do get killed. Some of them by man, some of them by other animals. Some of them get old and hungry and can't hunt anymore—and they die. It's not nice—but it's the way it is.

"Traps can be—can be terribly mean things. Like the trap that caught the beaver. Good trappers know how to set the traps so that the animal doesn't suffer as much. But they always suffer some. I admit that. And I don't like it either. But I need the money from the pelts. That is how I live."

Kendra did not stir. He wondered if she was listening. He wondered if she was still hurt. Still angry with him.

"I am always sorry about the animal. About the fact that I take their life in order to make a living—to have pelts to sell so that people can have warm clothes for our harsh winters. But I try—I try hard not to make the animals suffer very much."

Kendra sat in silence, thinking seriously about what he had said.

"I wish—I wish that I could tell you I won't trap anymore. But I can't. And I don't want to lie to you. So I won't tell you that it doesn't hurt the animals. I know it does. But trapping—trapping is a way of life. If we raised animals—cows or sheep or even chickens—for our use—our food and our clothing, they would have to die too. Traps are perhaps a more cruel way to die, but if one is a good trapper the animals can be spared suffering. I'm sorry, Kendra, but that's the way it is."

Kendra sat quietly in his arms, pondering what he had said. The beaver with its dangling paw and plaintive cries still disturbed her. She shut her eyes tightly, trying to block out the sight—the memory. Then she stirred and turned to face her grandfather, her arms stealing about his neck.

"I don't hate you, Papa Mac," she said, her words trailing off in sobs.

He rocked her back and forth, holding her close, wishing that he could shield her from the ugliness of the trapline. Wanting to shield her from the ugliness of life. But he could only hold her and weep, his tears mingling with the blond hair that rested against his cheek.

Chapter Eight

Acceptance

Kendra's sixth and seventh summers varied little from the previous ones. She and Nonie worked together as a team gathering leaves and tender shoots, roots and berries in their baskets. Kendra's sharp eyes were often the first to spot the wild produce, and her keen nose the first to smell the pungent odors that led them in the right direction.

Oscar, big for his breed, had grown to full size and with Kendra's patient training had become a dog that quickly obeyed her commands. Kendra's grandfather, Papa Mac, teased that Oscar ate better than anyone else in the cabin. It was true that Kendra fussed over him and fed him accordingly. The dog was also strong and sturdy, his chest broad, his legs sinewy. Papa Mac, voicing pride in the dog, declared that he would make an outstanding lead dog for a sled team.

The words were not lost on Kendra. In her mind was the picture of the team she hoped to one day have as her own.

She managed to find it in her heart to hope for a good winter's catch on her Papa Mac's traplines, though she still inwardly cringed at the thought of the instruments of death. But she never could run her hands over the softness of the pelts with pleasure as she had done as a small child. She could not see them now without thinking of the animals that they had once been, roaming free and wild in the mountainous forests.

But more and more Kendra was understanding the words her grandfather had spoken—the truth of the laws of nature. Life was hard. Life was violent. The strong took from the weak. Indeed, took of the weak. Kendra had witnessed a wolf pack bringing down a moose. She had seen a lioness dragging a new kill back to her den of cubs. She had watched the bears sweeping salmon from the stream. "The weak will feed the strong," her Papa Mac had explained simply, and though Kendra had at first hated it, had fought against it, she gradually learned to accept it.

Nonie did not lift her arms and cry her chilling lament of "Aiyee" over the kills of nature. She reserved her plaintive cry for the acts of men. Kendra wondered about it and wished to ask the elderly Indian woman, but something held her back. Kendra did not feel free to question Nonie. She did feel she could ask her grandfather.

"Papa Mac," she said one night as they sat on their porch watching the sun dip behind the outline of distant mountains, "why does Nonie say 'Aiyee' like she does?"

"That is her people's way of expressing grief," he answered her. Even then his memory went back to the younger Kendra who had troubled him deeply by echoing Nonie's cry.

"She did it for the beaver—but she didn't do it for the moose," puzzled Kendra.

He sat for a moment in silence, not that he didn't know the answer, but because he wasn't sure how to explain it to the young girl.

"Nonie—and her people—accept the ways of nature. That is normal . . . and right." He hesitated. "But Nonie—and her people—fear that—that their gods—nature—might be angry with man for taking for himself. Oh, they know that animals are here for man to use. They hunt. They fish. They must or they would never survive. But when an animal dies—on behalf of man—then Nonie—and many others—feel that they must mourn that animal so that the spirits—whatever they are and wherever they are—realize that they did not take pleasure in the death of their animal brother. If they don't mourn sufficiently, they are afraid that the spirits might decide to take their lives."

"Is that right?" asked Kendra, her eyes large in her childish face.

"That's the story I was told," said Papa Mac.

"But it is right? Do the spirits really do that?"

"What spirits?" Papa Mac's words were abrupt. Then his tone softened. "Look, Kendra. I don't mind Nonie telling you her little tales about the loon or the mountain lion—but I don't like her filling your mind with all that stuff about spirits and taboos and evil omens. That's all nonsense, Kendra. Indian myth. The earth is not our mother. The beaver is not our brother. Animals don't have spirits that prowl about at night looking for revenge. These are all just—stories—like the ones I read to you at bedtime. Just stories. I don't want you to think of Nonie's tales as anything but—tales. That's her way of life—and at times I think she really believes all that nonsense—but we don't, Kendra. We know better."

Kendra felt a strange stirring somewhere deep inside. She had believed Nonie's stories. She had let them become a part of her. Now Papa Mac was saying that there was no truth in them. But she wanted them to be true. She wanted to feel akin to nature. To have that sense of being a part of something so much bigger than herself.

She wished with all her heart that she could turn to her grandfather and say stoutly, "You are wrong. They are not just stories. There *are* spirits. Good spirits and bad spirits—just like Nonie says. I know. I can—can feel—something."

But Kendra did not say the words. Looking into the intense, dark eyes of her grandfather, she did not dare to say the words. Papa Mac knew about such things. Papa Mac did not believe. Papa Mac might be angry with her if she believed.

She swallowed away the lump in her throat, but deep within herself she felt a sudden pain—an empty spot where something had lived before. What had it been? Belief? Hope? Kendra did not know. She just knew that now it was gone—slain by the words of the grandfather she loved. But what would she ever find to fill its place?

⚜   ⚜   ⚜

The long summer evenings were a joy to Kendra, for it was then that her grandfather told her to get out the books and they would read and study together.

Kendra loved the books. She loved the words on the pages. It was a marvel to her when she first learned to read and discovered for herself that she now had the key to unlock the mysteries of those pages.

The lessons in sums were not as popular with Kendra. All of the numbers made little sense to her.

Then her grandfather began to use more realistic equations. "If you had three weasel pelts, four lynx, two wolves, and three beavers, how much flour, salt, and coffee could you purchase?"

On the wall in her grandfather's cabin was an updated list of the worth of a pelt. He changed and posted it as frequently as the prices fluctuated. Kendra always ran to the list and figured out the worth of the furs, then scrambled back to the table to his last journal entry on the prices of the kitchen supplies at the local store. It made the problems fun to solve, and Kendra always felt proud when her grandfather praised her work.

But the simple problems in arithmetic also did something else for Kendra, though neither her grandfather nor she were aware at the time what was happening. But something was being born within her—the desire to have her own trapline. To add up those pennies and dollars from the furs to her own account. It seemed to the young girl that with all the furs she watched her grandfather pile carefully in the sturdy shed behind the cabin, her grandfather must be getting terribly wealthy in his trade. Someday, she decided silently as she worked the sums, someday she would be counting out pelts of her own.

❧   ❧   ❧

"Mother Earth mourns," said Nonie, and Kendra lifted her head and looked about. What did Nonie mean? But Kendra did not ask. Over the years they had spent together, Kendra had learned from Nonie many of the ways of the Indians—and one of those ways was to wait in silence for an elder to speak further.

"I saw black crow—blackest crow ever. But sad. His eyes were dark. His feathers no longer glistened in sun."

The words that at one time would have filled Kendra with a delicious chill failed to stir her. Papa Mac had said that Nonie's tales were untrue. Just Indian myth. They no longer had the power to move her.

"He speaks," went on Nonie. "He speaks of Mother Earth. She mourns in sorrow. Soon we too will mourn. All will mourn."

Kendra turned her back and lifted her chin. Nonie's story was a bit silly. Just as Papa Mac had said, it was just a foolish omen. Something that the elderly lady was making up to try to frighten her.

"We pick—for Mother Earth," went on Nonie. "Berries of all kind. We scatter them by the first moon in the moon ripples of the lake water. Maybe Mother Earth will forgive."

Kendra wanted to argue. They needed the berries for themselves. They needed to clean and dry them in the warm summer sun so they would have them to sweeten their porridge on the long, cold winter mornings. The berry bushes had not yielded as well as in other years. They had to fight with the birds and the animals for their possession. To pick them and scatter them on the moon ripples of the lake was ridiculous.

But Kendra did not argue. Nonie spoke with such confidence. What would happen if they did not appease Mother Earth? Would she turn on them with thunder and lightning? Would the skies pour down balls of icy hail that would destroy their already shriveling garden plants? Kendra wished to deny the words that Nonie was speaking, but in her heart she felt a tingling of fear. What if? What if Nonie was right and her grandfather was wrong? What then? Could they really afford to challenge Nonie's strange gods?

When Kendra had filled her basket with the luscious wild fruit, she silently passed it to Nonie. She wouldn't take part in the little ritual herself, but if Nonie had the power to protect them from the anger of the gods, then Kendra would not interfere.

⚜   ⚜   ⚜

"Would you like to go with me?"

George turned to his young granddaughter, who was watching him load the canoe in preparation for a trip to the post. It had been some time since Kendra had made the trip. She seemed to prefer to stay at home with Nonie, roaming the nearby woods and meadows, gathering her berries and herbs, studying the wildlife that teemed around them.

But today her eyes held wistfulness. Was she getting bored with her life in the woods? Was she longing for a bit of excitement? Civilization?

At his question, Kendra's eyes seemed to deepen in their green intensity, but no other change took place in her countenance.

"Choosh," said George under his breath, "she's been isolated in the wild too long. Now she doesn't even let her feelings show."

He lifted his head to study his granddaughter and asked again, "Would you like to?"

She nodded mutely. She longed to go. Something within her was stirring. She knew not what. Maybe it was just a silent longing to spend extra time with her grandfather.

"Go tell Nonie. She won't need to stay. Get your things. We may get caught in the rain, so you'd better take an extra coat."

Kendra ran to do his bidding, and in spite of herself a smile played about her lips.

"You'd better tether Oscar," her grandfather said when she returned, breathless and carrying a small bundle under her arm.

Kendra hated to tie her dog. All the sled dogs were tied about the clearing, but Oscar did not like to be tethered. Kendra lifted her eyes to her grandfather and pleaded silently.

"What if he runs off?" he asked in answer to her unasked petition.

"He won't," she dared to promise.

She turned to Oscar and pointed to the porch where he often lay in the sun. "Stay," she said firmly.

Oscar crossed to the porch and lay down, but a whine of protest lifted his sides and seemed to be reflected in the shadowing of his eyes.

"Stay," Kendra said again as she stepped from the bank into the loaded canoe.

It was wonderful to feel the gentle rock and sway of the canoe as they glided over the swift flowing water. Up and around the sharp bend they went, and Kendra could picture again the sight of the beaver fighting for its life against the trap that held it. Though the picture still made her feel sick inside, she pushed it firmly from her. It was a way of life. Acceptable. Ugly—and painful—but acceptable.

She let her glance fall to the pile of carefully wrapped pelts. The returning canoe would bear flour and salt and coffee and yard goods and all the other supplies they so desperately needed for survival. Kendra sighed deeply and reached out a hand to let it trail in the cool stream.

They passed by the Indian village, and Kendra nodded greetings to the children who played about the bank. She recognized a few of them by name. Nonie had provided the information on the few trips they had made together to the little settlement. But George did not like Kendra to spend much of her time with the other children. He feared that if she learned more of their ways, she would have even greater difficulty when she had to go back to the city for her education.

George had been putting off sending Kendra out. He knew that it had to be done. He knew that he had waited longer than he should have. But she was doing well. She could read almost anything he handed her—with understanding. And she was quicker at working out sums than many of the adults he knew. Still, she did need to go out. Back to the city. She needed to learn about her own culture. Her own people. She needed to learn the social graces that would identify her as civilized. He knew that. But it was so hard to let her go. To think of the long days without her about the cabin.

George rested the paddle for a moment and let the small craft drift as he studied the face of his grandchild. She was doing fine—wasn't she? She was happy. Content. Nonie was caring for her. Nonie with all of her ridiculous scare stories. He did hope that she had stopped feeding the child all the nonsense about ghosts and wandering spirits. He had talked to her about it on more than one occasion. Kendra hadn't brought the tales to him of late. Did that mean they had stopped—or had Kendra chosen not to discuss them with him anymore?

Kendra felt his eyes upon her and lifted her head to look at him. The green eyes were so large and intense. The small oval face so much like his Mary's. He could not hide the love—the pain—that he was feeling inside. He forced a smile to crinkle the corners of his eyes, make his mustache twitch at the sides of his mouth. "Happy?" he asked simply.

Kendra nodded. She was happy. Totally at peace with herself and her world. She tilted her head and listened for the return call of the whiskey jack, then nodded again.

"Except for poor Oscar," she said to her grandfather. "I wish he could have come. He hates to stay alone."

"He has all the other dogs for company," her grandfather answered.

"But he doesn't want the dogs for company," argued Kendra. "He wants us. He thinks he's people."

George threw back his head and laughed good-naturedly. It was the first time Kendra had heard him laugh so generously for a long time. A smile played about her lips, and before long she felt a little giggle rising in her own throat.

From then on the trip became a shared delight. They chatted and laughed and teased each other as they had not done for a long time. Both of them enjoyed it. It was a breaking of silence. A bonding together. A release from a thought prison that had held back full communication.

We need to do this more often, thought George. *She needs to be able to talk and laugh. She is not silent by nature. She should not be forced into that mold. She needs to talk and to be free to share her feelings. She needs to be with me more. Be less with Nonie.*

And George decided that he would find ways to integrate the child more into his style of living.

Chapter Nine

Fire

There were visitors at the fort. The trader's brother and sister-in-law had come from a city somewhere to visit him in his "wilderness."

Kendra tried not to stare at them, but she could not help feeling interested. As her grandfather accepted a cup of hospitality, the trader's thick bitter coffee, Kendra sat on a pile of furs and listened to the conversation and studied the faces before her.

"Your granddaughter?" Kendra heard the visiting woman ask. "How nice." Then she turned to Kendra and gave her a big smile.

"How long has she been with you?" the woman asked.

George had to stop and do some calculating. "Past four years now. Almost five," he answered, surprising even himself at the time that had quickly passed.

The woman cast another glance at the slight young girl in her simple shirt and buckskins. Her blond braids were in sharp contrast to her tanned cheeks.

" 'Course she goes out every winter," speculated the woman.

"Oh no," George said quickly. "She has been with me the whole time."

The woman's eyes showed her surprise. She did

not hold back but spoke her mind quickly. "Where does she get her schooling?"

It was more than a question. It was an accusation.

"I teach her," George answered, his voice getting deeper with his need to defend the circumstance.

"But—" began the woman.

"And I dare say she can read better for her age than any of those city kids," he went on, tempted to call Kendra to him to show off her ability. He did not do so. He felt it would be unfair to the child to drag her into their little dispute.

The lady cast another glance at Kendra and seemed to concede the point. Then she licked her lips, doubt still showing in her eyes. "What about her religious training?" she challenged further.

George stirred uncomfortably. He put no stock in religious training, whether one was raised in the wilderness or the middle of the city. Did he dare to speak his feelings to the woman before him? Would he take the stand of an infidel in front of the whole trading post? If he did, how might it affect the future of Kendra?

He swallowed the words he wished to say and replied simply, "You think the wilderness has no God?"

The woman nodded in silent agreement. She could not argue that point. She saw the work of God everywhere she looked in this wide, open, beautiful country.

The subject was dropped, the coffee finished, and the bartering begun.

❧   ❧   ❧

"I have something I would like to give you," the

woman said, approaching Kendra as her grandfather was loading the canoe for their return trip.

In her outstretched hand she held a silver chain, and on the chain was a strange, delicate figure.

"What is it?" asked Kendra.

"The cross," said the woman. "You wear it about your neck—like this."

She placed the necklace around Kendra's neck and fastened it securely.

"Is it an amulet?" asked Kendra.

"A—a what? No—no nothing like that. We don't wear it like a—like a charm. We wear it simply as a—a remembrance."

"Oh-h," said Kendra. But she had no idea what the woman was talking about.

"You are a very pretty girl," went on the woman, reaching out to stroke the blond head of hair. She smiled. "And rather intriguing too. A young Scot in Indian dress. You make quite a picture."

Kendra did not fully understand the words. She had no idea what the woman was carrying on about.

"Are you a Scot?" Kendra asked. She knew the woman was not Indian.

"Oh no." The woman chuckled merrily. "I'm German," she said.

Kendra supposed that the words should mean something to her—but they did not. She had nothing with which to identify them. So she tucked the word away for future reference and studied the woman carefully.

She looked kind. Her eyes were clear and direct. Her mouth curled easily into a smile. She was neat and pleasing. Her body looked strong and sturdy. Kendra concluded that it must be fine to be German.

George McMannus was approaching. The

woman stepped back and smiled at Kendra again.

"Perhaps we will see you again sometime," she said pleasantly.

Kendra nodded, then turned to follow her grandfather to the canoe. Her fingers reached up to feel the cross that dangled from the chain around her neck. It was a pretty thing. Shiny and simple. Kendra had never had anything like it before. She was anxious to show it to her grandfather.

The two pushed off in the canoe for their return up the river. Papa Mac was much too busy easing the canoe out into the stream and around all the other canoes that bobbed up and down on their moorings to be distracted by Kendra's new possession.

Kendra watched, noticing how skillful he was with the paddle and subconsciously noting how to handle the oar with the most efficiency.

When they had waved for the last time to the group clustered at the water's edge and the canoe dipped behind the first bend in the river, Kendra sat back and relaxed. It was all paddling upstream now, but her grandfather had made the trip many times and seemed not to tire as the paddle dipped rhythmically into the cool, clear stream, thrusting them ever forward against the pull of the current.

"Look what the lady gave me," Kendra finally said, her fingers still on the silver cross.

"What lady?" he asked absently, not even glancing up at her. He was intent on easing their way around an outcropping of rock in the stream bed.

"The German lady," said Kendra. "The one visiting the post."

But before her grandfather could even respond, Kendra changed the topic with, "What's a German?"

His eyes still on the rocks as he steered the canoe carefully through the maze, he replied, "A race of people. They come from Germany."

"Where's Germany?" asked Kendra.

A frown furrowed his brow. He had been priding himself on Kendra's advanced education. But the truth of the matter was there was so much that he wasn't teaching her. So much that he couldn't teach her. She needed lessons in geography. In history. In social studies. He didn't have the time or the ability to teach her what she needed to know. No—he would have to send her out. It wasn't fair to the child to keep her from school.

Deeply troubled, he sighed. He did not wish to spoil their time together by bringing up the subject. When they had spoken of it before, Kendra had always begged for a bit more time. But now—? The woman had been quite right, though it galled him that she had dared to question him on the raising of his granddaughter. But she was right. Kendra needed to go to school.

He would keep her with him throughout the summer, but he would write a few letters and when the fall arrived again, he would take her to the city.

"Where'd you get that?"

For a moment Kendra was puzzled by her grandfather's question. They sat at their evening meal together, Oscar stretched out on the floor beside Kendra's chair. Then Kendra noticed that his eyes were studying the chain with the lovely silver cross attached hanging around her neck.

"The woman gave it to me," Kendra explained, eyes shining.

"What woman?"

"The German woman—at the post." Kendra fingered the cross and lifted it so that she and her grandfather could get a better look. "She brought it to me when I was waiting for you to put everything in the canoe. She said it's a cross."

"I am well aware of what it is," he responded, but he didn't sound pleased or excited about Kendra's gift.

She looked at him, not understanding the gruffness in his voice.

"Don't you like it?" she dared to ask, disappointed.

"I guess it's harmless enough," he replied carelessly. But Kendra could sense that he was not pleased with the gift.

Still, he had not said that she couldn't keep it.

Perhaps he just didn't think it was pretty. Already Kendra had noticed that her grandfather was drawn to things she and Nonie were not; the reverse was also true. She would show the cross to Nonie. She felt quite sure that her response would be quite different.

"Look what I've got."

Kendra had run down the path to meet Nonie. Grandfather was still at the house preparing the dogs for a trip to the bush to haul firewood. Nonie approached the cabin slowly, her ever-present herb basket on her arm.

"Look!" said Kendra again and lifted the silver cross for the woman to see.

Nonie's eyes brightened. She may not have understood the cross, but she did understand silver jewelry. "Good!" she said to Kendra.

Kendra was quite pleased with herself. Nonie had pronounced the gift as something worthwhile.

"A lady gave it to me," she explained as she skipped along beside Nonie toward the cabin. "A German lady."

The old woman stopped short, stared at Kendra with dark, brooding eyes, then said, "German. P-f-f-t." She spat in the dust of the trail.

Kendra's eyes shadowed. She did not understand the response. Nonie had liked the gift. Now she looked at it with contempt, spitting out her word with the one angry exclamation.

"P-f-f-t," said Nonie, and she spit again.

Then without another word to the girl, she resumed her silent steps toward the cabin.

Kendra turned to follow, her eyes troubled with questions, her mind filled with deep confusion and sorrow.

There was something bad about Germans. Maybe she shouldn't have accepted the gift. Maybe she should take it off now and throw it into the lake as an appeasement to the moon ripples. Would Mother Earth—or some other unseen being—be angry with her? What might be the consequences? Kendra shivered at the thought.

Wordlessly she followed Nonie. When she reached the cabin, she cast a glance at the woman. Noticing that her back was turned, Kendra reached up and slipped the silver chain over her head. She would take no chances.

For a long moment she stood and looked longingly at the pretty cross. She hated to give it up, but she really had no choice. Tonight she would steal down to the edge of the waters, and when the first moon cast its gold over the ripples of the lake, she would cast her gift into the deep. She hoped there would be a loon. If a loon cried at just the right time—the time that the moon first turned the ripples gold—it would be a good omen. Any spell that might have been cast over her would surely be broken.

Kendra hoped that she would never again have to face the curse of a German.

❧   ❧   ❧

There was a strange crackling sound up on the roof. Kendra wondered if a bird or squirrel was doing something quite out of the ordinary. She listened for the sound to come again.

Nonie had stopped what she was doing and tilted her head to listen too.

The sound came again. This time Nonie's head jerked up quickly. "Come!" she said to Kendra and reached out to nudge her toward the door.

Kendra frowned in puzzlement—not because of the command but because of the urgency with which it was spoken.

"Come," said Nonie again, and the two of them pushed through the cabin door at the same time.

It was then that Kendra noticed a different smell. In the air about the cabin a new color of smoke drifted leisurely.

"What is it?" Kendra asked, fright making her voice tremble.

"Fire," said Nonie. "Fire on roof."

Kendra lifted her eyes to the sloping roof of the cabin. Sure enough. The smoke was curling upward, caught by the gentle breeze and spiraling around the chimney.

"Get pail!" shouted Nonie, and after one wild glance at the woman, Kendra ran for the pail that stood on the bench by the door.

"Water," barked Nonie.

With terror making her heart constrict, Kendra dashed for the stream and scooped up a pail of water.

Nonie had already placed the ladder against the side of the house. Now she took the pail from Kendra's numb fingers and turned to mount the ladder. Her knees were stiff, her shoulders bent. Kendra feared that the woman would fall in her attempt.

"Let me," she said, taking the pail back. "I will do it."

When Kendra looked over the side of the roof line, she could see that the fire had started in the chimney. The flames were now extending beyond the stonework and reaching angrily toward the sky. Kendra pulled herself up onto the roof and struggled with the heavy pail of water.

She crept as close to the flames as she dared and flung the water with all of her might. She heard the sizzle and sputter as the water collided with the fire, but even as she watched, the hungry flames flared up again. The water had little effect.

By the time Kendra scrambled back down the ladder, Nonie was there with another pail of water. They exchanged pails and Kendra remounted the ladder.

Again and again she climbed the ladder—up and down. The flames had escaped the chimney now and were licking at the dry shingles of the roof.

But each time Kendra threw another pail of water on the flames, she seemed to make a small bit of headway. Not much. But as the dry shingles soaked up more and more of the cold river water, the fire seemed to lose a bit of power in the struggle.

Kendra's face burned. Her arms ached. Her back felt as if it were broken, and with all the trips up and down the ladder, her legs seemed like jelly. She wondered if she would be able to fight on.

But she did. She climbed and dumped every pail that Nonie dragged up to her. And finally the flames flickered, struggled, then ceased.

Kendra was ready to collapse. What if they had lost their cabin? What if they had lost their home? The traps? Her books? Their supplies? Everything they owned was in that cabin. What if they had lost it all?

She climbed stiffly down the ladder for one last time and collapsed on the cool ground beside Nonie. Both were exhausted, soot-covered, both flushed from the heat of the fight.

"Mother Earth angry," said Nonie between gasps for breath.

Kendra immediately thought of the silver cross given to her by the German. Her grandfather had said that it was harmless. But Papa Mac had not understood about Nonie's gods. Had not realized how angry they could be.

She had thrown it away. Given it to the gods of the lake. She had been careful that the first light of the moon was tinting the ripples of the water. But no loon had called. There had been two loons on the lake. Kendra had pleaded in her heart for one of them to call to the other, but they had stubbornly refused. Was that the problem? Were the loon brothers also angry?

Kendra buried her head in her arms and began

to weep. It was so hard. So hard. So hard to keep all the spirits happy. She hadn't meant to make them angry. Had tried so hard to undo the damage. It seemed there was just no way to live at peace with the spirit world.

George McMannus spent the next two days patching the roof of the cabin, and as he worked he often shook his head in wonder. How had the elderly Indian woman and his young granddaughter managed to save the structure? He couldn't imagine the number of trips she must have made up and down the ladder. Again he was thankful that he kept the tall pines and spruce from encroaching too closely on the space around the cabin. If the fire had spread to tree branches, they would never have saved the cabin. There would have been a forest fire that might have taken a large sweep of the area. He might even have lost his little girl to the flames.

He should not have been so careless. He knew well that chimneys need frequent cleaning. He knew that a buildup of soot and wood tars could be disastrous. Why hadn't he paid closer attention? Why hadn't he checked it sooner?

It was another reminder to George that his cabin, miles from civilization, was really not a proper place for a young girl. He pulled out the letter he had penned a few weeks earlier and went to the post to send it off to the head mistress of the girls' school. He had to make proper arrangement for Kendra. He could put it off no longer.

Chapter Ten

School

"Why do we need to go to the city?"

He was sure Kendra already knew the answer to her question. He had explained it carefully to her before they left the cabin. But he answered her again, "So that you may go to school."

"But why do I have to go to school?" she argued. "You teach me."

"Yes—I have taught you—some. But there is so much more to learn than I've been able to teach you. You need to learn about lands and peoples and discoveries and inventions. I can't teach you all of those things. I don't know about them—and I haven't got the maps or charts or books that tell about them."

Kendra was silent. To his relief she had not resisted the trip when he had first told her about it. But he did wonder if she was feeling the change more deeply than she dared to let on.

"You will like it at school. There will be other girls of your own age. You will make many friends."

"I already have friends," said Kendra stubbornly.

"What friends?" He wondered if Nonie had been sneaking her off to the village when he wasn't around.

"Nonie," said Kendra. "Nonie and Oscar."

George McMannus smiled, but he also felt sadness. He should have brought the young girl out earlier and let her have a chance at being a part of the real world.

"When do I go to school?" she asked him. "How many more days?"

"We'll have a whole week before school starts," he answered, trying to put some enthusiasm into his voice. "Mrs. Miller is going to help us get you ready for school. She knows how to shop for young girls. We might even pay a visit to Mrs. Weatherall—if you'd like. Remember her?"

Kendra did remember. Slightly. She had liked the woman well enough. But she wasn't sure she wanted to pay a visit.

"Would you like that?" her grandfather pressed.

"I don't think so," Kendra replied simply, her head turning from him. He did not push the subject further.

"We will do your shopping then," said her grandfather. "That should be fun."

Kendra looked down at her soft buckskin garments. Her feet were still comfortably shod in her moccasins. She wasn't sure if she wanted to shop or not. Oh, she supposed it would be nice to have new things instead of the clothing that Nonie had sewn for her. But she just wasn't sure she wanted to give up the things with which she was familiar.

"Who is Mrs. Miller?" she asked instead.

"She is a friend of mine from many years back."

Kendra knew that. What she really wished to know was what kind of a person the woman was. Was she old? Young? Kind? Difficult? Talkative or silent? Who was Mrs. Miller?

"You will like Mrs. Miller," her grandfather continued. "She never had a family of her own but she . . ." He hesitated. They had not talked of Mary for many months. At last he willed himself to continue. "She loved your mother very much," he said softly. "Almost like she was—was her own daughter. After your—your grandmother died, Mrs. Miller helped your mother with her clothes and—and even her wedding."

Kendra stirred. It was the first in a long time that she had been reminded of the mother she could barely remember.

"Is she Scotch too?" she asked, wishing to have some point of contact.

"No. No, she is German."

Kendra's head came up, her eyes reflecting her deep shock.

The man had no idea what the one simple word meant to Kendra. Again she saw the flashing dark eyes of Nonie as she spat in the dust of the path and hissed out the words, "German. P-f-f-t." And spit again.

"What's wrong?" asked her grandfather, sensing her discomfiture.

"Germans are bad," she said in a whisper.

"What do you mean?"

"They're bad."

"Who told you that?" he asked her. "Where did you get that idea?"

"Nonie. Nonie spit. She—"

"Nonie?" His mind scrambled to try to figure out the meaning of her words. Then a light dawned.

"Oh, that. Nonie shouldn't say such things. Should know better."

"But—"

"There was a trapper in the area once," he went on to explain. "He was a bad trapper. He stole from other traps and made a great deal of trouble for everyone. Including Nonie's husband, who was still alive at the time and trapping south of the settlement. Eventually the Mounties came and got the man. They put him in jail somewhere, I guess. We've never heard of him again. He was German. It's true. But, Kendra—you never should judge a whole race of people because one of them is bad. It doesn't work that way."

Kendra still looked doubtful.

"I knew a bad Scotsman once," her grandfather went on. "He drank whiskey—all the time. Then picked fights with anyone who came along. He was a Scot. I am Scot. Does that make me bad?"

Kendra knew that it didn't. Still she could not voice a reply.

"And I knew a bad Indian once," her grandfather went on. "He never wanted to work a trapline. Never hunted for food. Never wanted to do anything except steal from his neighbors. He watched the other cabins, and whenever the people were not at home, he slipped in and stole from their traps and belongings, their food supplies and leggings. He was Indian. Nonie is an Indian. Does that make her a bad Indian?"

Kendra shook her head slowly. She knew that it didn't. She loved Nonie.

"We must never—*never* judge a race by one person—or a person by a race. Each individual must be allowed to be good—or judged bad—on their own merit, their own behavior. Do you understand, Kendra?"

The words were spoken softly but firmly. Kendra

sensed that her grandfather felt very strongly on the matter.

She nodded her head again.

"Maggie Miller is about the finest woman you will ever meet," her grandfather went on. "She nursed your grandmother for months before—" He couldn't finish the thought. "And Henry, her husband, another German—he risked his life to save mine. He still bears the scars on his hands. No, Kendra. One bad German does not make a race of bad Germans any more than one bad Scot makes a race of bad Scotsmen."

Kendra looked at him solemnly. When it came to taking sides with the one or the other, Kendra was willing to accept the word of her grandfather over Nonie's.

❦　　❦　　❦

"George. Come in! It's been a long time."

Kendra judged the woman at the door to be Maggie Miller. The long journey had finally ended, and she and her grandfather stood on the stoop with small cases in hand.

"Come in. Come in," the welcoming voice continued. "I'm so glad to see you. It's been such a long time."

She drew them in. There was a strange and delicious aroma in the room. It smelled spicy and warm—reminding Kendra of a warm summer day in the berry patch.

"And this is Kendra?" The woman's arm reached out to draw Kendra close. "My, how you've grown! And such a pretty girl, too. Your mama would be so proud of you."

Kendra felt herself pulled close. She could smell the scent of the woman. So different from the way Nonie smelled. There was no hint of cured leather. No odor from open fires. No lingering smells of the cooking pots. Kendra did not recognize any of the strange aromas, so she felt neither welcomed nor repelled by them. They were simply new. Different. Like the house that enclosed her. It was strange. With furnishings and "things" all around her. Pictures on walls, more chairs than there were people. Books. Lamps. Baskets cradling various objects. Coats on hooks. Blankets draped here and there. It looked cluttered and busy to Kendra, who was used to stark simplicity.

She kept her eyes to the floor in the manner she had learned from the Indian women, but she was so tempted to peek around her, taking in all of the strange sights and feelings.

Mrs. Miller released her, and Kendra stepped back, not really feeling comfortable in the arms of the woman.

"Sit down," Mrs. Miller said to them both, and George moved to an overstuffed chair with a multicolored blanket draped over it and lowered himself with a sigh of contentment.

"How's Henry?" he asked before his body had even settled in.

"Not good, I'm afraid." The woman's eyes shadowed. "He gets a bit weaker every day."

George did not allow himself the comfort of the chair. He rose quickly and crossed to the bedroom where he knew the man to be. Mrs. Miller nodded and moved toward the kitchen. Kendra did not know what to do, so she followed her grandfather.

"Hello, Henry," he said to the man who lay prostrate on the bed. "It's George. I should have come sooner . . ." The words trailed off.

Kendra saw her grandfather reach down and take the limp, wasted hand in one of his strong, sun-browned ones. He turned the hand over and stared for a long moment at the scar on the back of the hand. Kendra too saw the scar. The scar that her grandfather had told her about. She saw her grandfather's jaw working with emotion as he held the motionless hand. Then he laid it gently down on the covers and reached to brush the scanty gray hair back from the man's face.

He turned then, surprised to see Kendra standing so near to the bed of the invalid.

"This is Henry," he said quickly, as though he felt an explanation was in order. She nodded. She knew. She also saw in her grandfather's eyes the terrible pain he felt in seeing his friend so helpless.

❦   ❦   ❦

George stayed with Henry while Mrs. Miller took Kendra shopping for the new clothes she would need for her school year.

In a way, it *was* exciting. Kendra saw things she had never dreamed existed. Pretty things. Delicate things. Colorful things. Over and over she wished she could share her experience with Nonie. She wondered if Nonie's eyes would light up and pronounce them good, or if she would stop and spit in the dust.

Kendra wasn't quite sure what she thought about the new world. The world that she had quite forgotten. It fascinated her and seemed to draw her, yet she felt strange and uneasy with all the strangeness.

When the week was up and time to enter the new school approached, Kendra's wardrobe was ready. Mrs. Miller herself had done much of the sewing. The new nightgowns and undergarments were ready. The stockings, shoes, and school uniforms were already carefully packed in the new case.

But as Monday drew closer, Kendra was more and more sure that Martha Adams' School for Girls was not where she wanted to be. She wanted to climb aboard the boat with her grandfather and return to the place that was familiar. She wanted to go home to Nonie. To bury her face against the warm, soft side of Oscar. But Kendra did not even try to tell her grandfather how she felt. She did not speak with the German woman who fussed about her, hemming skirts and fitting bodices. Kendra buried the feelings deep inside, but at night when she went to bed, she pulled Dollie from her worn suitcase and later cried into the plump, soft body of the old rag doll.

Chapter Eleven

Pain of Separation

It was terribly hard to say goodbye. George consoled himself with the fact that he was doing what was right for the child. Kendra had no such consolation. She saw the separation as a painful situation totally beyond her control. Nor could she see that there was anything to be gained by the whole endeavor.

She did not weep. Not as she was held in the arms of her grandfather and commended for being such a brave young lady. She did not even weep as she watched his tall back disappear beyond the strong wooden door of the girls' school.

The tall, stern-looking young woman whom she was to call Miss Bruce said a crisp, "Come," and Kendra turned to follow, much as Oscar followed her commands.

"This will be your room," the young woman said. "You will share it with three girls. Stella Lange, Ruth Winters, and Rebecca Joyce. That bed will be yours. You may use the two bottom drawers in the chest by the window. Unpack your things and place them neatly in the drawers. Your case will be picked up for storage.

"Mind you hurry now. It will soon be time for the lunch bell."

She turned on her heel and was gone.

Kendra stood, her whole body trembling. But she did not cry. The words of the woman had come so fast, so brisk, that Kendra wondered if she had understood them. She couldn't think. Couldn't remember. What had she said? Kendra looked at the bed. Had she said something about the bed? Oh yes. This was her bed. The three other beds in the room belonged to—to somebody else.

Kendra let her eyes wander over the room. They lighted on the case that held all her new things. The woman had said she was to unpack her new things. Where was she to put them? She couldn't remember. Couldn't unscramble all the words that had poured out in such quick and utter confusion. In storage? But storage where?

Kendra knew about storage. Her grandfather had a loft in the cabin for storage of supplies. He had a shed out back for storage of pelts. He had another little shed for storage of materials for mending sleighs and harness and all sorts of other things. It held some tools too. Simple tools.

But where were the storage sheds for the girls' school?

Kendra opened her suitcase and carefully took out all the new items. She piled them on the bed that she was told would be hers. The little piles kept toppling over, and she knew she would never be able to keep them together to carry to the storage shed.

There was a nice white sack over the pillow at the head of her bed. Kendra decided to borrow it. Item by item she began to load all her belongings into the case. All except Dollie. Kendra looked about the room to make sure she wasn't being watched and stuffed the rag doll under her pillow. She had the feeling she was going to need her precious companion over the coming days.

The pillowcase was getting full by the time Kendra finished, but she managed to stuff the last pair of long stockings into the sack.

"I do wish I didn't have to store them," she whispered to herself. "I think Papa Mac was expecting me to wear them." She looked down at the dress she was wearing. She guessed that it would have to do—maybe for a long time. She wished she had brought her buckskins.

"Now, where is the storage shed?" she asked herself, and lifting her bundle she traveled the long hall and pushed her way out the door that led to the rear of the property.

She managed to find a shed, but the door was locked. Kendra did not know what to do, and then she spotted a window above her that was slightly open.

"If I could find a ladder," she murmured. She laid down her sack with all of her belongings and looked about. There on the side of the shed was a ladder. Kendra felt relieved to find that her problem would be solved so quickly and easily. She placed the ladder against the side of the building, hoisted her bundle and started up. Difficult climbing with her arms so full, she nearly lost her balance and fell.

She managed to push her bulky load through the open window. She heard the funny sound as it landed on the floor in the shed. Then there was a tinkling sound as though something else had landed on the floor as well. Kendra held her breath—but nothing more happened.

By the time she climbed back down the ladder and placed it back where she had found it, she was panting from her excursion. Somewhere a bell was ringing. Kendra puzzled over it. She was not used to hearing bells.

Then she remembered the words of the woman. There was to be a lunch bell. What did that mean?

As Kendra entered the building through the door from which she had left, she could hear scurrying feet off in the distance. Someone else was in the building. They were on their way—somewhere.

Kendra studied the puzzle of doors. She couldn't remember which one had been hers. She made her way down the hall, peeking in room after room. She was totally confused. The young girl who could have found her way through the forest trails without benefit of compass was thoroughly mixed-up by all the doors that looked alike yet led to different places.

At last she noticed a bed with a different pillow. It looked lumpy and bare and out of line. "That's mine," she said with some satisfaction. All the other pillows still had their cases. All the other pillows were placed evenly and neatly at the head of each bed.

Yes, it was hers. Dollie was still hidden under it. Her open valise was still sprawled across the floor. She closed the case and fastened the clasp.

What was she to do now?

She decided that the only thing she could do was to wait. She pulled Dollie out and tried to straighten the pillow to match the other ones on the beds in the room. Perhaps she should have dumped her things through the storage window and brought back the case so that her pillow wouldn't look different from the others.

It was too late now. There was no way she could retrieve what she had deposited in the shed.

With a deep sigh she looked for a place to sit. There was only one chair in the room and it was across the floor from her. What if it belonged to someone else? Perhaps it would be safer if she sat on the bed. But the bed was so white and smooth that she didn't dare sit on it.

At last she sank down to the floor, Dollie clutched tightly in her arms.

But Kendra had no idea what she was waiting for nor how long she might have to sit there. She didn't think much of this girls' school. She had been told that she was sent here to learn. She had expected to be able to use all the new clothes Papa Mac and Mrs. Miller had provided. She had been told about books and maps and all manner of interesting things that would help her to learn about the world.

But there was nothing. Nothing but a room with stark white beds. Papa Mac was gone and she was all alone. She didn't know where she was or how to ever get back to Bent River Crossing again. She didn't know how to find Nonie. Or Oscar. She was alone. Alone. And so frightened and lonely. Besides all that—her feet hurt in the tight, stiff new shoes. Kendra reached down and slipped them off. She hated them. She wanted her comfortable moccasins back. She wanted to go home. She just wanted to go home.

Kendra curled up on the hard board floor with Dollie held tightly in her arms. She longed to cry, but she refused to allow herself even that small comfort.

❧   ❧   ❧

George McMannus walked slowly. He had delivered Kendra as he had known he must do. Martha Adams' School for Girls was known to be a good one. It would be good for Kendra. The first few days might be hard, but she would quickly adjust. She was a bright little thing. She would soon have everything in the place all figured out. She would soon make friends with the other little girls.

He had done the right thing. He knew that. But he had not done the easy thing.

No. He was miserable. He knew that he would likely be miserable for months to come. How long? How long was the school term before Kendra could come home again? Not until spring. Not until almost summer. He didn't know if he'd ever be able to stand it.

He knew that the winter ahead would be the loneliest winter of his life. He hoped that he would be able to endure it. That he could make it through. He wouldn't even have Nonie moving silently about the cabin. There would be no need for Nonie to come now. There would be just him and Oscar. He thought of the sled dog. He was really too big to be taking up room in the cabin. It was totally unnecessary. He had a warm, thick coat. He would be as comfortable out of doors as any of the other team members. But for the first time, George felt thankful that Oscar was a cabin dog. It wouldn't be quite as lonely. At least he would have the pampered dog to talk to.

It was going to be a long winter. An awfully long and lonely one.

❧   ❧   ❧

"Kendra! What are you doing?"

It was the stern-looking young woman who stood over Kendra, her brow furrowed, her eyes flashing frustration. "You missed your lunch."

Kendra struggled to her feet, Dollie hanging limply from her hand. She had no words to answer. She wasn't quite sure of the question.

But it came again. "What are you doing? You were told to put away your things and come for the lunch bell. We have strict rules. If you miss the lunch bell, there will be nothing to eat until the supper hour. And if you miss that—nothing until breakfast. Do you understand?"

Kendra nodded. There was so much she did not understand, but she felt she had understood those few severe words.

"Come now," said the woman. "It is time for your first class."

She wheeled on her heel and Kendra obediently stepped forward to follow.

"And leave that—that worn-out—rag—behind," hissed the woman, motioning toward Dollie.

Kendra looked down at the doll that still dangled from her hand. Then she looked about the spotless, bare room. Dollie would look so out of place.

"Put her in the drawer where you put your clothes."

Kendra stood stark-still. She remembered then. She was to have put her clothing in the chest. In the chest with the drawers. She was to have the two at the bottom. But she had put her clothes in the storage shed. She had made a dreadful mistake.

"And where is your pillowcase?" a disturbed and angry voice demanded.

"I—I needed it," Kendra stammered. She still stood holding Dollie. Slowly the doll was lifted until Kendra was clutching her tightly against her chest. Her large green eyes were dark. There were no tears. Kendra was beyond that.

"And get your shoes back on," ordered the woman, totally beside herself.

Kendra didn't know what order to try to fill first. She lowered Dollie to the wooden boards of the floor and sank down beside her, reaching for a shoe as she did so. She hated to put the miserable things back on her aching feet. They hurt. And they made noise when one walked.

"Now—about that pillowcase—where—?"

Just then another woman entered the room. She was shorter than the blustering woman who stood before Kendra. And she was not as thin, nor as straight. Nor did she look quite as sour.

"You have found her," the woman said, and there was both concern and relief in her voice.

"She was right here in the room—the whole time," answered the younger one, annoyance still evident in her voice.

Kendra was sitting on the floor struggling with her shoe. She said not a word, though her thoughts reminded her that she had not been in the room "the whole time." She had gone to the shed.

"I told her plainly to come at the lunch bell, Miss Jennings." The woman went on to explain to her elder that she had done her job properly but had not been obeyed.

"Perhaps she didn't know where the dining room is. Did you tell her that?" the older woman inquired softly.

The younger one seemed flustered. "Well, we must get her to her class. We don't want her late so she disturbs the others," Miss Jennings said. The one called Miss Bruce bent and snatched Dollie off the floor from Kendra's side and moved quickly to the chest of drawers.

"She has done something with the pillowcase." The thin one fairly spat out the words. "I was trying to get to the bottom of it."

She leaned and jerked open the drawer, then straightened with a horrified look on her face.

"She hasn't even unpacked her clothes!" she exclaimed, then wheeled back to Kendra.

"Why didn't you unpack as you were told."

"I—I did," floundered Kendra.

The woman turned back to the empty drawer before her. "No, you didn't," she denied hotly. "There's not a thing in here."

Miss Bruce spun around and lifted Kendra's case from the floor, opening the latch with hands that trembled with anger.

"There's nothing here either," she said, her face filled with unbelief. "What did you do with them, child?"

"Perhaps she put them in the wrong drawers," suggested the other woman.

"They wouldn't fit." But even as the younger woman said the words, she crossed to the chest and pulled out one drawer after another. Kendra's things were not there. "What did you do with them?"

"I—I—" Kendra could not meet the angry eyes.

She lowered her head, her eyes on the floor.

The older woman, Miss Jennings, had not left the room. She seemed to sense Kendra's deep discomfiture. Kendra heard the swishing of skirts and felt a hand placed on her head.

"What is it, child?"

Kendra longed to weep but she stood silent. As tall as she could. Completely still.

"Did you unpack?" asked the woman. Her voice did not sound harsh and angry, just concerned.

Kendra nodded her head.

"Where did you put them?"

"In the storage shed," answered Kendra.

"What storage shed?"

"The one at the back—down the hall."

"But the shed is always to be locked."

Kendra nodded again. It was locked.

"How did you get in," the voice above her went on.

"I put them through the window," said Kendra in a small, trembling voice.

Kendra heard a sharp intake of breath. It came from the tall, brisk, angry woman.

"Miss Bruce—find the gardener and check the storage shed," ordered the older woman, her voice even and controlled. "Kendra—come with me. We'll have a little talk."

Kendra was led from the room with its four beds, through the hall, down some steps, and to a small office.

"Sometimes first days can be confusing," Miss Jennings commented as they walked.

Kendra sat down on the big chair indicated to her and nodded her head silently.

"Miss Bruce asked you to unpack your things

and put them in the drawers?" It was more a question than a statement. Kendra nodded again.

"So why didn't you?" The question was direct and firm but without accusation.

"I got mixed up. I thought she said to put them in the storage shed."

"In the storage shed? Why did you think that?"

"I forgot. She—she—I think she said the case was for the storage shed."

"The pillowcase?" The woman sounded confused.

"No. The clothes case. When it was empty," explained Kendra without looking up.

"The suitcase?"

"I don't have suits," replied Kendra, and for the first time she lifted her eyes.

A small smile played about Miss Jennings' lips. She lowered her own eyes to the hands that were clasped together on the desk in front of her. "And the pillowcase?" she asked Kendra.

"I couldn't carry the clothes. They kept unpiling," said Kendra. "I borrowed it."

The woman nodded.

"Did you hear the lunch bell?" she went on, changing the direction of their conversation.

"I heard—something," admitted Kendra.

"But you didn't come to lunch. We have rules that one must be at lunch."

Kendra nodded. She had heard about the rule. Even talking about lunch made her stomach growl. She'd had nothing to eat since early morning.

"Were you shown the dining room?" asked Miss Jennings.

Kendra nodded her head. She and her grandfather had been given a tour of the school. But it was so big and had so many halls and doors and steps up and down. It wasn't like her familiar home area where one could travel by landmarks.

"Would you take me to the dining room?" Miss Jennings stood as she asked the question and motioned for Kendra to lead the way. Kendra knew she must obey, so she nodded again and stepped from the door.

But she couldn't remember. She had no idea which way to turn. She went to her left and started down the long hall. They came to steps and Kendra didn't know whether to take the ones that went up or the ones that went down. She decided to go down.

Another long hall. Should she go left—or right. She took a deep breath and turned left.

"Kendra—" The voice stopped her. "Kendra, you will never get to the dining room this way. It's on the bottom floor at the end of the hall."

Kendra wasn't sure what to do. What would the woman do with her now? She didn't know. Along with her confusion and loneliness a new emotion filled her. Fear. Kendra was quite unaccustomed to fear, but it shook her young body now.

"Come," said the woman, and she extended her hand. "It's already too late for you to join your first class. We will get you some soup and bread. But this must not happen again—understand. I am waiving the rule this one time because you did not know where to find the dining room, but in the future we will expect you to be at meals on time. There will be no bowl of soup should this happen again."

Kendra trembled. She had no intention of missing a meal in the future.

"We will henceforth appoint a classmate, a big

sister, to help you get acquainted with the layout of the building."

There were a few words that Kendra had not understood, but she felt that she knew the woman's meaning.

She was glad to accept the offered hand and be led to the dining room.

Chapter Twelve

Adjustments

It was not a good start for Kendra. The feelings of being left on her own in an alien environment lingered with her even after she had eaten her bowl of reheated split pea soup and a slice of dark bread. The bread tasted fine, but Kendra didn't like the soup and wished she could refuse it. But she was hungry, and the lady who sat down opposite her told her that she was to eat. Kendra ate obediently, but she did not enjoy the strange soup and felt her stomach threaten to refuse it on a couple of occasions.

When the bowl was finally empty, Kendra pushed it back with no intention of asking for more.

"Now—we must show you the classroom. We won't go in. The rule is that one must be on time for class. If students don't get there before the door closes, they do not get in."

It seemed to Kendra that there were rather a lot of rules.

Miss Jennings stood up and Kendra stood with her. As soon as the woman took a step, Kendra was at her heels. She was reminded of Oscar, and with the thought came another wave of loneliness. How was Oscar doing without her? Was the dog as lonesome as she?

They walked together down the hall. Kendra heard her unfamiliar shoes clicking against the hard board floors, a strange sensation to be hearing each step. She was used to walking silently except for the possible rustling of dried leaves that had tumbled to the trail.

She missed the sound of the leaves. They whispered to her as she walked through them—not the loud clunk, clunk as did the solid boards.

They came to some steps. These, too, were wooden, and Kendra noted the hollow sound as they thumped their way up the stairs.

Then they traveled down another hall, and Miss Jennings stopped and pointed at the door with one hand and raised the other to put a finger before her lips. Kendra had no plans to utter a sound. She wouldn't have needed the warning. But with the pointed finger and the quiet "sh-h-," Kendra did not even dare to breathe.

"This is the classroom you will be attending," the woman whispered.

Kendra's eyes grew larger. If there was one redeeming factor about going to school, she felt she would discover it behind this closed door. Her grandfather, Papa Mac, had spoken excitedly about all the things she would get to learn and be able to share with him when she returned to their home at Bent River Crossing. Kendra could hardly wait.

"Since class has already started, you may go to the library," Miss Jennings went on. "We mustn't waste precious time. I will give you a reading assignment and expect a report at the end of the normal class time. When rules are disobeyed we give library assignments. This is your first day and there seems to be some excuse for your failure to follow orders—but we cannot set new precedents. The other girls will expect to see you studying—not loafing."

Kendra had no idea what the library was. She did understand that she was going there as a result of her failure to obey instructions, so the library must be a place of punishment.

Dejectedly she followed the woman. They traveled the hall and Miss Jennings pushed open a large wooden door with a word on it that said "Library."

"Remember the rule," spoke the woman before they entered. "There is to be no talking in the library. Any communication with the librarian must be written clearly on a slip of paper and handed to her in silence."

More rules. Kendra began to wonder if there was ever an end to them.

Miss Jennings stepped in and Kendra followed. She had expected a horrid place—one of some kind of wicked torture, but instead what she saw was a room with shelves and shelves of books. To the side were two long tables with straight-backed wooden benches tucked along them. At one end was a desk where a woman sat with her head bent over a book. Kendra could see nothing but a pile of red-gold hair and the tip of an oval-shaped chin. In front of the woman was a lettered sign that read "Miss Dorcas. Librarian."

Miss Jennings motioned Kendra to one of the benches. Kendra went obediently and sat down quietly while the woman moved on. She searched along a shelf while Kendra's eyes traveled over the room. Never had she seen anything so breathtaking. Papa

Mac had been right. She would be able to learn all sorts of things.

Before Kendra was able to take in all that was around her, Miss Jennings was back. In one hand she held a book and in the other a sheet of paper and a pencil. The paper said "Report," and then some instructions. "Complete your report on your assigned reading, sign your name, and hand it to the librarian before leaving the library." The rest of the sheet was blank except for faint lines across the paper.

Kendra stared at the sheet. She wished she could ask what a report was, but she had already been told sternly that one was never to speak in the library. She looked up at the silent woman before her and said nothing.

Then the woman leaned over, and with the pencil still held in her hands she wrote on Kendra's sheet of paper: "Assigned reading—pages 1–20," and handed the sheet and the pencil to Kendra.

Kendra was still puzzling when Miss Jennings left the room. But she turned her attention back to the book that had been laid on the table before her.

She had never seen the story before. It was called *The Mystery of the Yellow Crow*. Kendra had never seen a yellow crow. She couldn't even imagine one. She began the book with some reservation.

By the time she reached page twenty, the story had barely begun. Hardly noticing that she had completed the assigned pages, Kendra kept reading. The purpose of reading a book was to discover what happened.

Somewhere a bell rang. Kendra scarcely heard it. The farmer and his wife had just decided to paint their house a nice bright yellow.

Kendra kept reading, turning pages quickly in her growing enthusiasm over the story. The blank paper still lay on the desk before her. From somewhere in the distance Kendra could hear the voices of children playing as they took their playground break from classes, but the sound did not even register. The story now had her totally enthralled.

She was almost to the end when she felt a presence near her. The librarian was standing close to her table, looking down with a frown at the blank sheet of paper. She pulled a pad and pencil from her skirt pocket and wrote in big letters: "Where is your report?"

Kendra held her breath. She took the offered pencil and put in small letters on the bottom of the pad: "I don't know."

The woman frowned even more deeply. Then she pointed to the sheet that had been left on the table beside Kendra's book. She wrote again. "You have not written your report. The library is closing for the supper hour. You should have finished the twenty pages easily."

Kendra looked back at her book. It had one hundred and six pages. She had two more to go.

"That will be two demerits," Miss Dorcas's long white slim fingers wrote on a fresh sheet of the little pad.

Kendra had no more idea about demerits than she did about reports. She shrugged her slim shoulders, anxious to return to her book.

The librarian was nodding toward the door and reaching for the book that Kendra held. Kendra realized that the librarian wanted the book. Reluctantly she handed it over. The last two pages would unlock the mystery, but the book was being taken from her. Mutely, Kendra watched as it was returned to a shelf.

Miss Dorcas turned and came back to the table. She pointed to a line that said, "Place your name here," and Kendra picked up the pencil and wrote in neat script, Kendra Marty. The woman took back the pencil and wrote in big letters all across the page: REPORT NOT COMPLETED. TWO DEMERITS. Then she took the paper with her and returned to her desk. With one more nod of her head she indicated that Kendra was to leave the room. The girl got up and moved toward the heavy wooden door. She didn't know where she was or where she was to go next. She had no idea what the rule was about leaving the library. She only knew that she was confused and alone and that she had not been able to finish the story. She would never be able to tell her Papa Mac what had happened.

❧   ❧   ❧

"Are you Kendra?"

A girl stood beside the big library door seeming to be waiting for her to exit. Kendra was surprised to see her and even more surprised to hear her question.

She nodded silently, wondering what was going to happen now.

"I'm to be your big sister," the girl went on, but she didn't sound one bit happy about her assignment.

Kendra just nodded again.

The girl was older than she was. Perhaps eleven or twelve, Kendra decided.

"It's almost supper," the girl went on. "Have you washed?"

Kendra had washed that morning before she had left Mrs. Miller's house. She was about to say that she had when the girl spoke again.

"It's the rule that we all have to wash our hands. We get a demerit if we don't."

Kendra still wondered what a demerit was.

"Have you washed your hands?" asked the girl again.

"I washed this morning at Mrs. Miller's," Kendra managed to say.

"Not this morning," said the girl in exasperation. "We have to wash before every meal."

Kendra hung her head. She had not washed.

The girl led her to a large room with many basins and a long row of towels hanging on pegs on the wall.

"That's your towel," said the girl, pointing to a peg. "Hurry or we'll both be late and we'll both get demerits."

Kendra washed quickly and was soon hurrying along behind the briskly walking figure in front of her.

"We can't run or we'll get a demerit," the older girl informed Kendra over her shoulder.

They were breathless by the time they reached the dining room, but they did manage to duck in just before the big door closed.

"That was close," said the older girl under her breath. "We were almost late—and I'm starving. I never would've lasted 'til breakfast. Next time don't be so slow."

Kendra nodded.

"That's your place," said the girl and motioned

to the empty chair beside the one she moved toward at the table. Kendra was about to take her seat, but the girl hissed crossly, "Don't sit down. We haven't said grace."

Kendra looked around the room. All the other girls were standing silently behind their chairs, their hands placed on the chair back.

Kendra imitated what she saw.

"Bow your head," whispered the girl beside her sharply, and Kendra bowed her head.

Soon someone began to speak. "For all we are about to receive, may we truly be thankful. May we honor thee in our walk, our talk, and our thought. Amen."

As soon as the last word was spoken there was a scraping of chairs, and the girls all around her took their seats. After a moment of confused hesitation, Kendra followed.

The food was served by two older girls who walked up and down the tables and spooned a portion onto each plate. As soon as Kendra had received her scoop, she picked up her spoon and took a bite.

"Don't eat yet," the girl beside her ordered in a harsh whisper. "We have to wait until everyone is served."

Kendra cast a nervous glance about the room and dropped her spoon beside her plate. She didn't know if she should spit out the food or swallow it quickly. Which action would reap the least demerits? She dared not chew. Some pair of stern eyes would surely see her.

"And don't use your spoon," the voice beside her continued. "Use your fork."

From then on Kendra watched the older girl

carefully. She did not make one move until her leader had made it.

The supper was green beans—fixed in a very strange way that made them taste funny—mashed turnips and a small slice of roast meat. The meat was bland and tough to chew. Kendra did not like that either.

Silently she ate her supper. She longed for some of Nonie's good stew. It had so much more flavor with its garden vegetables and its herbs from the forests. Kendra was sure she would not be able to swallow the stuff that had been set before her. She did enjoy the half slice of bread.

❧   ❧   ❧

Gradually Kendra began to understand about the life at the girls' school. When in doubt, she watched the other girls. Her sharp eyes and quick wit kept her from more demerits. As it was, Kendra had amassed far too many demerits before she had learned the system. And she had discovered, much to her dismay, that a total of six demerits could earn one cleaning duties, and eight demerits sent one to the office of Mrs. Adams herself. Ten demerits meant a strap, and with a dozen demerits the doors of the esteemed school closed on you forever, sending you home totally disgraced.

As much as Kendra longed to return home, she did not wish to disgrace her grandfather, so daily she tried her hardest to evade the dreaded demerits.

She enjoyed the classes, even though they were a puzzlement to her in the beginning. She wished she could just read and do sums, but the teachers seemed to expect all manner of strange procedures. Kendra did discover what a report was and once she knew, she did the assignment well and on time.

Her favorite place was the library, and while other girls often seemed to think of the room as some specialized form of school torture, Kendra could not get enough of the books on the shelves and would gladly have spent her recess times buried in a book rather than shyly standing back from the games on the playground.

But rules were rules. Each girl had to have daily exercise, so Kendra reluctantly made her way to the backyard as well.

Kendra did not feel at home with her new roommates. She was not used to having the company of other girls. And the girls from the school already had their special friends. Nor were they inclined to befriend someone new. Instead, they teased and giggled and picked on Kendra when no one else was around to admonish them.

Kendra never fought back. Never told her superiors. Instead she withdrew, becoming more and more the butt of cruel jokes and girlish pranks.

In spite of her determination to comply with the wishes of Papa Mac, Kendra was unable to shake her deep loneliness. Day after day she yearned for home. At first it was just a hollow, empty longing somewhere deep inside her. A feeling of not belonging with all the busy, noisy girls who already had their friends and did not really need or welcome a young stranger. The shared bedroom seemed crowded and stuffy at night. The clothes she wore were uncomfortable and stiff. Her shoes hurt her feet constantly. She could not remember all the rules. People frowned at her and prompted her and gave her orders that she could not understand. She just didn't like it. She didn't like it at all, and she longed with all her heart to go home to Papa Mac and Nonie and Oscar.

Day by day her longing increased until it was so painful she couldn't sleep at night or swallow her food at mealtime. She became pale and listless—even her schoolwork suffered for lack of concentration. Miss Bruce always seemed to be fussing at her for one reason or another, and her teacher, Miss Spooner, fretted and stewed and sent repeated reports to the office of Mrs. Adams. At length Mrs. Adams herself called the girl in.

"Are you not feeling well, Kendra?" she asked.

Kendra shook her head. Her eyes looked dull, her face, tanned and healthy at her arrival, now looked wan and pale.

"Where are you sick?" asked the woman.

Kendra could not answer the question. She felt sick all over. Right from the very depth of her soul—the very pit of her stomach—the very core of her being.

At last Mrs. Adams, as the head of the institution, felt it her duty to notify George McMannus. In her letter she tried to assure him that she was sure the illness was nothing serious. That the girl would soon perk up again. They now had her on tonic morning and night.

But Kendra did not improve. Most of her food was still left on her plate, and when a staff member insisted that she clean up the plate, she promptly brought it all back up again. She was not forced to eat again.

Mrs. Adams was about to send off another letter when there was a knock on her door.

George McMannus stood there. It was already the trapping season. He could ill afford the time to make a long trip to the city. But he had to check on Kendra. He had to know what was ailing his little girl.

⚜   ⚜   ⚜

"I'm taking her home, Maggie."

George had just tucked his granddaughter into the bed made for her on Maggie's cot and sat beside her until she dropped off to sleep. She had lost weight and looked so pale that he feared there must be something terribly wrong with her.

"Shouldn't she see a doctor first?" asked Maggie, who agreed that the child was not well.

"Mrs. Adams said that she had her thoroughly checked by the school physician—twice. He could find nothing wrong with her."

Maggie sighed and poured buttermilk into two tall glasses.

"I should have kept a closer eye on her," she berated herself.

"You couldn't. Not with Henry needing you full time here," George quickly responded. He sat in reflective thought for a few minutes and then went on. "I'm not sure that it would have helped anyway. I have a feeling she is just pining for home."

"So what will you do?" asked Maggie. "She does need schooling."

George sat stroking his beard. Maggie noticed that it showed faint streaks of gray. They were all getting older.

"Mrs. Adams said that Kendra is a smart little thing. She already has the basics. With extra books to study, she feels that Kendra will be able to get most of what she needs. At least she won't be illiterate."

"She reads everything," chuckled Maggie. "I heard her reading that *Almanac* while I was getting supper on and you were feeding Henry."

There was silence for many minutes. With a sigh, George broke it with, "Henry's getting weaker, isn't he? I could scarcely get him to swallow a little soup."

Maggie nodded her head. Every day it seemed that Henry lost a little more of his strength. Tears moistened her eyes.

"It's hard," she said. "Hard to just watch him waste away day by day."

George nodded. He didn't know how Maggie kept on going. She must be worn to exhaustion.

"Can I ask for further hospitality?" he asked her, sorry that he could be a burden but hoping he might be able to give her a hand with Henry's care for a few days and let her get some much-needed rest.

"Of course," replied Maggie. "You know you can."

"I need to do some shopping for books for Kendra. And a globe. Mrs. Adams said that it is important for her to have a globe. Get the feel of the world around her. Especially since she is so isolated. And history books and . . . There is so much she needs that I can't get for her out there. Mrs. Adams said she should have a weekly newspaper. Wouldn't do much good. The mail only comes in about once a month. Sometimes less if it should storm or the rivers flood."

He sighed deeply and rubbed at his beard again.

"I've not done right by her, Maggie," he said with remorse.

"You've tried," responded his friend. "You've done your best. No one can do better than that."

"But she looks so frail. So pale. They said she hasn't been eating—or sleeping. That she just sat around looking forlorn and forsaken."

"That'll all change quickly," Maggie dared to promise.

"You should have seen her when they brought her to the office. I'll never forget her eyes. They—they looked like she couldn't believe I was really there. Like I was a ghost or something. And then she just threw herself into my arms and hung on. Like she was afraid to let go. She didn't even cry—just clung to me. I—I—it was almost more than I could take."

He brushed the back of his hand against his cheek. "If I had only known—how bad it really was—I would have come for her sooner," he finished.

"But you didn't know."

Silence again. He stirred restlessly in his chair. "No," he said at last. "I didn't know. I figured that she would adjust and be happy. I thought that I was the only one—suffering."

"You missed her, didn't you?" said Maggie softly. It was not really a question but an observation.

"Terribly. I—for the first while I thought that I was going to—to go stir crazy. And that dog of hers sure didn't help. He kept pacing the cabin, whining and moaning, and then he would go to her bed and cry like she was dead or something. I couldn't stand it. I spent as much of my time away from the cabin as I could find excuses to leave."

"You'll both be much happier with her home again," Maggie assured him.

She looked toward the door that led to the bedroom. Henry had not really been able to offer companionship for many months. Years. And yet he was still with her. She knew he would not be with her for much longer. He was so weak. She knew it would be better for him. But my! How she would miss him. Just to know that he was there brought her a measure of comfort. Just to be able to talk with him. Tell him about her day. Even if he couldn't understand or respond. She did not look forward to being alone.

"We weren't made to be alone," said Maggie softly and reached into her apron pocket for a hankie.

Chapter Thirteen

Home Again

They left for home as soon as George was able to find the needed books and school supplies for Kendra. George remembered their first trip and the excited, chattering young girl. Now she was quiet, studying everything about them with wide, haunted eyes. He tried to draw her out, tried to coax back some of her former merriment, but she did not respond. George hoped that once they got back to Bent River Crossing and Nonie and Oscar, she would return to being his beloved Kendra again.

❧   ❧   ❧

"Look," said Kendra, and for the first time on the entire trip George heard excitement in her voice. "There's Nonie!"

"Where?"

They were still some distance from the Crossing, but they could see a number of figures moving about the shore. George found it hard to believe that Kendra could actually pick out Nonie.

"Right there," insisted Kendra, "by that clump of willows."

And she was right. When the wagon neared the small post, a lone figure moved silently from among the willows across the river and waded right into the water toward them. Kendra didn't wait for Nonie to come to her. She jumped from the wagon before George could even summon her to be careful and plunged into the stream to wade toward Nonie.

They embraced each other, the elderly lady in her deerskin garments and the young girl, whose thin face made her large green eyes look even bigger and greener. The shallow, cold waters of the Bent River swirled and eddied about their skirts. The tears that had not been free to fall when Kendra had welcomed her grandfather were now released. Nonie just held her, one hand on the blond head, the other pressing Kendra to her as she rocked back and forth. "Nayeea, nayeea," she cried over and over. George recognized it as Nonie's prayer of thanks to the spirits for bringing back the child.

"I suppose we'll have to go through that all over again," he muttered to himself. "If the old woman has her way, she'll make a pagan of the child."

George promised himself that he would watch more closely and try to keep Nonie from putting foolish notions in the young girl's head.

☙ ❧ ☙

Kendra was anxious to get back home to the cabin. George knew that the main reason was to see Oscar. The girl could hardly wait to hug her dog again.

"Do you think he will remember me?" she asked her grandfather, apprehension edging her voice.

"Oscar?"

She nodded.

"Do you remember him?" asked George, teasing her a bit to try to get her to talk more.

Kendra nodded her head. "Of course," she said. Her voice was little more than a whisper.

"Well, dogs have even better memories than humans do," said her grandfather. "Guess there's not much chance that he will have forgotten you."

Still Kendra's face did not relax or her eyes lose their look of fear.

"He won't be at the cabin when we get there, you know," her grandfather reminded her. "I left all the dogs with old Two Tooth."

Kendra remembered. She was sorry she'd have to wait, but she knew that her grandfather could not have left the dogs at home with no one to care for them.

"When will we get them?" she asked softly.

"I'll go for them first thing in the morning," he promised.

She sighed. It would have to do. Then she turned and let one hand trail in the cold river water. She was very tired. It had been a long, long trip— but she would be so glad—so glad to be home.

❧   ❧   ❧

True to his promise, George left early the next morning to go for the dogs. He was gone long before the sun had stirred itself from the night's repose. Nonie silently entered the cabin and crossed to the bed. She stood and watched the child as she slept. She was so pale and thin. Nonie's thoughts went to her medicine baskets. She knew the very thing to get Kendra well and strong again. She would make up the herbal tonics that night and bring them with her in the morning. She would be sure to put some in the stew and porridge each time she cooked. Soon Kendra would be running and smiling again.

Nonie let the two big tears that rolled down her withered cheeks go unheeded. To interfere with one's tears might make the rain gods feel they had been slighted. Next spring they might hold back the rain. Nonie did not wish to risk their wrath.

Nonie crossed to the rocking chair near the fire and eased her body into its wooden embrace. The warmth from the open fire felt good on her chilled bones. It would not do to stir about. She would sit quietly while Kendra slept. The girl needed her rest.

❧   ❧   ❧

Oscar bounded into the cabin, seeming to be well aware that Kendra had returned even before he reached her little corner bed with its mattress of fresh moss and spruce boughs. With an excited yip he pushed his nose against her and rooted at the covers that partially hid her face.

Before her eyes were even open, Kendra's hand came up to clasp a handful of the long, silvery coat. Oscar licked at her cheek and her eyes opened wide.

"Oscar," she squealed and bounded up to hug him and bury her face in his long hair.

Nonie rose from her chair. It was time to stir now. Time to put on the breakfast porridge. Time to carry on with life. Things were back to what they should be.

❧   ❧   ❧

It took several days for the old way of life to be reestablished. George had to return to his traplines, and Nonie came to stay with Kendra. She was always there when Kendra awoke in the mornings and they spent their days together, sometimes chatting, sometimes silent, often taking their baskets and heading for the woods. Gradually a feeling of security and peace began to steal over the young girl. She began to eat again and put on the weight she had lost. She romped in the out-of-doors with Oscar or helped Nonie with the chores. The late autumn sun and cold fresh air flushed her cheeks and added vitality to her body. Kendra was at home again.

Chapter Fourteen

Plans

"I'm going to build onto the cabin," George announced one morning while they shared their breakfast porridge.

Kendra lifted her head.

"You need your own room," he went on. "On which side of the cabin would you like us to build?"

Kendra couldn't keep the shine from her eyes.

"My very own room?" she asked him.

They were crowded in the small cabin. Especially since Kendra had so many books and school supplies to spread about.

"Your very own. This makeshift curtain stuff doesn't work too well."

It sounded too good to be true. Kendra took her time thinking about it. She wasn't sure where the best place would be. If her room was to the east of the cabin, she could watch the morning sun, while on the west of the cabin, she could watch the sun set beyond the mountain range. The east was closer to the stream. On warm summer nights she would be able to open her window and listen to its laughter. Yet the west was closer to the groves of forest trees. The birds would be so close it would seem that their singing was with her in her room.

"I'll—I'll check," said Kendra, going outside to

walk slowly around the cabin.

At length she made up her mind. Her room would be built on the east. It was not a large room, but it was plenty big enough, with its own fireplace and two windows. Two windows, Kendra exulted. One that looked to the east and another that looked to the south. She could hardly believe her good fortune.

George made a built-in bunk, and Nonie and Kendra gathered the spruce boughs and soft moss for the mattress. George also built a simple table-desk close to the fireplace and put a number of shelves along one wall.

Kendra moved in all her books and lined them up so she could read the titles. It was so much nicer than having them in stacks on the floor.

Nonie gave her a large bearskin rug that she placed in front of the fireplace. She could picture herself curled up there on long winter evenings, her head bent over the pages of one of her books. It made a nice picture. Kendra felt contentment wash over her.

When Kendra was totally moved in and settled, she heaved a deep sigh, then turned to her grandfather, who stood studying the work of their hands. "You can visit me sometimes, Papa Mac," she informed him generously.

He laughed heartily. "I'll just be beyond the door," he informed her.

Secure and happy, Kendra felt a world apart in her own place.

❧   ❧   ❧

The year that Kendra turned eleven included a

cold, damp summer. The garden did not produce as it should have. Even the berry trees in the nearby woods had been caught by a late frost so were producing little fruit. Nonie and Kendra tramped the trails gathering herbs and roots, but Kendra often saw Nonie lift her face toward the sky, fear filling her voice as she uttered words of pleading.

Nonie had ceased telling Kendra Indian tales. In a way she missed them. At times it had been frightening, knowing that one's life was in the hands of the unseen spirits. Spirits that seemed so difficult to please. But Kendra knew her grandfather did not approve of the stories. He dismissed them as fairy tales and informed Kendra that they had no foundation of truth.

There were so many mysteries. So many unanswered questions. Something deep within Kendra longed for answers.

"If the Old One didn't make the world, how did it all get here?" Kendra dared to ask her grandfather.

"There are theories," he answered vaguely. Personally, George McMannus didn't put much more stock in some of the usual theories than he did in the Indian tales. They didn't quite add up to logical conclusions.

"What theories?" asked Kendra.

"I'll get you a book on it the next time I am in the city," the man replied. Kendra was impatient to study about the theories. Would they answer her burning questions? It was hard for her to wait. She knew that grandfather might not go to the city again for many months—or even years.

She nodded. She would have to accept her grandfather's answer.

"What would you like for your birthday?" Her grandfather surprised her with his sudden change.

Kendra did not hesitate. She had been thinking of what she wanted. "I want to go with you on the trapline," she said quickly.

"You want to—? Why?"

Kendra did not back down. "So I can learn to help you—with the traps and the skinning and the caring for the pelts."

He looked thoughtful. He shook his head slowly. "The trapline is no place for a child," he said, his voice soft.

"But I'm getting big now," protested Kendra.

He smiled. She was getting tall for her age. But she was still a child.

"It gets pretty cold and stormy sometimes," he went on.

"I won't go on those days. Just the nice ones," put in Kendra.

He thought for a moment longer. "We'll see," he said slowly.

"That isn't a birthday gift," protested Kendra. " 'We'll see' means maybe. A birthday gift has to be real."

George chuckled softly. "Okay," he said. "I'll take you—at least—at least three times. How's that?"

It wasn't all that Kendra had hoped for, but it had to be enough for now.

❦　　❦　　❦

Word came from Maggie that Henry had passed away. George mourned his friend, but he was not able to make the long trip out for the funeral. He knew that the news should bring relief. Henry would not be suffering any longer. Maggie would not be driven to exhaustion caring for an invalid. But even so, even with his reason telling him that things were better now, he could not help but grieve. Maggie was going to be so lonely in the days ahead. He sat down and wrote her a long, long letter.

George chose the first of Kendra's trips on the trapline carefully. The sky was clear, the day bright, and the temperature moderate for a winter's day in the area. Even so, he had misgivings. He had not forgotten the words of a very young Kendra when she had turned from him, pain in her eyes and screamed, "I hate you. I hate you."

How would Kendra respond to seeing animals caught in the traps? It was not a pretty sight.

But Kendra surprised him. She turned her eyes from the first animal, an otter, curled and frozen, his head resting on the very trap that held him prisoner on the red-stained snow.

From then on, Kendra spoke of the animals in terms of the price of the pelt. Her knowledge surprised George. He had not realized just how much she had learned about the worth of furs and how to tell a fair skin from a superior one.

He took her again the next day. It was fun to have her company on the trail. George lost count of their trips after their third time out together. From then on, she went often. Kendra was soon more than company. She was actually a great help.

❧   ❧   ❧

A storm moved in, dropping the temperature and swirling snow about the cabin.

"I don't think you'd better come with me today," George announced firmly. Kendra looked out on the storm. It was one of the worst she had seen in her few winters.

"I don't think *you* should go either," she told him.

"I have to," he answered without even giving it thought. "The traps need to be checked every day."

Kendra knew that George always traveled the line each day when he had the traps out.

"Why?" she asked now, surprising her grandfather. "The animals won't stir about in this weather anyway."

"But there may be something in a trap already."

"You can get them when the storm is over," said Kendra.

"I don't want them to suffer needlessly," put in her grandfather.

Kendra looked up, her eyes big. "They're dead," she reminded him frankly.

Her words caught George totally by surprise. Yes. They were dead. Any trapped animal would be dead in a very short time in the frigid temperatures. But what if—what if—? No, he wouldn't take that chance. He would not have an animal suffering through a storm.

❧   ❧   ❧

Nonie no longer made her trips to the cabin when George was away from home. Kendra did not need child care. But the girl missed Nonie. Often on the days that she didn't go with George to check the traps, she paid a call on Nonie in the settlement. The elderly woman always welcomed her with smiles and soft words. Kendra knew she was loved.

The years were telling on Nonie. She seemed to much prefer the fireside to stirring about outside in the cold.

George made sure the elderly woman had a constant supply of wood. He often wished he could stack the fireplace logs up beside her door and then be done with it. But he knew that wouldn't work. Any of the other residents would feel quite free to use from the pile as well, and Nonie would soon be out of fuel for her fire.

So every other day George had to take Nonie another load, which he placed in her cabin. The time cut dreadfully into his workday, but he feared that Nonie would go cold if he didn't care for her.

Kendra also helped, gathering wood from the nearby forests and carrying it in her arms to the old woman's cabin. It was a chore that kept both George and Kendra busy over the winter months.

⚜   ⚜   ⚜

When Kendra was thirteen, one of George's team members produced a summer litter. Kendra spent much of her time playing with the puppies. By the time they had been weaned, she had made her picks. "I want this one and this one and this one . . ." she told her grandfather. She didn't stop until she had pointed out five of the eight puppies.

"What are you planning to do with all those dogs? They do need to be fed, you know."

"I'll make them work for their keep," Kendra said confidently.

"Work. How?"

"I'll use the old sled," said Kendra. "I can haul the firewood to Nonie and get supplies from the trading post and—and—"

"Whoa," laughed her grandfather. "I get the picture. But are you sure? A dog team is a lot of work."

"I know," replied Kendra. "But they are a lot of help too."

Kendra got her pups and could hardly wait until they were big enough to start training for the sled.

❦   ❦   ❦

Kendra sat at the table close to the crackling fire. The night was cold again. She could hear the wind moaning outside the log frame, but she paid little attention to its mournful song. Her nose was buried in a book. George had sent for a new supply by mail. Kendra drank in the information, but it never seemed to be quite enough. She had so many unanswered questions. If Nonie's stories were just myth, then how did things really come to be? Kendra had studied nature enough to be dissatisfied with trite answers. There had to be a logical reason for the universe with all of its complexity and intrigue. There just had to.

She lifted her head suddenly. Her eyes looked off into the distance, past the shadows of the flickering lamplight, her thoughts far away.

"I want a trapline of my own," she said suddenly, turning to her grandfather.

The wish was out. She had dared to voice it.

George looked up from the trap he was cleaning,

surprised by her words. She had been working with him on the traplines now for three winters. She handled the snowshoes as if she had been born with them as an extension to her feet. She could mush the dogs and handle the sled. George had spent time with her in rifle practice until he had total confidence in her ability to wisely and accurately use the gun. She knew the rules of the trail, could read the signs, and knew the laws of survival. She had become skilled at skinning without damaging the pelts. She could work the skins carefully over the stretchers, putting on just the right pressure without causing rips or weak spots. Kendra was a real product of her wilderness setting and quite at home in her surroundings.

Still George hesitated. Was he ready to let her have her own trapline? It didn't seem the right place for a young girl. He knew the dangers. Many an experienced man had lost his life to the trapline.

"Do you really think—?" he began, but Kendra stopped him.

"You've been my teacher," she said frankly. "And I think you've done it well. Nonie says I know as much as some of the village men."

George could not hide his smile. In his thinking, Kendra knew a good deal more than most of them.

"I don't know," he said again. "Some of those traps—"

"I won't use the biggest ones. I'll just go for the smaller game," offered Kendra.

"But the—the weather? The cold?" George thought of the bitter winds and the times when he had feared that he himself might perish in a storm.

"I'll be careful," put in Kendra. "I'll keep my line closer to the cabin."

"Of course—if it was really cold you could leave things go for a day or two," her grandfather thought out loud. "Lots of trappers do."

"I—I wouldn't want the animals to suffer," Kendra echoed her grandfather's own words. "I'll be careful."

George nodded, still reluctant to let the young girl have her own traps. But he was the one who had raised her in the wilderness—taught her the only way of life she knew. Was it fair of him to deny that she use what she had learned?

"I'm going to save my money," went on Kendra. "I'm going to go out to school."

George was caught off guard by her statement. "But you—you didn't like school."

Kendra had said nothing about wanting more schooling. Had she been thinking about it? Longing for it? Why hadn't she spoken? He would have sent her.

But even as the thoughts raced through his mind, he felt a stab of fear follow them. If Kendra left, his own life would be so empty. So void of any meaning. He quickly chided himself. He had to think of the child—not his own selfish desires.

Kendra looked at her grandfather, her eyes clear, her gaze steady. "I think I am ready now," she said frankly.

"But—but you will be—be older than all the other girls. They—" George was stroking his beard, his eyes intent on the face of his granddaughter.

"Oh—I don't plan to go to *school* school. I want to go to university. There is one in Edmonton—and they let girls attend. I read about the graduation exercises in that paper that came midsummer," said Kendra. "If I study real hard, and read all the books I can find—then I think I can be ready for it. Maybe by the time I am seventeen—or eighteen."

George let out the breath he had been holding. Seventeen—or eighteen. That still gave them a little time. He wouldn't have to face the thought of losing her for some time yet. He relaxed.

Then his mind switched back to the traps. He supposed it would not be fair to refuse her request. After all, because of him she was who she was.

"We'll see," he answered with a nod of his head.

Kendra smiled to herself. When her grandfather responded in that fashion, she most always got what she wanted.

Chapter Fifteen

Visitor

Kendra stamped her feet on the wooden step and pushed the door open with a mittened hand. It was cold. Even colder than she had expected it to be. She was glad to be home. Glad to be back to the comfort of the cabin, though it too would be cold until she got a fire going.

She closed the door behind herself and pulled off her heavy fur-lined mittens. Even with the protection of the fur, her fingers felt numb. She blew on them as she crossed to the fireplace and knelt to arrange kindling wood in a little pile for lighting. She was glad that there was never a shortage of fuel. Her grandfather saw to that.

With thoughts of her grandfather Kendra frowned. She wished he were home. She hoped he was okay. He had so many more miles to travel than she did. His trapline took him the entire day. It was now shortly past noon—and bitterly cold. He would be kept busy coaxing the dogs along. They would wish to bury themselves in the snow and curl up to keep warm.

"I wish he'd just forget the rest of the line and head for home," she spoke aloud, her words sounding strange in the stillness of the cabin.

She reached for the can that held the matches

and removed one. Never did she need more than one match to start a fire. Now as she held the match to the tinder-dry kindling, she noticed that her fingers still felt numb. Her fears concerning her grandfather deepened.

"He likely won't even get anything in the traps. It's too cold for the animals to be moving about."

She had checked her own traps and found nothing.

A dog barked, followed by a chorus of yelping. Kendra lifted her head. For a moment her heart quickened. Perhaps her grandfather was returning early. But she quickly changed her mind. Her dogs were not welcoming her grandfather's team. The barking indicated that a stranger was approaching.

Kendra looked up at the frosted window. She knew that she would see nothing through the iced-over pane of glass, so she rose and crossed to the door. They never had visitors unless another trapper dropped by for a cup of coffee and a bit of a chat, and that happened so rarely that Kendra couldn't remember the last time.

A team of only four dogs pulled up before the cabin. Kendra was not used to seeing a sled pulled by a team of four. All the trappers around their area used at least six dogs on their sleighs. She did not recognize anything about the fur-bundled figure who moved around the sled, then spoke sharply to the dogs who dropped down quickly to the snow. His head bent into the wind, he moved forward toward the cabin.

Kendra stepped back, holding the door open for the stranger. He didn't see her until he was about to step up onto the small porch. Then his head came up and he paused.

"Thank the good Lord!" he uttered with a strange accent. "I feared I would never reach a cabin alive."

Kendra said nothing, just nodded the man inside and closed the door quickly behind him. He pushed back his fur parka. His beard was covered with ice.

"I thought I would die on the trail," he added. "I prayed for a cabin. Someplace to take shelter."

"I'm sorry," said Kendra indicating the fireplace. Her little flame had burned up the kindling and gone out while she was at the door. "I just got in. I haven't even got the fire going."

"Well, at least I am out of the frigid wind," the man went on, drawing off his heavy mittens. "Here—let me start the fire for you," he said.

He bent before the fireplace and reached for kindling. Kendra bit her tongue. He was using far more of the precious fuel than was needed to get a fire started.

"Where are your matches?" he asked.

Kendra handed him the coffee can. He struggled with the lid. Kendra noticed that his fingers were clumsy. Likely he was even colder than she had been. With the fourth match he finally got a flame. Kendra wished she could ask him to move aside so she could carefully add larger pieces of wood to the fire. She was afraid to speak so watched as he bumbled the job and had to start all over with fresh kindling, depleting their precious supply still further.

"Why don't you thaw your hands in water," said Kendra, indicating the basin in the corner. "Your fingers must be half frozen." The man nodded and got up from his knees, and Kendra seized the opportunity to take over the fire lighting.

"The water's frozen," the man said as he turned from the basin.

Kendra had thought that it might be. "I'll get some snow," she said. "It works just as well."

But she didn't go for the snow until she was sure the fire had taken hold and would be ready to receive larger chunks of wood.

"It will soon be warm," she told the man. "I'll build a fire in the stove too."

She hastened to start the second fire and then took the basin from the shelf to scoop up some snow.

"Just use a little at a time," she said. "Frozen fingers need to be thawed slowly."

"I don't think they are frozen—yet," said the man. "But they sure are cold. It wouldn't have been much longer until more than my fingers would have been frozen."

Kendra nodded. Again she thought of her grandfather.

"Are you here alone?" the man asked her.

"No. My grandfather is out checking the traps," replied Kendra and reached for her heavy mittens. "I've put some water on for tea," she said. "You take off your wraps and sit by the fire as soon as it starts giving off some warmth. I need to care for the dogs. I'll tether yours at the north side of the house."

The man nodded. "You are an angel of God," he told her.

Kendra puzzled over his strange words as she stepped out into the cold air and began to unharness and tether the sled dogs. As soon as her own team was unharnessed, she moved to care for the four dogs of the stranger. When she had them all securely tied, she went to the shed for frozen meat for the dogs.

A loud clamor greeted her as she returned with their daily portions of meat, but soon all the dogs were much too busy eating to be making further noise. Kendra cast one last glance around the circles to be sure she hadn't missed any animal and returned to the cabin.

She could feel the heat as soon as she opened the door. It was a pleasant welcome on such a cold day. She shrugged from her furs and hung them on the peg on the cabin wall.

The man was standing in front of the fireplace, his furs tossed on the floor behind him, his hands spread to the blaze.

"Don't warm up too quickly," Kendra cautioned him.

"I couldn't warm up too quickly," he replied with a laugh.

Kendra did not wish to argue. She crossed to the stove and added a bit more wood under the kettle. It would soon be singing and she would be able to make them tea.

"My name is John Blackman," he told her.

Kendra responded with her name and then said, "I'm going to start a fire in my room. Why don't you pull the rocker up to the side of the fire?" *At least then he won't get faint and collapse,* thought Kendra as she went to build the fire in her bedroom fireplace.

When she came back to the room, the man was sitting in the rocker. His face was flushed, his eyes glazed. Kendra hastened to make the tea. She wished to coax him away from the direct heat.

"This will help warm us," said Kendra. She placed the tea on the table and drew two cups from the shelf. Then she sliced some bread and spread it with blueberry jam.

Mr. Blackman left the rocker and joined her at the table. Kendra breathed a sigh of relief.

For several minutes they sipped their tea in silence. The warmth of the liquid seemed to loosen his tongue.

"I just came from Bent River Crossing," he told her. "I'm on my way to Kenakee Falls."

Kendra looked up. Kenakee Falls was a long way from their area.

"Fellow at the trading post tried to talk me into staying on there until there was a break in the weather. I should have listened to him. Didn't realize how cold it was."

Kendra nodded.

Kenakee Falls was another Indian settlement. There was not even a post there as far as Kendra knew. Why would this white man be heading there?

It was not polite to ask another's business, so Kendra waited for Mr. Blackman to go on.

"We are going to start a church there," he said. "Take religion to the Indian people."

Kendra felt her eyes widen. The Indians had religion. Her grandfather maintained that they had far too much religion for their own good. Why would this outsider want to take them more?

Kendra poured more tea.

"We hope to start churches all through the area," the man went on.

Kendra remembered pictures of churches from one of her books about Europe. They were huge buildings with spires and turrets and beautiful windows. But Kendra wondered how, and why, this man and others would build such a building for the Indians.

"We have asked God to bless us so that by 1930 there will be no more pagans in northwest Canada."

Pagans. Kendra did not know the word. But the man was speaking with such intensity that she knew his cause touched him deeply. Kendra made a mental note to look up the word in her dictionary later that evening.

"Have you always lived here?" Mr. Blackman asked, changing the conversation.

"No," replied Kendra. "I came from north of Edmonton when I was almost four."

"Have you been back?" asked the man.

"To Edmonton. Once," said Kendra. "To school."

"Of course," said the man with a nod of understanding. Kendra did not bother explaining further.

"And you live with your grandfather?"

Kendra nodded.

"No grandmother?"

"My grandmother died before I was born," replied Kendra.

"And your folks?"

"I lost them the spring before I came with Grandfather."

Mr. Blackman shook his head sympathetically. "You poor thing," he said solemnly.

"I've liked living with Grandfather," replied Kendra simply. "He's been good to me."

The man seemed about to get up, and Kendra was afraid he would cross to the fire again. He'd had a chance to warm up a bit and the tea would have helped considerably. Still, she worried that it might be too much heat too soon.

"Would you like to lie down on Grandfather's bed for a while?" she asked him. "There's a heavy blanket there that you can just pull over you."

To her relief he nodded his head. "I am a bit done in after the trip," he said. "That wind was almost more than I could fight against. Might not hurt to just rest for a few minutes."

Kendra watched with relief as he settled himself and pulled the blanket up to his chin. Soon soft snoring filled the room. Kendra was relieved to hear the sound. She turned her thoughts back to her grandfather. She did hope he would soon be home.

❧   ❧   ❧

The man slept the entire afternoon. Kendra moved about quietly as she prepared the evening meal. She wondered if the aroma might waken him, but still he slept.

Kendra kept an eye on the faint sun that hung listlessly on the western rim of the sky. She longed to hear the sound of her grandfather's team. It would soon be dark. Was he okay?

Kendra was placing another log on the fire when she heard Oscar cry out. Oscar was always the first of her team to be alerted to something. His yip was quickly followed by welcoming staccato yaps. Kendra knew that her grandfather would soon be home. She reached for her fur jacket and heavy mittens. She would take care of the team and let him enjoy the warmth of the cabin.

❧   ❧   ❧

After the supper hour the two men had a long visit in front of the fireplace. George had many questions to ask Mr. Blackman about the world outside.

"Edmonton is growing quickly," the man informed him.

George nodded. He had not been out to Edmonton for some time. He had been getting all of the supplies he needed at the local post or else ordering them in. He had not even been to see Maggie since Henry had died. He chided himself about that fact.

"And Calgary is becoming quite a city as well," the man went on.

"But you are from the East?" asked George.

"From England originally," replied the man. "But I've been in Canada for seven years now."

The visit continued. Kendra listened quietly as she washed up the supper dishes and melted the snow she would need for the next day's water supply. She found the discussion of the outside world most interesting, and it served only to intensify her longing for answers.

Why was this man coming from the cities to the far reaches of the wilderness? Why did he think that the Indian people needed more religion? Her grandfather assured her that religion was of no consequence. Why bother with it then?

Kendra finished the last of her chores and went to her room to look up the word *pagan* in the dictionary. "A heathen; idolater," the book told her. Kendra frowned and flipped back through the pages until she came to the word *heathen*. This had a bit more. "Heathen. One who does not believe in the God of the Bible; one who is neither a Christian,

Jew, nor Mohammedan; an irreligious person; pagan."

Kendra read it over again. "One who does not believe in the God of the Bible," she said to herself in a whisper. "What is the Bible?" She had never heard Nonie speak of the Bible. Yet her grandfather said that Nonie could find a god under every stone and behind every bush. It was all very strange.

❧   ❧   ❧

The next morning the wind had calmed and the sun was shining feebly, though it was still cold. After their visitor had been breakfasted and sent on his way back to the trading post to wait for better weather before traveling on to Kenakee Falls, Kendra dared broach what had been troubling her mind.

"Papa Mac," she said, "are we pagans?"

"Pagans?" His head came up and his eyes darkened. "That fella say something?" he asked her.

"No. Not really about—about us. But—he said they hope that by 1930 there will be no pagans left in northwest Canada," said Kendra.

Her grandfather surprised her by chuckling. "He did, did he? Seems to me he's taking on a pretty big job."

"He's going to Kenakee Falls," went on Kendra.

"I know. He told me," said George, shrugging into his heavy coat. It was time to check the trapline again.

"I looked up pagan in the dictionary," went on Kendra.

"And—?" prompted her grandfather.

"It said 'heathen.' And then it said that a heathen is a person who doesn't believe in the God of the Bible. Which one is that?"

George couldn't help but chuckle again. Nonie had introduced Kendra to so many gods. Yet none of them came from the Bible. At least not to his knowledge—though he would have admitted that he knew very little about what the Bible contained.

Then he quickly sobered. Maybe it wasn't so amusing after all.

He answered slowly, "Really doesn't matter much as far as I can see," said George as he drew on a mitten. "It's all just a bunch of stories. Just different versions, that's all."

"So we are pagans, then?" pressed Kendra.

He reached out and pinched her cheek. "Some folks might call us that," he answered truthfully. "Isn't the way I think of it."

"But who—who is the God of the Bible?" asked Kendra.

Her grandfather turned to the door and Kendra knew that he would soon be out on the trail again. "Just the white man's version of the Indian myths," he told her, and with a nod he left the cabin, closing the door firmly against the cold.

Chapter Sixteen

Hard Winter

The cold snap continued. Kendra now dreaded the daily round of checking the traps. She feared more for her grandfather than for herself, but he insisted that they needed the money from the furs and went out each day as usual.

Kendra, too, left the cabin each morning as soon as it was light enough to see the trail. In spite of the weather, she did have fair returns from her traps. Each day she tallied the little account she was saving toward her schooling. She really had no idea how much money it would cost, but she knew she would need to work hard to save enough if she wished to go in her eighteenth year.

The cold weather was hard on their wood supply. Kendra watched as the pile that had seemed so big in the fall grew smaller and smaller every day. She still took Nonie a sleigh filled with wood every other day. The cold made it necessary for her to pile the wood a little higher on the sled. The dogs sometimes complained about the load, but Kendra preferred one hard trip to two lighter ones and helped ease the burden by throwing her weight behind the sleigh on the upgrades. Nonie needed to have wood for her fire.

It seemed that every task was just a bit harder

in the inclement weather. Kendra's fingers often felt numb, her cheeks close to freezing in spite of her efforts to keep exposed skin from frostbite. The river ice had to be chopped to reach water for the pail or else she had to thaw snow to fill the water buckets. She didn't know which task was the most difficult to take and alternated the one with the other.

Kendra began to wonder if there would ever be a break in the weather. Just after the first of the new year, there was some relief when the temperature climbed and the sun actually shone on the frigid world.

❧   ❧   ❧

"Have you had any trouble?"

The words came from the red-coated Mountie who shared their supper table. He was the second visitor they'd had in the space of a few months.

"No," said George after giving the question some thought. "I haven't noticed anything out of the ordinary."

"Well, we've had reports that someone has been tampering with traps in the area. I'm going on up to Wingate to ask a few questions and see what I can find out. I'll be back through in a week or two. I'll stop around and see if there's any reason for concern."

George nodded. Stealing from traps was a serious offense. Trappers would not tolerate it. If, in fact, someone was caught in the act, the person making the discovery might well take matters into his own hands. It was no wonder that the Mountie was concerned.

The conversation was not lost on Kendra. She said nothing, but a few discomforting thoughts began to whirl in her thinking. Her traps had not been doing as well of late. She had feared that perhaps she was trapping out the area—that the smaller animals had moved on to another range. But maybe—maybe someone else was taking advantage of her traps.

After the Mountie had thanked her for the meal, shrugged back into his heavy parka and left the cabin, Kendra still mulled over his words. Had she missed something? Were there signs that she should have caught?

"Papa Mac," she said after George had returned to the cabin, "I wonder if I have had someone bothering my trapline."

George looked up from the moccasin he was lacing. "You've spotted something?" he asked.

"Well—no. That is—nothing in particular, but it does seem as if I've had poor catches lately. I've been very careful when setting the traps to hide them well and cover the scent and sprinkle fresh snow over my tracks. And I never take the team too close.

"There are still animal tracks through the area. It seems the game is there—I'm just not having the catch that I should have. At least I'm not *getting* the catch."

George lowered himself to the chair by the table and proceeded to put on his other moccasin.

"Well—keep a sharp lookout," he advised. "If anything looks suspicious let me know."

Kendra nodded.

They both put on their warmest outer wear.

They were facing another day on the trail to check the traplines.

"I knew it," said Kendra, bent over her trap. "Someone *has* been stealing."

Anger filled her. It was hard work running the trapline. If someone wanted the benefit of trapping, they should be willing to do the work for themselves. It wasn't fair to reap from another's labors.

Kendra lifted the tuft of hair that clung to the sprung trap, indicating that an animal had been caught. But there was no carcass anywhere to be seen.

The next trap held an otter. Kendra noted that the fur was at its prime. It should bring a nice price on the market.

But as she left the packed trail and neared the next trap, she noticed that the snow had been rearranged as though something had scuffled around in it. There had been a new fall of snow and Kendra saw no footprints or snowshoe indentations showing through it. But perhaps the culprit had been sly enough to use a small twig to brush at the spot or else had sprinkled handfuls of powdery snow to cover any tracks that might have been left behind.

The more she studied the area around the trap, the more sure she was of her suspicions and the more incensed she became. She took off her mitten and brushed her hand through the new layer of snow. There were blood stains and scattered pieces of hair just beneath the surface. There *had* been an animal caught here, and it was now gone.

Who would do such a thing? Surely it wasn't one

of the area trappers. But it had been a hard winter. Every trapper was finding it difficult to travel out in the intense cold. Perhaps someone had decided that there were easier pickings closer to the settlement. Surely, though, the people in the area knew whose trapline lay so close at hand. But maybe that was the problem. Maybe they reasoned that a young girl would not be smart enough to read the signs. Maybe she was being taken advantage of simply because she was a girl.

The thought made Kendra even angrier. She found her mind reviewing each trapper in the area, white and Indian alike, trying to sort out which one might stoop to such lowness.

It was a mental exercise that disturbed her and really profited nothing. She tried to push aside the troubling conjectures.

"Someone has been bothering my traps," Kendra said to George that evening. Her green eyes flashed anger as she spoke the words.

"You're sure?"

"I'm sure. Two of them had catches that had been taken before I got to them."

"Did you find prints?"

"No. The thief is smart. He covers his tracks well. All I found were signs of the animals."

"What animals?"

"It was hair from a lynx at the first trap. The second was a fox. It had snowed enough to hide the prints, and whoever was there had disguised things pretty well."

George sat silently. "I don't like it," he said at last. "Anyone who will rob a trap will be desperate enough to do almost anything. I'm not sure that you should go out again until after that Mountie has been through."

"But I have the traps set. I need to check them," argued Kendra.

"Maybe I should take your line tomorrow."

"You have your own line to care for. The day isn't long enough for you to cover both."

George knew that was true. He really couldn't argue further.

"Well, I don't like it," he said. "Not one bit."

Kendra did not like it either. If someone was stealing from her traps, then someone was desperate and dangerous. She would have to be doubly cautious as she made her daily run. She hoped she could depend on Oscar to alert her if danger was about.

❧   ❧   ❧

The next day Kendra did her run with a loaded rifle near her on the sled. She hoped she would not need to use it, but she must be ready to take action if it was necessary.

"Just bring your traps on in until this is settled," her grandfather had suggested, but Kendra hated to give up the peak trapping season when she needed the money for her schooling.

"I'll be careful," she promised, and he reluctantly agreed to let her go.

Nothing unusual caught her attention. She picked up four catches and reset her traps. She was glad to hurry home. Nonie needed another load of wood.

❧   ❧   ❧

Four days later Kendra had another trap robbed. Again there had been a snowfall, so she had little hope of picking up any signs. But it made her uneasy in spite of herself. She decided not to tell her grandfather. He would just worry. She did hope that the Mountie would be back soon. The whole thing made her feel edgy. She traveled with the loaded rifle slung over her shoulder.

❧ ❧ ❧

Oscar shifted in his harness and sniffed at the air. Kendra, who traveled closely behind the team, saw the hackles rise along his neck.

"He senses something," she said to herself and reached for the gun on her shoulder.

There was a bend in the trail ahead, and just beyond, a small windfall where Kendra had carefully concealed a trap. Oscar's lifted head pointed in that direction, his sharp ears upright to catch the faintest stirring. He lifted his nose and sniffed at the air. Kendra heard a quiet growl come from his throat.

"Lay," she ordered softly and Oscar dropped immediately to the snow, and the other team members quietly followed suit.

Kendra hesitated. Should she leave the entire team where it was or might she need Oscar? She hesitated for only a moment, then fell to her knees and with a few quick movements had Oscar out of his harness.

"Heel," she commanded in a whisper, and Oscar dropped in close beside her.

The trap was out of sight beyond a stand of spruce. It had been hidden from view along an animal trail that crossed through fallen timber. Kendra knew that once she rounded the bend, she would be exposed to full view. She stopped and slipped off her snowshoes. She did not wish to be encumbered if there should be a tussle. On moccasined feet she moved slowly forward, Oscar following her like a silent shadow. The hair on his neck stood raised, his teeth were bared and ready, but no sound came from his throat or his softly padded paws.

Kendra cocked her gun. She was ready to face whoever was at her traps. She hoped with all her heart that it wouldn't be someone she knew. It would be hard enough to pull the trigger if it was a stranger in the sights.

"Go for his left shoulder—but well above the heart," she told herself as calmly as she could. "If he still threatens, take his right arm."

Then what would she do with him after she had wounded him? It would be a race with the dog team to get him to help before he bled or froze to death. Perhaps she should just turn and flee for home in the hopes that he would not spot her, for if he did he would most certainly be the one firing his gun and he wouldn't be shooting to wound.

No, it was too risky. Better to face him than to turn her back. She had to follow through now.

She took a deep breath and stepped out into the open. Her trap lay just ahead.

For a moment Kendra saw nothing. Whoever was at the trap was apparently bending over close to the ground. Kendra lifted her rifle and sighted toward the spot. Had he already been alerted? Was he hiding behind the fallen log with his sights trained on her? Kendra willed her hands to remain steady even though she was trembling inside.

A head rose above the log. Kendra squinted against the glare of the morning sun on the whiteness of the newly fallen snow. She had to see clearly—to focus on the face of the enemy.

Curious and challenging eyes stared back at Kendra and Oscar. A deep growl crossed the space between them, and Oscar echoed it with a growl of his own. The wolverine snarled more loudly, his teeth bared around their grip on the animal carcass he held in his mouth.

Kendra stood transfixed. So here was the thief. The dreaded wolverine. For one moment she held steady, and then her finger squeezed the trigger. He might charge—or he might bolt for cover. She could not wait to see. He had to be stopped. There would be no peace for any of the trappers as long as he prowled the woods stealing from them.

As the report of the rifle echoed across the still morning air, Kendra's whole body shuddered. It was hard enough to shoot a hated forest thief. She was so thankful that it hadn't been a fellow human in her sights. She lowered the gun, hands trembling. Had it not been an animal, she knew she never could have pulled the trigger.

❧   ❧   ❧

The Mountie stopped by again on his way back through. Kendra gave her report. He nodded his head solemnly.

"One wolverine can cause an awful lot of havoc," he admitted, "and they can cover several miles. Stealing here—stealing there. Making trapper doubt neighboring trapper. I've seen it before. I'm glad you got him."

Kendra smiled. She was glad too. He'd had a re-markably fine fur. It would add to her funds for university.

Chapter Seventeen

More Trouble

Kendra finished her morning run and prepared the two pelts taken from her traps. She was getting ready for a trip to see Nonie when she heard Oscar setting up a howl.

From the sound of Oscar's greeting it was her grandfather's sled entering their clearing. But it was just past noon. Her grandfather should not be returning for several hours. He could not possibly have finished his run. Kendra moved to the door, a frown creasing her smooth forehead.

Her grandfather was not running behind the team as she expected him to be. Surely his team had not deserted him. That was unheard of. But where was he?

Kendra strained to see up the trail. Was he following somewhere behind the sleigh?

But as the team drew near Kendra noticed that the sled had a load. Was the morning catch that profitable to make such a pile in the sleigh?

Kendra hurried forward as the dogs pulled up to the front of the cabin and dropped to the snow. Their sides were heaving, their tongues lolling to the sides of their mouth. Kendra knew they had been pushed hard on the trip.

"Give me a hand."

Kendra's attention jerked from the team to the sled. The mass in the sleigh bottom was her grandfather.

"What happened?" she asked, panic in her voice as she reached out to him.

"A moose. A moose came at me. Got my leg."

Kendra heard the pain in his voice. Terror seized her. How badly was he hurt? How could she ever get help?

"Can you make it to the house?" she asked him.

"I think so. If you help me."

He was a big man and heavy to lift. With a bit of help from the strength still in his arms they managed to get him up and on his one good leg. Then with Kendra for support, they moved slowly to the cabin.

"Get Nonie," George said with a husky voice as Kendra lowered him to his bed.

"Let me see first," said Kendra. She had noticed that one pant leg was soaked with blood. She could not leave him bleeding while she traveled to fetch Nonie. He might bleed to death before she could return.

Kendra reached for the skinning knife she carried in the side of her moccasin and slashed away the pant leg. The wound beneath made her shut her eyes and fight against fainting. The moose had given her grandfather an awful gash.

"How is it?" George managed to ask between clenched teeth.

"It's bad. Deep, I think. But if we can keep the infection out, it should heal okay."

"Get Nonie," George said again.

"Nonie is sick in bed," replied Kendra. "I was just leaving to take her some broth and firewood."

"What will we do?" George groaned as he asked the question.

Kendra tried to quiet her racing thoughts. She had to think clearly.

"I have medicine here," she said, trying hard to keep her voice calm in spite of her trembling. "Everything that Nonie has, I have. You lie still and I'll fetch it. It's in my room."

Kendra went for her roots and herbs. She had to think carefully, to sort out which use each one had. She had to be sure that she didn't make an error and use the roots for stomach pain in place of the roots for clotting, or the herb for toothache in place of the pain-killer. She also needed the bitter herb to fight infection and the gum from the spruce for healing.

It took some time for Kendra to clean the wound, treat it, and get it bandaged. George was in a cold sweat by the time she was done. She covered him with the blanket and moved to put her supplies back where they belonged. She still had not cared for the dog team, and Nonie still needed wood for her fires and the broth for her meal.

Her grandfather's trapline had not been covered, but she could not possibly see to it before dark. For the first time, it would not have its daily checking.

Kendra pulled on her heavy coat. "Try to rest," she told her grandfather. "I will put your team down for the night and make a fast trip to Nonie's. I'll be back as soon as I can."

George opened his eyes slowly. He tried to smile but it was more of a grimace. "Pesky nuisance," he managed. One hand stole up to tug at his beard.

Kendra moved forward and tucked the covers up around his chin.

"Sleep," she whispered. "I'll be right back."

When she returned from the dogs, she was thankful to find him sleeping. He needed to rest. He had lost a fair bit of blood, but Kendra was thankful that the bull's antlers had not seemed to break any bones or tear any muscles. With time he should heal. But it would be a while before he could travel the trapline again. Kendra prepared herself for some difficult days.

❧   ❧   ❧

It was impossible to care for both traplines alone, so Kendra brought in her own traps and took the trail daily to cover the trapline of her grandfather. He fussed and fretted but there was little he could do. They needed the furs from the winter catch to make it through to another season.

❧   ❧   ❧

Spring was making promises to return to the land. George had not yet taken over his trapline again, but when it came time to take the pelts to the post, he informed Kendra that he was well enough to drive one of the teams.

"Are you sure?" cautioned Kendra.

The leg had been healing nicely, but Kendra did not wish to take any chances.

"I'm sure," he insisted. "Stop pampering me."

They loaded the furs on the sleds and hitched the teams. Both of them knew that the winter had not been a good one. Usually their winter catch was twice as big as the one they now took to the post for trade.

"Well—it's not much," said George as he lashed the pelts on the sled, "but it might get us through until another season. Maybe our next winter won't be as bad as our last one."

Kendra nodded. She did hope things would improve. If they didn't, she might never get out to school.

With a shout to the dogs, both the sleds moved out onto the trail. They would follow the packed trail through the trees until they came to the bend in the river, and then they would travel the river ice into the settlement.

The morning held a hint of warmth. The snow had not yet left the area, but the sun now shone with some strength in its rays.

Kendra looked up at it and could not keep the smile from her lips. Nonie would have told her that Father Sun was getting over his anger with the world and was willing to give them all another chance.

They reached the river and moved out onto the windswept ice. It was much easier for the dogs to pull on the level. They increased their speed, and Kendra was afraid her grandfather's injured leg would make it difficult for him to keep up. She coaxed Oscar to set a more leisurely pace.

"We'll have to watch it around the beaver dam," George cautioned and Kendra nodded. She knew that the beaver dam could be dangerous. The water was deeper and the animals often made channels that would freeze over lightly. The channel ice could not carry the weight of a loaded sleigh.

Once they neared the dam, they slowed the

dogs, and George walked slowly ahead of the teams, sounding the ice with a stout stick. Kendra followed carefully, her eyes ever alert for thin ice that might lead to trouble.

They were almost beyond the spot when there was a sickening sound of cracking ice. Kendra cried out to her grandfather, but it was too late. Another crack. She watched in horror as his sleigh broke through the ice and slowly began to sink from sight in the gurgling water. The team struggled to hold it, pulling frantically against their leather harnesses. Kendra held her breath. Would the sled pull the entire team into the icy stream?

The dogs continued to scramble, their frightened yips filling the crisp morning air. Sharp toenails clawed at the slippery surface; then Shanoo went down with a cry, splashing nosily as she hit the water. She struggled against the current but it was no use. Kendra watched as the dog was dragged under, the water closing above her head with a satisfied gurgle.

Kendra's eyes jerked back to Natook who still fought for a foothold on the slippery ice that seemed to keep crumbling beneath him. He was losing ground quickly. Kendra looked on in horror, frozen to the spot, her thoughts whirling too quickly to make much sense. How much, and how many, were they to lose?

It was her grandfather who brought her back to her senses.

"Cut the harnesses," he called. "Cut the harnesses."

Kendra looked up to find George at the head of his team, clutching the harness of the lead dog and trying hard to keep the team from slipping farther into the gaping hole.

Kendra dropped to her stomach and inched her way across the ice. As she moved she reached down for the knife in her moccasin. Natook was still clawing and scratching at the edge of the breaking ice, about to slip into the river. Kendra was sure she would not make it in time.

She reached for the frightened dog and gave him a boost with all the strength she could muster. At the same moment her knife sliced through the strap that held him prisoner to the sleigh. She heaved again and the dog increased his scrambling, his claws digging at the icy surface. Kendra heard the ice groan beneath her. For one awful moment she was sure it would break again and she and the dogs would slip into the chilly water. She held her breath as she hoisted at the sled dog again.

Natook managed to get his feet back under himself as Kendra slashed at the harness that tied the other dogs to the weight of the sled.

At last the final strap was severed. Kendra lay panting. She heard the sound of the dogs as they scraped and scurried their way to the shore, fright still echoing in their whines.

"Get out of there," George called sharply and Kendra opened her eyes and forced herself to move, inching backward slowly in her prostrate position. She did not dare to try to stand. She did not even dare to draw herself up on her knees.

Where was her team? Had they gone down?

When Kendra thought she had slid far enough away from the danger zone, she rolled over slowly and looked around her. Oscar had the team in check. He stood before them, his eyes alert, ears back. The rest of the team lay silently where she had left them. The ice around them was still intact, but Kendra did not trust it for a minute longer.

She continued to slide her way back from the widening hole until she could safely rise to her feet. Then she called to Oscar and ordered him to bring the team off the ice to the safety of the riverbank.

Once they were all ashore, Kendra sank to the snow-packed ground. She was breathing hard and trembling from head to foot.

"We could have lost them all," said George, his voice edged with strain.

Kendra thought of Shanoo. The dog had no chance against the strong current. She had been swept under the river ice and carried downstream. Kendra closed her eyes tightly. It was too awful to even think about. But, like her grandfather had said, they could have lost them all.

Then Kendra thought of the load of winter furs.

"Is there any chance at all—?" she began, but George was already shaking his head.

"We'd never get it out," he answered her.

Kendra buried her head against her raised knees. It was so unfair. So unfair. They had needed every pelt. They'd already had a bad winter. What would they ever do now?

She felt a hand on her head. "We'll make it," her grandfather soothed. But his voice was tight with worry. She wondered if he really believed his own words.

"We'll make it," he said again. His words held more confidence now, as though speaking them gave him some assurance. Kendra lifted her head and looked at the teams lying about them on the snow. At least they still had their dogs. All but poor

Shanoo. And she still had Oscar. The ice had not broken under her weight while she fought at the edge of the hole to rescue the team. And, most important, her grandfather had not gone down. For that she was thankful. Perhaps they had a good deal to be thankful for after all.

Chapter Eighteen

Going Out

The summer was much kinder to them than the winter had been. Kendra planted a garden and tended it carefully. The vegetables kept their table supplied and produced additional food for canning and for their root cellar. Kendra spent day after day in the woods finding edible roots and berries. That, with the meat brought in from the hunt, kept them going over the summer and far into the fall. They got to the place where the flour and coffee ran out, but they managed to have food for their table.

Kendra did not even suggest that they pick up some supplies on credit as many of the other families in the area commonly did. She already knew her grandfather's feeling concerning spending money that one did not have. George believed in paying at the time of purchase and preferred to make do with less rather than run up a bill at the post.

It was almost Christmas when they took their first pelts of the season to the trading center and bought supplies they needed to get them through the rest of the winter. They both breathed a bit easier with the cabin's shelves stocked once again. It had been tough—but they had made it.

Kendra made a batch of fresh biscuits to go with

their usual meat and vegetable supper, and they ate them all at one sitting. It had been so long since they had enjoyed the taste of any kind of bread.

❦ ❦ ❦

The catch that year was a good one. Kendra began to hope she would be able to go out for school, after all. George brought the matter up every now and then to let the girl know he had not forgotten her plans.

"When do you want to go?" he asked one day as they worked together on next winter's supply of wood.

"I've been told classes start mid-September," replied Kendra. She did not have to ask her grandfather to what he was referring.

"And how much time will you need to be ready for classes?" he pressed further.

Kendra placed the wood length on the pile and straightened. She reached her hand up to brush wisps of blond hair back from her moist brow. "I don't know," she responded. "It's rather scary. I haven't been out for years."

George leaned his saw against a young sapling and dropped to the grass. It was hard work felling trees and sawing them into stove lengths. They could both use a rest. He patted the grassy ground beside him and Kendra took the few short steps to lower herself at his side.

"I've written to Maggie. She says you can stay with her for as long as you like," George said.

Kendra nodded. She was glad that Maggie Miller was in the city. She let her eyes drop to her worn and simple clothing. She certainly wouldn't be wearing these to the classroom. What would she wear? None of her clothes were suitable. Her wardrobe consisted of a strange combination of deerskin and simple cloth garments. Most of the materials for her skirts and blouses had been woven by the local Indians or purchased as yard goods at the trading post. In fact, she dressed just as the Indians in the settlement did. Practical clothing, made to endure and keep one warm.

Her eyes traveled farther—to the tips of her moccasined feet. Another change and one that she did not look forward to. She remembered when she had gone out for school before and how uncomfortable the stiff, awkward shoes felt. She would have to adjust to the shoes this time.

"I don't know," she said again as she stretched the ache from between her shoulders. She had some nagging doubts. Perhaps she shouldn't go out, after all. Her grandfather did need her to help with the work. It took both of them working hard just to survive.

"Would you rather I stayed here?" she asked him, her eyes still on her feet.

"Oh no," he assured her quickly. "I think you should go to school."

She didn't know if his words were encouraging or disappointing. Did she really want to go? Could she make it?

He seemed to sense her mood. "Of course, there will be some adjustments—at first," he commented. "But you're bright and quick—remember, I was your first teacher." They smiled at each other at those memories. "You'll adjust quickly," he went on. "And once you do—I think you'll really like it."

"You think so?"

"I'm sure you will. Just think of all of the new stuff you can learn."

Kendra longed to learn, but she still felt agitated.

"And you'll be all right?"

"Truth is," he said slowly, "I don't know how in the world I'm ever going to get along without you. Don't know how I ever got along without you before you came. I'm going to miss you—so much." He turned again to her. "But I want you to go—honest. I want you to learn about that big world out there. You won't want to live back here forever. It isn't fair. You need to know people. Other people. People your own age. You've never even had a playmate. Never even had a chance to play. I feel bad about it, Kendra. I—"

But she interrupted him. "There's no reason to feel bad. I couldn't have chosen a better way to live. Honest. I can't imagine living a life where you just—just sit around all day—being bored—and useless. I love it here. And I'll be back. I promise you that. I'll be back."

She leaned over and kissed his whiskered cheek.

❧   ❧   ❧

They left in the middle of August. Kendra fretted and stewed as she checked the woodpile, the storage shed, the supply shelves. Would her grandfather really be able to handle things all alone? She would be gone for the whole winter. Maybe two or three winters before she returned to the cabin. Would he really be able to manage?

The trip out meant days of weary travel while

Kendra silently wondered over and over if she was doing the right thing. George, silent as well, was sure his granddaughter was doing the right thing— the only thing—but he also knew that it was going to be awfully quiet and lonely when he returned home to the empty cabin.

When they finally reached the city, Maggie greeted them warmly. She had aged since Kendra had seen her last. George noticed it as well and knew that losing Henry had been terribly hard for Maggie.

Still, she was able to smile and chatter and inform them of all the new happenings in the city.

"We've got some lovely shops, dear," she told Kendra. "Whenever you wish to go shopping, I will be most happy to go with you."

Kendra was glad to hear that. She wasn't even sure what she should be shopping for. How did the young women who attended university dress? Did Maggie know? Would the sales ladies help her or were they just out to sell as many dollars of merchandise as they could? Kendra trembled every time she thought of her upcoming shopping trip.

George busied himself about Maggie's small home, fixing this and repairing that while Maggie and Kendra went out on shopping excursions. It wasn't quite as bad as Kendra had feared. The sales clerks were most helpful, though Kendra did feel that they would gladly have helped her spend every cent she had. She would not let them pressure her, and when she decided that the purchases for her wardrobe were sufficient, she gently but firmly said no to further suggestions.

The sewing of garments was the next step. Maggie was a good seamstress, but because she was afraid she was not up on the latest styles, she took advantage of the help of a neighbor. Between the two of them, they presented Kendra with an adequate and attractive wardrobe.

Kendra spent days trying to adjust to the shoes. There were many times she wished to lean down, slip them from her aching feet, and retrieve her worn moccasins, but she did not allow herself the pleasure. She had to learn to wear them or be the laughingstock of the classroom.

Another adjustment came in changing her hairstyle. Kendra was used to wearing it in two long braids that hung down over her shoulders. If her task was such that she didn't want the braids dangling in her way, she simply wound them around her head and pinned them securely.

But braids would not do on the university campus, however. Kendra knew that. But she wasn't quite sure how her hair should be worn. Again the young neighbor came to her rescue. She set about trimming Kendra's long blond locks.

"You have lovely hair," she said over and over. "Such a beautiful color—and so shiny."

Kendra had never given it much thought. It was just—hair. Different from the Indian neighbors, but hair nonetheless. Now she looked at it a bit more closely. It was a nice color. She was pleased about that.

"Now," the neighbor woman went on to explain, "the younger women are wearing it a bit looser at the front—with soft waves. You have a real advantage there because yours is naturally wavy. You bring it back like this. Give it a twist, then wrap it like so. Then you bring this section over here, fold this back this way, bring this around, tuck this in, and put pins in like this."

It looked so complicated. Kendra was sure she would never be able to do it. She regretted that she wouldn't be able to just braid her hair the way she was used to.

George accompanied Kendra when she went to the school to enroll. She did not tell him, but it was the most frightening experience of her life. She wanted to cling to his hand, to plead with him to take her home again, but she did neither.

It was not a large school, but to Kendra the halls felt strange, the many unknown faces slightly threatening.

"There's nothing to be afraid of. Stop your trembling," she chided herself over and over. But her heart pounded, her stomach hurt, and her hands shook anyway.

She was quizzed about her knowledge. That made her tremble even more, but the results seemed to satisfy the officials, for soon she found herself being handed the papers that told her when and where she would be expected to show up for her classes. She was in.

She decided to accept the gracious invitation and stay with Maggie. At least she could save herself one additional adjustment—and perhaps a few dollars as well. Besides, Maggie expressed a genuine desire to have her company, and George seemed most anxious that she agree to the arrangement.

George stayed on until she was settled into her new surroundings and schedule. Kendra knew he would need to leave soon to prepare for the winter trapping season. He knew it as well, but he seemed to hate the thought of leaving.

Along with Kendra, Maggie hated to see him go. "I didn't realize how many little things needed fixing," she told him. "Henry—Henry wasn't able to care for such things his last years, and I didn't know how to go about them. Seems one broken or worn-out thing just leads to another. It is so nice to have everything in good order again."

"I was happy to do it," replied George. "Gave me something to do while you ladies were shoppin' and snippin'."

Kendra laughed. She knew he would have been terribly bored if Maggie hadn't found little chores for him around the house.

❧   ❧   ❧

A full week of Kendra's classes had passed before George announced that he would be returning to Bent River Crossing. Kendra was adjusting well, though she occasionally had moments of intense nervousness. She still often trembled as she thought of how much "catching up" she had to do in some of the subjects. But she was willing to work hard.

She hadn't as yet made any new friendships, but she did have a few nodding acquaintances. In one class the teacher had singled her out for introduction to the entire class and asked her to share a bit about life in the wild. Kendra, blushing with embarrassment, had managed to give a brief report. It must have created interest, for after she was done a number of students had questions. She fared far better in giving direct and informative answers to the queries, and when she finally took her seat there was appreciative applause. Kendra felt that the students were friendly and open and that, given a bit of time, she would be able to make friends. She told her grandfather so and he seemed pleased.

"The belle of the classroom," he beamed. "I knew you would be."

"Oh, Papa Mac," said Kendra, hanging her head, her cheeks flushing, "it's not like that at all."

"Well, it will be. Just you wait and see. It won't take those teachers—or the other young people—long to see that you are a very special person."

Kendra smiled in spite of herself.

And then her glance fell on her hands. She had soon realized that hers were the only rough and calloused hands among the school's young women. Embarrassed, she wriggled uncomfortably on Maggie's sofa and ended up with her hands tucked under her new gray wool skirt.

Chapter Nineteen

Stirrings

"How are your classes going?"

Kendra frowned at Maggie's question. The classes, for the most part, seemed to be going just fine. Yet for some reason Kendra couldn't explain, she felt she was not enjoying them as she had anticipated.

"Perhaps it's just that I miss home and Papa Mac and Oscar so much," she told herself night after night when she was tempted to cry silently into her pillow. "I will get used to the noise and commotion of the city. It will just take a while."

But every day added to Kendra's discontent.

Now as she hesitated, Maggie read in her eyes her secret yearnings.

"You miss home." Maggie's simple statement was filled with understanding. "Some of these adjustments are hard and they take time," Maggie went on. "But it will come. You haven't had time to make friends yet."

Kendra wondered if time was the issue. Perhaps she just didn't fit in. She had been raised so differently. She thought differently, liked different things. Even dressed differently in spite of the fact that she had tried so hard to imitate the other girls.

"I don't know, Aunt Maggie," she finally answered with a deep sigh. "I—I just feel that—that something is missing. I don't quite fit. I'm like—like a hawk trying to swim. I just don't understand some of the ideas. I—"

"But you will," said Maggie with complete confidence. "It takes time."

Kendra thought for a while. Perhaps her problem was that she really didn't *want* to be like the others. They all seemed so—so patterned. So programmed. If one said something was so, all the others agreed. Did she really want to be like that? She wasn't sure. Perhaps that was her problem. Maybe she just wasn't open to change.

"I don't know," she said hesitantly. "I think it might just be me."

"Nonsense," said Maggie, rising from her chair to bring the apple cobbler. "Don't rush yourself." As though still carrying on the same subject, she added, "I had a letter from your grandfather today."

Kendra lifted her head. She'd already had three letters from her grandfather in spite of the inadequate mail service. Two of them had arrived together. Every letter made Kendra so lonesome she wondered if they brought pleasure or added to her misery.

"How is he?" she asked quickly.

"Oh, he's fine. Just fine. He's missing you awfully though. Says that Oscar still sits and whines."

It was almost more than Kendra could bear. She clenched together the hands that lay in her lap and willed tears out of her eyes.

"He says they've already had some snow," Maggie continued, unaware of Kendra's struggle as she cut the cobbler. "Not too cold yet. Just a flurry. He doesn't think it will stay."

"No," Kendra murmured. "It likely won't stay. We get those storms that move through and it always gets nice again."

"Says Nonie's doing well," Maggie added. "He was over to take her some wood the day he wrote. He knew you'd be wondering about Nonie, so he said for me to be sure to tell you."

Kendra longed to see Nonie. The Indian woman had been like a grandmother to her in many ways. Kendra did not know what she would have done without Nonie in those early years.

"Nonie had a flying squirrel drop down her chimney and scatter fireplace ashes and soot all over the place. Luckily the fire had died out and the squirrel didn't suffer none from the fracas. But Nonie sure had a mess to clean up."

Kendra couldn't help but smile. It must have been quite a shock for the squirrel. She could picture the little creature being greeted with a loud shrieking, "Aiyee! Aiyee!" It must have been frightened half to death.

"Not much other news, I guess. He was just wondering how we are getting on."

Kendra accepted the dish of apple cobbler. Maggie was a good cook. Kendra was enjoying all sorts of new and delicious food. But tonight she didn't feel much like eating.

❧   ❧   ❧

"Miss Marty. May I walk with you?"

Kendra looked up to find a tall young man standing beside her, books tucked under his arm just as she did. Kendra had noticed the young man before. He sat just behind her and to her left in English Literature class. Other students shifted from one seat to another, but this young gentleman, like Kendra herself, always got to class early and always chose the same seat.

Kendra nodded and resumed her steps. They didn't have much time between classes.

"May I introduce myself," he said as they walked. "I'm Carl Mandrake."

Kendra nodded, aware of that fact.

"So how are you enjoying the class?" he continued.

Kendra dipped her head slightly. She always loved literature. Yet if she were to be honest, she was not overly impressed with the professor, so she wasn't sure how to answer the question.

"Personally," he went right on, "I find old Prof Flanders absolutely"—He stopped and glanced around to make sure there was no one else within earshot—"boring," he finished conspiratorially.

Kendra couldn't help but smile. He had echoed her own feelings. She felt it a shameful waste for a professor to take an interesting subject and treat it with such lack of enthusiasm.

"Hear he teaches philosophy as well," the young man went on. "I'm avoiding that one if I can."

"Thanks for the tip," Kendra replied with another smile. "I think I'll try to do likewise."

They had almost reached their classroom.

"I was wondering," said the young man, suddenly sounding rather out of breath and in a hurry, "if you would like to join us on Friday night. We're having a party at Nancy's house. I've been invited and she said we might bring a guest."

Kendra stopped walking. She had never been invited out before—never been to a party. What would she wear? How should she act? Did she really wish to go?

"That would be very nice," she heard a voice answering and was surprised to discover that it was her own.

"Good," he said. "Write down your address and I'll get it after class. I'll pick you up at eight."

All through class Kendra's mind kept whirling. What had she done? She hardly knew the young man. She had no idea what sort of a fellow he was. She had even less of an idea of how the young entertained themselves at a party. She should not have said yes. Perhaps she should just write him a little note and tell him she had changed her mind. Several times during the class Kendra felt his eyes upon her. She dared not turn her head even slightly for fear their eyes would meet.

At the end of the class period she slipped him a note with Maggie's address. She wanted to avoid looking at him, but it didn't seem the polite thing to do. She glanced at him briefly and was rewarded with a warm smile. Kendra flushed and hurried off to another class. She would not see him again until the next day. In the meantime she hoped she would have a chance to chat with Nancy, a girl she knew slightly. She just had to learn a bit more about the coming party.

🌼   🌼   🌼

Normally Nancy was surrounded by a noisy, fun-loving group of her five or six special friends. But this time, Kendra noticed, she was sitting alone in the small cafeteria. Kendra breathed a sigh when she spotted her and concluded that the others must not have been dismissed from their final class yet. She took a deep breath, walked forward, and put her best smile in place. "May I join you for a minute?" she asked.

Nancy looked surprised, then nodded.

Kendra took the seat opposite the girl and sipped at her cool drink. Then she swallowed quickly and decided she had better talk fast. Nancy's crowd might soon be arriving.

"Carl has asked me to accompany him to your party on Friday night," she began, noting the surprised look that crossed Nancy's face.

"Good," she smiled, and Kendra hoped she truly meant the single word.

"I was wondering," continued Kendra before she had a chance to lose her nerve, "what we plan to do—so I'll know how to dress for it."

Relaxed again, Nancy smiled a second time and leaned forward.

"Oh, we won't do much. We mostly just hang around and talk and eat and maybe dance a bit to the gramophone. I have some great records. Papa got them the last time he traveled to Chicago."

Kendra nodded, her own smile still carefully in place.

"So you aren't dressing formal?" she asked. She had heard the word used and finally figured out what it meant in terms of present-day wear.

"No. No. Just come—comfortable. Whatever—" said the young woman with a flick of her wrist.

Kendra could hear a chattering group entering the room. She looked up to see Nancy's usual bevy of cohorts. Nancy stood and waved wildly. "Over here," she called across to them.

Kendra stood and smiled. "Thanks," she said.

"Oh, you don't have to leave," put in Nancy. "There's room for you to join us."

But Kendra gathered her armful of books.

"Thanks," she said again, "but I really have to go. I have loads of homework."

"Homework?" said Nancy with a shrug of her shoulder. "I really can't be bothered." She laughed.

❧   ❧   ❧

Kendra was so nervous as she dressed for Friday evening's outing that her hands trembled. She was ready much before eight and sat on Maggie's couch watching the clock and nervously fidgeting.

"I think it's so nice that you can go out with the young people," Maggie exclaimed for what Kendra judged must have been about the tenth time. "And you look so nice," enthused Maggie. Kendra again felt doubts that she may have picked the wrong outfit.

"What did you say this boy's name is?"

Kendra licked dry lips and swallowed. "Carl," she said. "Carl Mandrake."

"Mandrake. I don't believe I've heard that name in the city."

"No. No, I believe he is from out of town. Somewhere south, I think," replied Kendra. She had a vague recollection of a comment made in class, but she couldn't remember what it was. She had paid little attention at the time.

"Well, I do think it's so nice," said Maggie again as she reached for her scissors to clip a thread on her needlework.

"Your grandfather will be pleased as well," went

on Maggie. "He has worried some that he kept you in the woods too long."

Kendra smiled. But it was a halfhearted one. She was too nervous to fully appreciate Maggie's comment.

"Well, I told him that I was sure you'd do fine. It just takes time, that's all. One can't come into a new situation and feel perfectly at home immediately. It takes time."

Kendra thought she heard steps on the wooden sidewalk. She rose swiftly to her feet and crossed to the window. There was no one in sight.

She sat back down and fiddled with the buttons on her shirtwaist front. Was the shirtwaist too plain? Too tailored for such an outing? She glanced at the clock. She did wish she had decided on the other one, but she wouldn't have time to change now. It was almost eight o'clock.

Kendra, beginning to hope that she had been forgotten, didn't hear a knock till twenty past eight. But when Maggie opened the door, Carl Mandrake stood on the step. He smiled congenially and introduced himself to Maggie. Kendra grabbed a light shawl and went to meet him. If Maggie got started talking, they would never get away, she reasoned.

Carl made no reference to the fact that he was late and no apologies for keeping her waiting. Kendra tried to shrug it off. Perhaps that was how young people generally made arrangements—with a great deal of flexibility.

It was fifteen blocks to Nancy's house, but it was a nice evening and Kendra enjoyed the chance to stretch her legs and breathe in the fresh evening air. She walked farther than that each day to get to classes. Maggie had fretted about the distance to the university, but Kendra felt it was a short stroll after being used to following the dog team for miles each day.

As they walked, Carl made light conversation. He was easy to listen to. His little puns made Kendra laugh. She began to feel that the evening might not be so bad after all. Perhaps she had done the right thing in agreeing to go out.

When they reached Nancy's house, there was a noisy crowd already gathered in the backyard. Carl led Kendra directly down the sidewalk, past the flower garden, and to a back patio. Kendra could tell that he was familiar with the place.

"Hi, Carl" greeted them over and over as they neared the group of revellers. "Hey, Carl." "How you doing?" "What took you so long?"

Kendra listened to the boisterous shouts. It seemed that Carl was popular with the crowd. It made her feel rather good to be out with such an important young man.

But the feeling didn't last very long. Though a good deal of attention was showered on Carl, Kendra was rather ignored. She managed to find a spot to sit on a low bench almost in the shadows, and from her perch watched the party going on around her.

Kendra wasn't sure what she had expected, but certainly more than the chattering, bantering, teasing, and flirting that went on. Now and then a couple drew back into the shadows, more interested in each other than in the rest of the party guests.

There was lots of food. And drink. Much of it was alcoholic. Kendra had never seen people drink before. Her grandfather abhorred the use of alcohol. But the young people at the party did not share his perspective. Even some of the young women present shared the bottles passed around.

Now and then Carl seemed to remember her. He would look around, spot her on the bench she had not left all evening, and wave his hand at her merrily. Once he brought her some of the party food. It tasted strange to Kendra, and she was glad she had taken only a small portion. At least she wouldn't have to force down a lot of something she didn't like.

The hour got later and later. The air became chillier. The party grew noisier. Kendra suppressed yawn after yawn. She began to shiver. She was afraid the neighbors would soon be complaining. She longed to go home.

"Hey, Kendra. Join the party," someone called.

"Come on, Kendra," said Nancy, finally acting the hostess. "We are going in to dance."

There didn't seem to be anything else to do. Kendra followed.

The dancing was even noisier and livelier. Kendra wished she could cover her ears. She was used to quiet, to silence—except for the sliding of the sleigh runners over the crisp winter snow or the call of a loon in the cold evening air. Even the whole dog team baying at once wasn't as loud as this group.

"Want to dance?" The young man who spoke to her was a stranger to Kendra. She did not know him even from any of her classes.

Kendra shook her head. "I'll just watch," she replied and tried to smile. She had no idea how to take part in one of their dances. All she had ever seen were the dances connected with the Indian festivities at the settlement.

He shrugged and left to find another partner.

Carl was having fun with a young woman in a full navy skirt and a puffy-sleeved blouse. When she twirled, her skirts lifted, both surprising and embarrassing Kendra. But the young woman did not seem to mind. Round and round they whirled, laughing and breathless.

The party went on and on, and Kendra's desire to go home nearly overwhelmed her. But Carl was having such a good time she feared he would never wish to leave.

"You wanna dance?' he asked her breathlessly between pieces played on the gramophone.

Kendra shook her head.

"Can I get you a drink?" he asked solicitously.

Kendra shook her head again.

He nodded. It seemed to be fine with him if she wished to just sit. He looked around for another dance partner.

Kendra waited until the music started and the couples began to swing and sway; then she gathered her shawl about her shoulders, slipped quietly from the room, and started the long walk home.

Chapter Twenty

Amy

At first Kendra was angry—angry with Carl for asking her to the party and then nearly forgetting she was even there. Angry with Nancy for not making more effort to include her in the evening's activities. Angry with the other young guests who gave her a nod and then went about having a good time. But, mostly, angry with herself for not fitting in. They had already branded her as a girl "from the sticks." She had just proved to them that she was.

Tears threatened to form, but Kendra willed them away in the manner she had learned from her childhood. She would not cry.

"I just don't fit," she scolded herself. "I just don't fit. I'm as—as awkward and—and different as a— a crow with a flock of bluebirds."

Kendra was almost halfway home when a new thought came to her.

"I don't need to fit. I really don't. If I'm not comfortable with the 'in crowd,' I don't need to fit. Why was I trying to fit with them anyway? They aren't what I want to be. What I wish to become. They don't even take life seriously. They don't study. Half of them will never make it through the year. They party. They drink too much. They—" Kendra stopped. She need not go on with her accusations.

She had no more right to judge them than they'd had to judge her.

"I don't fit!" she said to finish her tirade. "And that's that! They have a right to be who and what they want to be, but I don't have to try to mold myself into their way of living. I can still be me."

Once she had worked it through, Kendra felt much better about the evening. Perhaps good had come of it after all. She now did not feel so pressured to be part of this strange new world. She could take it one day at a time, and pick and choose what she liked from it and feel perfectly free to reject what did not suit her. She was here to learn—to become a wiser and better person because of the experience. There was no reason for her to throw that away just to be one of the crowd.

"Besides," she reminded herself honestly, "there are lots of young men and women who are here to learn. Perhaps—in time—I will get to know some of them."

❧   ❧   ❧

"Did you have a nice time?"

Maggie was still up, clad in a warm fuzzy robe and pretending to be reading.

Kendra managed a smile. The night was a bit chilly and she had only had her light shawl along. She felt cold in spite of her brisk walking pace. She shivered slightly.

"It—it was different," she managed.

Maggie laid aside her book, concern filling her eyes.

"Oh, it was all right," Kendra quickly added to ease the woman's fears.

"Would you like a cup of hot cocoa," asked Maggie, "or have you been eating all evening?"

"No. No," said Kendra. Some of them had been eating for a good part of the evening, but she had not. "I haven't eaten much at all, and a cup of cocoa sounds wonderful."

They went to the kitchen and Kendra was glad for its warmth. Maggie had kept the fire going in the big cookstove. The teakettle was still humming contentedly on the back of the range.

Kendra lowered herself into one of the wooden chairs, and Maggie went to stir up two cups of cocoa.

For a few moments silence settled over them. Maggie broke it, seeming to search carefully for words. "That—that Carl—seems like a—a nice young man."

Kendra wanted to laugh. All the anger and frustration had totally left her. She had drawn back—distanced herself from the laughing, celebrating party-goers. It seemed strange now that she had even tried, or thought of trying, to be one of them.

And then quite suddenly, catching her unaware, she felt an unusual sadness. Carl *was* a nice young man. Sort of. He had been fun to talk with. He had asked her out. He had tried to look after the young girl half-hidden in the shadows, unable to come out and join the crowd. He had brought her something to eat. Had checked now and then.

She didn't feel angry with Carl now. Nor did she feel superior to him. But she did feel sorry—in a strange way. Carl was failing. In almost every class. It was not a well-kept secret. She was sure it was not because Carl needed to fail. He had a good mind and would do well if he chose to use it instead of spending his time partying. She felt sorry about Carl and wondered what the future held for him.

Maggie placed the steaming cup on the table in front of her.

"Yes," said Kendra as she stirred the frothy brew. "He *is* nice. It was good of him to invite me tonight." She lifted her eyes. "But, Maggie—I'll not be going to one of their parties again. I don't—don't have anything in common with them. I've decided to take my time and—and pick my own friends. It might take a while—but good friends are worth it—don't you think?"

Maggie nodded, then smiled slowly. Her eyes looked off into the distance seeing another time and other faces. "George and Polly McMannus were friends like that with Henry and me—for ever so long," she said, looking at Kendra. "They stuck through thick and thin—even when we didn't see one another that often. When one has friends like that—you don't really need many." She smiled at Kendra and wished such a blessing for her.

༝ༀ   ༝ༀ   ༝ༀ

"You're still lonesome too, aren't ya?"

George ruffled the fur of the big dog beside him and then patted the large, soft head. Oscar responded with a whine and a tongue licking at the hand.

"Thought we'd have got used to it by now," the man murmured. "But we haven't—have we? Cabin still feels just as empty. Sometimes I wonder if I'll ever be content to be alone again."

George continued to stroke the head. He had never allowed a dog in to share his cabin until Kendra had coaxed to have Oscar inside. Now it didn't seem right to make the dog go back outside with the others. Besides, George rather needed his company on the long, cold winter nights cooped up inside near the fire.

"What did I use to do with my time?" he went on. "I don't remember the time dragging like it seems to do now. How did I spend those long evenings? Reading? Working on the furs? Just loafing? I don't know. It seems like I now have more hours than I have jobs to fill them. I don't like the feeling, Oscar. Not at all."

George was not conscious that his left hand reached up to stroke agitatedly at his full beard.

From somewhere out in the night a lone wolf howled and the sled dogs set up a chorus in response.

Oscar pulled away from the man's hand, a deep rumble starting down in his chest.

"What's the matter? The wilderness calling? You wish to be out? Free?"

But no. George was sure that Oscar would not welcome freedom. He was restless. Lonely. That was all. Oscar did not wish to rush out into the night in answer to what he was feeling any more than George himself did.

The big dog returned from his pacing and pressed up against George's knee, still whining.

"She'll be back," George said as he reached out to stroke the silky fur. "She'll be back. Before we know it spring will come again and she'll be back."

But even as he spoke the words, George wondered. Would Kendra really want to return to her home in the wilds? Would she ever be content again to dress in buckskins and furs and mush a team of huskies? He half hoped that she would not. She deserved more than what life here could give her. He really didn't want this hard and lonely life for his little girl. But oh, how he would miss her—did miss her. The very thought of her not coming back brought a lump to his throat that he could not swallow away. He curled his fingers deeply into the fur of the large animal. He needed something to hang on to.

❧   ❧   ❧

At Monday morning's English Literature class, Carl dropped into his usual desk, breathing hard from hurrying. His eyes, a bit hesitant, lifted to Kendra's. He looked a bit apologetic.

Kendra smiled. He responded quickly, easily, seeming to be relieved that she was not angry. "Hi," he said, shifting his books around on the desk top.

"Hi," she replied, then turned her attention back to the front of the room and the professor who had just entered.

Nothing more was said between them until the class ended. The teacher had called for assignments, and Kendra noticed that Carl had nothing to turn in. Another assignment missed. Kendra could not help but wonder how much longer Carl would be allowed to stay in the class.

As she gathered her books to leave, Carl fell in step beside her.

"So what did you think of poor Walter?" he asked, referring to the story they were studying in class.

Kendra laughed lightly. "I think he made his own problems," she answered.

"You don't think he was a victim of circumstance?"

"No more than you or I—or anyone, for that matter," responded Kendra.

"But look at the poor ol' chap," went on Carl in mock sympathy. "Married to that woman. Needing all that money. Having that poor job."

Kendra smiled. "He married the woman—he spent money he didn't have. He picked the job because it was undemanding."

Carl chuckled. "So you won't give the unlucky ol' boy a break?"

Kendra shook her head. "We all make our choices," she replied. "He made bad ones."

Carl sobered suddenly. They walked in silence. At length Carl spoke again.

"Do you think that's what the author is trying to say?" he asked seriously.

"No," replied Kendra after some thought. "I think the author was trying to picture Walter just as you have described him. A victim. But I don't agree. There are victims in the world, of course. Real victims. But they are the people who've never had choices to make. Not the ones who have made bad choices."

"Youch. You're tough," said Carl with a mock grimace, and they both chuckled.

Nothing was said about the Friday night before. No reference. No apology. No accusations. Kendra was happy to forget the whole event.

"See you on Wednesday," said Carl when they reached the end of the hall where Kendra turned one way and he the other.

Kendra nodded and smiled. She was glad that things could continue just as they had been.

❧   ❧   ❧

On Tuesday Kendra hurried to tuck her books together and follow the class from the room. She did wish she didn't have classes back-to-back that were located from one end of the building to the other. She always reached her late-afternoon biology class breathless and flushed. She was feeling frustrated with the class anyway. What she had hoped would provide her with many answers was instead filling her mind with troubling thoughts and even more questions.

Just ahead of her, two students nearly collided, jostling to avoid each other, smiling in embarrassment and fighting to stay in control of their armloads of books.

"I'm sorry," Kendra heard the young man apologize, but it was obvious he was in a big hurry to get to his next class.

"My fault," replied the girl. "I was too deep in thought." She managed a smile. He gave her a smile in return and they both hurried on.

Kendra was about to push the little incident from her mind. It happened frequently in the narrow halls as students rushed back and forth to classes. But just as she neared the spot where it happened she noticed some sheets of paper on the floor. They must have fallen from the books of one or the other of the students. She stopped to scoop them up. They might be important. She stood and looked down the hall in the direction both students had gone, but they were no longer in sight. She did not have time to run after them nor did she have time to check the papers at present, so she slipped them into one of her own class books. She would try to sort it out later. She did hope that if they indeed were important, there would be a name on one of the sheets.

It wasn't until Kendra was doing her homework that evening that she remembered the sheets of paper. She pulled them from her text and scanned the page to look for a name. At the bottom of the one page was one word, written in smooth, elegant script, "Amy."

Amy? Was that the name of the girl? Was this a class assignment? Would she be looking frantically for the copy? Kendra had so little to go on. She didn't remember seeing the girl in any of her classes.

"It looks like poetry," mused Kendra. She began to read the lines.

> Trees
> So new-born
> They still look
> Sticky-wet.
> They
> Haven't
> Even gathered
> Any air-dust yet.

Kendra reread the little verse. She liked it. It was strange to her, this new form. But she liked the thought. She had seen trees like that. In the spring. With the new green leaves just unfolding, looking fresh and new—and yes—just a bit sticky as they uncurled from the firm wrapping of the bud.

Kendra turned to the next sheet.

Who put the stars in the evening sky?
Who gave the waters their azure blue?
Who set the rainbow up on high?
And sprinkled the grasses with morning dew?

Who hid the fawn with its dappled sides?
Who taught the salmon to swim the brooks?
Who buried gold in the heart of the earth?
Planted wood violets in shadowed nooks?

Who told the crocus that spring had come?
Brought the butterfly from the cocoon?
Who put the song in the robin's heart?
Governed the tides by the distant moon?

Kendra felt a strange stirring of her heart in response to the poem with its reference to the nature she loved and the questions it raised. She was so moved she could scarcely continue reading. This was what she wanted to know. This was what her heart cried out for. The answers. She needed the answer.

She let her eyes fall back to the page she held in a trembling hand.

Who put the "wonder" within my breast?
Set off the "joy bells" within my soul?

Kendra turned the page, but the back of the sheet was empty. Was there another sheet? There had to be. The poem had not given her the answer. There had to be more. There just had to.

But there was nothing more. Kendra turned the page again and slowly reread the poem. Line by line she pondered the thoughts. Here was a kindred spirit. Here was someone who thought as she thought. Wondered as she wondered. Had she—this Amy—found the answer to all the unasked questions? Oh, she must have. Kendra could sense a—a contentment—a peace in the writing. It was not written as by one who was still searching in frustration to find the answers. There had to be more to the poem.

Kendra looked again at the last two lines. Yes. There was more. The meter, as well as the content, called for it. There were at least two more lines to the poem. Perhaps they held the secret. Kendra scrambled through her textbook hoping to find another page of script. But there was none.

"Oh, I do hope she hasn't lost the last part," cried Kendra inwardly. "What if she dropped another sheet and I didn't see it? What if she dropped it farther on?" The very thought made Kendra feel panicky. Maybe she would never find the answers to her questions.

She had to find Amy. She had to. She focused mentally on remembering the girl she had seen briefly in the hall. She was of medium height, with dark hair and eyes, a nice, rather shy smile, glasses—yes, glasses. Not many of the students wore glasses. Perhaps she could find her by her glasses. She had to find her. Somehow.

Chapter Twenty-one

Encounter

For the next two weeks Kendra walked the halls scanning faces. She was so intent on trying to find Amy that she could hardly concentrate on her schoolwork. She even went to the office and asked if anyone had inquired about missing assignment copies.

"No," came the answer. "I suppose we could hold the sheets here in case anyone asks concerning them," he added, but Kendra was reluctant to give up the pages.

"I'll just keep looking for her," she replied hurriedly. "I'm bound to run into her again."

But Kendra was beginning to doubt her own words. Would she ever find the girl? Had the unknown Amy needed the pages to fulfill an assignment?

By the end of the third week, Kendra wondered if she must give up. It seemed that Amy was not to be found. Dejectedly Kendra loaded her arms with her homework for the weekend and started home. She would never find her now. She wondered if she would even remember what the girl looked like.

It was a cold day. The wind blew from the north and whipped at Kendra's heavy coat as though trying to tear it from her shoulders. Kendra braced herself against it and pulled her collar snugly up to her chin. It was on days like this that she wished she still had her fur parka.

"I wonder how Nonie is doing?" she asked herself. She missed Nonie. Missed the smile and the friendly chatter. Even missed her silence as she moved wordlessly about the cabin. Nonie had been like a grandmother. A replacement for the woman Kendra had never known.

Kendra's thoughts then turned to her grandfather. She wondered often how his winter's trapping was going. He had helped considerably with her university costs. Had he kept enough money back to get himself through the long, hard winter? Did he have ample supplies? Kendra did hope so, but she had been reluctant to ask. She worried about her grandfather, and she felt some guilt for leaving him on his own just so she could fulfil her selfish desire to learn at the university.

"I may as well have stayed at home," she said sadly. "I really have not found answers anyway. Not to the real questions. It—it seems that the answers are—are as lost as I am."

Kendra fought against a sudden gust of wind that whipped sharp ice crystals against her exposed cheek, making it sting.

"I think I'll just go home." She surprised even herself. "Back to Papa Mac and Nonie and Oscar."

But as quickly as her heart began to beat with the excitement of the thought, Kendra dismissed it. She couldn't quit in the middle of a term. That would be a waste. That would not please her grandfather. He had not raised a quitter. Kendra amended her statement. "I'll go home just as soon as I finish my first year," she told herself and felt sorrow and loneliness fill her being again. It seemed such a long time to wait.

Had Kendra been one to give way to tears, she would have let them fall now. She felt deep, inconsolable sorrow. She was so lonely for the life she knew. So disheartened over what she had failed to find. All she wanted was her own familiar room with its Hudson Bay blankets, its kerosene lamp, its crackling fire in the hearth, and Oscar lying on the bear rug beside her moss and fir-bough-covered bed. All she wanted was her shelf of books and the stirring of her grandfather in the small room beyond her door.

But Kendra knew she must finish what she had started.

She was glad for Maggie Miller. The friend of her grandfather's had been most kind. Kendra was sure that, despite her strong resolve, she would never have been able to finish the year were it not for Mrs. Miller.

Another gust of wind caught her, almost wrenching the books from her arms. She clutched them closer and turned to ward off the chilly blast.

Just as she turned back she bumped into someone. Startled, Kendra caught herself and looked to see who it was. A young woman was returning her gaze, her eyes as wide open in surprise as Kendra's.

"I'm—I'm sorry," said the young woman quickly. "I—I'm afraid I wasn't watching."

"My fault," replied Kendra, but the wind seemed to snatch her words away.

"It's the wind," began the girl and she pushed back her heavy scarf. Kendra found herself looking at the girl from the university hallway. She had found her.

"Amy?" she said in unbelief.

The girl looked even more surprised. "Do I know you?" she asked simply.

"No. No," said Kendra, shaking her head. "But I've—been looking for you. For weeks."

Amy looked confused. "Why don't you come in," she offered, turning to indicate the small house in front of them.

"You live here?" asked Kendra. It was only a few blocks to Maggie's house.

"Yes," replied the girl and took Kendra's arm.

They hurried toward the house against the push of the wind.

Once inside, the door firmly closed behind them, they turned to face each other again. Amy pulled off her scarf, revealing her face. Yes, it truly was her. Kendra saw the same dark eyes, the same soft smile. Kendra took a deep breath and grinned.

"I thought I'd never find you," she admitted.

"Come in," said Amy, pointing to the sitting room. "Take off your coat—and tell me why you've been looking for me."

Kendra quickly shrugged out of her coat and picked up her textbook with the folded pages that bore the two poems.

"You dropped this—in the hall one day. You ran into someone and I found these on the floor."

She handed the pages to the girl.

"Oh—these. I wondered where they went." Amy looked up and smiled. "Thanks—for returning them."

"I was afraid you'd need them for an assignment, and I'd get them back to you too late," continued Kendra.

"Oh—no. Just—just some of my—musings. I'm

always—scribbling down thoughts here and there. I just—"

"Do you have the rest of it?" asked Kendra before she could check herself.

Amy looked down at the sheets she held. The short poem about the trees was on the top.

"Not that one. The other one," put in Kendra. "The one with—with all the questions."

Amy turned to the second sheet and let her eyes fall to the bottom lines.

"Did you finish it?" prompted Kendra.

"Oh—yes. Yes, I finished it."

"Would you—would you mind terribly if—if I saw the—ending?" asked Kendra. She wondered if she was being terribly rude. If it was right to ask someone to share something so personal. She flushed at her own boldness.

"That is—if you wouldn't mind," she finished lamely.

Amy's chocolate brown eyes met hers evenly. "It's not really very good," she apologized. "I just—just scribble things down to—to sort things out for myself."

"It's beautiful," enthused Kendra. "I could almost see it. Hear it. Just like—" She stopped.

"Sit down," invited Amy. "I'll see if I can find the last few lines."

Amy was gone for several minutes.

When she returned she was shaking her head. "I can't find it right now," she said. "I'm sorry. It must be with some of my other books."

Kendra stood, disappointment filling her whole being. She had been so close to an answer. Now she had nothing.

"Would you like a cup of tea?" Amy asked.

"Thank you—but I must be going. Aunt Maggie will be worried if I don't show up soon."

The girl nodded.

"Well, I'll keep looking for the lost sheet," she promised Kendra. "If you live nearby, then stop again and perhaps I will have found it."

"Oh yes, could I? You wouldn't mind? I don't want to be a—a pest."

"I wouldn't mind at all," Amy began and then quickly added, "You say that you do live nearby? And you go to the university? It's strange that we haven't met before. We must walk the same sidewalk every day."

She was smiling again and Kendra smiled in return.

"It seems strange that after searching and searching for you for three weeks that I would find you living almost in my own backyard," Kendra acknowledged.

"I stay here with my aunt and uncle," Amy said. "I'm really from out of town. A farm kid, actually. I'm hoping to be a teacher."

Kendra was pulling her heavy coat on again. She did hate to go, but she didn't wish to worry Mrs. Miller.

"What are you majoring in?" the girl asked.

"I—I haven't decided on—on anything yet. Just a general course. Though I admit I picked the subjects that interest me."

"Like?"

"Literature—and the sciences."

"Ugh," said Amy. "My most *un*favorites. I like math and history."

"I guess that explains why we haven't met before," said Kendra as she leaned to pick up her books.

"Well—we must remedy that," put in Amy. "Now that we are acquainted, we must make the most of it. I could use a friend."

Kendra did not trust herself to speak. The words spoke to her very soul, and it responded with all the longing that was within her. But she could only nod her head.

She was about to leave when Amy spoke. "Wait. I don't even have your name—or where you live."

"It's Kendra. Kendra Marty," she replied. "And I live on Ninety-Sixth Street with Mrs. Maggie Miller—a friend of my grandfather's."

"What time do you go to class on Monday?" asked Amy.

"I—I walk past here about eight o'clock," replied Kendra.

"I have to leave by seven-thirty," continued Amy. "It's a shame we couldn't walk together."

"Oh, I can be here by seven-thirty," quickly promised Kendra. "No problem at all."

"Are you sure?"

"I'm sure."

Kendra turned back to the door. She really had to go.

"I'll see you on Monday then," said Amy. "Oh, but before you go, you must meet my Aunt Sophie. Just one minute," and she dashed through the adjoining door. Kendra heard voices but she couldn't make out the words. Soon the door pushed open again and a matronly woman made her appearance as she wiped her hands on her printed apron. Amy followed closely behind her.

"Aunt Sophie, this is Kendra. She goes to the

university too. We just rather—rather bumped into each other."

The last words were said with a grin. Kendra smiled and reached to shake the hand that was extended.

"We are going to walk together on Monday," went on Amy. She sounded as excited as Kendra felt.

"It's nice to meet you, Kendra," said the older woman.

Kendra thought the lady had such beautiful warm eyes. She hated to turn from them.

"I must go," she apologized. "Mrs. Miller will be waiting."

"Do stop in anytime," the woman offered, and Kendra could feel the sincerity of her words.

"Thank you," she managed to mumble, then turned to go out into the cold.

She could scarcely slow down her anxious feet. She could hardly wait to get home to tell Mrs. Miller. She had a strange, wonderful feeling that she had found a friend.

❧   ❧   ❧

Over the weeks that followed, the two new friends exchanged many ideas between them. The girls walked to and from university with each other almost every morning. They visited back and forth, studying together, sharing hot cups of cocoa and freshly baked ginger cookies.

The deep, dark empty feeling that had been loneliness gradually began to leave the heart of Kendra. It was so much nicer when one had a friend.

✹ ✹ ✹

"I've finally found it," said Amy breathlessly as she waved a sheet of paper under Kendra's nose. "I had almost given up."

Kendra's brow furrowed in perplexity.

"The rest of the poem," Amy reminded her and Kendra took a deep breath. She had almost forgotten the poem. She had been so relieved to have a friend that her quest for answers had been temporarily set aside.

"Oh!" she exclaimed now, almost squealing in her eagerness. "The poem."

"I brought the first page too," put in Amy. "Just in case you have forgotten how it starts."

Kendra accepted both sheets and began to read aloud.

Who put the stars in the evening sky?
Who gave the waters their azure blue?
Who set the rainbow up on high?
And sprinkled the grasses with morning dew?

Who hid the fawn with its dappled sides?
Who taught the salmon to swim the brooks?
Who buried gold in the heart of the earth?
Planted wood violets in shadowed nooks?"

Who told the crocus that spring had come?
Brought the butterfly from the cocoon?
Who put the song in the robin's heart?
Governed the tides by the distant moon?

Who put the "wonder" within my breast?
Set off the "joy bells" within my soul?
Who gave a reason to even exist?

Made earth a "mission" and heaven a "goal"?

Mere chance occurrence? Complete mystery?
Of course there's a reason, if only we prod.
Nature demands it—and so does my heart.
There's only one Answer. Only one God!

Kendra looked up from the page. She liked the
poem. Something within her responded to it. But
she didn't understand it. Not really. She felt a moment of deep disappointment. She still didn't have
her answer. Even Nonie had told her this much.

Her eyes returned to the last few lines. She read
them over again.

Mere chance occurrence? Complete mystery?
Of course there's a reason, if only we prod.
Nature demands it—and so does my heart.
There's only one Answer. Only one God!

Only one God! Did Amy really believe that?

"I—I really don't understand . . ." began Kendra
hesitantly.

"I told you I'm not a very good poet," shrugged
Amy. "I—I guess the poem was—just for me. To express how I feel about—about God creating everything. About—the—the purpose of life."

"But—" began Kendra. That was exactly what
she didn't understand. Who was God? Her grandfather had told her that God existed only in the
myths of the white people. The Indians called Him
by another name—The Great Spirit or the Old One
or some other rather mysterious title of honor.

"I like the poem," Kendra was quick to assure
Amy. "I really do. But I— Do you really think—? I
mean, do you really believe—about—about God?"

Amy's eyes widened. "You don't?" she asked, incredulous.

Kendra opened her mouth and then closed it again. Somewhere deep within her was a little voice that wished to say that she did believe. But how could she believe in One she had never known? She shrugged her shoulders and tried to smile.

"I really don't know much about Him," she informed the other girl, trying hard to make the words sound casual and of little importance.

Amy seemed to have recovered. "How about this?" she said. "Would you like to come to church with me on Sunday?"

"Church?"

Kendra had doubts about church. She had heard some very strange rumors about what went on there.

"Yes. I go with my aunt and uncle to a church near here. It's not big—but they really are nice people. I felt at home almost at once."

Kendra hesitated. "I don't know," she stalled. "I promised Mrs. Miller that I'd give her a hand with a quilt on Sunday."

"Maybe another Sunday then," replied Amy easily, seeming quite willing to make it another time.

❧　❧　❧

There was something different about Amy. The more time they spent together, the more Kendra sensed the difference. Even though Amy was buoyant and outgoing, she was just so much more settled than others her age. So at peace with herself and her world. So confident that things were under control.

But whose control? Amy admitted to not being in charge of her own life, her own fate. She made frequent references to God. She talked just as though she herself knew this mystic being. Yet there was no fear in her voice when she spoke of Him as there had been when Nonie talked of one or another of the spirits.

Kendra was puzzled.

"How did you—learn—so much about—about this white man's spirit?" Kendra dared to ask one day.

"Who?" asked Amy, puzzled.

"This—this God," replied Kendra.

"God? Oh, He's not the white man's spirit. Or the white man's God. He's everyone's God—the Creator God. He doesn't belong to the white man any more than the—sun or moon belongs to the white man."

"But—?"

"He created all men. All things."

It sounded like more myths.

"But how do you know this?" asked Kendra.

"It's all in the Bible—the whole story," replied Amy, not one bit put off by Kendra's asking.

"The Bible?"

"You don't have a Bible? I'll lend you one. You can read it for yourself."

❦   ❦   ❦

Kendra did read it for herself. Over the weeks that followed she spent every minute she could spare reading the account for herself. Deep within her she felt she had finally found the answers to her questions. It was not a myth. It was *truth*. There really was a God in heaven—just as she had wondered, had suspected all along. He really *did* create the universe. All the things that Amy's poem had referred to and so much more. Kendra was glad to discover such a God—but she was just a bit afraid of Him, too.

"I think I'd like to go to church with you on Sunday," Kendra surprised Amy by saying. They had been doing homework together on a Saturday afternoon. Kendra thought she might as well say the words before Amy asked her again. Amy always seemed to offer another invitation each Saturday.

Amy's eyes lit up. Kendra knew that she was pleased that her standing invitation had finally been accepted.

As Sunday followed Sunday, Kendra began to put all the pieces together. There was a God. Not a mystic, unknown someone, out there somewhere. A real Person, a revealed and understandable God. He created people, who sinned. This caused a chasm between human beings and their Creator. They hid from God and at the same time turned their backs on Him and wished to be left on their own.

But God loved the creation of His mind, His hands. He knew that the people He had created were lost—blinded—and left to the devices of the Evil One. He had a plan whereby mankind could once again be restored to a place of fellowship. Sin had to be dealt with, had to be justified. Kendra supposed that it must have been the hardest part of the plan for a holy God to carry through. It meant sending His Son, His only Son, to take the penalty of death for people—the sinners.

No one had to tell Kendra about the reality of sin. Deep within her own heart was a feeling of guilt. She wasn't sure she could have listed the things that made her guilty—but she knew that her heart was not right in the eyes of her Creator. The knowledge troubled her, but she wasn't sure what to do about it. She knew one thing. She could not stop attending the services. She hungered for the truths that were taught. Nor could she quit reading the borrowed Bible. She was sure that it was the only place where the true answers might be found.

❧   ❧   ❧

"I know you are well familiar with the text of the morning," said the pastor, "but I feel we should return to it often so that we might never lose the wonder—the marvel—of what it says to us. That an almighty, eternal, holy, and just God would love us—me—and you—so much as to send His only Son to Calvary to bear the penalty for our sins and grant to us, through the name of Jesus Christ our Savior, forgiveness of our sins and life everlasting. Turn with me to the third chapter of the gospel of John."

Kendra did not stir. She held the open Bible in her hands silently as others about her rustled with the pages of their Books. Something had clicked in her mind with the words of the speaker. That was it. That was it! God loved her. God had sent His Son—for her, Kendra Marty—that she might have her sin forgiven and be granted everlasting life.

A sob arose in her throat. Her head dropped and before she hardly knew what was happening she was saying, "God, please forgive me—please help me—" The prayer quickly turned to one of thanksgiving. "Thank you—oh, thank you, Father," her heart cried. "Thank you, Lord Jesus."

A peace, a warmth began to steal over her soul, washing away doubts, confusion, and frustration. It was true. It was true. She knew it as surely as she knew anything. It was not a myth. There was a God. He loved her. He sent His Son to take her penalty of death. She was free. Free and forgiven.

The tears rolled down her cheeks as she turned the pages of her Bible to locate the morning text. The preacher was beginning his sermon. But Kendra was already marveling over the truth of the message.

Chapter Twenty-two

A Meeting

"You look all bubbly this morning," Kendra remarked to Amy as the two fell into step for their walk to morning class.

"I am. I'm going home for the Easter break. I can hardly wait. I haven't been home since Christmas and it seems an awfully long time."

Kendra's eyes shadowed. She hadn't been home for what seemed like ever so long. Now that she had answers—the real answers to life—she longed to get back to her grandfather so she might share her good news. She had written him a long, long letter, but it had been so hard to try to express all that she felt, all she was discovering, on paper.

And she wished to see Nonie again. To tell the dear Indian woman that she now knew just who the Great Spirit was that Nonie spoke of. The woman was so close—yet so far from the truth. There weren't lots and lots of gods dwelling in the hills, the trees, the sun, the moon. There was only one God—who made all things. And human beings were not fashioned by Mother Earth who took from herself to bring people forth. Humankind was designed by the Creator who breathed into the new creation the breath of life, making each one the only created being with a living soul.

Kendra could hardly wait to explain it all to the woman who had been her guardian, her mother, her grandmother—all in one.

Kendra turned her attention back to Amy, happy for her upcoming visit.

"They are picking me up tomorrow night," Amy went on excitedly. "And Mama suggested that I bring you along. Oh, can you, Kendra? I would so love to have you."

Kendra stopped walking. Was she hearing right? Was Amy really asking her to share her wonderful long Easter week at her farm home?

"Can you?" prompted Amy again.

"I don't know," replied Kendra. "I'll have to talk with Aunt Maggie."

"Oh, I hope you can. I would love to have you meet Mama and Papa and Reynard and Thomas and Carry and Nell. I would—"

But Kendra had grabbed her hand to stop her. If Mrs. Miller didn't agree, it would be difficult enough to endure without making lots of plans that would never happen.

"I'll ask," promised Kendra, her whole being filled with excitement. She had heard Amy speak of her family many times and always thought how wonderful it would be to have brothers and sisters. A real family.

All during the classes of the day, Kendra kept thinking about the possibility of going home with Amy. Would Mrs. Miller think it was okay or would she hesitate to take responsibility for the decision? Kendra prayed, as she had learned to do, many times throughout the morning and afternoon. She finally came to the place where she could honestly leave her deep desires in the hands of her newfound God.

"As you will," she whispered and felt a measure of peace. Whatever God worked for her would be for her best good.

"Do you want me to come with you to ask Mrs. Miller?" asked Amy on their return home. "I will— and explain everything—if you wish."

Kendra shook her head. It was in God's hands. "Aunt Maggie is not unreasonable," she hastened to say. "If she feels that she isn't stepping out of line by giving permission, she'll let me go. I know she will. After all, I'm not a child."

Amy nodded. "Oh, I do so hope you can come," she said. "I do hate to leave you here all alone—and Easter week, too."

❧   ❧   ❧

Mrs. Miller did not even hesitate to grant her permission, even though she had a few reservations about the new "faith" that Kendra often spoke about. Mrs. Miller had never been a religious person and she knew that George McMannus was not in any way religious either. What would George think of Kendra's embracing of a faith?

Mrs. Miller had written a letter to George. Hers too was a long letter, trying her best to describe what had happened to Kendra. But Mrs. Miller really didn't understand what it was.

"She has not gone 'off,' " her letter stated. "She was lonely before and seemed a bit disturbed. Now she is more settled and seems to enjoy the little church where she goes. I think that having Amy Preston for her friend has been good for her. There doesn't seem to be anything to worry about. I will keep my eyes and ears open and let you know if anything happens that doesn't seem right."

George had written back to Maggie through the first available post.

"When Kendra went off to university," he wrote, "I fully expected that it would change her thinking on many things. Though, I admit, I didn't expect this. But she is a bright girl. She has her own life to live. She must make up her own mind on such things. I will not try to sway her or change her thinking. I do hope that she continues to hold steady. I wouldn't want her becoming fanatical or mystical about this new religion she has taken on."

Kendra knew nothing of the exchange of letters. She had told her grandfather about her experience in her own way. His reply to her had been carefully penned.

"I am glad that you have discovered an answer that suits you," he had written. "We all have the right to find an inner peace in our own way."

Then he had gone on to speak of the sled dogs, the winter's catch, and the cold weather. Kendra knew that she hadn't been able to make him understand.

Now as Kendra excitedly packed a small valise for her trip home with Amy, she thought again of her grandfather. Oh, if she could only go home. If she could only sit and have a long chat with him. She was sure that he would be as excited as she was about discovering the Truth.

Arrangements were made to travel with another student who was going to Amy's home community. It was a long drive by team. They had to make one stopover on the way. Amy and Kendra shared a small room over the kitchen of a farmer who took overnight paying guests.

"This works perfectly for me," said Amy. "It's a place to stop for the night and we'll be home by noon tomorrow."

Kendra was so excited, she could hardly sleep. Tomorrow she would discover for herself what a real family was. There had only been herself and her grandfather for as long as she could remember. She had a few scattered mental images of a laughing mother and a teasing father, but not enough for her to put together any kind of picture of a home life.

The two girls had a simple, early breakfast the next morning and started out again with their travel companion at the reins. The morning was bright, but the day still held the chill of early spring. Kendra was glad for the heavy coat that kept the brisk breeze from freezing her bones.

"We are almost there. Just over that next hill!" Amy exclaimed. "I can hardly wait."

Kendra felt the tingle go through her body.

❦   ❦   ❦

"I wish Reynard would hurry. I'm starved," said fourteen-year-old Thomas.

Amy laughed. "You're always starved," she teased him.

Kendra looked again at the young boy. He was tall and lanky, almost red-headed, but his eyes were much like Amy's. Carry, who was coming from the kitchen with a platter of fried chicken, looked much more like her mother, slight and much fairer, with a sprinkling of freckles across her upturned nose, and eyes more the color of blue cornflowers. Nell, the baby of the family at age eight, was brown-haired, her hair done in two long plaits much as Kendra had worn her own blond hair for many years. Except Nell's darker braids were enhanced by two large green velvet bows.

"You know that Reynard will be here just as soon as he can," said Mrs. Preston, entering the room with a bowl of vegetables in each hand.

Kendra had been informed that Reynard worked in the nearby town and rode horseback to and from his job each day. And that was all she knew. She was so busy studying the other members of the family that she had given very little thought to the one still missing.

Mr. Preston entered the room, his face shining from a recent wash at the kitchen basin. He was a big man, dark like his oldest daughter. His coloring was ruddy from working outside, and his hands reminded Kendra of her grandfather's. His face lighted easily into a teasing grin. He flashed one at Kendra now.

"Have you ever seen such an impatient brood?" he asked her. "Sort of reminds one of a nest of young magpies. Every one wants to be fed right now. I'm sure your family is much more civilized."

Kendra smiled. "I was the one and only," she admitted. "And for some time I've been the one *getting* the meal. Grandfather was most patient in waiting for it."

Then Kendra looked back at the table groaning with its burden of delicious-smelling dishes. "But I never fixed anything like this," she added. "Our meals were very simple."

They heard the kitchen door open and close again.

"Finally," breathed Thomas with a mock groan. "He's finally here."

Kendra could hear steps in the kitchen. Reynard had stopped to wash at the corner basin.

"Let's be seated," said Mr. Preston, and the family moved in to claim the chairs around the table. One chair remained—directly across from Kendra.

She sat silently, her hands in her lap, her eyes on the vacant chair. Steps sounded behind her, and she sensed more than saw someone stop briefly and lean over to place a kiss on top of Mrs. Preston's head.

"Good evening, Mama," a low voice said.

"Reynard, I'd like you to meet Amy's guest from the university. This is Miss Marty. Kendra Marty."

Kendra turned slightly. She wasn't sure if she should stand or stay seated. She was about to rise, a smile tilting her lips, when her eyes met the eyes of Reynard.

She had expected a boy. She really didn't know why. All the Preston children had been just that— children. Kendra had thought Amy was the family's eldest. Now as she lifted her eyes she discovered, to her discomfort, that she was looking into the eyes of a young man. Dark, warm eyes, in a sensitive and pleasant face. Amy's eyes. But the resemblance stopped there. Reynard was fairer than his sister, slim of frame, and thoughtful in demeanor. Amy was rather sturdy like her father, full of enthusiasm for life.

Kendra did not rise after all. She sucked in her

breath, lowered her gaze, and sank back into her chair. She had been so totally unprepared.

"Good evening, Miss Marty. I'm pleased to meet you," the same even voice was saying. There was warmth in his voice as well. Kendra looked up just long enough to see a hand extended toward her. She accepted it and was given a brief but sincere handshake.

"Let's eat," spoke up Thomas. Reynard chuckled and moved to take his seat.

All through the evening meal Kendra felt nervous and fidgety. She was afraid to lift her eyes for fear he might be looking her way. Yet she felt compelled to steal little glances at the man opposite her at the table. Why hadn't Amy warned her? She would have been much better prepared had she known that this brother was *not* one of the children.

But Kendra chided herself. What difference would it have made? And what could Amy have said? "I've got this older brother who is all grown up—and terribly good-looking?" No. Most certainly not. Besides, Kendra doubted that Amy even thought of her brother in that fashion.

"Stop it," she told herself. "You have rubbed shoulders with many young men in your classes, in the halls, in the cafeteria. You've even had an evening out with one of them. You've never acted like this before. Stop it."

And Kendra willed her wildly beating heart to slow its mad pace and allow her to enjoy the fellowship of the family supper table.

❧ ❧ ❧

After the dishes had been washed and returned

to the cupboard shelves, Amy took her seat at the piano in the family living room and invited Kendra to join her. They sang many of the songs from church. By now they were familiar to Kendra. She enjoyed singing and could join in wholeheartedly. One by one other family members joined them. Only Thomas, whose voice was changing, held back from the song fest.

Never had Kendra felt such joy. So this was what it was like to be a part of a big family. She had missed so much. She couldn't help but envy Amy.

After the singing they sat around the kitchen and drank hot cocoa and ate sugar cookies. The laughter and chatter rang through the room, and Kendra was reluctant to leave it, even though her eyes would hardly stay open.

"We need to get you two to bed," said Mr. Preston. "You'll never make it up for church in the morning."

Kendra smiled. She was tired. But she hated to break the spell of the evening.

"We'd better go," said Amy with a yawn. "We have lots more nights to be together. I guess we don't have to stay up all night on our first one."

Reluctantly Kendra rose to follow her friend. With a few changes in the family's usual sleeping arrangements, the girls would be sharing Amy's old bedroom. Kendra prepared to say good-night. Her eyes quickly traveled around the room to each family member. But when she got to Reynard, she found him looking at her. Her cheeks colored faintly, her words got all tripped up in her thinking, and she turned to follow Amy from the room.

Chapter Twenty-three

Back to the Wilderness

Kendra was deeply stirred by the Easter service. It was her first Easter as a new Christian, and as the pastor told the story of the Crucifixion and what it cost the Father to send the Son—and the Son to be obedient to His Father—tears filled her eyes. Wiping them away on her handkerchief, she never had felt such love.

On the ride back to the farm, Amy started singing and soon the others had joined in. Even Thomas dared to join them in spite of his voice cracking embarrassingly every now and then.

It was a glorious experience for Kendra. Already she felt a part of this wonderful family who had taken her in so quickly and completely.

The dinner was a simple but delicious meal. Kendra, used to a stew or Indian-style bannock, thought it a feast. She enjoyed every part of it right down to the apple pie.

After the dishes had been washed and put away, they played a family game together. Kendra had never played a game before and had to be taught the rules. She caught on quickly and soon proved to be a very competitive player.

When the menfolk prepared for evening chores, Kendra begged to go with them. She was anxious to see the farm and how it operated. She drew on a borrowed chore coat and set off with young Thomas, whose duty was to slop the pigs and feed the chickens.

"I'll gather the eggs," volunteered Kendra and began to move the day's "rent" from the boxed nests to her basket.

Kendra didn't care much for the pigs. They smelled awful to her sensitive nose and they pushed and shoved to get at the food in the trough, nearly knocking her off her feet.

"Now I know why it's an insult to call someone a hog," Kendra quipped as she removed herself to a safe distance and brushed at the dust on her coat.

They visited the barn where Reynard was milking a Jersey cow and laughed as he fed a barn cat with a long stream of frothy milk directly from the cow. Then they moved on to the horses, and Kendra patted each one in turn and fed them handfuls of hay. Mr. Preston was working with the horses. Kendra was especially taken with a big bay with a bold slash of white down the front of his face.

"That's Duke," said Thomas. "He's Reynard's horse. He rides him to work every day."

"Where does he work?" asked Kendra casually.

"In Stewart."

"Doing what?"

"He's a banker."

Kendra had expected a farm boy to be working at something quite different than banking. In fact, she didn't know much about banking at all. She and her grandfather had never had need of a bank. They bartered for their furs, trading them for needed supplies and accepting cash for the difference or leaving the funds for credit at the small post.

Kendra nodded and tucked the information away. Secretly she wished that Reynard was in some other occupation. A schoolteacher or keeper of books or even a clerk in a store. She had heard things about hard-hearted bankers who used their position to further their own ends.

But Kendra said nothing more, just continued to stroke the big bay and offer him handfuls of hay that he could easily have reached on his own.

When they returned to the house, Kendra spent a good deal of time at the kitchen basin. Even so, she couldn't wash all the smell of the barns away. It clung to her clothes and her hair, and she was embarrassed as she joined the family at the supper table.

No one seemed to notice. At least no one made comment. Kendra was glad for that and hoped her trip to the barn was not advertised by her very presence.

❧   ❧   ❧

The week went too quickly. Kendra put every thought of returning to the city out of her mind. How could Amy stand to be away from her family? Kendra wondered. Why, if she herself had a family like that, she would never leave home. Then Kendra thought of her grandfather. He was just as dear. She loved him just as much—yet she had left. Left him alone to run the trapline when she knew he needed her help. Guilt clutched at Kendra. Again she resolved that just as soon as the term was over, she would return to her grandfather. And she would not leave him alone again.

❧ ❧ ❧

"Would you like to go for a walk?"

Kendra was just wiping the last of the supper plates that Amy had washed in the large dishpan. She placed the dish on the stack in the cupboard and turned slowly. Reynard stood before her, her shawl in his hands, and a teasing smile playing about his lips.

Kendra managed a smile of her own.

"Does she really have any choice?" quipped Amy, looking on.

"Of course she does," replied Reynard good-naturedly. "I know where to hang this up again."

But Kendra wiped her hands on the flowered apron, hung the dish towel on its bar, and turned so Reynard could drape the shawl over her shoulders.

"It looks like a nice evening for a walk," she replied.

"That's exactly what I thought," said Reynard and winked at his sister.

They followed the worn path through the barnyard, down the lane, and beside the small stream. Kendra had never ventured very far from the farm buildings before and enjoyed the walk. She was not used to leisurely strolls after running behind the dog team or walking at a fast pace to and from her classes.

But this walk was totally unhurried.

"Thomas says you work in a bank," Kendra dared to comment. "What do bankers do?"

If he was surprised at her question, he did not

show it. "Mostly books," he answered. "I started as a teller in the tell and—"

"The tell?" puzzled Kendra.

Reynard laughed. "Have you ever been in a bank?" he teased.

Kendra smiled and shook her head. She had to admit that she had never been in a bank.

"But I've heard stories about bankers," she added, her bantering tone not entirely covering her concern.

"Like—foreclosing mortgages and driving out widows and forcing beautiful young girls to marry them or be sent out penniless?"

Kendra had to laugh.

"I've heard those stories too," said Reynard.

"Are they true?" asked Kendra, still a hint of teasing in her voice but seriousness as well.

Reynard shook his head. "Would I still be single if they were?" he asked in mock innocence.

It was Kendra's turn to smile.

"What do you do?" she asked after a pause. "Seriously."

"Seriously? I'm pretty good at being serious. At least that's what Amy is always telling me. 'Oh, don't be so serious.' She says it often. Well, maybe I am serious—but there's always so much to think about—to ponder. Do you mind serious men?"

Kendra faltered. "Well—I—I don't know. I mean—I—I've never given it any thought. I—to tell you the truth, I've never thought too much about—about men at all."

"I like that," Reynard affirmed. "I've noticed that many girls your age seem to be thinking about men—or boys—all the time."

"But Amy doesn't—"

"Amy is too scattery to be thinking about any one thing for more than a minute at a time," laughed Reynard. Then with deep sincerity, "And I love her—just as she is."

Kendra nodded mutely.

"Now Carry. Carry is quite different. Already Carry does a good deal of thinking about boys." Again Reynard chuckled.

They walked in silence for a few more steps; then Reynard said, "But you asked about banking. Banking, for me, is mostly numbers. Good numbers. Bad numbers. People who have money in the bank and people who owe money to the bank. We are there to lend money if it is needed, but the big man at the top, whoever he is, he likes to be paid back. So far we have no bad debts. Oh, some people have struggled and had to have an extension on a loan. But we haven't had to foreclose on anyone or drive widows from their houses." He smiled again.

"And a teller?" prompted Kendra.

"A teller is at the cash drawer. Taking in deposits for accounts and cashing notes for customers," he explained.

"Oh," said Kendra. It really didn't sound complicated. "But you don't do that anymore?"

"Not anymore." Reynard stopped to pick up a flat stone and skip it across the small pond formed by a beaver dam in the stream.

"Ever watched beavers work?" he asked her.

"Yes," said Kendra softly.

"Kind of neat little fellows," Reynard remarked.

Kendra nodded. She did not say that she had not only watched them work, she had worked over them, skinning them out, stretching and tacking their hides on the forms, taking their pelts to the trading post. The thoughts racing through her mind made her shiver. Perhaps Reynard wouldn't think much of her occupation either.

"Are you cold?" asked Reynard and slipped out of his jacket and draped it over her shoulders before she could even answer.

They walked on together. It was easy to chat with Reynard. Kendra felt that she had gotten to know him quite well over the week she had spent at the Prestons. Although he was gone for work during the day, he seemed to slip so easily into the family circle at night when he returned. He always stopped to wash in fresh water at the family basin, then proceeded to the table where the family was usually waiting for him. Always he stopped on the way to his chair to bend over and press a kiss on his mother's brow or cheek or hair with an easy, "Good evening, Mama."

Kendra often wondered about this little ritual, but it seemed so sincere, so simple, that she couldn't question it. If she had a mother, she would want to do the very same thing.

"Are you enjoying university?" Reynard's question brought Kendra's attention back to the present.

"I—I guess so," began Kendra. Then she went on. "It hasn't been what I had expected—to be truthful. In fact, the answers that I was really looking for—about nature, creation, my inner longings, God—I wouldn't have even found them if I hadn't met Amy. University really doesn't give you the answers for all of that. There is so—so much taught about *things*. Knowledge. All for the head. Nothing for the heart."

Reynard nodded in understanding.

"But it's good—if one wants to be something—like a teacher—or a doctor—or . . ."

Kendra finished lamely, giving her shoulder a slight shrug.

"And you don't plan to be any of those things?"

"No. No, I just came because I wanted to learn. I'd never been to school—except for a few horrible months. Papa Mac—Grandfather—taught me, and then when I was old enough I studied on my own. And I had all of these—these unanswered questions. Nonie—the Indian woman who took care of me—tried to answer some of them with her Indian tales. I—I think I could have believed her, but Papa Mac said they were only myths. Totally untrue."

Kendra stopped. She still felt a sadness deep down inside. Sadness for all people who did not know or believe the truth.

"Nonie's close," she went on. "She really is. She just doesn't know who God really is—or that there's only one God—who made and controls everything."

Reynard nodded again. "You care deeply for Nonie, don't you?"

Kendra drew a breath. It was hard to put into words. She stood there, gazing out over the rippling pond water. Her thoughts traveled back to a very young, terrified child being held in comforting arms, breathing in the smell of woodsmoke from the bosom that cradled her. She thought of carefree days tramping through the woods, gathering herbs and roots and berries and learning how to use them.

She remembered an older Nonie, spending most of her time in her caned chair in front of her fire. But always, always when Kendra opened her door and called a greeting, the tired eyes lit up and a smile carved itself on the wrinkled face.

"Yes," she answered with a great deal of feeling. "Yes—I love Nonie. She—and Papa Mac have been all the family I've known."

"Do you—do you ever feel cheated—about the way you were raised?" asked Reynard.

Kendra turned to face him fully. The last light of twilight mixed with the first soft rays of the rising moon to caress cheeks and hair with a soft halo. Her green eyes deepened, sparkling with the intensity of her feelings. "Oh no," she said with sincere fervor. "I feel singularly blessed."

❦   ❦   ❦

"Reynard is coming to the city."

Amy greeted Kendra with the news as soon as they joined together for their walk to class.

Kendra's eyes lifted. She couldn't explain the sudden little flutter she felt inside.

"What for?" She managed the simple question without her voice giving her away.

"He's on some bank business—a training session or something."

"When?" asked Kendra, her eyes focused on where she placed each step.

"He comes next Monday and stays until Friday," replied Amy. "Aunt Sophie is afraid he'll be terribly bored in the evenings with no farm chores to do, but I assured her that he'll likely be able to think of something."

Kendra looked at her friend. Amy was about to burst into a giggle. Kendra felt her face flush. Surely Amy wasn't implying that Reynard would be interested in spending some time with her. But she knew by Amy's face that she was indeed making such an inference. Kendra's flush deepened.

❦   ❦   ❦

At the rap on the door, Kendra shifted in her seat at the book-strewn table. Mrs. Miller rose to answer the summons, casting a curious look Kendra's way. They did not often have visitors.

"Good evening," Kendra heard a deep, even voice say. "Is Miss Marty in, please?"

"And who shall I say is calling?" Mrs. Miller was asking, but Kendra was already crossing toward the door.

"Reynard?" she said.

"You weren't expecting me?"

"Well, I—I—"

"I should have written, but I didn't have your address. I wrote Amy. She was supposed to tell you."

"Well—she did—I mean she said you were coming to the city. She said . . ." Kendra faltered to a stop and held the door open.

"I do hope I'm not imposing—"

"Oh no. No, not at all. Come in. This is—I'd like you to meet Mrs. Miller. Mrs. Miller, Amy's brother Reynard. Reynard Preston."

Mrs. Miller smiled warmly and chatted easily for a few minutes, then turned and went back to the kitchen, leaving the two in the living room.

"I see you are studying," said Reynard, motioning toward the books on the table. "I'm afraid—"

"Oh no," quickly replied Kendra. "I've finished what needs to be done. I always work ahead."

"I thought—I wondered if you might like to go

for a cup of coffee in that little shop up by Aunt Sophie's?"

Kendra smiled. She had never been in the little coffee shop and had always secretly longed to join the university crowd who sometimes gathered there, just to see what it was like.

"I'll get my shawl," she said with no hesitation.

☙　　☙　　☙

They managed to spend much of the evening together each night of the week Reynard was in town. Kendra cautioned her heart over and over not to become involved, but she wasn't sure that it was paying much attention to her words.

On the last night before Reynard was to go home, they walked the river trail together. When they came to a bench, Reynard brushed it off and offered Kendra a seat.

"I've been hoping you'll be able to come out to the farm with Amy again. Guess it's getting too close to the end of the term now, but you could come as soon as classes are over."

He reached down and took her hand and Kendra did not resist.

"I'd—I'd like to," she managed, her voice little more than a whisper.

"Maybe we could even find a job for you—in town. The—"

"In town? A job?"

"Just for the summer. I know that when classes start again you'll—"

"I'm not coming back," said Kendra softly.

He looked surprised. Then his eyes began to shine.

"Well—if you're planning to get a job here," he said, "it might better be there. Then you'll be near—all the time."

Kendra lowered her gaze. "I'm not—not planning on a job—here either," she said.

He reached out and lifted her chin so he could look directly into her eyes. "What are you planning?" he asked seriously.

"I'm—I'm going back. Home. To my grandfather. He—he needs me. I never should have left him in the first place."

Kendra tried to pull away from the hand that held her prisoner so that she could turn her face from him. She didn't want to see the look that had flooded into his eyes. His fingers tightened around the hand he held.

"Do you have to?" he asked.

Kendra turned to him again and nodded slowly. "I have to," she replied, her voice deep with emotion. "I have to. He needs me. Nonie needs me. I have to—to tell them—about God. That I've found the answer."

His voice brightened. "Then you'll be back?"

Kendra looked up at him, then lowered her gaze. She shook her head slowly. "No. No, I'll not be back. Papa Mac needs me."

Silence hung heavily about them. Kendra felt chilled—isolated.

"Could—might we write?" asked Reynard, his voice husky with emotion.

Kendra raised her eyes to his. She shook her head slowly.

"I—I don't think it would be—wise," she managed in little more than a whisper as she pulled her hand out of his. "It—would only make it—harder."

❧   ❧   ❧

Kendra had expected her trip back to the wilderness to be one that filled her heart with joy. It would be so good to see her grandfather. Wonderful to visit Nonie again. A treat to be welcomed by Oscar. But there was little joy in Kendra's heart as she packed her small cases, crated her acquired belongings, and boarded the boat for the first leg of the journey.

Had she done the right thing? Would she one day be sorry? Would it be purely selfish for her to stay?

She thought again of her grandfather—and of Nonie. Of their need to learn of the God Kendra had come to love. But couldn't she just tell them and then return to the city? Back to Reynard? Kendra longed with all of her being to come back.

"No. No," she told her weeping heart. "I can't. I just can't leave Papa Mac all alone again."

Chapter Twenty-four

Change of Plans

"It won't be long now, Oscar," said George. The dog team was gathered on the shore to wait for the incoming wagon bringing supplies to the post. And along with the supplies, Kendra was coming home. George had debated about bringing the canoe to transport Kendra back to their little cabin. It would have been much faster. But he had harnessed Kendra's dog team to the wagon-sled with Oscar in the lead and taken the overland trail. He knew the big dog would be almost as glad to see Kendra again as he himself.

So they stood together and waited, the dust in the distance announcing the coming of the supply wagon. She was almost home.

"It's been a long winter, hasn't it, boy?" George spoke further to the dog, his fingers curling in the long silky neck hair of the animal, then twining around and uncurling again. "Long—and miserable. But that's over now. She's almost home."

Oscar responded with a whine, his tail scattering dry leaves as it swept the ground and he looked up into the face of the tall bearded man who towered above him.

"You know—I think you sense that something is about to happen. Something out of the ordinary."

Oscar whined again.

The wagon drew closer. George squinted his eyes and tried to pick out Kendra. There was a blur of color on the wagon. The freight hauler had more than one passenger.

"Sure hope she's on there," he mused more to himself than the dog.

But with a quick move, Oscar jerked from his hand and ran excitedly toward the approaching wagon.

"Oscar!" called George. "Oscar!" But the dog paid no attention.

George heard a frequent sharp yip as the dog closed the distance to the approaching team.

"Sure hope he don't go and spook those horses," George muttered as he followed absently after the dog. "Well—one thing's for sure. She's on there."

Just as George spoke the words a figure disengaged herself from the wagon and dropped to the ground, then fell to her knees. Kendra reached out her arms just as Oscar flung himself at her, nearly knocking her over. George watched as the two of them rocked back and forth, Kendra hugging and Oscar licking and wagging until he nearly exhausted both of them. George swallowed and reached up to wipe unwanted moisture from his eyes. Perhaps the brilliant summer sun was just too bright.

❧　　❧　　❧

Kendra walked about the familiar cabin, letting her hand run over the rough boards that formed the sparse furniture. She had never realized before just how plain, how bare it was. But it was home, and she was glad to be there. She looked at the pile of crates and cases her grandfather had stacked in the corner of her bedroom, then lifted the top-most box.

"If I hurry I can get it all unpacked before I have to get supper," she told herself and started at the task. She nearly tripped over Oscar who refused to let her out of his sight. She reached down to give his head an affectionate pat.

"There's someone I sure would have liked you to meet," she murmured to the big dog, and then sighed. In spite of her joy at being home again, there was the shadow of leaving someone behind who might have become very important in her life.

❧   ❧   ❧

Kendra did not wait to talk about her new faith. She brought up the subject with her grandfather that very night as they sat together after they had shared their simple meal.

"I found what I was looking for, Papa Mac," she said and noticed that he seemed to draw back.

"I'm glad," he responded carefully, and he sounded sincere.

"There really is a God," went on Kendra. "But He is so much more than just an—an unknown Someone out there someplace. He is real and He is personal and He gave us His Word, the Bible, so that we might understand all about Him."

Her grandfather nodded.

"But we—all of us—have cut ourselves off from Him. Because of sin—because of sinful, selfish choices we make.

George stirred in his chair.

"God said that if Adam and Eve, the first people, sinned they would die. But they chose to sin anyway." Kendra shook her head. It was almost beyond her comprehension that those two created beings could go ahead and do such a thing when it had been forbidden by God himself.

"The only way God could restore the relationship and have the penalty paid for people's sin was to send a substitute—a sacrifice. His Son, Jesus."

George shifted again. "Really, Kendra—" he began, but Kendra wasn't finished.

"He died for us—in our place. But that's not— not quite enough," Kendra hurried on. She wanted to be sure her grandfather had the complete picture before they stopped to discuss her newfound truth.

"We can—"

This time George did stop her. He held up his hand, his signal for silence. Even the dogs did not dare to bark or whine when George McMannus held up his hand in such a fashion.

Kendra silenced, but her eyes were pleading with the big man who sat before her.

"I think we need an understanding here," said George slowly. "I have let you speak your piece. I am glad you've found—what you were looking for. Some people—well, they seem to need—religion."

Kendra opened her mouth. The words wished to gush forth. She hadn't needed religion. She needed God. She needed a Savior. Everyone did. But George lifted his hand again and Kendra's mouth closed.

"Now—I grant you that right," went on George. "Heaven only knows you have had precious little to cling to in your short lifetime. I grant you that right. But—"

George stopped and ran his fingers through his graying beard. "I don't, Kendra. I'm—I'm just fine the way I am. I'm not *seeking*. I'm not restless. My soul isn't looking for answers."

He stopped again and looked at the young girl. "Do you understand? Do I make myself clear?"

Kendra nodded, swallowed hard, and blinked back tears. Then she nodded again and lowered her gaze.

"Good," said the man, and he rose from the table to his full height. "Now, let's have no more of this serious talk. I want to hear all about your year of university. Come—leave the dishes. Pull your chair up to the fire and let's visit."

Kendra picked up her chair and crossed the short distance to the fireplace. George pulled his chair up beside her, and Oscar crowded in between the two.

George reached down a hand and stroked the big dog.

"We've missed you so much," he admitted. "Oscar and I—we been 'bout to drive each other crazy. It's good to have you back, girl. Mighty good to have you back."

❧   ❧   ❧

When Kendra lay in her bed that night, her grandfather's soft snoring reaching her from the room beyond and Oscar curled up close beside her bed on the bearskin rug, she thought again of the earlier conversation. Large tears formed in her eyes and trickled down to her pillow. She had hoped so much that her grandfather would respond to her words. Had prayed for so many months that she would be able to say the right thing—in the right way. But it hadn't turned out that way. Not at all.

"Perhaps it will take time," she whispered to herself in the darkness. "I must be patient—and obedient—and show him—prove to him that it's real."

But Kendra still felt sorrow. She was concerned about her grandfather. What if something happened to him before she had a chance to live her new life before him, before he had opportunity to see that faith in God was real—and obtainable?

❧ ❧ ❧

Early the next morning Kendra and Oscar headed out for the little settlement. She had to see Nonie. All the way along the trail that led through the tall pines and spruce, Kendra prayed.

"Help me to be wiser with Nonie, Father," she kept praying. "Help me to say things so she will understand. So she will accept."

When she reached Nonie's small cabin, she opened the door and called out as she always did. There was a stirring in the far corner where the furs were piled to form a bed.

"Amo-chika?" called Nonie in a weak voice.

"Yes—it's me," replied Kendra and hurried to the elderly woman.

Kendra fell on her knees beside the bed and wrapped her arms around Nonie's frail body.

Nonie reached with a trembling hand and felt the girl's face, her hair. Kendra realized with a painful wrench in her heart that the old woman no longer could see.

"Oh, Nonie," she cried, "I am so glad to see you."

Nonie answered with words of her own tongue— soft, clucking, contented words that reminded Kendra of a hen gathering her chicks to the safety of her wings.

"You're back," Nonie said in English.

"I'm back," said Kendra.

"When you go again?" asked the old woman.

"No. I'm not going again," said Kendra firmly. "Papa Mac needs me here."

Nonie said nothing. The sightless eyes turned toward the smoked wooden ceiling. She uttered more words in her own tongue.

"Nonie," said Kendra, sitting back on her heels and taking the old familiar hands in her own, "I made the most amazing discovery when I was gone. All those stories you told me—about how the world was made—about the spirits—the good ones who help us and the evil ones that try to harm us—well, it's true. I mean—there really are good and evil spirits."

Nonie nodded silently. It was not news to her.

"But there is only *one* God," went on Kendra. "One God who made everything. And Mother Earth, she didn't make us. *God* did. He made the earth too. Everything. He is the one and only God. There aren't gods in the rocks or gods in the hills or gods in the bear or mountain lion."

Nonie looked frightened by Kendra's bold words. Would the girl call down the wrath of angry spirits?

But Kendra went on with confidence. "There is only *one* God—and He loves us. He is so filled with love for us that we never have to live in fear. We can love Him in return. You see, He made us."

"White man's god," said Nonie.

"No. No—*not* the white man's God. *Everyone's* God. He made all mankind. He placed them in a beautiful garden and told them not to eat of the tree that was planted there. But they did not listen. They deliberately—" Kendra stopped. What was a word that Nonie might understand? "They set their hearts to disobey," went on Kendra, her voice intense with emotion. "They would not listen to His voice. They shut their ears. Turned their faces."

Nonie stirred on her pallet.

"But God still loved them. He had said that the punishment for sin—for not obeying His word—would be death. Mankind would die—apart from God. They could not go to the new home—new forest He made for them. They would need to go to a terrible place—where all was pain and deep sorrow.

"God could not go back on His word. He had given His pledge—extended His hand. But because He still loved the people He had made—He had a plan. He sent His own Son—His only Son—and *He* died in place of the whole human race—white people *and* Indians. Took the—the curse on himself." She paused for a moment and took the old woman's face in her hands.

"It's true, Nonie. It's all in the Bible—the big Book. We can know this God. This *only* God. We never need to be afraid of all the evil spirits. God is greater. He is—His medicine is stronger. Much stronger. All we need to do is to believe in Him. To accept His great plan for us and ask Him to take away all the—the evil from our hearts. Oh, Nonie"—Kendra was in tears—"don't you see? A religion without a Savior is just not good enough. Jesus is the Savior—the only Savior—for us all. We can't do anything about our sinful hearts by ourselves—no matter how hard we try. But He can—and He will."

The woman had quietly listened to all that Kendra said. Her eyes gazed into emptiness. Kendra put one arm again around the frail body, the fingers of her other hand brushing lightly against Nonie's cheek.

"It's true, Nonie," Kendra said again, unmindful of the tears that ran down her cheeks.

Nonie shook her head slowly. Sadness seemed to pour from her very soul.

"White man's god," she said again.

"No, Nonie. *Your* God. *Everyone's* God," insisted Kendra.

"Too late," said Nonie, and she lifted weary and frail shoulders in a slight shrug.

"No. It's *not* too late. It's not. You can ask Him to forgive you right now. You can believe, right now. It's *not* too late."

Nonie shifted her slight weight. Kendra eased back gently and Nonie seemed to sink deeper into the furs that formed her bed.

"Too late," said Nonie again with resignation. "I live with Indian gods. I die with Indian gods. Too late."

"But, Nonie, you—"

"You go now," spoke the feeble lips. "Come tomorrow."

Kendra hated to leave. She knew the old woman had very little strength left. How much longer might she be with them? Would she listen to Kendra's plea on another day?

Kendra knelt in silence.

"You go now," Nonie repeated.

Tears again squeezed from Kendra's eyes and rolled slowly down her cheeks.

"You'll—you'll think about what I have said?" she asked the elderly woman, patting her hand.

Silence.

"Will you?" persisted Kendra.

"Make Amo-chika happy?"

"Yes—yes, it will make me *very* happy if you'll

just think about it. Think carefully about what I have said."

Nonie nodded.

"Then, I think," she said solemnly.

It was the best Kendra could do. She slowly rose to her feet and left the cabin, Indian fashion, without a backward glance.

An Indian boy brought the news the next morning. Nonie had died sometime during the night.

George and Kendra would not be expected to attend the burial. The Indians would conduct the ceremony in their own way. Kendra mourned alone by her beloved stream. In the distance she could hear the beating of the funeral drums, too far away to hear the accompanying dirge that would be the death chant. Kendra wept bitterly. She had failed. She had come home too late. In the short time, she had not been able to make Nonie understand. She had been unable to effectively share her faith with the two people she loved the most. Nonie was gone. Her grandfather had forbidden her to speak. She might just as well have stayed in the city. She might just as well have encouraged the courtship of Reynard. For the first time since she had wept on the graves of her parents as a frightened and lonely child, she cried until she had no more tears.

George knew the death of Nonie was hard on his Kendra. He watched her as she moved about the cabin or tended the small vegetable garden or took her basket and headed for the woods, Oscar at her heels.

She was in deep mourning, and he did not know how to help her—what to say. He didn't know if he should draw out her feelings or let her deal with them in her own way, in her own time.

At last he could stand the sorrow-filled eyes no longer. She was sitting on the small bench at the front of the cabin where she often spent her evenings listening to the sounds of the closing day and drinking in the peace that seemed to seep from the twilight. George sat down beside her and spoke of Nonie's death for the first time.

"I know it has been terribly hard on you to lose Nonie," he began.

Kendra could not answer. Her tears were falling again.

"I'm—I'm sorry," he continued. "Truly sorry that you—that you have to face another sorrow. Another death."

"It wasn't just her death," Kendra said in a trembling voice.

"Not her death?"

"Not really. It was—it was just that she—she wasn't ready to die."

The words tore again at Kendra's heart.

"I—don't think I understand," said her grandfather.

"I—I went to see Nonie. To tell her about God. To tell her that she could—could have her sins forgiven—could know God as her—Savior," sobbed Kendra. She was sobbing openly now.

"You wanted to change her religion?" he asked softly, but there was a hint of accusation in his words.

Kendra's head came up. "I wanted to share with

her the Truth," she said frankly, and he could see the fervor in her eyes. She really believed in what she had embraced.

There was silence. George shifted a bit. At last he spoke again.

"She didn't want to listen?"

"Oh—she listened. She let me say—say it all—but then she said—she said He is the white man's God. I couldn't make her—understand that He isn't. That He made all mankind. That He loves us all."

"I see," said George.

There was silence.

"Did she send you away?"

"She was very weak—and tired. She said for me to go and come again the next day."

"So she wasn't angry with you?"

"I—I don't think so. She called me—Amochika—just like she did when I was little. Remember? She said—she'd—she'd think about what I said if it would make me happy."

"She said that?"

Kendra nodded.

They sat in silence, each deep in thought. George spoke first.

"Then, she did that," he said simply.

Kendra looked up at her grandfather, not understanding his words.

"If Nonie gave her word, she also fulfilled it," said George.

"You mean—?"

George hesitated, then said, "If she was still able to—to think—straight—then Nonie pondered your words. Now I don't know if—if she believed them. But she thought about them."

"Oh, God." The words escaped from Kendra's

lips without her being aware of them. It was a prayer. It was an earnest plea. It was a bit of heartfelt praise. Just two simple words, but her whole heart was wrapped up in them.

What if Nonie had thought on her words? What if she had actually understood them? *What if she had believed?* "Father, I leave Nonie's soul in your hands," she whispered.

❧　　❧　　❧

At least in some measure, things returned to a normal summer routine. George went about his daily tasks and Kendra quickly seemed to slip back into the role she had left when she went away to university. But there was a difference somehow. Kendra's faith set her apart. She had a confidence, a peace, even as she moved about the cabin. George often heard her humming little snatches of song, and he had the feeling that she was in her room reading her Bible or praying in the early mornings or late evenings. He didn't know how he knew—he didn't actually see her—but he felt it.

Another fall came and went and soon winter was with them again, wrapping them in its chilling arms with falling snow. Kendra harnessed the dogs and put out her traps. She did not take pleasure in the death of the animals, but she and her grandfather were trappers and they had to make a living.

After the long winter, Kendra was glad to see another spring breathe through. As Easter drew near her thoughts were more and more on the wonder of it all—God's creation, His redemption for that creation. It was a joyous time. She recalled the previous Easter and her time spent with the Preston family. In spite of the happiness within her soul, she felt a tug of sorrow—of loneliness. Things might have been so different had she not been needed by her grandfather—by Nonie.

But Kendra breathed a little prayer, leaving her life and her future in the hands of the God she had learned to trust. He knew what was best. She could trust Him.

❧   ❧   ❧

"Where is he?" Kendra said aloud for the umpteenth time.

She paced the floor again and looked out the window. It was already getting dark. Her grandfather should have been home from the woods long ago. He always came home long before sundown from logging out firewood.

Kendra went to the door and stood listening to the sounds of the approaching night. In the distance a wolf howled, and Kendra saw the hackles on Oscar's neck rise in response. She placed a hand on the dog's head without thinking, her eyes still hopefully straining to make out an approaching form in the darkness.

Then she returned to the kitchen, picked up a lantern, and drew a few matches from the can near the stove. She shrugged into her light jacket, slipped her knife into the side of her moccasin, and turned to Oscar.

"Let's go," she said to the dog. "We've got to find him."

She moved quickly through the forest with the lantern unlit until the darkness closed in around them. Then she stopped, drew a match from where she had tucked it in her sash and lit it.

Without a word to the dog at her side she hurried on. They both knew the trail to the fallen timber where her grandfather had been working. Oscar walked in step beside her, his ears forward, his eyes alert. Once or twice Kendra felt him tense and knew that some animal was near them in the heavy forest growth. With Oscar at her side, she didn't feel any concern.

By the time they reached the deadfall, it was completely dark. Kendra could only see within the brief circle of light cast by the lantern. She depended on Oscar's sharp nose and basic instincts to help find her grandfather.

"Find him, Oscar," she told the dog.

The dog moved forward, head up, nostrils pointed into the wind. Now and then he whined, but he did not stop nor look at Kendra, so she knew he had not yet picked up a scent.

"Papa Mac! Papa Mac!" she shouted every now and then as they wound their way through the fallen trees and discarded branches.

She was about to give up when Oscar stopped with his head turned, his whole body tensed.

"What is it?" Kendra asked, moving forward to place her hand on the dog's neck.

A whine escaped Oscar's throat. He turned and looked at her. Then whined again.

"Go ahead," she told him. "Find him."

The dog moved forward and Kendra followed closely. "Papa Mac!" she cried out again. "Papa Mac, where are you?"

A faint reply returned to her, borne on the sporadic breeze.

Both girl and dog surged forward.

They found him pinned by a log he had been working to cut free from a tangle of fallen trees. Kendra put the lantern on a nearby stump and quickly set to work with the handsaw, saying encouraging things to the man as she worked. "I'll have you out of here in no time," she told him. But the trunk was thick and Kendra was perspiring from hard work and nerves by the time she finished the task. She had to saw through the trunk again in order to get the log to a size she could move by herself. The minutes seemed to expand into hours before she was able to lay aside the saw and put all her remaining energy to moving the heavy section of log.

At last she managed to pull it off her grandfather and let it drop with a crash among other forest debris. She was panting heavily. George lay quietly, and Oscar's tongue reached now and then to lick the sweat from the man's brow.

When Kendra felt she could breathe again, she rose to her feet and picked up the lantern.

"You should be able to get up now," she gasped out. "Your leg is free."

Her grandfather did not move.

"Papa Mac," prompted Kendra, turning the lantern so she could she his face. It was white with pain. Kendra dropped on her knees beside him.

"I—I can't—get up," he managed to say. "The—leg—it's—" He could say no more.

Kendra crawled along his body until she reached the leg that had been under the log. She lifted the lantern and was relieved to see no blood. Then she noted the odd way the limb was lying. "I'll get the team," she said.

"You—you can't," groaned her grandfather.

"With the wagon-sled," went on Kendra. "I'll bring the wagon-sled."

He shook his head. "You'll never—get it anywhere near here—with all the tangle," he gasped through stiff lips.

Kendra looked around her. He was right. She'd never be able to bring anything into this part of the forest. Dead trees fell in every direction, mingling with others in a wild tangle of limbs and branches.

She felt panic. What was she to do?

Quickly she made herself think through her options. She couldn't leave him where he was. But she couldn't move him very far. She only had Oscar to help her, and he didn't even have a harness.

"I'll make you a bed—of spruce boughs," she began. She had to begin somewhere. She had to do something. "Then I'll—I'll start a fire. That will keep us until morning. Then—then I'll figure out a way to get you back to the cabin."

With the axe her grandfather had brought with him, she set to work cutting branches from the spruce and interwove them until she had formed a bed close beside him that was softer and warmer than the ground. Carefully she dragged and pushed her grandfather until she had him eased onto it. Then she began to clear and scrape away a spot to build a fire. She had to make it as close to her grandfather as she could, but she could not take a chance on setting ablaze any of the dry, tangled underbrush about them.

When she had all the loose boughs out of the way, she dug down with her knife until she reached cold, damp ground. This would make a safe base for the fire.

Carefully she gathered small sticks and dried

grasses and drew another precious match from her sash.

In a few moments her little fire was blazing. Kendra noticed her grandfather extend his hand toward the flame, flexing his fingers. In spite of the fact that it was midsummer, the nights were cold.

"You make a good fire," he said calmly, as though they were camping out.

Kendra smiled. "I know," she replied. "My grandfather taught me. He said, 'Make a little fire. One that you can sit close to. White men make a big fire. Have to sit way back—and freeze. Indians make a little fire. Can cuddle up close—and keep warm.' My grandfather is a wise man."

In spite of his pain, George chuckled.

"Now I'm going to leave you—for a while," Kendra went on.

"What are you going to do?"

"I've piled up enough wood, right there to your left, so that you can keep the fire going. I'm going to the cabin. Get some supplies. I'll get some blankets and food and Oscar's harness and some hides and be back soon. Come morning we'll make a travois. We'll get you out of here. I'll be back as soon as I can. Oscar will stay with you."

"You're going alone?" asked George.

"I have my knife," replied Kendra with more confidence than she felt.

"Take Oscar. I'm fine. I have the fire."

"I'll feel better if you have Oscar too," Kendra insisted calmly. "I'll have the lantern."

Nearby an owl hooted.

"I heard that fellow before," George said, his voice low. "I thought—I thought for a while there he was calling my name."

Kendra's head came up sharply. "Nonsense," she said quickly. "You are going to be just fine. Once we get you home—get that leg patched up."

"Maybe," he answered softly. "Maybe."

"I'll hurry," said Kendra. "I'll be back just as quickly as I can."

She turned to go.

"Kendra."

His call stopped her. She turned to him, lifting high the lantern so she could see his face.

"I—I really did think that—that maybe this was *it*. Oh, not because of the—the Indian legend about the owl—but because—because of the pain—the fact I couldn't move."

Kendra felt horror wash all through her. She knew now his leg had been hurt badly. That it was likely broken in more than one place. But she didn't expect him to die. Surely, not—that.

"Kendra," he said again, and she heard his voice tremble.

"I—I didn't know if—if I'd make it—if you'd find me—in time—but—but I thought about what you said. I thought a lot about it. I did it. I—I prayed. I—asked for His help. His forgiveness. You were right. He really is there."

With a cry Kendra fell on her knees beside her grandfather and let the tears fall on his plaid woollen shirt.

He stroked her hair and whispered softly to her.

"It's all right. Even if—even if I don't make it. Even if— It's okay. I'm ready now. I'm ready. Honest."

Chapter Twenty-five

A Heart at Rest

"Do you mind—very much—leaving the wilderness?" George asked his granddaughter.

They were on the boat, all their belongings stacked around them. They both knew they had said a final goodbye to the little cabin they had called home for so many years. They had not brought much with them. There really hadn't been that much. Their personal items, Kendra's pile of books—and Oscar. Kendra could not bear to give up Oscar. All the other sled dogs had been sold—bartered off—to the trader at the post. The traps and skinning knives and snowshoes and sleds, the crude cabin furniture, garden tools and axes—it all had been sold to various trappers in the area, the canoe given to an Indian boy from the settlement. Gone. It was all gone now. A total way of living. A total life.

Kendra sighed deeply. She had loved the wilderness. She had loved it all. She had been happy there, communing with the God of nature. Her God—once she had discovered who He was. But she did not say the words. There was no turning back. She managed a smile.

"We need to get that leg of yours taken care of," she said simply.

She watched his hand stroke absentmindedly at his beard.

Both of them busy with their own thoughts, they sat in silence, their eyes on the moving treeline along the riverbank.

George broke the spell. "I've really been a pesky nuisance, haven't I?"

"A nuisance? Of course not," Kendra was quick to declare.

Her mind went back to the time of the accident. How frightened she had been when she knew how badly hurt he was. She feared that she would never be able to get her grandfather out of the tangled bush with only Oscar and the makeshift travois to help her. But she had done it. She had given him some of Nonie's special root medicine. It had killed the pain some so he could endure the bumpy journey back to the cabin. But the ride had been hard on the badly broken leg. Kendra was afraid it might have been further damaged in the transport.

It was healing now—to a measure. At least he was no longer in constant pain. At least he could move about on it—in a way. But they both soon had come to the realization that he would never be able to run the trapline again. Kendra offered to take over for him, but he refused to hear of it. There seemed to be only one thing to do. To sell what they had and move out.

A movement on the shore drew Kendra's attention. She saw Oscar's head come up, his ears perk forward. She reached for him and laughed softly.

"You see that moose? I suppose you'd just love to have a merry chase," she teased her dog. She rubbed his ear and the deep rumble in his chest subsided. It was going to be very different for Oscar in the city. For a fleeting moment Kendra wondered if she had done the right thing to bring the animal from his wilderness home. All three of them were facing major adjustments.

They moved into a small house just down the street from Maggie. Even before they were settled, Kendra made arrangements for George to see a city physician. His prognosis was not good. There might be a bit that could be done for George's leg, but it would never be restored to full use.

"You are lucky to have it at all. I'm surprised it healed as well as it did. Must have been five or six breaks there. You were lucky. Just plain lucky."

"I had a good nurse," said George. Then he added thoughtfully, "And a wonderful God."

The doctor just shook his head as though he still couldn't understand.

Kendra worried. Her grandfather was too young, too energetic, to be confined to a small house on a city lot. Would he be able to manage the enormous changes?

Kendra finally found a job doing housework for a wealthy family. It did not pay especially well, but it gave her a steady income and that was all they really needed.

George took over the household duties. Kendra was surprised at how easily he seemed to assume the role. But then he had been a bachelor for many years, she reasoned.

He also spent a good deal of time at Maggie's, puttering around her yard, working her garden, repairing anything that was broken.

The two old friends shared cups of coffee on the wide veranda and chatted over years that used to be. George took advantage of opportunities that arose to talk with Maggie about his newfound faith. Soon she was joining him and Kendra for the short walk to the little church each Sunday morning. The two prayed with more intensity, hoping that it would not be long until Maggie made her own commitment to the Lord.

❧   ❧   ❧

"Kendra!"

At the sound of her name Kendra wheeled around. It sounded like—yes, it was!

"Amy!" she cried in return and the two friends ran to throw their arms excitedly around each other.

"What are you doing here?" they asked in unison. They both laughed.

"I think we need to sit down and have a good talk," Amy prompted. "Do you have time for a cup of tea?"

"I'd love to," replied Kendra, and they hastened to the nearby small cafe, chattering as they went.

"I'm teaching here in town," explained Amy. "Oh, so much has happened since I saw you last. I'm engaged. To a wonderful man. We're to be married in September."

"Wonderful!" exclaimed Kendra.

"Now that you're back—you can be my maid of

honor. Oh, will you? Please—don't run off on me again."

Kendra laughed. "I'll not be running anywhere," she said. "Papa Mac broke his leg—badly. He won't be able to work the trapline anymore."

"Oh, I'm sorry. Where is he?"

"Here—in the city."

"Can't the doctors—?"

"No," said Kendra, shaking her head. "But—it's really not so bad. He's adjusted far better than I hoped. He has the house—and his puttering—and Aunt Maggie."

They found a table and sat down.

"Now," said Amy, "I want to hear all about what has happened since I saw you last. Then it's my turn."

They both laughed again. It was so good to be back together.

But what Kendra really wanted to know—what she could hardly wait to hear—was about Reynard. If Reynard was still single—or if he had found himself a girl—maybe even a wife.

❧   ❧   ❧

"You look beautiful," said Kendra, and she leaned over to kiss her friend on the cheek.

Amy did look beautiful, absolutely glowing. Kendra had never attended a wedding, and Amy was the first bride she had ever seen, and the sight nearly took her breath away.

Kendra seemed to fit right back into the Preston family when she went out to the farm for the wedding. She was amazed at how much the younger siblings had grown when she saw them all the evening before at the rehearsal. Thomas was as tall as his father. A big boy, sturdy and strong with an easy grin and an interest in anything that might qualify as a sport. Carry was slim and pretty and yes, very aware of male attention, just as Reynard had said. Nell was more subdued than she had been as a bouncy, energetic eight-year-old. But she was just as loving, and Kendra often felt the young girl close beside her, seeming to wordlessly ask for an arm to draw her close.

Reynard—was *not* married. Kendra's heart had skipped when she heard the news. Still, she knew that she had no claim on Reynard, even if she did have deep feelings for him. They had exchanged no promises, made no commitments. She did not know if Reynard still cared at all for her—in that fashion. In fact, she had no assurance that he had ever cared—in that way—unless his look, his manner were assurance. Or the pressure of his hand on hers. Kendra clung to a hope. A dream.

She turned her attention back to Amy, Amy the bride.

"Walt is a blessed man," she said with sincerity.

Amy smiled. "Oh, Kendra—I'm so happy—I could just burst."

She gave Kendra an impetuous squeeze.

"I—I just hope that you—that you will one day feel—just as I feel," enthused Amy. "In love. Blissfully happy. So—so loved and blessed."

Kendra blinked back tears. She wasn't sure why she suddenly felt like weeping. She was experiencing too many emotions, all wanting expression.

❧   ❧   ❧

"Would you care to take a little walk?"

Reynard whispered the words very close to Kendra's ear. The wedding was over. The bride and groom had left in a flurry of goodbyes, beaming first at each other, then at the family and guests who were to be left behind. Now the guests, too, had departed and Kendra was helping gather the wedding gifts and pack them into boxes. She looked up at Reynard and nodded.

"I suppose—"

"Those will be looked after," he assured her.

Kendra smiled. "That's easy for you to say," she teased.

"Promise. I'll help you when we get back—if they aren't already boxed up."

It was a warm evening. There was no need for Kendra to get a shawl. They left the church together and strolled slowly down the lane that led them away from the small church building.

"You had me very worried," said Reynard softly.

Kendra looked up to meet his serious eyes.

"I was afraid I might never see you again."

Kendra lowered her glance. "I—I had—had thought the same," she admitted.

Reynard reached for her hand and Kendra interlaced her fingers with his.

"I've—thought about you, Kendra," he continued.

Kendra was unable to respond.

"And I've prayed." Silence followed. Then he chuckled softly. "How I've prayed." He laughed again. "Did you feel prayed for?" he asked her quietly.

Kendra lifted her eyes again. "I—I felt—at

peace," she answered honestly. "Strangely at peace. I—I—"

Kendra wished to tell him how much she had missed him. How distraught she felt at the thought she would never see him again. But she wasn't able to say the words. Instead, she answered quietly, "In spite of my circumstances—I felt that—that God would work it all out—in the right way for—for all of us."

His fingers tightened on hers.

"So He brought you back."

Kendra nodded. "He—He brought me back. Not—not in the way I had—had hoped. I mean, I certainly would not have asked that Papa Mac be—be—"

"Of course not. But his accident *did* make him think about God—about his salvation," Reynard reminded her.

Kendra nodded. She still could not think about that without tears of joy.

"So—I guess lots of good came of that accident—for many of us," he continued.

He stopped and turned to her.

"Kendra," he said softly. "You must know how—how I feel about you. Would it—would it be presumptuous of me to ask if—if I might call. I know that it won't be—quite as I would like—me being here and you in the city. But I could come as often as possible on weekends—and we could write. It would be okay now—wouldn't it?"

He went on before Kendra could give her answer. "I know that—that it isn't the way a young lady might wish to be courted—but—but—"

Kendra lifted a hand and rested it against his chest. He seemed so apologetic—so troubled by their situation. She did not wish him to think she felt cheated by their awkward arrangement.

But she didn't know quite what to say—or how to say it.

The silence seemed to stretch out between them.

"That is—if you feel the way I do," Reynard said at last.

Kendra could not look up into those intense brown eyes. She was afraid they would look into her very soul and discover the love that filled her being.

He reached for the hand and drew her a bit closer.

"Do you, Kendra?" he asked softly, placing a finger under her chin, lifting her face so she had to meet his eyes. She remembered the other time, long ago, when he had done the same thing. She had been enamored with him then. She loved him deeply now.

"Kendra—I've prayed so much—about us. About what God might have in mind—for our future. All I ask—all I dare to ask is that you—grant me the opportunity to—to try to show you—how much I care."

Kendra nodded mutely.

He smiled then, one of relief. "I'll come to see you as often as I can. I promise. I'll try to make it next weekend."

Kendra still could not speak. She was too overcome with emotion. She had prayed too. When things had looked so—so impossible. When she could only place her life in the hands of God and ask that His will be done. When it seemed that she might never see Reynard Preston again. But now— But she couldn't bring herself to tell him all that. Not now. Not yet.

He did come. That very next weekend. And as often as he could over the months that followed. George McMannus soon came to recognize the sound of Reynard's eager steps on the broad sidewalk. Even Oscar would lift his head from the mat where he rested and cock his ears forward. Then he would turn to look for Kendra, who always seemed in such a hurry to get to the door.

"Kendra's in the house."

George McMannus straightened up from the rose he was pruning and looked at the young man who stood before him, his hat held in nervous hands.

"I—I know, sir. At least—that's what I was counting on."

Surprise showed in the older man's eyes.

"I—I wished to see you, sir," went on Reynard, his eyes lifting from his hat.

"Me?" Oscar moved from the shade of the tree where he had been watching the proceedings and pushed against the younger man for a bit of attention. Reynard reached a hand down absentmindedly and rumpled the dog's ear. Oscar pressed more closely against him.

"Well," said George, "let's get in out of the sun."

He turned to lead the way to the back door.

"I—I would like to talk to you here—first," Reynard said. Then added quickly. "If you don't mind."

George stopped and turned, eyes narrowed, as though trying hard to see through the young man before him to study his very thoughts.

He waved a hand at the bench that stood beneath a large poplar and Reynard moved toward it.

Reynard did not make George wait. He lifted his head, took a deep breath, and hurriedly began. "I'm—sure you must know how I feel about Kendra."

George nodded.

"I—I wish to marry her, sir."

He stopped and toyed with his hat. George watched him, sensing his nervousness and feeling empathy, yet at the same time aware of some discomfort of his own. He had known this would come. He couldn't possibly keep her forever. Yet— He wished there were some way to put it off. To hold on to her for just a bit longer.

He drew in a big sigh, turning his gaze off somewhere in the distance, his left hand stroking his graying beard. He wasn't ready to answer—yet.

"I'm asking you, sir, for her hand in marriage."

At last George stirred himself. He turned to look at the eager, nervous young man. There was no one to whom he would sooner entrust his little girl.

"What does Kendra say?" he asked.

Reynard looked surprised. "Oh, I wouldn't ask Kendra before asking you, sir. I need your permission—for that."

George looked steadily at the young man. He nodded silently. "Then perhaps you should ask her—now—with my permission," he said, fighting to keep his voice even and controlled.

Without rising from his seat, he turned toward the house.

"Kendra," he called, and Kendra answered through the open window.

"Can you join us?"

When she came from the house, Kendra was surprised to see Reynard. She hesitated, reaching down to nervously toy with the hem of her apron.

Reynard stood to his feet, his eyes on Kendra's face. George waited a moment, then said, "This young man has just asked for your hand in marriage." Both men heard the sharp intake of Kendra's breath.

Silence followed while Kendra cast a glance toward Reynard. He looked at her pleadingly as he shifted nervously from one foot to the other.

"How do you feel about it?" asked George. "Do you wish to marry him?"

It seemed too blunt. So—so sudden. Kendra lowered her gaze, her hands still twisting in the apron.

"Well—?"

Kendra lifted her eyes and looked directly into those of the young man.

"Yes," she said, and her voice was strong. "Yes— I wish to marry him."

Reynard stepped quickly forward and reached for Kendra's shoulders.

"I guess it's settled then," said George. But no one seemed to be listening.

The two stood close to each other, their eyes exchanging promises of love. George knew he had been forgotten. He cleared his throat loudly and Reynard stirred, his cheeks coloring slightly.

"You'd better get that girl out of here and let her know how special she is," suggested George. "There are too many nosy neighbors for you to be saying it here in the garden."

"Thank you, sir," Reynard said, and his voice was filled with excitement. Confidence.

George watched them go. One hand reached down to stroke Oscar, who had moved to press up against his knee, the other reached toward his beard.

Though he fought against the tears, they could not be held in check. His little girl had left childhood behind and entered womanhood. He had known it would come. Should have been prepared, but it all seemed to have happened so quickly. Wasn't it only yesterday that he had stood in the garden of the Home, bracing himself for the meeting with a nearly four-year-old. Now—now—

He wiped carelessly at the tears with his flannel sleeve. If only—if only Mary could see her now. A beautiful young woman—vibrant—in love.

He had to let her go—with his blessing.

W9-BAN-639

VOCABULARY CARTOONS

Building an Educated
Vocabulary with
Visual Mnemonics

Sam, Max, and Bryan Burchers

New Monic Books, Inc.

www.vocabularycartoons.com

Aneila ♡ M

Manufactured in the United States of America.
Library of Congress Catalog Card Number: 96-96399
ISBN: 978-0-9652422-7-1
Illustrations: Bryan Burchers, Lee Horton, David Horton, Beryl "Woody" Woodman, Joe Toth,
Andrew Grimm.
Cover Design: Bryan Burchers, D.T. Publishing
Setup & Typography: Sam Burchers III

Library of Congress Cataloging-in-Publication Data
Burchers, Sam
  Vocabulary Cartoons
Sam "Max" Burchers, Bryan Burchers, & Sam Burchers, III
        p.   cm.
  Includes index.
  ISBN 978-0-9652422-7-1
  1. Vocabulary Cartoons - United States.
II. Title

                                                    96-96399

New Monic Books
P.O. Box 511314
Punta Gorda, FL 33951
(941) 575-6669
www.vocabularycartoons.com $12.95

ACKNOWLEDGEMENTS

The Educators

Our gratitude to the following educators who contributed their expertise in making this book possible.

Larry Marsh - Language Arts Teacher
North Ft. Myers High School, North Ft. Myers, Florida

Judy Baxley & Nancy Wiseman - Language Arts Teachers
Mariner High School, Cape Coral, Florida

John LeClair & Christine Miller - Elementary School Teachers
Deep Creek Elementary, Punta Gorda, Florida

Joe Baxley - Elementary School Teacher
Pine Island Elementary, Pine Island, Florida

Beth Crosby - Elementary School Teacher of the Year 1996
Diplomat Elementary, Cape Coral, Florida

Sue Williams - Elementary School Teacher
Liberty Elementary, Pt. Charlotte, Florida

The Artists

Our special thanks to staff artists **Bryan Burchers, Lee** and **Dave Horton, Beryl "Woody" Woodman** and contributing artist **Andrew Grimm** and **Joe Toth**. Their collective talents provided the essential quality of zany humor and outrageous bizarreness that make cartoon mnemonics memorable.

Contents

Introduction

WHAT THIS BOOK IS ALL ABOUT

This book is about having fun while learning new words easier and faster than you have ever thought possible. You may laugh at many of the 210 cartoons in the book, but don't for a minute think the cartoons are just for your amusement. Each and every cartoon is a vocabulary learning tool in the form of a mnemonic device.

A mnemonic (nuh MON ik) is a fancy word which simply means "assisting the memory." Memory experts tell us mnemonics are just about the best way to remember anything.

RHYMING MNEMONICS

A rhyming mnemonic is a form of word association where you rhyme a word you want to learn with a word you already know. Here's an example of a rhyming mnemonic you probably are already familiar with. It is the famous one that teachers often use to help their students remember the date Christopher Columbus discovered America. It goes like this: "Columbus sailed the ocean BLUE in fourteen hundred and ninety-TWO."

BLUE, of course, rhymes with TWO. See how rhymes can be helpful in remembering things? In this book you will find that every word you wish to learn is rhymed with a word you probably already know.

VISUAL MNEMONICS: PICTURES IN YOUR MIND

There is a famous expression that says "a picture is worth a thousand words."

For most people it's easier to remember pictures that are seen rather than sounds that are heard. Anything that can be visualized as an object is much easier to remember.

All human beings have something like built-in cameras

inside their heads. When you know what a banana looks like and you hear the word, your mind automatically makes a mental picture of a banana.

MAKING A PICTURE WITH A SUBSTITUTE WORD

Unfortunately, most words we use to communicate with do not make pictures. In that case we find substitute words that do make pictures and use them for words that do not.

Take the word PARRY. PARRY means to protect yourself from a blow; to avoid skillfully; to turn aside and evade. For example: "George PARRIED the blow by jumping to one side."

PARRY is not a word that makes a picture. But there are words that sound like PARRY that do make pictures.One word that rhymes with Parry is PEAR.

To make a mnemonic (memory aid) we take these two words, PARRY and PEAR, and put them together into a cartoon picture.

*"The **PEARS PARRIED** each other's fencing movements."*

We have now combined a RHYMING mnemonic and a VISUAL mnemonic; making it twice as easy to remember a new word. Of course, two pears with arms and legs and swords makes a ridiculous picture. But the crazier the picture the easier it is to remember.

From now on, when you hear the word PARRY and you don't remember the definition, just think of what it sounds like. It sounds like PEAR. Now think of the two words together, PARRY and PEAR. You'll remember the picture of two PEARS PARRYING and that will tell you the meaning of PARRY is to protect yourself by skillfully avoiding a blow.

That's all there is to remembering new words with the aid of mnemonic vocabulary cartoons.

First, RHYME a word you do know with one you do not, and then see the two words in a PICTURE together.

Vocabulary Cartoons make learning new words easy and entertaining. You will be amazed at the magic of mnemonics as your vocabulary grows and grows.

ABDUCT

(ab DUKT) *v.*

to kidnap or carry off by force

Sounds like: **DUCK**

"ABDUCTED DUCKS"

- ❑ The Evil Knight planned to **ABDUCT** the queen when she came alone to the village.

- ❑ Our basketball team was **ABDUCTED** by aliens who carried them off to the planet Mars.

- ❑ The neighbor's boy **ABDUCTED** our pet pig, and we paid a ransom of a box of cookies to get him back.

GUERRILLAS

(ger RIL uz) *n.*

members of an irregular military force operating in small bands behind enemy lines

Sounds like: **GORILLAS**

"GORILLA GUERRILLAS"

- ❏ The **GUERRILLAS** stormed the town and then fled back into the woods before the army troops arrived.

- ❏ **GUERRILLAS** often have to seal and capture equipment from the enemy as they have none of their own.

- ❏ Jack's mom said he and his friends were a bunch of house **GUERRILLAS**, but she loved them anyway.

BUFFOON

(buh FOON) *n.*

one who amuses with jokes and tricks;
a bumbling or ridiculous person, a fool

Sounds like: **BABOON**

*"A **BUFFOON** of a **BABOON**"*

- ❑ Robin is a **BUFFOON**. At the party he stood on his head and sang *Jingle Bells*.

- ❑ A little **BUFFOONERY** sometimes is a welcome thing at a dull gathering.

- ❑ Uncle Jed warned his nephew that his **BUFFOONISH** behavior did not belong at the dinner table.

FLOUNDER

(FLOWN dur) v.

to move clumsily; to struggle or proceed with difficulty; also a flat fish (n.)

Sounds like: **FLOUNDER (fish)**

"A FLOUNDERING FLOUNDER"

☐ The dog **FLOUNDERED** through the mud attempting to find his master in the dark night.

☐ Jack started his speech but began to **FLOUNDER** when he couldn't find his notes.

☐ The ship **FLOUNDERED** in the storm.

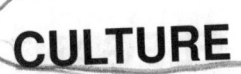

CULTURE

KUL chur) *n.*

the developed pattern of one's
knowledge, beliefs and behavior

Sounds like: **VULTURE**

*"**VULTURES** with **CULTURE**"*

- ❑ The **CULTURE** of ancient Egypt has been studied perhaps more than any in mankind's history.

- ❑ It is in most **CULTURES** to be nice to your fellow man.

- ❑ A **CULTURED** person often reads great literature, appreciates fine art and eats good food.

ELEGANT

(EL uh gunt) *adj.*
characterized or exhibiting
elegance; excellent

Sounds like: **PELICAN**

*"An **ELEGANT PELICAN** is a very fine bird."*

□ The presidential ball was an **ELEGANT** affair.

□ The Princess was dressed in an **ELEGANT** Thai silk gown for the ball.

□ The ever-popular playwright, Tennessee Williams, wrote **ELEGANTLY** about the decadent South.

INHABIT
(in HAB it) *v.*
to live or dwell in

Sounds like: **RABBIT**

"RABBITS INHABIT holes."

- ☐ Ants **INHABIT** ant hills.

- ☐ People **INHABIT** houses and buildings.

- ☐ Dinosaurs **INHABITED** the Earth millions of years ago.

GOAD

(gohd) *v.*

to urge, prick or push; anything that pricks, prods, or urges (*n.*)

Sounds like: **TOAD**

*"Never **GOAD** a big **TOAD**."*

- ❑ Because he was so tall, Michael's friends **GOADED** him to try out for basketball.

- ❑ Her friends called Helen "chicken" and **GOADED** her into becoming a cheerleader.

- ❑ Bill's bad grades **GOADED** him into studying harder.

FERTILE

(FUR tul) *adj.*
able to reproduce children, seeds,
or fruits; highly productive

Sounds like: **TURTLE**

"*A FERTILE TURTLE*"

- Mabel is our **FERTILE** cow and has a calf every spring.

- The village was located in a **FERTILE** valley where many farms grow vegetables.

- Most fiction writers have **FERTILE** imaginations.

AQUEDUCT

(ACK wa dukt) *n.*
a large pipe or conduit for carrying
water from a distant location

Sounds like: **AQUA DUCK**

*"**AQUA DUCKS** working on an **AQUEDUCT**"*

- ❑ **AQUEDUCTS** that carry liquids can be opened, like ditches, or closed, like pipes.

- ❑ **AQUEDUCTS** can be made of stone or wood, as well as steel and plastics.

- ❑ The Romans built huge **AQUEDUCTS** to bring water to their cities.

REVIEW #1: Match the word with its definition.

1. abduct - (duck)
2. guerrillas - (gorillas)
3. buffoon - (baboon)
4. flounder - (flounder)
5. culture - (vulture)
6. elegant - (pelican)
7. inhabit - (rabbit)
8. goad - (toad)
9. fertile - (turtle)
10. aqueduct - (aqua duck)

a. irregular military
b. move clumsily
c. large water pipe
d. to kidnap
e. to live in
f. to prick or prod
g. highly productive
h. a joker
i. products of humans
j. exhibiting excellence

Fill in the blanks with the appropriate word. The word form may need changing.

1. The speaker began to _____ when he couldn't find his notes.

2. The Romans built _____ to carry water to their cities.

3. Bryan's friends _____ him to try out for the tennis team.

4. The _____ child was returned to his parents by the police.

5. A _____ person often reads great literature.

6. Ants _____ ant hills.

7. The princess was dressed in an _____ gown at the ball.

8. _____ troops often capture weapons from their enemies.

9. Mabel is a _____ cow and has a calf every spring.

10. Robin stood on his head and acted the _____ at Larry's party.

PRANCE

(prants) *v.*

to act or walk about in a lively manner

Sounds like: **DANCE**

*"The majorette came **PRANCING** down the street, leading the parade in a high-stepping **DANCE**."*

- Rodney was a real showboat; every time he made a touchdown he **PRANCED** about as if he thought he was "hot stuff."

- Cindy's horse was trained to **PRANCE** in the most regal manner.

- Ricky **PRANCED** down the hall after getting straight As on his report card.

ENCROACH

(in KROHCH) *v.*
to intrude gradually upon the
rights of another; to trespass

Sounds like: **ROACH**

*"**ROACHES** will **ENCROACH** wherever there is food."*

- With an **ENCROACHING** anxiety, I made my way to where the crashed car lay on its side.

- The weeds from the adjacent vacant lot continued spreading with each rain until they **ENCROACHED** into our vegetable garden.

SMITTEN

(SMIT in) *adj.*

very much in love

Sounds like: **KITTEN**

*"A **SMITTEN KITTEN**"*

- The **SMITTEN** young man carried a bouquet of flowers for his girlfriend.

- After receiving a birthday card from Laura, Nathan was **SMITTEN**.

- Brad Pit ran out of the restaurant with a group of **SMITTEN** girls trailing behind him.

ALLUDE

(uh LOOD) *v.*

to refer to casually or indirectly

Sounds like: **RUDE**

"WOULD YOU LIKE A SPOON?"

*"Not to be **RUDE**, the hostess only **ALLUDED** to her guest's manners."*

- ❏ The letter Mark received **ALLUDED** to something that happened in his college days.

- ❏ The merchant often **ALLUDED** to his military days as the best time in his life.

- ❏ It is **RUDE** to **ALLUDE** to how much money a person has.

FLEET

(fleet) *n.*

a group of cars, boats, or other type of vessels

Sounds like: **FEET**

"The Postal Service's new FEET FLEET"

- The Navy's Seventh **FLEET** patrols the waters off China.

- A **FLEET** of new automobiles arrived at the Ford dealership today.

- The Spanish **FLEET** was sunk by a hurricane in 1765.

PARALLEL

(PEAR uh lel) *adj.*
running alongside;
two lines equally distant

Sounds like: **PAIR of Ls**

*"The **PAIR of Ls** are **PARALLEL** in
the word **PARALLEL**."*

- ❑ The lives of the Baker twins **PARALLEL** each other because they are so much alike.

- ❑ Christine's favorite gymnastic event is the uneven **PARALLEL** bars.

- ❑ A **PARALLELOGRAM** is a geometric figure with opposite sides **PARALLEL** and the same length.

HORIZONTAL

(HOR uh ZON tul) *adj.*
parallel to level ground;
at right angles to vertical

Sounds like: **HORIZON**

*"Something in a **HORIZONTAL** position is parallel to the **HORIZON**."*

- The police car has a **HORIZONTAL** stripe painted along it's side.

- People sleep in a **HORIZONTAL** position.

- I placed the painting in a **HORIZONTAL** position on the wall.

VERTICAL

(VUR tuh kul) *adj.*

straight up and down; a direction at right angles to the horizon

Sounds like: **ICICLE**

"ICICLES always tend to be VERTICAL."

- ❑ The **VERTICAL** clearance of doors in most houses is six feet eight inches.

- ❑ When we hear that something is plumb, we know that it is **VERTICAL**.

- ❑ A **VERTICAL** cliff of sheer rock was to be found at the top of the mountain.

BLISS

(bliss) *n.*

great happiness; joy

Sounds like: **KISS**

*"The prince was in **BLISS** when he
gave Sleeping Beauty a **KISS**."*

- ❑ The mother was in **BLISS** when she held her newborn baby.

- ❑ Jane and Glen said their vacation to Hawaii was pure **BLISS**.

- ❑ Dad's is in pure **BLISS** when he gets to set on the couch and watch his football games all day long.

DRENCH
(drench) *v.*
to wet thoroughly, to soak

Sounds like: **BENCH**

*"Grandma got **DRENCHED** waiting on the **BENCH**."*

- ❏ The cat was **DRENCHED** from the rain.
- ❏ The rainstorm **DRENCHED** everyone in the stadium.
- ❏ Agnes **DRENCHES** herself in cheap perfume.

REVIEW #2: Match the word with its definition.

1. prance - (dance)
2. encroach - (roach)
3. smitten - (kitten)
4. allude - (rude)
5. fleet - (feet)
6. parallel - (pair of ls)
7. horizontal - (horizon)
8. vertical - (icicle)
9. bliss - (kiss)
10. drench - (bench)

a. very much in love
b. to refer casually
c. a group of vehicles
d. running alongside
e. straight up and down
f. act in a lively manner
g. great happiness
h. to intrude or trespass
i. right angles to vertical
j. wet thoroughly

Fill in the blanks with the appropriate word. The word form may need changing.

1. I was _____ when I was caught in the rain without an umbrella.

2. The weeds from the vacant lot _____ into our yard.

3. The _____ distance along the ground was ten feet.

4. It is considered rude to _____ to how rich you are.

5. A _____ of new cars arrived at the Ford dealership today.

6. The _____ distance to the top of the tree was twenty feet.

7. The mother was in _____ when she held her newborn baby.

8. The friends have _____ interests when it comes to sports.

9. Ricky _____ down the hall after getting straight As on his report card.

0. After receiving a birthday card from Laura, Nathan was _____.

Vocabulary Cartoons

SHUN
(shun) *v.*
to keep away from;
to take pains to avoid

Sounds like: **SUN**

"At the beach, Dad would always
***SHUN** the **SUN**."*

□ Ralph was **SHUNNED** by everyone in his class because he rarely took a bath.

□ She thought she was a princess and **SHUNNED** all her friends.

□ In large cities it is wise to **SHUN** dark streets at night.

RESIDENT

(REZ uh dent) *n.*
one who lives in a place

Sounds like: **PRESIDENT**

*"The **PRESIDENT** and his family are **RESIDENTS** of the White House."*

- ❑ Although Jack had been a house guest for two years, he was only a visitor and not a **RESIDENT**.

- ❑ We used to live in Ohio, but now we are **RESIDENTS** of Texas.

- ❑ Upon entering the United States, an immigration officer will ask to see your passport to prove you are a U.S. **RESIDENT**.

RUTHLESS

(RUTH lis) *adj.*

having no compassion
or pity; cruel; merciless

Sounds like: **TOOTHLESS**

*"**TOOTHLESS** Captain Gums
was a **RUTHLESS** pirate."*

- The **RUTHLESS** hurricane caused a ten mile swath of destruction through the middle of the state.

- **RUTHLESS** Coach Ashton made his players run fifty laps around the field.

- The **RUTHLESS** behavior of Captain Bligh caused a mutiny aboard his ship.

OBSOLETE
(ob suh LEET) *adj.*
out of date; no longer in
use or in fashion

Sounds like: **FLEET**

*"The Norwegian Viking **FLEET** is **OBSOLETE**."*

- ❏ Jet engines may some day make propeller-driven airplanes **OBSOLETE**.

- ❏ The horse may be **OBSOLETE** transportation, but it is still a fun way to take a ride.

- ❏ **OBSOLETE** technology made it difficult for the old computers to keep up with the modern ones.

MAGNATE
(MAG nate) *n.*
a rich, powerful, or
successful business person
Sounds like: **MAGNET**

*"A **MAGNATE** attracts money like a **MAGNET**."*

- William Hearst was America's greatest newspaper **MAGNATE**.

- Oil **MAGNATES** own the oil rights in oil fields.

- Donald Trump is a powerful and wealthy real estate **MAGNATE**.

DESPITE

(dis PYTE) *n.*

in spite of, notwithstanding

Sounds like: **WRITE**

*"Sammy the snake, learned how to **WRITE**
DESPITE having no hands."*

- ❑ We had a great time at the picnic **DESPITE** the rain.

- ❑ We went to the movie **DESPITE** the fact we had
  already seen it.

- ❑ **DESPITE** his bad table manners, Ralph was a good
  dinner guest because he helped with the dishes.

CONCEAL
(kun SEEL) *v.*
to keep from being seen;
to put out of sight; hidden

Sounds like: **CON SEAL**

"The **CON CONCEALED** his pet **SEAL**."

- We could hear the airplane but could not see it **CONCEALED** above the clouds.

- Erin found it difficult to **CONCEAL** her feelings from others.

- We tried to **CONCEAL** Arnie's pet elephant in the garage, but he was **UNCONCEALABLE**.

CLIMATE

(KLIME ut) *n.*

refers to weather conditions; typical weather for an area; attitude

Sounds like: **CLIMB**

*"As a climber **CLIMBS** a mountain, the **CLIMATE** gets colder."*

- ❑ South Florida has a sub-tropical **CLIMATE** consisting of warm breezes and sunshine.

- ❑ When it started to rain, there was a **CLIMATE** of optimism among the farmers that the dry season was over.

- ❑ After showing her parents her bad report card, the **CLIMATE** was not right for Tanya to ask for her allowance.

42

SWELTER
(SWEL tur) *v.*
to become exceedingly hot
Sounds like: **SWEATER**

*"**SWELTERING** in a **SWEATER** is not
the coolest way to diet."*

- ❑ The dog **SWELTERED** in the summer sun without any shade.

- ❑ Our air conditioner broke and we began to **SWELTER** in our rooms.

- ❑ The **SWELTERING** temperatures in a green house create optimum conditions for growing plants.

WEAN

(ween) *v.*
to withdraw from any
type of habit

Sounds like: **TEEN**

*"How to **WEAN** a **TEEN** away from
the family telephone"*

- ❑ Baby bottles filled with warm milk are used to **WEAN** babies from their mother's milk.

- ❑ Her folks tried to **WEAN** Mable off her ice cream habit by giving her a teaspoon of sugar every hour.

- ❑ Homer **WEANED** himself off cigarettes by biting his finger every time he wanted a smoke.

REVIEW #3: Match the word with its definition.

shun - (sun)
resident - (president)
ruthless - (toothless)
obsolete - (fleet)
magnate - (magnet)
despite - (write)
conceal - (seal)
climate - (climb)
swelter - (sweater)
0. wean - (teen)

a. to keep away from
b. rich, powerful
c. refers to weather
d. cruel; merciless
e. in spite of
f. one who lives in a place
g. put out of sight
h. out of date
i. to become hot
j. to gradually withdraw

Fill in the blanks with the appropriate word. The word form may need changing.

1. Ellen had difficulty _____ her feelings.

2. Mothers use bottles to _____ their babies from breast feeding.

3. Florida has a tropical _____.

4. When the air conditioner broke, we began to _____ in our room.

5. William Hearst was a wealthy newspaper _____.

6. Our teacher was so _____, she gave us three hours of homework every night.

7. It is wise to _____ dark streets at night.

8. Jet engines may someday make propeller airplanes _____.

9. We had a great time at the picnic _____ the rain.

10. April and I are _____ of Texas.

SHODDY

(SHOD ee) *adj.*
of poor quality or make;
dishonest

Sounds like: **BODY**

*"Frankenstein may have been famous, but he
sure had a SHODDY BODY."*

- ❑ Jill thought the quality of the toys in the store was **SHODDY**.

- ❑ Mary told her friend that leaving her alone at the mall was a **SHODDY** thing for him to have done.

- ❑ Harry quit work because he said it was a **SHODDY** job at a **SHODDY** company.

TRANSPIRE
(tran SPIRE) *v.*
to happen; to become known

Sounds like: **VAMPIRE**

*"At nightfall it **TRANSPIRES** that **VAMPIRES** wake up."*

- After the dance it **TRANSPIRED** that the bus had a flat tire.

- Andrea wanted to know what would **TRANSPIRE** if she refused to come to school on Fridays.

- A fight **TRANSPIRED** after Tom was hit in the face with a water balloon.

HOAX

(hokes) *n.*
a practical joke; something
intended to deceive

Sounds like: **JOKES**

*"David's **HOAX** turned out to be a bad **JOKE**."*

- ❑ H.G. Wells **HOAXED** the public with his report of an alien invasion.

- ❑ A common **HOAX** is when innocent people are cheated out of their money.

- ❑ The rumor that a lion had escaped from the zoo was only a **HOAX**.

QUALM
(kwalm) *n.*
a feeling of illness;
a disturbing feeling

Sounds like: **CALM**

*"Even though the lake was **CALM**, the fishermen had **QUALMS** about their safety."*

- Elizabeth felt stomach **QUALMS** after eating three hamburgers

- The pilot had **QUALMS** about flying after hearing the news about bad weather.

- Liars have no **QUALMS** about telling lies.

HARSH

(harsh) *adj.*
unpleasant to the
senses or conditions

Sounds like: **MARSH**

*"Life in the **MARSH** can be **HARSH**."*

- ❑ It was a **HARSH** winter, and the cold forced the animals to stay in their holes.

- ❑ The **HARSH** words of criticism made us cringe with regret.

- ❑ We heard three **HARSH** sounds and then a thump in the night.

FAMINE

(FAM un) *n.*
a drastic, wide-reaching
shortage of food

Sounds like: **FAMILY**

*"The **FAMILY** suffered through the
worst **FAMINE** of the century."*

- Many people starve to death during **FAMINES** around the world.

- The worst **FAMINES** of this century have occurred in African nations.

- Harry said he was **FAMISHED** and wanted to know if dinner was ready.

ADJACENT

(uh JAY sunt) *adj.*
adjoining, next to;
near or close

Sounds like: **JASON**

*"No one liked sitting **ADJACENT** to **JASON**."*

- ❑ Mary lived in a house **ADJACENT** to the grocery store.

- ❑ The baseball park and **ADJACENT** lands are city property.

- ❑ My apartment shakes when my **ADJACENT** neighbor plays his drums.

WARY

(WEAR ee) *adj.*
alert, cautious;
on guard, watchful

Sounds like: **HAIRY**

*"Always be **WARY** when you wake up and
feel something **HAIRY**."*

- It is good to be **WARY** of strangers coming to your door selling things.

- Donna was **WARY** of snakes in her yard.

- We were always **WARY** of making mistakes in our chemistry experiments.

DREAD

(DRED) *v.*

to be in terror of; to fear greatly

Sounds like: **BED**

*"Billy sometimes **DREADED** going to **BED**."*

- Many people in Japan live in **DREAD** of earthquakes.

- Shirley **DREADED** her annual dental checkups.

- Most people **DREAD** spiders and snakes and wiggly things.

AGHAST

(uh GAST) *adj.*
shocked; frightened;
terrified; taken back

Sounds like: **GHOST**

*"The **GHOST** was **AGHAST**."*

- [ ] After the fire, we were **AGHAST** at the destruction to our home.

- [ ] Evelyn was beside herself, absolutely **AGHAST** that she wasn't invited to Mary's tea party.

- [ ] Even veteran homicide detectives were **AGHAST** at the murder scene.

REVIEW #4: Match the word with its definition.

1. shoddy - (body)
2. transpire - (vampire)
3. hoax - (jokes)
4. qualm - (calm)
5. harsh - (marsh)
6. famine - (family)
7. adjacent - (Jason)
8. wary - (hairy)
9. dread - (bed)
10. aghast - (ghost)

a. of poor quality
b. to become known
c. anticipate with distaste
d. disturbed feeling
e. practical joke
f. on guard, alert
g. shortage of food
h. unpleasant conditions
i. shocked, frightened
j. near or close

Fill in the blanks with the appropriate word. The word form may need changing.

1. People in California live in _____ of earthquakes.

2. We were _____ at the destruction of the fire.

3. We heard _____ sounds and a thump in the night.

4. Mary's house was _____ to the grocery store.

5. The students wanted to know what would _____ if they skipped school.

6. People often become ill during _____.

7. It is wise to be _____ of strangers who come to your door.

8. After eating three hamburgers, Elizabeth felt stomach _____.

9. The toys in the store were of a _____ quality.

10. The story that Ed had won the lottery was a _____.

Vocabulary Cartoons

HYPNOTIZE
(HIP no tize) *v.*
to put into a sleep-like state
Sounds like: **HIPPO EYES**

*"**HIPPO EYES** are famous for **HYPNOTIZING**."*

- The patient was **HYPNOTIZED** and experienced no pain during the operation.

- The exciting performance of the trapeze artists **HYPNOTIZED** the audience.

- Sue went to a **HYPNOTIST** and requested that he **HYPNOTIZE** her to stop smoking.

DOVETAIL

(DOVE tail) *v.*

to combine or unite into a unified whole;
fit together harmoniously

Sounds like: **DOVE TAILS**

*"**DOVE TAILS** that **DOVETAIL**"*

- The carpenter cut the boards so they **DOVETAILED** perfectly.

- The engineers had the idea to **DOVETAIL** the two bridges so that they would come together as one.

- The strikers **DOVETAILED** their arms and marched down the street in protest.

GAPE

(gape) *v.*

to become widely open, separated;
to stare in amazement

Sounds like: **APE**

*"The **GAPING** mouth of an **APE**
devoured the grapes."*

- The deep pit **GAPED** before him; if he stumbled and fell there would be no rescue.

- There were **GAPING** differences between what each witness told the police.

- When he won the lottery, he shook his head and **GAPED** in amazement.

OUTFOX

(out fox) *v.*

to outwit; to overcome by cunning or cleverness

Sounds like: **FOX**

*"It's hard to **OUTFOX** a **FOX**."*

- The burglar **OUTFOXED** the police by escaping up the chimney.

- Our teacher was hard to **OUTFOX**. She had already heard every possible excuse for skipping school.

- Many times mothers will pretend to let their children **OUTFOX** them.

AFLOAT

(uh FLOAT) *adj.*
a floating condition;
circulating about

Sounds like: **GOAT**

*"A **GOAT AFLOAT**"*

- The canoe was **AFLOAT** in the stream.

- During the flood, our living room was **AFLOAT** half way to the ceiling.

- Rumors were **AFLOAT** that the principal was going to be transferred to another school.

CARP

(CARP) *v.*
to complain

Sounds like: **CARP (fish)**

THE WATER'S TOO COLD!

MY FINS HURT!

"CARPING CARPS"

- It was tiresome listening to Molly **CARPING** about her sore foot.

- **CARPING** about the weather does not good because you can't do anything about it.

- Sometimes a little **CARPING** in a restaurant when you are getting bad service gets results.

ENDORSE

(en DORSE) *v.*

to give approval or support

Sounds like: **HORSE**

*"A Kentucky Derby winning **HORSE** **ENDORSES** his ointment."*

- ❏ Many teachers **ENDORSE** the idea of free lunches for themselves.

- ❏ Famous athletes make a lot of money **ENDORSING** sports products.

- ❏ Banks require customers to **ENDORSE** their checks before they will pay them.

REMAINDER

(re MAIN dur) *n.*
what is left when a part is taken away;
those left behind

Sounds like: **REINDEER**

*"Because Santa couldn't take all the **REINDEER**,
Comet became the **REMAINDER**."*

- The **REMAINDER** of the pie was put away where dad couldn't find it.

- For the **REMAINDER** of the year we had to take a cut in pay.

- When all the beds were filled, the **REMAINDER** of the team slept on the floor.

AMBLE

(AM ble) *v.*

to walk slowly; walk with a leisurely gate

Sounds like: **CAMEL**

*"Caravan **CAMELS** on long journeys rarely run; they **AMBLE**."*

- After school, Alexander and Tom **AMBLED** down the road to the fishing hole to catch their dinner.

- "**AMBLE** on out here," the dance instructor said to the new student. "Let's see some of your moves."

- Jack walked with an **AMBLING** quality, as if he hadn't a care in the world.

ENROLL

(in ROHL) *v.*

to make or become a member;
to sign up for something

Sounds like: **MOLE**

*"A **MOLE** waiting to **ENROLL**."*

- His dad took Jack to school to **ENROLL** him in the first grade.

- In order to vote in an election you must **ENROLL**.

- Leslie wanted to **ENROLL** in the history class, but the **ENROLLMENT** was already filled.

EVIEW #5: Match the word with its definition.

- hypnotize - (hippo eyes)
- dovetail - (dove tails)
- gape - (ape)
- outfox - (fox)
- afloat - (goat)
- carp - (carp)
- endorse - (horse)
- remainder - (reindeer)
- amble - (camel)
- enroll - (mole)

a. to float
b. what is left over
c. wide open
d. give approval
e. to complain
f. to sign up
g. a sleep-like state
h. to walk slowly
i. unite harmoniously
j. to outwit

Fill in the blanks with the appropriate word. The word form may need changing.

1. The patient was _____ so she wouldn't experience any pain.

2. Banks require customers to _____ their checks.

3. For the _____ of the year we saved our money.

4. Soldiers are always _____ about something.

5. The canoe was _____ in the stream.

6. Our teacher was hard to _____.

7. The father took his children to _____ in school.

8. After school Tom _____ down to his favorite fishing hole.

9. The carpenter cut the boards so they would _____.

10. Pete _____ in amazement when he won the lottery.

SUCCOR

(SUCK ur) *n.*
help; relief; assistance

Sounds like: **SOCCER**

*"Cheerleaders giving **SUCCOR** to an
injured **SOCCER** player"*

□ Doctors provide **SUCCOR** to their patients.

□ The police often provide **SUCCOR** to those injured in
automobile accidents.

□ Wounded soldiers are **SUCCORED** by medics in
battlefield conditions.

FOWL

(fowl) *n.*
any type of bird;
the meat of that bird

Sounds like: **FOUL**

*"A **FOWL** hit by a **FOUL** ball"*

- ☐ Turkey is the **FOWL** of choice for Thanksgiving dinner.

- ☐ Phil raised **FOWL** on his farm, mostly chickens and ducks.

- ☐ Snow geese are **FOWL** that fly south in the winter.

- ☐ Quail are a favorite **FOWL** in gourmet restaurants.

RUNT

(runt) *n.*
undersized; a small
animal or person

Sounds like: **BUNT**

*"The **RUNT** laid down a **BUNT**."*

- ☐ The **RUNT** of the litter is always Karen's favorite.

- ☐ Silver was my **RUNT** pony, but I loved him all the same.

- ☐ Jack's father affectionately called him "**RUNT**," a misnomer because Jack was the biggest member of the family.

PREVAIL

(pree VAIL) *v.*

to be victorious; to persuade

Sounds like: **SAIL**

*"The boat with the biggest **SAIL PREVAILS**."*

❑ His coach **PREVAILED** upon Joshua to stop moaning about the team's loss and get ready for the next game.

❑ The **PREVAILING** winds were out of the north most of the summer.

❑ "Justice **PREVAILS**," is an expression that means good has won over evil.

FERVOR

(FUR vur) *n.*

intensity of feeling or expression

Sounds like: **FEVER**

"*Babe Butterfinger had such **FERVOR** for baseball he even played with a **FEVER**.*"

- Avid sports fans have such **FERVOR** for their teams they often argue during the games.

- The fans at the ballgame were split booing and cheering with equal **FERVOR**.

- As a mark of his dedication and **FERVOR** for the violin, Zachary practices six hours a day.

WAD
(wod) *n.*
a small mass of soft material
squeezed into a ball

Sounds like: **SOD**

*"A big **WAD** of **SOD**"*

- After working all summer, Joey had a good **WAD** of money stashed away to buy books for school.

- Jake stood before the principal and **WADDED** his cap into his pocket.

- The detective found a small **WAD** stained with blood behind the sofa.

AVERT

(uh VERT) *v.*
to ward off; to turn away;
to keep from happening

Sounds like: **HURT**

*"The quarterback found a way to **AVERT** getting **HURT**."*

- ❑ We **AVERTED** our eyes from the solar eclipse.

- ❑ The truck driver **AVERTED** an accident by driving onto the median.

- ❑ **AVERTING** disaster is often times a matter of luck.

ZIGZAG

(ZIG zag) *n.*

a series of turns in different directions that nevertheless proceed in a general direction

Sounds like: **TAG**

*"When playing **TAG**, **ZIGZAG** to avoid being **TAGGED**."*

- ☐ The blind person **ZIGZAGGED** his way across the unfamiliar room.

- ☐ The trail **ZIGZAGGED** through the hills.

- ☐ **ZIGZAGGING** through the defenders, the quarterback ran for a touchdown.

WHIMSICAL

(WIM zuh kul) *adj.*
erratic in behavior; unpredictable;
having a quaint or fanciful quality

Sounds like: **SWIM POPSICLE**

*"A **SWIMMING POPSICLE** is a **WHIMSICAL** notion."*

❑ Todd's suggestion to have a grape catching contest with our mouths was a **WHIMSICAL** idea.

❑ Children's stories often have **WHIMSICAL** plots; Cinderella is one example.

❑ Bathing suits fashionable in the 19th century seem **WHIMSICAL** to us now.

SCAMPER

(SCAM pur) *v.*

to run; to go hastily of lightly

Sounds like: **HAMPER**

*"The laundry **HAMPER SCAMPERED**
to the finish line."*

□ The dogs **SCAMPERED** across the lawn to the house.

□ The cat **SCAMPERED** after the rolling ball.

□ We planned to **SCAMPER** past the guards when their backs were turned.

REVIEW #6: Match the word with its definition.

1. succor - (soccer)
2. fowl - (foul)
3. runt - (bunt)
4. prevail - (sail)
5. fervor - (fever)
6. wad - (sod)
7. avert - (hurt)
8. zigzag - (tag)
9. whimsical - (swim popsicle)
10. scamper - (hamper)

a. to go hastily
b. approach indirectly
c. to turn away
d. a small mass
e. intensity of feeling
f. to overcome
g. a bird
h. undersized
i. relief; assistance
j. erratic behavior

Fill in the blanks with the appropriate word. The word form may need changing.

1. Children's stories often have _____ plots.

2. The football player _____ his way to a touchdown.

3. Joe found a small _____ of lint in his pocket.

4. Ralph has _____ for his new job.

5. The _____ of choice for Thanksgiving is turkey.

6. We all agreed to _____ our eyes when the scary part of the movie appeared.

7. The _____ of a litter is the smallest one.

8. Doctors provide _____ to their patients.

9. Our team _____ over the opposing team.

10. The car _____ its way up the crooked hill.

AGILITY

(uh JILL uh tee) *n.*
the quality or state of being nimble,
quick in movement or adaptable

Sounds like: **KILL A FLEA**

*"It takes **AGILITY** to **KILL A FLEA**."*

- It takes physical **AGILITY** to become a good gymnast.

- Chess players must have considerable mental **AGILITY**.

- Cats are so **AGILE** that when they fall they always land on their feet.

WAIL

(wail) *v.*

to cry out loudly

Sounds like: **TAIL**

*"Cats **WAIL** if you rock on their **TAIL**."*

- ❑ The relatives of the deceased **WAILED** at her grave.

- ❑ Visiting his uncle's ranch, Billy heard the scary **WAILING** of a coyote in the night.

- ❑ Ghosts are supposed to make **WAILING** sounds inside haunted houses.

PASSIVE
(PASS iv) *adj.*
inactive; acted upon but
not acting in return

Sounds like: **MASSIVE**

*"Once quite active, Rex got so MASSIVE
he became PASSIVE."*

- Hector had a **PASSIVE** attitude about life and seldom left his home.

- Shirley played a **PASSIVE** role and went along with whatever her sister wanted.

- For sick people in recovery, **PASSIVITY** can be a positive thing.

CATAMARAN

(KA tuh muh RAN) *n.*
a boat with two parallel hulls

Sounds like: **CAT**

"A CAT CATAMARAN"

- **CATAMARANS** are fast sail boats.
- **CATAMARANS** are good for sailing in shallow waters.
- We rented a **CATAMARAN** at the beach this summer.

ACCLAIM

(uh KLAME) *n.*

enthusiastic public praise and approval

Sounds like: **FAME**

*"**ACCLAIM** is often the consequence of **FAME**."*

- When Janet became a movie star in Hollywood, she received enough **ACCLAIM** to last a lifetime.

- The entire student body came out and **ACCLAIMED** the returning football team.

- The mayor said he did not seek **ACCLAIM**; he just wanted to help the city become a safer place to live.

INNATE

(IN nate) *adj.*
possessed at birth, inborn;
a natural characteristic

Sounds like: **HATE**

"*Dogs have an **INNATE HATRED** for cats.*"

- Hang gliding presents definite **INNATE** dangers for the participants.

- Most animals have an **INNATE** intelligence about finding their way to water holes.

- Carl says he **INNATELY** knows when his wife is going to be mad at him.

UNDERDOG
(UN der dog) *n.*
a loser or predicted loser in a
struggle or contest

Sounds like: **UNDER DOG**

*"The **DOG UNDER** the rug is definitely
the **UNDERDOG**."*

- ❏ Some people find it more fun to root for the
  UNDERDOG in every sporting event.

- ❏ Because our class had never won the tug-of-war, we
  were considered the **UNDERDOGS**.

- ❏ Everyone expects the favorite to win; therefore, when
  an **UNDERDOG** wins, it comes as a surprise.

RETRIEVE

(rih TREEV) *v.*
to recover; to find and
bring back; to get back

Sounds like: **RETRIEVER**

"RETRIEVERS will RETRIEVE anything thrown."

- Eric swam to the bottom of the river to **RETRIEVE** his favorite fishing lure.

- Peter was able to **RETRIEVE** all the lost data on his computer.

- Janet searched for an hour before she **RETRIEVED** her lost purse.

COLOSSAL

(kuh LOS ul) *adj.*
enormous, gigantic; huge in
size, extent or degree

Sounds like: **FOSSIL**

*"A **COLOSSAL** FOSSIL."*

- The navy's aircraft carriers are **COLOSSAL** ships that carry as many as three thousand sailors.

- Borrowing my father's car without his permission was a **COLOSSAL** mistake.

- Jerry had a **COLOSSAL** ego and thought he was the most handsome guy in school.

PARAPET

(PAIR uh pet) *n.*

a low wall or railing

Sounds like: **PAIR OF PETS**

*"A **PAIR OF PETS** on a **PARAPET**"*

- ☐ My brother and I built a **PARAPET** of rocks around our play house to keep out the dog.

- ☐ When the house caught fire, John jumped from the balcony **PARAPET** onto the nearest tree.

- ☐ The soldiers hid behind a **PARAPET** so that they wouldn't be seen.

EVIEW #7: Match the word with its definition.

agility - (kill a flea)
wail - (tail)
passive - (massive)
catamaran - (cat)
acclaim - (fame)
innate - (hate)
underdog (under dog)
retrieve - (retriever)
colossal - (fossil)
0. parapet - (pair of pets)

a. quick in movement
b. to cry out
c. inactive
d. a low wall
e. boat with two hulls
f. public approval
g. natural characteristic
h. predicted loser
i. to bring back
j. enormous

Fill in the blanks with the appropriate word. The word form may need changing.

1. Joel was _____ in class and never volunteered to answer a question.

2. The cat let out a _____ when I stepped on her tail.

3. Acrobats at the circus have wonderful _____.

4. _____ are excellent boats for shallow water.

5. Aircraft carriers are _____ in size.

6. We were supposed to lose so people said we were the _____.

7. Tim left his notebook in class and asked a friend to _____ it.

8. Dogs have an _____ hatred for cats.

9. The soldiers hid behind a _____ made of stone.

10. When George won the tournament, he received high _____ from his coach.

FETCH

(fitch) *v.*

to go after and bring back;
to get as in a price

Sounds like: **STRETCH**

"A genuine rubber dog can
***FETCH** by **STRETCHING**."*

- John asked Paul to go out to the car and **FETCH** his briefcase.

- The old silverware **FETCHED** a good price at the charity auction.

- Her father's telephone call **FETCHED** Sue home for dinner.

PROTOTYPE

(pro toh TYPE) *n.*

an early or original example upon which later examples are based

Sounds like: **TOE TYPE**

*"The original **PROTOTYPE** of the **TOE TYPE**writer"*

- In 1903, the Wright Brothers' airplane was the **PROTOTYPE** of many future airplane designs.

- The first McDonald's restaurant was a **PROTOTYPE** of the thousands that are now everywhere.

- An inventor built a **PROTOTYPE** of a machine for peeling bananas, but nobody cared to copy it.

ABOUND

(uh BOWND) *v.*

to be numerous or in great quantity

Sounds like: **AROUND**

*"Animals **ABOUND AROUND** watering holes."*

- ❑ Mosquitoes **ABOUND** in the summertime.

- ❑ Walt Disney World **ABOUNDS** with tourists all year long.

- ❑ Henry has **ABOUNDING** love for his family.

ZEAL

(zeel) *n.*

showing great enthusiasm or devotion to a goal

Sounds like: **SEAL**

*"Sammy the **SEAL** catches fish with great **ZEAL**."*

- Rachel **ZEALOUSLY** attends her acrobatics class.

- Hal ate his burger and french fries with **ZEAL**.

- (A **ZEALOT** is a person with excessive **ZEAL**.) When the leader told them to jump, the **ZEALOTS** all jumped off the bridge.

QUACK

(kwack) *n.*

one who pretends medical knowledge
or skills that they do not possess

Sounds like: **QUACK**

*"A **QUACKING** duck who is a **QUACK**"*

- ❑ Sue took some **QUACK** medicine to reduce weight, but never lost a pound.

- ❑ Dr. Johnson was a **QUACK** and had no medical degree at all.

- ❑ Watch out for medical **QUACKS** who pretend they can cure incurable diseases.

SHAMBLE

(SHAM bul) *n.*

a scene or condition of disorder or destruction; to walk or go awkwardly

Sounds like: **CAMEL**

*"When the sheik left, his **CAMELS** made **SHAMBLES** of his tent."*

- ❑ The fighting soldiers left the town in **SHAMBLES**.

- ❑ The bored young man **SHAMBLED** down the street kicking a tin can.

- ❑ **SHAMBLING** from side to side, the wagon with a broken wheel couldn't stay on the road.

INEPT

(in EPT) *adj.*
awkward or clumsy; lacking
in ability or competence

Sounds like: **SLEPT**

*"Our **INEPT** watch dog **SLEPT**
through everything."*

- Clarissa always made the most **INEPT** suggestions about how to improve our work.

- The actors seemed bored and gave an **INEPT** performance of the play.

- The **INEPTITUDE** of the lawyer handling Jerry's case was disgraceful.

LITERATE

(LIT ur ut) *adj.*
having the ability to
read and write

Sounds like: **LITTLE RAT**

*"A **LITERATE LITTLE RAT**."*

- Switzerland is one of the most **LITERATE** nations in the world. Practically every Swiss citizen can read and write.

- In our educational systems, the goal is for children to become **LITERATE** by the fourth grade.

- Teaching illiterate adults to become **LITERATE** is a rewarding experience.

SPLICE

(splice) *v.*

to join or unite by interweaving the stands;
a joint made by splicing something (*n.*)

Sounds like: **MICE**

"SPLICED MICE."

- ☐ The sailor said he could **SPLICE** two short ropes to make one long one.

- ☐ The electrician **SPLICED** the two wires.

- ☐ The **SPLICE** we made came undone after we pulled on both ends of the rope.

EMBARK

(im BARK) *v.*

to go aboard some means of transportation; to set out on a venture

Sounds like: **BARK**

*"Indians **EMBARKING** in a **BARK** canoe."*

- They were scheduled to **EMBARK** the ship at noon.

- The nurse reminded us to get our vaccinations before **EMBARKING** on our trip to Africa.

- We **EMBARKED** on a journey to Africa to photograph the wildlife.

REVIEW #8: Match the word with its definition.

1. fetch - (stretch)
2. prototype - (toe type)
3. abound - (around)
4. zeal - (seal)
5. quack - (quack)
6. shamble - (camel)
7. inept - (slept)
8. literate - (little rat)
9. splice - (mice)
10. embark - (bark)

a. to set out
b. join at the ends
c. to bring back
d. ability to read/write
e. an original example
f. pretends skills
g. numerous
h. disorder
i. enthusiasm for a goal
j. awkward or clumsy

Fill in the blanks with the appropriate word. The word form may need changing.

1. After the riot, the restaurant was left in _____.

2. They were scheduled to _____ the ship at noon.

3. The electrician _____ the wires together.

4. Doctors are not supposed to be _____.

5. My father always approached his evening meal with great _____.

6. John asked his friend to _____ his briefcase.

7. Her husband was _____ at fixing things around the house.

8. Switzerland is one of the most _____ nations in the world.

9. Animals usually _____ around a watering hole.

10. The first McDonald's restaurant was the _____ of all those to follow.

WAFT

(wahft) *v.*

moved gently by wind or waves; something conveyed through the air; a gentle breeze

Sounds like: **RAFT**

*"To get **WAFTED** out to sea in a **RAFT** isn't necessarily a pleasant surprise."*

❑ A gentle morning breeze **WAFTED** through the open window.

❑ The smell of cooked bacon **WAFTING** through the cabin let everyone know breakfast was almost ready.

❑ As Jennifer lifted the lid of the pizza box, a delicious aroma **WAFTED** through the room.

AWRY

(uh RYE) *adj.*

twisted or turned; wrong, amiss

Sounds like: **TIE**

"Ed's first attempt to TIE a TIE went AWRY."

- The wind blew the window shades **AWRY**.

- When it started to rain, our plans to go to the beach went **AWRY**.

- The campaign went **AWRY** when the candidate refused to make further speeches.

PERTURB

(pur TURB) *v.*

to make uneasy; to upset

Sounds like: **DISTURB**

*"It highly **PERTURBS** hornets when you **DISTURB** their nests."*

- ❑ It **PERTURBED** Bill's father when Bill took the family car without permission.

- ❑ The manager told his salesmen he was **PERTURBED** about the drop in sales for the year.

- ❑ Traveling by air is **PERTURBING** when the planes are behind schedule.

BULLETIN

(BUL uh tun) *n.*
a brief announcement of public interest;
a small publication published regularly

Sounds like: **BULLET**

*"The mob's **BULLET BULLETIN** board"*

- ☐ Our teacher posted the test results on her **BULLETIN** board.

- ☐ There are weather **BULLETINS** all day long on the television weather channel.

- ☐ Our club **BULLETIN** lists the dates of all meetings and special events.

FELON

(FEH lun) *n.*
a person convicted of
a serious crime

Sounds like: **MELON**

*"**FELON MELONS** going off to jail"*

- A person convicted of a **FELONY** may be punished by imprisonment in a state prison.

- Stealing a car is considered a **FELONY**.

- The police arrested a man for carrying a gun with **FELONIOUS** intentions.

STIFLE
(STY ful) *v.*
to hold back

Sounds like: **RIFLE**

*"A **STIFLED RIFLE**"*

- The jungle heat was **STIFLING** and we sought shelter in a cave.

- It was a boring party and Jack **STIFLED** a yawn and looked at his watch.

- The revolt was **STIFLED** and the culprits were arrested.

POROUS

(POR us) *adj.*
filled with holes

Sounds like: **POOR US**

*"**POOR US**, we get **POROUS**
every hunting season."*

- Natural sponges are **POROUS** marine creatures used for soaking up liquid.

- You can't have a **POROUS** roof and not expect it to leak.

- (Something **POROUS** is said to have **POROSITY**.) **POROSITY** is an essential quality of oil bearing rocks.

LIMBER

(LIM bur) *adj.*
flexible; exercise so as to
become limber

Sounds like: **LUMBER**

*"**LUMBER** from the rubber tree
is very **LIMBER**."*

❑ Ballet dancers have **LIMBER** muscles.

❑ The team **LIMBERED** up by doing stretching
exercises before the game.

❑ Diane was a **LIMBER** athlete, but she is no longer as
flexible as she once was.

ENAMOR
(in NAM ur) *v.*
to inspire with love; captivate

Sounds like: **HAMMER**

*"Duffy is **ENAMORED** of **HAMMERS**."*

- ❑ Jack was **ENAMORED** of the idea of going to the Naval Academy and becoming an admiral.

- ❑ Bill said what **ENAMORS** him is a good book.

- ❑ The **ENAMORING** quality of dogs is their devotion to their owners.

UTTER

(UH tur) *v.*

to speak; absolute; complete

Sounds like: **BUTTER**

*"When the **BUTTER** begins to **UTTER**"*

☐ Jean asked Max not to **UTTER** another word until he heard her side of the story.

☐ Harry and Billy crept into the cemetery in **UTTER** darkness.

☐ The **UTTER** daring of the ice box raid was beyond belief for two small dogs and a pet monkey.

EVIEW #9: Match the word with its definition.

<table>
<tr><td>. waft - (raft)</td><td>a.</td><td>to speak</td></tr>
<tr><td>. awry - (tie)</td><td>b.</td><td>to inspire with love</td></tr>
<tr><td>. perturb - (disturb)</td><td>c.</td><td>a gentle breeze</td></tr>
<tr><td>. bulletin - (bullet)</td><td>d.</td><td>filled with holes</td></tr>
<tr><td>. felon - (melon)</td><td>e.</td><td>twisted or turned</td></tr>
<tr><td>. stifle - (rifle)</td><td>f.</td><td>to hold back</td></tr>
<tr><td>. porous - (poor us)</td><td>g.</td><td>to disturb</td></tr>
<tr><td>3. limber - (lumber)</td><td>h.</td><td>brief announcement</td></tr>
<tr><td>). enamor - (hammer)</td><td>i.</td><td>flexible</td></tr>
<tr><td>0. utter - (butter)</td><td>j.</td><td>a serious criminal</td></tr>
</table>

Fill in the blanks with the appropriate word. The word form may need changing.

1. Jill asked Jack not to _____ another word.

2. Sponges are _____ marine creatures.

3. What _____ Bill of a girl is her cooking ability.

4. It was a boring party and Janet _____ a yawn.

5. A person convicted of a serious crime is a _____.

6. Our teacher posted the class grades on the _____ board.

7. The wind blew the window shades _____.

8. Ballet dancers have _____ muscles.

9. It _____ bees when you disturb their nest.

10. The smell of bacon cooking _____ through the cabin.

ADAGE

(AD ij) *n.*

a short traditional saying;
a proverb

Sounds like: **ADD AGE**

*"As we **ADD AGE**, we learn there
is truth in **ADAGES**."*

- Today, many large companies post **ADAGES** on their bulletin boards to inspire their employees.

- Our salesman, Homer, entertains his customers with an **ADAGE** for every occasion.

- "Give me liberty or give me death," is a famous American **ADAGE**.

CALAMITY

(Kuh LAM uh tee) *n.*
an event that causes great
misfortune; a disaster

Sounds like: **CLAM CITY**

*"A **CALAMITY** in **CLAM CITY**."*

- ❑ **CALAMITY** Jane was a figure from the old west who was aptly named because many misfortunes befell her.

- ❑ The movie was a **CALAMITY**; it cost twenty million to make and audiences hated it.

- ❑ Henry is a reckless driver and a **CALAMITY** waiting to happen.

SURVIVE

(sir VIVE) *v.*
to remain alive, to continue
living or existing

Sounds like: **STAY ALIVE**

*"Those who **SURVIVE, STAY ALIVE**."*

- Red Riding Hood is a children's story that will **SURVIVE** for centuries to come.

- The tomato crop **SURVIVED** the winter freezes.

- The campers went into the forest and **SURVIVED** on berries and edible plants for an entire week.

DISMANTLE
(dis MAN tul) *v.*
to take apart, pull down,
disassemble

Sounds like: **MANTLE**

*"Termites **DISMANTLING** the fireplace **MANTLE**"*

- We **DISMANTLED** the bicycles and packed them in shipping boxes.

- It was necessary to **DISMANTLE** the engine in order to clean it.

- **DISMANTLING** furniture is an everyday event for movers.

SLEAZY

(SLEE zee) *adj.*

of cheap quality; of low character

Sounds like: **FLEAS**

*"A **SLEAZY** dog with **SLEAZY FLEAS**."*

- ❑ The only place with rooms available was a **SLEAZY** hotel.

- ❑ Many tabloids are essentially **SLEAZY** gossip about celebrities.

- ❑ James bought a **SLEAZY** raincoat that leaked when it rained.

FALTER

(FALL tur) *v.*
to become weaker;
to be unsteady

Sounds like: **ALTAR**

*"The groom **FALTERED** at the **ALTAR**."*

- Paul's determination **FALTERED** when he saw the size of the mountain he hoped to climb.

- Tony stammered and **FALTERED** when it came his time to speak to the class.

- The swimmers **FALTERED** as the waves pushed them back.

ENCUMBER

(en KUM bur) *v.*
to weigh down unnecessarily;
to burden; to impede action

Sounds like: **CUCUMBER**

*"An **ENCUMBERED CUCUMBER**."*

- The boy scouts feared their canoe trip might be **ENCUMBERED** by a storm that afternoon.

- Favored to win the race, Stephanie came in second because she was **ENCUMBERED** by a sore ankle.

- His home was **ENCUMBERED** by a loan from the local bank.

EMBED

(im BED) *v.*

firmly fixed in a surrounding mass

Sounds like: **IN BED**

*"You can get **EMBEDDED IN BED** when you jump on it."*

- ❏ To **EMBED** wire in concrete will make the concrete stronger.

- ❏ A splinter was deeply **EMBEDDED** in Rachel's finger.

- ❏ Telephone poles are **EMBEDDED** deep in the ground so that they won't fall over.

OBTAIN

(ub TAIN) *v.*

to gain possession of; to acquire

Sounds like: **STAIN**

*"The clumsy waiter helped Joe **OBTAIN** a **STAIN**."*

- ❏ Henry **OBTAINED** permission to go swimming with his friends.

- ❏ Walter wanted to know the best way to **OBTAIN** a pass to the zoo.

- ❏ **OBTAINING** the ability to speak a second language makes it easier to travel abroad.

INTUITION

(in TOO ish uhn) *n.*
knowledge gained without
reasoning or proof

Sounds like: **INTO FISHIN'**

*"It didn't take **INTUITION** to know
Mr. Smith was **INTO FISHIN'**."*

❑ Joe said his **INTUITION** tells him the robbers will try again this week.

❑ Mary was a very **INTUITIVE** salesperson and knew how to sell her products.

❑ Allison's **INTUITION** told her not to drive to the grocery store while it was raining.

REVIEW #10: Match the word with its definition.

1. adage - (add age)
2. calamity - (clam city)
3. survive - (stay alive)
4. dismantle - (mantle)
5. sleazy - (fleas)
6. falter - (altar)
7. encumber - (cucumber)
8. embed - (in bed)
9. obtain - (stain)
10. intuition - (into fishin')

a. to surround
b. to weigh down
c. of cheap quality
d. a short saying
e. to be unsteady
f. to acquire
g. a disaster
h. to take apart
i. knowledge without reason
j. to remain alive

Fill in the blanks with the appropriate word. The word form may need changing.

1. The swimmers _____ in the high seas.

2. Her _____ told her it was best to stay home and not go to the dance.

3. John bought a _____ raincoat in a flea market.

4. The old professor had an amusing _____ for every occasion.

5. The spear was deeply _____ in the ground.

6. The earthquake was a _____ for the residents who lost their homes.

7. Red Riding Hood is a children's story that will _____ for centuries to come.

8. The horse moved slowly because he was _____ by three riders on his back.

9. It was necessary to _____ the engine in order to repair it.

10. Henry _____ permission to skip school on Monday.

Vocabulary Cartoons

RAGE

(rage) *n.*

violent, explosive anger;
a fad or craze

Sounds like: **CAGE**

*"Oscar **RAGES** when put into **CAGES**."*

- ☐ The crowd went into a **RAGE** when they heard the announcement that the concert was just cancelled.

- ☐ Going barefoot to class is the latest **RAGE**.

- ☐ The home owner **RAGED** at the firemen for coming late to the fire.

BURDEN

(BIRD in) *n.*
weighed down; an oppressive load;
something to be endured

Sounds like: **BIRD N**

*"The big **N** was a **BURDEN** for the **BIRD**."*

- The hikers carried their heavy **BURDEN** up the hill.
- Having eight children has been a **BURDEN** for her.
- George was **BURDENED** with sad memories of his long illness.

SCURRY

(SKUR ee) *v.*
to go or move quickly
in a hurried manner

Sounds like: **FURRY**

*"When a **FURRY** bear came up the tree, the
squirrels **SCURRIED** for cover."*

- ❑ The girls **SCURRIED** about and hurriedly dressed so as not to be late.

- ❑ We heard small feet **SCURRYING** up the stairs.

- ❑ The rabbits scampered and **SCURRIED** up the hill until they reached the cabbage patch.

DIVULGE
(duh VULGE) *v.*
to make known; reveal, tell

Sounds like: **BULGE**

*"The **BULGE DIVULGED** what
happened to Larry."*

- ❑ Harry would never **DIVULGE** something told to him in secret.

- ❑ The scientist **DIVULGED** information about UFOs that was top secret.

- ❑ The robbers never **DIVULGED** where they had hidden the gold.

ZANY

(ZAY nee) *adj.*

silly, funny; crazy but likable

Sounds like: **RAINY**

*"On **RAINY** days, frogs sing, dance and act **ZANY**."*

- ❑ We went to a crazy movie at the mall on Saturday night. It was really **ZANY**.

- ❑ The **ZANIEST** people I ever saw were an entire fraternity of guys trying to get into a telephone booth at the same time.

- ❑ It's good to see a little **ZANINESS** in young people having a good time.

FRENZY

(FREN zee) *n.*

a state of wild excitement

Sounds like: **FRIENDS EAT**

*"Every time I invite my **FRIENDS** over
to **EAT**, they go into a **FRENZY**."*

☐ The frightened dogs yelped and ran about in a
FRENZY.

☐ The sharks attacked the dead fish in a **FRENZY**.

☐ A **FRENZIED** commotion in the hallway caused a
crowd of students to gather.

CULPRIT

(KUL prit) *n.*

a person guilty of doing
something wrong

Sounds like: **PAW PRINTS**

*"The **PAW PRINTS** led to the **CULPRIT**."*

- ❏ The **CULPRIT** who swiped the tennis balls should put them back.

- ❏ Our dad is the **CULPRIT** who left the water running.

- ❏ It is the job of the police to catch **CULPRITS**.

SCOWL

(skowl) *n.*
an angry frown or
to make any angry facial expression (*v.*)

Sounds like: **OWL**

"SCOWLING OWLS"

- The witch's **SCOWL** scared the trick-or-treaters.

- George was a **SCOWLER** and always had a frown on his face.

- It is unfortunate that Mr. Smith has a natural **SCOWL**, everyone thinks he's angry.

DIVERGE
(duh VURJ) *v.*
to go in different directions
from a common point

Sounds like: **DIVERS**

*"When the octopus appeared, the **DIVERS DIVERGED**."*

- ❏ The search party met at the road crossing and then **DIVERGED** to search for the lost puppy.

- ❏ Our children all had **DIVERGENT** careers.

- ❏ The campers **DIVERGED** from the path and took a shortcut home.

JAR

(JAHR) *v.*

to bump or shake; to have an irritating effect

Sounds like: **JAR**

*"A **JARRING** experience by a **JAR**"*

- ☐ It was a **JARRING** experience when Mrs. Marsh told us that half the class had failed the exam.

- ☐ Rock and roll music **JARS** my parents' ears.

- ☐ The size of the whale **JARRED** the sensibilities of the crowd gathered on the beach.

EVIEW #11: Match the word with its definition.

. rage - (cage)
2. burden - (bird 'N)
3. scurry - (furry)
4. divulge - (bulge)
5. zany - (rainy)
6. frenzy - (friends eat)
7. culprit - (paw prints)
8. scowl - (owl)
9. diverge - (divers)
10. jar - (jar)

a. angry frown
b. explosive anger
c. to weigh down
d. to bump or shake
e. crazy but likable
f. move hurriedly
g. go in different directions
h. to reveal
i. a guilty person
j. wild excitement

Fill in the blanks with the appropriate word. The word form may need changing.

1. Mom wanted to know who was the _____ who tracked mud through her clean kitchen floor.

2. The movie was good, but was it _____.

3. Making a speech in a noisy room is a _____ experience.

4. The hikers _____ from the path and took a shortcut home.

5. The mountain climber carried a heavy _____.

6. The witch's _____ scared the trick-or-treaters.

7. We told the girls to stop _____ about and get dressed.

8. Never _____ anything told to you in secret.

9. The crowd went into a _____ when they heard the announcement that the concert was just cancelled.

10. The excited dogs barked and ran about in a _____.

INERT

(in URT) *adj.*
inactive, sluggish

Sounds like: **IN DIRT**

*"Worms are **INERT IN DIRT** during the winter."*

□ After Thanksgiving dinner, the family sat around and remained **INERT** the rest of the day.

□ The **INERTNESS** of pigs must be an inherited quality.

□ (To be **INERT** is an act of **INERTIA**.) When the motor quit, the car lacked **INERTIA** and rolled to a stop.

RAZE

(rays) *v.*

to level to the ground;
to tear down or demolish

Sounds like: **RAYS**

*"The alien **RAYS RAZED** the city."*

- The demolition team **RAZED** the building so that a new one could be constructed.

- Beach erosion has **RAZED** the good bathing beaches where we live.

- Bombs **RAZED** the town until not one building was left standing.

CREVICE

(KREV us) *n.*

a crack forming an opening

Sounds like: **CREVASSE (kruh VAS)**

*"A small **CREVICE** sometimes grows into a large **CREVASSE**."*

- Walter's lucky coin fell into a **CREVICE** between two stones and was never seen again.

- The farmer's weathered face was covered with wrinkles the size of small **CREVICES**.

- (A large **CREVICE** is called a **CREVASSE**.) The mountain climber's fingers slipped from a CREVICE in the rocks, and he fell into a CREVASSE a thousand feet deep.

NOVELTY

(NAHV ul tee) *n.*
newness

Sounds like: **NOVEL**

*"The first **NOVEL** was a **NOVELTY**."*

- The kids rode their new bikes all day until the **NOVELTY** wore off.

- When first invented, television sets were only an interesting **NOVELTY**.

- Visiting Walt Disney World for the first time is an enjoyable **NOVELTY**.

PALTRY

(PAWL tree) *adj.*

insignificant; of little value

Sounds like: **POULTRY**

"PALTRY POULTRY"

- Jake left the waitress a **PALTRY** tip because her service was poor.

- The **PALTRY** cowards ran from the battle and refused to defend their country.

- The lawyer was inexperienced and could manage only a **PALTRY** defense for his client.

DELECTABLE
(dee LEK tuh bul) *adj.*
pleasant, delightful, savory, delicious
Sounds like: **LICK THE BOWL**

*"Granny's pudding was so **DELECTABLE**, the family **LICKED THE BOWL**."*

- The guests said the dinner was **DELECTABLE**.

- All the frozen dinners look **DELECTABLE** in the grocery store, but sometimes the food is not as good as it looks.

- There is nothing that smells more **DELECTABLE** than bacon frying on an open campfire.

PERIL

(PEAR il) *n.*

something dangerous or risky; the condition of being in danger or at risk or harm

Sounds like: **PEARL**

*"The **PERILS** of **PEARL** diving."*

- Because he skipped school, Billy was in **PERIL** of losing his part in the school play.

- It is **PERILOUS** to ride a bicycle on the highway at night.

- One **PERIL** of sky diving is you could land in a cactus patch.

LULL

(lull) *v.*

to cause to sleep or rest;
a temporary period of calm (*n.*)

Sounds like: **DULL**

*"The movie was **DULL**; it
LULLED us to sleep."*

- ❏ The high winds finally **LULLED**.

- ❏ Laura's mom **LULLED** her to sleep by singing a soothing song.

- ❏ A **LULL** in the storm gave us a chance to run to our cars and get to safety.

DOUSE

(dows) *v.*

to immerse in liquid; to drench

Sounds like: **HOUSE**

*"Firemen **DOUSE** the burning **HOUSE**."*

- The fire started in the kitchen, but Billy had the good sense to **DOUSE** the flames before they spread.

- I quickly **DOUSED** the rumor I was leaving the school to study abroad.

- Mother **DOUSED** our dog in flea spray.

DERELICT

(DER uh likt) *adj.*
deserted, abandoned,
neglected; a bum (*n.*)

Sounds like: **DEER LICKED**

"DEER LICKING DERELICTS"

- A **DERELICT** ship, rusty and unpainted, lay anchored at the dock.

- Our coach was **DERELICT** in her duties and often missed team practices.

- **DERELICTS** who beg in the streets are often the product of broken homes and poor education.

REVIEW #12: Match the word with its definition.

1. inert - (in dirt)
2. raze - (rays)
3. crevice - (crevasse)
4. novelty - (novel)
5. paltry - (poultry)
6. delectable - (lick the bowl)
7. peril - (pearl)
8. lull - (dull)
9. douse - (house)
10. derelict - (deer licked)

a. to tear down
b. neglected, deserted
c. to immerse in liquid
d. inactive
e. period of calm
f. dangerous
g. delicious
h. newness
i. of little value
j. a crack

Fill in the blanks with the appropriate word. The word form may need changing.

1. Thanksgiving dinner looked _____.

2. The first novel was a _____ to readers.

3. A _____ ship was anchored at the dock.

4. Billy was in _____ of getting bad grades for his poor classroom conduct.

5. The demolition team prepared to _____ the building.

6. Snails are mostly _____ creatures.

7. Walter's lucky coin fell in the street and rolled into a _____.

8. Mother _____ our dog in flea spray.

9. A _____ in the rain gave us a chance to run home.

10. The unfriendly waitress received only a _____ tip.

Vocabulary Cartoons

NOURISH

(NUR ish) *v.*

to feed and provide the other things
necessary for life and growth

Sounds like: **NURSE**

*"A **NURSE's** job is to **NOURISH** the sick."*

☐ Jack had a petting zoo and **NOURISHED** the animals
with loving care.

☐ We **NOURISHED** hope that the mountain climbers
would make it back down the mountain safely.

☐ The baby was badly **MALNOURISHED** an in need of
NOURISHMENT.

SHACKLE

(SHAK ul) *v.*

to restrain or confine someone or something; a restraint (*n.*)

Sounds like: **TACKLE**

*"The guard **TACKLED** the last **SHACKLED** prisoner."*

- ❑ The **SHACKLES** of ignorance prevent many people from reaching their true potential.

- ❑ The dogs were **SHACKLED** within the small confines of the walled garden.

- ❑ Holding one's breath underwater is a **SHACKLING** experience.

FUTILE

(FYOO tul) *adj.*
having no useful result;
not successful; of no importance

Sounds like: **FLUTE**

*"Playing the **FLUTE** underwater is **FUTILE**."*

- ❑ It is **FUTILE** to argue that the moon is made of cheese.

- ❑ It was a grand idea, but the band's efforts to raise a million dollars for the school picnic was **FUTILE**.

- ❑ (**FUTILITY** is the condition of being **FUTILE**.) Randy's hope to run a three minute mile is an exercise in **FUTILITY**.

EXPLORE

(ex PLOR) *v.*

to search for or travel for the purpose
of discovery; to investigate carefully

Sounds like: **FLOOR**

*"Toddlers like to **EXPLORE** on the **FLOOR**."*

- John and his friends went to Alaska to **EXPLORE** for gold.

- Billy wanted to **EXPLORE** the old haunted house on Halloween.

- The **EXPLORATION** of the North Pole took six months.

CRAM

(kram) *v.*

to fill completely or with more than is normally or easily held; to force into a tight place; to study hastily

Sounds like: **EXAM**

FINAL EXAM TODAY

*"It appeared that Jimmy **CRAMMED** too much for his **EXAM**."*

- ❑ We tried to **CRAM** our clothes into one small bag, but it split open on the way to the airport.

- ❑ The hungry guest **CRAMMED** half a turkey into his mouth.

- ❑ The streets were **CRAMMED** with cars after the game.

WRENCH

(rench) v.

to pull or turn suddenly; to twist or sprain;
a sudden surge of emotion; a tool used for
holding or turning an object (n.)

Sounds like: **WRENCH**

"A WRENCHING WRENCH"

☐ Harry **WRENCHED** his ankle playing basketball.

☐ The audience felt a **WRENCHING** pang of sorrow for
the orphan in the movie.

☐ It was a **WRENCHING** experience to visit my sister in
the hospital.

TURNCOAT

(turn koat) *n.*

a person who goes over to the
other side; a renegade; a traitor

Sounds like: **TURN COAT**

*"Benedict Arnold was a **TURNCOAT** in the American
Revolution (who **TURNED** his **COAT**
in favor of the British.)"*

❑ Herman became a **TURNCOAT** when he quit the
Panthers and went over to the Bulldogs.

❑ When the going gets rough, **TURNCOATS** show their
true colors.

❑ It's hard to call Butch a **TURNCOAT** on account of his
changing sides every week.

RECITE

(ree SITE) *v.*

to speak aloud before an audience;
to tell in detail

Sounds like: **TIGHT**

*"Jimmy's mouth shut **TIGHT** when it
came his turn to **RECITE**."*

- ❑ It took an hour for Helen to **RECITE** all her problems
  with her older sisters.

- ❑ Last night's dance **RECITAL** was very interesting.

- ❑ Mike's **RECITATION** of his poems was met with great
  applause.

COMPILE

(kum PILE) *v.*

to gather together facts from different sources into a report or a book

Sounds like: **COME PILE**

*"The professors were invited to **COME** and **PILE** all their ideas together to **COMPILE** a book."*

- ❑ The authors **COMPILES** a special dictionary of aviation terms.

- ❑ The class was assigned the task of **COMPILING** the records on the baseball team for the past ten years.

- ❑ History books are usually the **COMPILATION** of many events.

DETAIN

(di TANE or dee TANE) *v.*
to keep from proceeding; delay, retard;
to keep in custody, confine

Sounds like: **THE TRAIN**

"The bandit DETAINED THE TRAIN."

- Our ship was **DETAINED** for three months in the Panama Canal because it had developed a leak in the hull.

- The customs agents **DETAINED** the man for three hours while they searched his luggage for drugs.

- The defensive tactics of the rebel forces were designed to **DETAIN** their enemies' advances.

REVIEW #13: Match the word with its definition.

nourish - (nurse)
shackle - (tackle)
futile - (flute)
explore - (floor)
cram - (exam)
wrench - (wrench)
turncoat - (turn coat)
recite - (tight)
compile - (come pile)
detain - (train)

a. to restrain
b. help grow
c. with no useful result
d. search for
e. a traitor
f. to gather together
g. to delay
h. speak aloud
i. turn suddenly
j. study hastily

Fill in the blanks with the appropriate word. The word form may need changing.

1. Benedict Arnold was a _____ during the American Revolution.

2. It is no fun to be in prison and wear a _____.

3. Harry felt a _____ pain in his arm when he fell to the ground.

4. The writer wanted to _____ all his ideas into a book.

5. We tried to _____ all our clothes into one suitcase.

6. The high wall outside the fort was built to _____ the enemy.

7. A nurse's job is to _____ the sick.

8. It took an hour for Elizabeth to _____ all her problems.

9. John went to Alaska to _____ for gold.

10. It is _____ to argue with a stubborn person.

VEX

(veks) *v.*

to annoy; to pester; to puzzle

Sounds like: **PECKS**

"Woodpeckers VEX trees with their PECKS."

- □ It was a **VEXING** situation when Marlene made dates with two boys at the same time.

- □ We were **VEXED** with fear when we entered the haunted house.

- □ Karen **VEXED** me by always being late.

MINISCULE
(MI nus kyool) *adj.*
very small

Sounds like: **MINI SCHOOL**

*"Roger's **MINISCULE MINI SCHOOL**"*

- ❑ It only takes a **MINISCULE** crack in a dam to start a flood.

- ❑ Jane explained she had turned her back only for a **MINISCULE** moment, but it was long enough for her baby sister to stick her entire face into the lemon pie.

- ❑ The teacher gave us a **MINISCULE** amount of time to finish our math exam.

WADDLE

(WAH dul) *v.*
to walk with short steps swaying
from side to side

Sounds like: **BOTTLE**

*"Babies with **BOTTLES WADDLE**"*

- Ducks always **WADDLE** when they walk.

- Sailors on ships **WADDLE**.

- Larry **WADDLED** from the dinner table after eating his third helping of apple pie.

DETEST

(dee TEST) *v.*
to dislike intensely; to hate

Sounds like: **TEST**

"Dave DETESTS taking TESTS."

- ❑ Many people **DETEST** spiders and snakes.

- ❑ Alice has **DETESTED** swimming ever since she fell into the pool.

- ❑ Jack has a **DETESTABLE** habit of picking his nose during lunch.

REFRAIN

(ree FRAIN) *v.*

to keep oneself from doing, saying, or thinking something; a phrase that repeats itself in a song or poem

Sounds like: **RAIN**

*"Friendly clouds trying to **REFRAIN** from dropping their **RAIN**"*

- ❏ The sergeant could not **REFRAIN** from telling his new recruits they were a bunch of nerds.

- ❏ Some songs have a **REFRAIN** at the end of every stanza.

- ❏ The police **REFRAINED** from making any arrests until they had collected all the evidence.

WINDFALL
(WIN fall) *n.*
unexpected good fortune; something
blown down by the wind

Sounds like: **FALLING WIND**

*"A **WINDFALL** caused by the **FALLING WIND**."*

- ❑ Helen's aunt died and her inheritance was a **WINDFALL**.

- ❑ A **WINDFALL** of apples blew down in the storm and ruined the farmers crop.

- ❑ The Smiths won a million dollar **WINDFALL** in the lottery.

FRUGAL

(FREW gul) *adj.*
saving; sparing

Sounds like: **BUGLE**

*"What happens when a **FRUGAL** bugler buys a cheap **BUGLE**"*

- The poor farmers could only afford a **FRUGAL** meal of rabbit and sweet potatoes.

- To be **FRUGAL** does not mean to be cheap. Sometimes real **FRUGALITY** is to buy the best that will last the longest.

- "Save your pennies and the dollars will take care of themselves" is an expression of **FRUGALITY**.

THROTTLE

(THRAH tul) *v.*
to strangle; a valve or peddle
that regulates the flow of a fluid (*n.*)

Sounds like: **BOTTLE**

*"When you want to **THROTTLE** a **BOTTLE**"*

- ❏ Phil's mom threatened to **THROTTLE** him if he tracked dirt into the house one more time.

- ❏ The race car was speeding at full **THROTTLE** when it crossed the finish line and won the race.

- ❏ When we reached the fishing hole, the captain **THROTTLED** back the engine.

IMPALE

(im PALE) *v.*

to pierce through with any sharp pointed object

Sounds like: **PAIL**

*"An **IMPALED PAIL**"*

- ❑ The sales clerk **IMPALED** his sales order on a nail.

- ❑ Roger fell on a stick and **IMPALED** his hand.

- ❑ Butterfly collections usually consist of dead butterflies that have been **IMPALED** and placed in display cases.

GARBLE

(GAR bul) *v.*

to confuse, to jumble

Sounds like: **GARGLE**

"Henry, you sound GARBLED when you GARGLE."

- In the hurricane, the sinking ship's radio message was **GARBLED**.

- Suzy was so excited she **GARBLED** everything she wanted to say.

- We couldn't finish building the dog house because the instructions were **GARBLED**.

REVIEW #14: Match the word with its definition.

1. vex - (pecks)
2. miniscule - (mini school)
3. waddle - (bottle)
4. detest - (test)
5. refrain - (rain)
6. windfall - (wind fall)
7. frugal - (bugle)
8. throttle - (bottle)
9. impale - (pail)
10. garble - (gargle)

a. a swaying walk
b. saving; sparing
c. to pester
d. unexpected fortune
e. tiny
f. dislike a lot
g. not to do something
h. to strangle
i. to jumble, confuse
j. to pierce through

Fill in the blanks with the appropriate word. The word form may need changing.

1. Woodpeckers _____ trees with their pecks.

2. When Henry is angry he cannot _____ from speaking his mind.

3. Helen was very _____ and rarely spent money on herself.

4. The sinking ship's radio message was _____.

5. Roger fell on a stick and _____ his hand.

6. Jack's unexpected _____ was when he won the lottery.

7. It only takes a _____ leak in a dam to start a flood.

8. The race car was speeding at full _____ when it crossed the finish line.

9. Ducks _____ when they walk.

10. Many people _____ spiders and snakes.

Vocabulary Cartoons

PACIFY

(PAS uh fye) *v.*

to have a calming effect

Sounds like: **PACIFIER**

*"**PACIFIERS** are great for **PACIFYING** crying babies."*

- The nurse was unable to **PACIFY** the patient when he learned his was had also been injured in their auto accident.

- The troops were **PACIFIED** when they had a hot meal and a good night sleep.

- Johnny declined to be drafted into military service and declared himself a **PACIFIST**.

BILK

(bilk) *v.*

to defraud, to cheat or swindle;
escape paying one's debts

Sounds like: **MILK**

"BILKING MILK"

- Laura's sister **BILKED** the cookie jar until she was finally caught.

- The **BILKING** practices of the insurance salesman finally landed him in jail.

- Ed came to the conclusion that he was being **BILKED** by his brother-in-law.

EXPEDITE
(EK spuh dite) *v.*
to speed up the progress of something

Sounds like: **EXTRA MIGHT**

*"Super Stork's **EXTRA MIGHT** helped
EXPEDITE his large baby shipment."*

- When the war broke out the army needed all supplies to be **EXPEDITED** to the front line.

- Jean's telephone call to her travel agent **EXPEDITED** delivery of the airplane tickets.

- In order to keep productivity high, many factories hire an **EXPEDITER**.

COMMUTER

(kah MYOO tur) *n.*
a person who travels from home
to work and back

Sounds like: **COMPUTER**

*"A **COMMUTER COMPUTER** on his way to work"*

- Students in Alaska often **COMMUTE** a hundred miles each day because schools are so far away.

- Many **COMMUTERS** in big cities have car pools and take turns driving to work.

- **COMMUTING** long distances from home to work is much easier now that there are freeways.

MAR

(mar) *v.*

to render less attractive, less useful;
to spoil to a certain extent

Sounds like: **CAR**

*"Dad, don't get excited; your **CAR'S** only
MARRED a tiny bit."*

- Our vacation was **MARRED** by stormy weather.

- Our coach was afraid we might **MAR** the gym floor with our baseball shoes.

- Tina's natural physical beauty was **MARRED** by her disagreeable personality.

GENTEEL

(jen TEEL) *adj.*
polite; refined

Sounds like: **FIN FEEL**

*"Porpoises are **GENTEEL** in nature and
don't mind a friendly **FIN FEEL**."*

- Jane was born into a high society where the people are taught to be **GENTEEL**.

- Even though John was a tough football player, he was an aristocrat with **GENTEEL** qualities when he was off the playing field.

- One who is **GENTEEL** has the quality of **GENTILITY**.

RUE

(roo) *v.*

to feel regret or sorrow

Sounds like: **SHOE**

*"Hillbilly Bob **RUED** the day he agreed to wear **SHOES** into town."*

- Jenny told Bob he would **RUE** the day he stepped on her toes.

- Phil **RUED** the day he decided not to go to college.

- Josh was a **RUEFUL** figure when his bike was stolen. (**RUEFUL** means inspiring pity or compassion.)

PLUMB

(plum) *adj.*

straight up and down, vertical;
completely, utterly

Sounds like: **THUMB**

*"Whenever you give the 'THUMBS up' sign,
your THUMB is PLUMB."*

- The **PLUMB** line recorded the water depth at eighteen feet.

- The telephone pole stood **PLUMB** to the ground.

- The water barrel is **PLUMB** full.

PRONE

(prohn) *adj.*
tending or inclined to
something; lying flat

Sounds like: **PHONE**

*"Teenagers are **PRONE** to spend hours on the
PHONE lying **PRONE**."*

❑ From a **PRONE** position it is difficult to skip rope.

❑ Jack and Jill are **PRONE** to go up almost any hill they
come across.

❑ Parents are **PRONE** to worry about their children.

WILT

(wilt) *v.*

to become limp, to droop down;
to be deprived of energy

Sounds like: **TILT**

*"Flowers **TILT** when they begin to **WILT**."*

- ❏ We **WILTED** after climbing the mountain in the summer heat.

- ❏ It was a **WILTING** day and everyone stayed inside and enjoyed the air conditioning.

- ❏ After a few days in the store, vegetables will begin to shrivel up and look **WILTED**.

pacify - (pacifier)
bilk - (milk)
expedite - (extra might)
commuter - (computer)
mar - (car)
genteel - (fin feel)
rue - (shoe)
plumb - (thumb)
prone - (phone)
wilt - (tilt)

a. one who travels back and forth
b. polite; refined
c. up and down
d. become limp
e. lying flat
f. to regret
g. to spoil
h. to speed up
i. cheat or swindle
j. to calm

Fill in the blanks with the appropriate word. The word form may need changing.

1. In big cities there are many workers who are daily _____.

2. John knew he would _____ the day he quit college.

3. The merchant was careful not to let his customers _____ him.

4. Our postman always tries to _____ delivery of Christmas packages.

5. Our coach warned us not to _____ the gym floor with our hard-sole shoes.

6. People of high society are thought to be _____.

7. The nurse was unable to _____ the patient.

8. From a _____ position it is difficult to skip rope.

9. Flowers tilt when they begin to _____.

10. The telephone pole was _____ to the ground.

HOSPITABLE

(hos PIT uh bul) *adj.*
receiving guests warmly;
having an open mind

Sounds like: **HOSPITAL**

*"An overly **HOSPITABLE HOSPITAL**"*

- The hotel guests were treated **HOSPITABLY**.

- Honduras has a climate **HOSPITABLE** to growing bananas.

- John has always been **HOSPITABLE** to new ideas.

UNWIELDY
(un WEEL dee) *adj.*
hard to handle or
manage; clumsy

Sounds like: **WHEEL**

*"The first **WHEELS** were a bit **UNWIELDY**."*

- The moving men had a heck of a time getting our **UNWIELDY** piano out the front door and down the steps.

- Pushing the stalled car off the highway was an **UNWIELDY** task.

- For a man of three hundred pounds, you would think Clarence would be **UNWIELDY**, but he sure could dance.

GRAPH

(graf) *n.*

a drawing that demonstrates the relationship between changing things

Sounds like: **RAFT**

*"Keeping a **GRAPH** on a **RAFT**"*

- ❑ Mr. Jones kept a **GRAPH** to show how much his apple tree had grown each year.

- ❑ A **GRAPH** of the population of the United States would show that it is growing more than two percent each year.

- ❑ On Wall Street, the stock brokers keep **GRAPHS** of the ups and downs of the stock market.

EXTREMITY

(ik STREM uh tee) *n.*
the outermost part or edge;
the greatest degree

Sounds like: **TRIM A TREE**

*"The gardener **TRIMMED A TREE'S EXTREMITIES.**"*

❑ In the coldest weather, a person's **EXTREMITIES**, that is, their feet and hands, suffer the most.

❑ The diver stood at the **EXTREMITY** of the cliff and dived into the sea below.

❑ Even in the **EXTREMITY** of his depression, Ray smiled bravely and was pleasant to those around him.

INCOME

(IN kum) *n.*
money received from work
or from investments

Sounds like: **BUM**

*"A **BUM** has no **INCOME**."*

- Mary was retired and received a steady retirement **INCOME** from the government.

- Harold lost his job five months ago and has had no **INCOME** since.

- Everyone pays taxes on their **INCOME**. It's called **INCOME** tax.

TIRADE

(TYE raid) *n.*

a long, angry, or scolding speech

Sounds like: **TIE RAID**

*"Mr. Cohen fell into a **TIRADE** when he discovered his children's **TIE RAID**."*

- When we lost the game by two points, our coach began an angry **TIRADE** that lasted an hour.

- John's mom went into a **TIRADE** when John wouldn't clean his closet.

- My boss flew into a **TIRADE** when I showed up for work late for the third time this week.

PROBE

(prohb) *v.*

an exploratory action; an expedition; an instrument used to explore or investigate (*n.*)

Sounds like: **ROBE**

*"Astronauts **PROBE** the lunar surface in their **ROBES**."*

- ❑ The doctor carefully **PROBED** the injured area with his metal **PROBES**.

- ❑ The expedition **PROBED** deeply into the heart of the Brazilian jungle.

- ❑ The school board is **PROBING** the reason for the teachers' strike.

COLLAPSE
(KAH laps) *v.*
to fall down; to fail; the complete loss of strength

Sounds like: **TOE TAPS**

*"All the **TOE TAPS COLLAPSED** the floor."*

- ❑ The runner **COLLAPSED** and fell down half way through the race.

- ❑ The weight of the circus fat man **COLLAPSED** the bed.

- ❑ Many buildings **COLLAPSED** during the earthquake.

COMPATIBLE

(kum PA tuh bul) *adj.*

suitable; capable of living or existing together in agreement and harmony

Sounds like: **PAT AND BULL**

*"**PAT AND** the **BULL** are **COMPATIBLE** roommates."*

- The fishing rod is **COMPATIBLE** with the fishing reel.

- Sarah painted her living room a color **COMPATIBLE** with the furniture she bought.

- The exotic palm tree we just planted my not be **COMPATIBLE** with our winter weather.

GALL

(gawl) *v.*
to irritate

Sounds like: **PAUL**

***"PAUL GALLED** everyone at the funeral."*

- Discourtesy **GALLS** most people as much as dishonesty.

- The saddle **GALLED** the horse's back.

- Sadie said she found it **GALLING** to be stood up by her date for the dance.

REVIEW #16: Match the word with its definition.

1. hospitable - (hospital)
2. unwieldy - (wheel)
3. graph - (raft)
4. extremity - (trim a tree)
5. income - (bum)
6. tirade - (tie raid)
7. probe - (robe)
8. collapse - (toe taps)
9. compatible - (Pat and bull)
10. gall - (Paul)

a. money from work
b. to irritate
c. living in harmony
d. outermost part
e. angry speech
f. a relationship drawing
g. to explore
h. hard to handle
i. having an open mind
j. to fall down

Fill in the blanks with the appropriate word. The word form may need changing.

1. We were afraid George would _____ when he heard the tragic news.

2. Telescopes _____ the skies to learn about distant planets.

3. _____ are helpful for observing changes in the stock market.

4. The hikers stood at the _____ of the cliff.

5. James had the _____ to come to the fancy wedding in his jeans.

6. John has always been _____ to new ideas.

7. Pushing the stalled car was an _____ chore.

8. A person in the midst of a _____ is not easy to talk with.

9. Most elderly people receive a retirement _____ from the government.

10. Bill and Jack are _____ friends.

MENTOR

(MEN tor) *n.*

a trusted advisor who is experienced and is teaching an inexperienced person

Sounds like: **MEN SOAR**

*"Their **MENTOR** taught the **MEN** to **SOAR**."*

- ❏ Joyce had many music teachers, but she considered Mrs. Livingston her only **MENTOR**.

- ❏ It is important in business to have a **MENTOR** who can advise you.

- ❏ Phil was more than a coach; he was a **MENTOR** to the young players on the team.

GORGE

(gorj) *v.*

to stuff oneself with food; also a steep narrow passage with steep sides

Sounds like: **GEORGE**

"GEORGE GORGED himself at every opportunity."

- ❏ A small stream ran through the **GORGE** below the cliffs.

- ❏ The team members **GORGED** themselves with pizza.

- ❏ All day without food, Jack **GORGED** his dinner like he hadn't eaten for a month.

TIMID

(TIM id) *adj.*

shy, hesitant, fearful

Sounds like: **TIM HID**

HAPPY BIRTHDAY TIM!

HEY, WHERE'S TIM?

FWEEEE!

"TIM HID at his own birthday party because he was TIMID."

❑ Our dog **TIMIDLY** approached the dinner table because he knew he was not allowed to beg for food.

❑ **TIMID** salespeople usually do not do well.

❑ The **TIMIDITY** of the welcoming committee was due to the fact they were not sure who they were supposed to be welcoming.

IDEAL

(eye DEEL) *adj.*
a situation said to be perfect; the best result or goal of something

Sounds like: **MEAL**

*"The **IDEAL MEAL**"*

- ☐ It was an **IDEAL** day for going swimming in the lake.

- ☐ **IDEALLY**, the best type of government would be one that didn't require taxes.

- ☐ The **IDEAL** location for a motel is next to a restaurant.

FRET

(fret) *v.*

to be troubled or worried

Sounds like: **PET**

*"Zachary's mom began to **FRET** when
his **PET** grew to full-size."*

☐ Carl **FRETTED** over every little thing.

☐ The team tried not to **FRET** their coach unnecessarily.

☐ Carla **FRETTED** away her vacation worrying about all the homework she still had left to do.

DAZE

(daze) *adj.*

a stunned or confused condition,
as with a blow, shock, or surprise

Sounds like: **DAYS**

*"After his car accident, Richard was
in a **DAZE** for **DAYS**."*

- ❑ The roar of the waterfall **DAZED** and deafened the tourists.

- ❑ Walter has been walking around in a **DAZE** ever since he won first place in the whistling contest.

- ❑ The contender was **DAZED** after he received a series of blows to the head.

BEHOOVE
(bee HOOV) *v.*
to be necessary, proper, or advantageous for

Sounds like: **MOVE**

*"I believe it **BEHOOVES** us to **MOVE**."*

- It **BEHOOVES** athletes to prepare for their sport by constantly practicing.

- We are **BEHOOVED** to meet with the governor upon his arrival.

- It **BEHOOVES** students to do their homework promptly and on time.

RATIFY

(RAT uh fye) *v.*

to approve something formally;
to confirm

Sounds like: **RAT AND FLY**

*"The **RAT AND** the **FLY RATIFIED** their garbage
agreement and shook hands on it."*

- ❑ The State of Texas **RATIFIED** an agreement with the State of Oklahoma.

- ❑ The latest law on crime was **RATIFIED** last month.

- ❑ The students met to **RATIFY** their decision to take an extra week off for Christmas vacation.

VAST

(vast) *adj.*
very large in intensity,
degree, or size

Sounds like: **MAST**

*"A **VAST MAST** creates problems for sailors."*

- A **VAST** amount of money was stolen from the bank.

- The **VASTNESS** of the universe we live in is almost beyond belief.

- There was a **VAST** difference between our opinions.

BELITTLE

(bee LIT ul) *v.*

to speak of or think of as unimportant;
to put someone down

Sounds like: **LITTLE**

*"Johnny felt **LITTLE** when Miss Tronkin
scolded and **BELITTLED** him."*

- ❏ It is not fair to **BELITTLE** another person's opinion when you aren't sure of all the facts.

- ❏ The students worked hard to collect rocks, but the field trip leader **BELITTLED** their efforts.

REVIEW #17: Match the word with its definition.

mentor - (men soar)   a. to be necessary
gorge - (George)   b. shy; hesitant
timid - (Tim hid)   c. a stunned condition
ideal - (meal)   d. put someone down
fret - (pet)   e. to worry
daze - (days)   f. to stuff oneself
behoove - (move)   g. very large
ratify - (rat and fly) h. formal approval
vast - (mast)   i. perfect
belittle - (little)   j. teacher

Fill in the blanks with the appropriate word. The word form may need changing.

1. John was in a _____ after the auto accident.

2. The students met to _____ their decision.

3. Jane is quiet and very _____ around other people.

4. It was an _____ day for going to the beach.

5. The children try not to _____ their mother over little things.

6. Professor Jones was my history _____.

7. It _____ students to do their homework on time.

8. Never _____ anyone's beliefs different from your own.

9. A _____ amount of money was missing from the bank.

10. As long as their is something to eat, Phil will _____ himself.

COLLIDE

(kuh LIDE) _v._

to come or strike together in a violent manner;
to meet in opposition; to disagree forcefully

Sounds like: **SLIDE**

"Two kids about to **COLLIDE** on a **SLIDE**"

- ❑ Both cars were wrecked when they **COLLIDED** on the highway.

- ❑ The opinions of the two attorneys **COLLIDED** over the way to settle the lawsuit.

- ❑ Mary and Sue were on a **COLLISION** course ever since both announced they would enter the beauty contest.

ATTRACT

(uh TRAKT) *v.*
to cause to draw near by
some quality or action

Sounds like: **ATTACK**

"The rare 'birdbath cat' has a sneaky way to
ATTRACT *its prey before it* ***ATTACKS."***

- The beautiful Florida beaches **ATTRACT** millions of tourists each year.

- Nails are **ATTRACTED** to magnets by magnetic force.

- Exciting rides are the major **ATTRACTIONS** of amusement parks.

VEGETATE

(VEJ uh tate) *v.*

to lead a life characterized by little physical or mental effort; also to grow as a plant grows

Sounds like: **VEGETABLE**

"VEGETATING VEGETABLES"

- Norma's husband hasn't had a job in six years. He just sits on the porch, eats cake and **VEGETATES**.

- After **VEGETATING** for three months during summer vacation, the kids were eager to return to school.

- When my vacation comes around in July, the only thing I want to do is to go to the beach and **VEGETATE**.

DUCTILE

(DUK tul) *adj.*

capable of being formed or shaped without breaking

Sounds like: **DUCK PULL**

"A DUCTILE DUCK PULL"

❑ Gold is a **DUCTILE** metal and can be drawn into thin wire or sheets.

❑ All children know how **DUCTILE** rubber bands can be.

❑ Plastic pipe is **DUCTILE** if heated.

WHET

(wet) *v.*

to sharpen as a knife;
to make keen or eager

Sounds like: **WET**

KNIVES SHARPENED

*"Dummy; I said **WHET**, not **WET!**"*

- The smell of bacon cooking **WHETTED** our appetite for breakfast.

- Champion tennis players **WHET** their skills by practicing every day.

- The knife thrower **WHETTED** his eagerness for the knife throwing contest by **WHETTING** his knives.

DISPUTE

(dis pyoot) *v.*

to argue; to question the validity of;
a verbal controversy; to resist

Sounds like: **THEY SHOOT**

*"In the old West, when in **DISPUTE**, **THEY SHOOT**."*

- ❏ The long running **DISPUTE** between Joe and Ed was never settled until Ed died.

- ❏ "I **DISPUTE** that argument, sir," said the senator from Georgia.

- ❏ There were many **DISPUTES** among the delegates when it came time to vote on the public transportation issues.

TOXIC

(TAWK sik) *adj.*
having the effect of a poison

Sounds like: **SICK**

*"Some snakebites are **TOXIC** and
can make you **SICK**."*

- ❑ Tobacco smoke is **TOXIC** to anyone who breathes it.

- ❑ A garbage dump contains many **TOXIC** materials such as oils and pesticide residues.

- ❑ Some shellfish contain a **TOXIN** that can make you sick if you eat them.

FLEE

(flee) *v.*

to run away from danger or trouble; to escape from

Sounds like: **FLEA**

"FLEAS FLEEING from FLEA spray"

- ❏ The golfers were told to **FLEE** the golf course if they heard a lightning storm approaching.

- ❏ The family quickly **FLED** from the burning house.

- ❏ The darkness **FLED** quickly when the dawn broke over the horizon.

SENILE

(SEE nile) *adj.*

the weakening of mental or physical abilities due to old age

Sounds like: **SEE THE NILE**

*"A lot of **SENILE** tourists visit Egypt and **SEE THE NILE** River."*

- ❑ My grandfather wasn't really **SENILE**. He has just always been forgetful.

- ❑ The **SENILITY** of the carpenter was obvious. His hands shook, and he had trouble seeing the nails.

- ❑ **SENILITY** sometimes accompanies old age.

OBSCURE

(ob SKYOOR) *adj.*

hard to understand; not clear or
distinct; hidden; not well known

Sounds like: **NOT SURE**

*"The signs were so **OBSCURE**, Tim was
NOT SURE which way to go."*

❏ The outline of the trees in the forest grew **OBSCURE**
as darkness fell.

❏ Jack was an **OBSCURE** artist, and his paintings were
known only to his relatives and friends.

❏ The directions dad gave us were **OBSCURE** and we
ended up getting lost.

REVIEW #18: Match the word with its definition.

1. collide (slide)
2. attract - (attack)
3. vegetate - (vegetable)
4. ductile - (duck pull)
5. whet - (wet)
6. dispute - (they shoot)
7. toxic - (sick)
8. flee - (flea)
9. senile - (see the Nile)
10. obscure - (not sure)

a. poisonous
b. run away from
c. to argue
d. mentally weak
e. hard to understand
f. strike together
g. to sharpen
h. easily shaped
i. to put out little effort
j. to draw toward

Fill in the blanks with the appropriate word. The word form may need changing.

1. Florida beaches _____ millions of tourists each year.

2. Gold is a _____ metal and is easily shaped without breaking.

3. Josh is so lazy, he sits on his porch and _____ all summer.

4. The outline of the mountains became _____ as darkness fell

5. The smell of hot apple pie will _____ the appetite.

6. The venom from poisonous snakes is _____.

7. The long running _____ between Joe and Ed was never settled until Ed died.

8. Grandfather isn't really _____; he has just always been forgetful.

9. Both cars were wrecked when they _____.

10. Fleas will _____ from flea spray.

Vocabulary Cartoons

NEOPHYTE
(NEE uh fite) *n.*
a beginner, a novice

Sounds like: **KITE**

*"Steve was a **NEOPHYTE** at
KITE flying."*

- Charlie was such a **NEOPHYTE** that he did know where to place the chess pieces on the board.

- Only a **NEOPHYTE** would forget to bring his bathing suit to a beach party.

- The young cowboys were **NEOPHYTES** at herding the cattle.

VOCATION

(voh KAY shun) *n.*
an occupation; a job; what a
person does for a living

Sounds like: **VACATION**

*"Some people have a **VOCATION** that is
more like a **VACATION**."*

- **VOCATIONALLY**, Marcie works as a beautician.

- In the evenings George went to **VOCATIONAL** school to study computer programming.

- George's **VOCATION** is an auto mechanic, but his **AVOCATION** is growing miniature orchids on the weekends. (A **VOCATION** is your job, while an **AVOCATION** is your hobby.)

FEAT

(feet) *n.*

an outstanding accomplishment

Sounds like: **SEAT**

*"An outstanding **FEAT** performed on a **SEAT**"*

- The bridge was a **FEAT** of engineering.

- Hercules was known for performing **FEATS** of great strength.

- Roger was precocious and could perform unusual **FEATS** of juggling even before he learned to walk.

GLOWER
(GLAU er) *v.*
to look or stare with dislike

Sounds like: **FLOWER**

"Never GLOWER at a FLOWER."

- ☐ The unfriendly track team **GLOWERED** at us when they climbed off the bus.

- ☐ **GLOWERING** at all the other cats, our cat scared them away from his dinner.

- ☐ Our friendly dog has such a fierce looking face that everyone thinks he **GLOWERS** at them.

CAPSIZE
(KAP size) *v.*
to overturn; upset
Sounds like: **CAP SIZE**

*"The **SIZE** of Tim's **CAP**
made him **CAPSIZE**."*

- ❏ The rescue ship saved the passengers after their boat **CAPSIZED**.

- ❏ Standing up in a wooden canoe is a sure way to make it **CAPSIZE**.

- ❏ The sailors held on to the sides of the boat after it **CAPSIZED**.

LATITUDE

(LAT uh tewd) *n.*
distance from North or South Pole;
permitting freedom or action or thought

Sounds like: **ATTITUDE**

*"Elizabeth's parent's **ATTITUDE** gave her plenty of **LATITUDE** in her pet selection."*

❑ Mrs. Miller was a teacher who gave her students a lot of **LATITUDE** in studying for exams.

❑ Circus high wire walkers have little **LATITUDE** as to where they must step.

❑ The ship sailed along **LATITUDE** 29 degrees north.

WARBLE

(WAR bul) *v.*
to sing or whistle in
a special way; to babble

Sounds like: **MARBLE**

*"When birds **WARBLED**, John threw **MARBLES**."*

- Swiss yodelers **WARBLE** from mountain tops.

- It takes a special talent to **WARBLE** like a bird.

- Canaries are known for their **WARBLING**.

- Jack said his barber was a big talker and **WARBLED** every minute he was in the barber's chair.

ANGUISH

(ANG gwish) *n.*

strong physical or mental pain

Sounds like: **SANDWICH**

*"Robert was starving and in such **ANGUISH**
he ate a rat **SANDWICH**."*

- The family suffered terrible **ANGUISH** until the baby was found unharmed.

- The **ANGUISH** of automobile accident victims crying out is a terrible thing to hear.

- We saw the **ANGUISHED** faces of the hurricane victims on television.

JOCULAR

(JAWK yuh lur) *v.*
to be jolly; fond of
joking or jesting

Sounds like: **JOCKEY**

*"A **JOCULAR JOCKEY** and his **JOCULAR** horse"*

- Everyone was laughing and in a **JOCULAR** mood at the school picnic.

- The band leader was fond of making **JOCULAR** remarks about his band members.

- People with **JOCULAR** natures smile a lot.

SUPPLE

(SUH pul) *adj.*
easily bent or folded; moving or changing easily

Sounds like: **SUPPER**

*"Alysia was so **SUPPLE** she could eat her **SUPPER** backwards."*

- ❑ The leather purse was **SUPPLE** and soft to the touch.

- ❑ Rose had a **SUPPLE** mind and was quick to follow any conversation.

- ❑ With the **SUPPLEST** of movements, the thief jumped out of the window and fled.

VIEW #19: Match the word with its definition.

neophyte - (kite)
vocation - (vacation)
feat - (seat)
glower - (flower)
capsize - (cap size)
latitude - (attitude)
warble- (marble)
anguish - (sandwich)
jocular - (jockey)
supple - (supper)

a. big accomplishment
b. sing or whistle
c. to be jolly
d. a beginner
e. freedom of action
f. occupation
g. ugly stare
h. easily bent
i. to overturn
j. strong pain

ill in the blanks with the appropriate word. The word form ay need changing.

1. It takes a special talent to _____ like a bird.

2. The rescue ship rescued the passengers after their boat _____.

3. Only a _____ would forget to bring his bathing suit to the beach.

4. The leather purse was _____ and soft to the touch.

5. Everyone was laughing and in a _____ mood.

6. The bridge was a _____ of engineering.

7. Our teacher gave us a lot of _____ about our home work assignments.

8. The family suffered _____ until they heard the good news.

9. George's _____ is that of an auto mechanic.

10. Our cat _____ at the other cats when they eyed his dinner.

SALIENT

(SAIL ee unt) *adj.*
prominent; something
that sticks out

Sounds like: **SAIL ANTS**

*"The **SALIENT** feature of **SAIL ANTS** are their large wings."*

- The mast is the **SALIENT** feature of a sailboat.

- The **SALIENT** feature of Dumbo, the elephant, is his large ears.

- The **SALIENT** part of Mrs. Morris' speech was that children should be given more quality time by their parents.

TREK

(trek) *n.*

a journey, or the leg of a journey especially long and difficult

Sounds like: **STAR TREK**

*"In the movie, **STAR TREK**, the star-ship Enterprise was on a **TREK** for new worlds."*

- The caravan slowly **TREKKED** across the mountains until they finally arrived at a large oasis.

- The **TREK** through the waist-deep snow made it difficult for the rescue party to reach the avalanche victims.

- The hikers were happy to finally reach the camp site after the long five hour **TREK** in the 90 degree heat.

FUMBLE

(FUM bul) *v.*

to mishandle something; to feel around awkwardly while searching

Sounds like: **TUMBLE**

*"It's dangerous to **FUMBLE** the ball and take a **TUMBLE**."*

❑ Jane **FUMBLED** through her purse to find her car keys.

❑ The cook **FUMBLED** with the hot plate of food.

❑ The detective **FUMBLED** the crime investigation.

TOPIC

(TOP ik) *v.*

a subject of discussion

Sounds like: **TROPIC**

*"In the **TROPICS** a weatherman's
TOPIC is often hurricanes."*

- Jim's father said worms were not a great **TOPIC** of conversation while they were eating spaghetti.

- The travel agent's **TOPIC** for the evening was Hawaii.

- Vacations are a good **TOPIC** about which to write a school report.

ERODE

(eh RODE) *v.*
to wear away or become worn away;
to eat away

Sounds like: **ROAD**

*"A heavy load can **ERODE** a **ROAD**."*

- ❏ We sat and watched the sand castle **ERODE** as the tide came in.

- ❏ Divorce was the only solution to their **ERODING** relationship.

- ❏ After the storm, the beach **EROSION** became so bad it actually threatened the foundations of many beach homes.

226

STRUT

(strut) *v.*
to walk proudly;a vain;
a pompous way of walking (*n.*)

Sounds like: **MUTT**

*"For a **MUTT**, Fido really can **STRUT**."*

- ❑ The expression of "**STRUT** one's stuff" means to show off as if expecting to impress others.

- ❑ The band leader **STRUTTED** in front of the band.

- ❑ Joan **STRUTTED** about the room trying to draw attention to her new dress.

RAKISH

(RAKE ish) *adj.*
dashing or stylish in manner;
having a streamlined appearance

Sounds like: **RAKE**

*"A **RAKISH RAKE**"*

- Sir William was definitely a **RAKISH** chap and sported around with others of the same class.

- Charles dressed **RAKISHLY**, always in the latest of fashion.

- The designer came up with a **RAKISH** design that we all liked.

METTLE

(MIT ul) *adj.*
courage; vigor and
strength of spirit

Sounds like: **MEDAL**

*"Walter received many **MEDALS** for
his **METTLE** in battle."*

❏ The true **METTLE** of Jim's tennis ability will be tested
in tournament play.

❏ A champion can always be counted on to test his
opponent's **METTLE**.

❏ For all her life's problems, my mother had as much
METTLE as the bravest soldier.

SKIMP

(skimp) *v.*

to be stingy or sparing; to deal with hastily or with poor material

Sounds like: **CHIMP**

*"**CHIMPS** never **SKIMP** on their favorite food."*

- On a tight budget, Martha served a **SKIMPY** meal of fish and rice with no vegetables or fruit.

- Walter always said if you **SKIMP** on non-essentials, you will have more money for the essentials.

- Paul had to concentrate on English, **SKIMPING** study time on history and geography.

ENTRAP

(en TRAP) *v.*

to catch in or as if in a trap

Sounds like: **NAP**

*"When butterflies **NAP**, that's when they are most likely to be **ENTRAPPED**."*

- ❑ The police hoped to **ENTRAP** the robbers if they tried to rob the bank.

- ❑ The prisoners were **ENTRAPPED** in a dungeon with no hope of escape.

- ❑ George was **ENTRAPPED** by a scheme which cost him his life savings.

REVIEW #20: Match the word with its definition.

1. salient - (sail ant)
2. trek - (Star Trek)
3. fumble - (tumble)
4. topic - (tropic)
5. erode - (road)
6. strut - (mutt)
7. rakish - (rake)
8. mettle - (medal)
9. skimp - (chimp)
10. entrap - (trap)

a. drop something
b. to wear away
c. to be stingy
d. dashing manner
e. to catch
f. vain way to walk
g. prominent
h. journey
i. courage
j. subject to discuss

Fill in the blanks with the appropriate word. The word form may need changing.

1. The mast is the _____ feature of a sailboat.

2. Vacations are good _____ about which to write a school report.

3. We sat and watched the sand castle _____ as the tide came in.

4. The band leader _____ in front of the band.

5. The children went on a _____ through the woods.

6. Marta served a _____ meal of rice and beans.

7. The designer gave a _____ design to the new automobile.

8. Jane _____ through her purse to find her car keys.

9. The police hoped to _____ the robbers.

10. My mother has as much _____ as the bravest soldier.

Vocabulary Cartoons

AWE
(aw) *n.*
wonder, respect, fear
Sounds like: SAW

*"Everyone was in **AWE** of Pierre's new **SAW**."*

❑ We were **AWED** by the size of the crowd at the Super Bowl.

❑ The picnic at Sue's house on Saturday was absolutely **AWESOME**.

❑ We were in **AWE** of the music we heard at the concert.

NIMBLE

(NIM bul) *adj.*

quick and light in movement;
clever and quick in thought

Sounds like: **THIMBLE**

*"You must be **NIMBLE** to dance on a **THIMBLE**."*

- Susan **NIMBLY** jumped over the fence to escape the charging horse.

- Our coach has a **NIMBLE** wit and makes jokes to keep the team loose.

- The **NIMBLENESS** of a deer running through the woods is quite impressive.

SOLITUDE

(SOL uh tewd) *n.*
being alone or isolated from others;
a lonely or secluded place

Sounds like: **SOLO DUDE**

*"A **SOLO DUDE** in **SOLITUDE**"*

- Prisoners who cause trouble in prison are often placed in **SOLITARY** confinement.

- The **SOLITUDE** of the mountains made Janet feel closer to nature.

- Jack felt lonely and deserted living in **SOLITUDE** away from others. (Being isolated is being alone or living alone, but **SOLITUDE** emphasizes the feeling of being alone.)

SUMMIT

(SUM it) *n.*
the highest point;
the highest level

Sounds like: **SOME SIT**

*"When mountain climbers reach the **SUMMIT**, **SOME SIT** to enjoy the view."*

- ❏ Reaching the **SUMMIT** of the hills surrounding Reno, Nevada, we could see the city below.

- ❏ When Mr. Chambers became president of MGM Studios, he attained the **SUMMIT** of his ambition.

- ❏ The **SUMMIT** of Babe Ruth's career was the year he hit sixty home runs.

FACADE

(fuh SOD) *n.*

the front of a building; a false appearance
or illusion of something

Sounds like: **FACE ODD**

"The **FACADES** of some buildings appear
to have **ODD FACES**."

- Paris, France is a city famous for having buildings with beautiful architectural **FACADES**.

- The Smith family maintained a **FACADE** of wealth although they were not rich.

- Movie studios build sets of towns that look real but are only the false front of buildings with nothing behind the **FACADES**.

ROBUST

(row BUST) *adj.*
full of health and
strength; vigorous

Sounds like: **ROW A BUS**

*"A **ROBUST** lad **ROWING A BUS**."*

- ❑ Each morning Jimmy's mother prepared a **ROBUST** breakfast of oatmeal and fruit.

- ❑ Weight lifters are usually very **ROBUST** individuals.

- ❑ Jane's flowers grew **ROBUSTLY** because she gave them lots of tender loving care.

OCCUPANT

(OCK ya punt) *n.*
condition of inhabiting;
one who occupies a particular place

Sounds like: **OCTOPUS PANTS**

*"An **OCTOPUS OCCUPYING** his **PANTS**"*

- Robert and Liz Myrtle have been **OCCUPANTS** of their Fifth Avenue apartment for forty years.

- When the police arrived, they demanded to know the name of the **OCCUPANT**.

- Many turtle habitats are **OCCUPIED** by interloper snakes who then become the main **OCCUPANTS**.

FRUITFUL

(FROOT ful) *n.*

producing something in abundance;
good results, beneficial, profitable

Sounds like: **FRUIT FULL**

*"Frank's **FRUIT** truck is **FULL**, and it promises
to be a **FRUITFUL** business."*

- Our meeting was **FRUITFUL**; we figured out how to bake a cake without sugar.

- Sharing an apartment together proved to be very **FRUITFUL**.

- Alexander Graham Bell had a **FRUITFUL** idea; it was the invention of the telephone.

ARMADA

(AHR mah dah) *n.*

a big fleet of warships; also used to mean an overwhelming number of something

Sounds like: **ARM**

*"An **ARMADA** of **ARMS**"*

- The Spanish **ARMADA** was a great naval fleet defeated by the English Navy.

- An **ARMADA** of mosquitoes attacked us as soon as we arrived at the picnic.

- An **ARMADA** of jet skiers was on the river last weekend.

UNRULY

(un ROO lee) *adj.*

difficult or impossible to control;
disobedient

Sounds like: **RULER**

*"An **UNRULY RULER**."*

- Fido was an **UNRULY** dog. If you didn't hold tight to his leash, he would run away.

- Janet's date was **UNRULY**. His hair was uncombed and his clothes were wrinkled.

- **UNRULY** children are generally undisciplined and difficult to control.

awe - (saw)
nimble - (thimble)
solitude - (solo dude)
summit - (some sit)
facade - (face odd)
robust - (row a bus)
occupant - (octopus pants)
fruitful - (fruit full)
armada - (arm)
unruly - (ruler)

a. a building front
b. highest point
c. full of health
d. fleet of ships
e. being alone
f. condition of inhabiting
g. profitable
h. quick and light
i. wonder
j. hard to manage

ill in the blanks with the appropriate word. The word form may need changing.

1. The police arrived at the house and wanted to know the name of the _____.

2. Weight lifters are very _____ individuals.

3. Many buildings on movie sets are just _____.

4. The _____ of Babe Ruth's career was the year he hit sixty home runs.

5. Our coach has a _____ wit and makes jokes with the team.

6. Fido was an _____ dog.

7. We were _____ by the size of the crowd at the stadium.

8. Sharing an apartment together was a _____ idea.

9. The _____ of the mountains made Jane feel close to nature.

10. An _____ of ships appeared on the horizon.

Review Answers

Review #1, page 23
Matching:
1-d
2-a
3-h
4-b
5-i
6-j
7-e
8-f
9-g
10-c

Fill in the Blank:
1-flounder
2-aqueducts
3-goaded
4-abducted
5-cultured
6-inhabit
7-elegant
8-Guerrilla
9-fertile
10-buffoon

Review #2, page 34
Matching:
1-f
2-h
3-a
4-b
5-c
6-d
7-i
8-e
9-g
10-j

Fill in the Blank:
1-drenched
2-encroached
3-horizontal
4-allude
5-fleet
6-vertical
7-bliss
8-parallel
9-pranced
10-smitten

Review #3, page 45
Matching:
1-a
2-f
3-d
4-h
5-b
6-e
7-g
8-c
9-i
10-j

Fill in the Blank:
1-concealing
2-wean
3-climate
4-swelter
5-magnate
6-ruthless
7-shun
8-obsolete
9-despite
10-residents

Review #4, page 56
Matching:
1-a
2-b
3-e
4-d
5-h
6-g
7-j
8-f
9-c
10-i

Fill in the Blank:
1-dread
2-aghast
3-harsh
4-adjacent
5-transpire
6-famines
7-wary
8-qualms
9-shoddy
10-hoax

Review #5, page 67
Matching:
1-g
2-i
3-c
4-j
5-a
6-e
7-d
8-b
9-h
10-f

Fill in the Blank:
1-hypnotized
2-endorse
3-remainder
4-carping
5-afloat
6-outfox
7-enroll
8-ambled
9-dovetail
10-gaped

Review #6, page 78
Matching:
1-i
2-g
3-h
4-f
5-e
6-d
7-c
8-b
9-j
10-a

Fill in the Blank:
1-whimsical
2-scampered
3-wad
4-fervor
5-fowl
6-avert
7-runt
8-succor
9-prevailed
10-zigzagged

Review #7, page 89
Matching:
1-a
2-b
3-c
4-e
5-f
6-g
7-h
8-i
9-j
10-d

Fill in the blank:
1-passive
2-wail
3-agility
4-Catamarans
5-colossal
6-underdogs
7-retrieve
8-innate
9-parapet
10-acclaim

Review #8, page 100
Matching:
1-c
2-e
3-g
4-i
5-f
6-h
7-j
8-d
9-b
10-a

Fill in the Blank:
1-shambles
2-embark
3-spliced
4-quacks
5-zeal
6-fetch
7-inept
8-literate
9-abound
10-prototype

Review #9, page 111
Matching:
1-c
2-e
3-g
4-h
5-j
6-f
7-d
8-i
9-b
10-a

Fill in the Blank:
1-utter
2-porous
3-enamors
4-stifled
5-felon
6-bulletin
7-awry
8-limber
9-perturbs
10-wafted

Review #10, page 122
Matching:
1-d
2-g
3-j
4-h
5-c
6-e
7-b
8-a
9-f
10-i

Fill in the Blank:
1-faltered
2-intuition
3-sleazy
4-adage
5-embedded
6-calamity
7-survive
8-encumbered
9-dismantle
10-obtained

Review #11, page 133
Matching:
1-b
2-c
3-f
4-h
5-e
6-j
7-i
8-a
9-g
10-d

Fill in the Blank:
1-culprit
2-zany
3-jarring
4-diverged
5-burden
6-scowls
7-scurrying
8-divulge
9-rage
10-frenzy

Review #12, page 144
Matching:
1-d
2-a
3-j
4-h
5-i
6-g
7-f
8-e
9-c
10-b

Fill in the Blank:
1-delectable
2-novelty
3-derelict
4-peril
5-raze
6-inert
7-crevice
8-doused
9-lull
10-paltry

Review #13, page 155
Matching:
1-b
2-a
3-c
4-d
5-j
6-i
7-e
8-h
9-f
10-g

Fill in the Blank:
1-turncoat
2-shackle
3-wrenching
4-compile
5-cram
6-detain
7-nourish
8-recite
9-explore
10-futile

Review #14, page 166
Matching:
1-c
2-e
3-a
4-f
5-g
6-d
7-b
8-h
9-j
10-i

Fill in the Blank:
1-vex
2-refrain
3-frugal
4-garbled
5-impaled
6-windfall
7-miniscule
8-throttle
9-waddle
10-detest

Review #15, page 177
Matching:
1-j
2-i
3-h
4-a
5-g
6-b
7-f
8-c
9-e
10-d

Fill in the Blank:
1-commuters
2-rue
3-bilk
4-expedite
5-mar
6-genteel
7-pacify
8-prone
9-wilt
10-plumb

Review #16, page 188
Matching:
1-i
2-h
3-f
4-d
5-a
6-e
7-g
8-j
9-c
10-b

Fill in the Blank:
1-collapse
2-probe
3-Graphs
4-extremity
5-gall
6-hospitable
7-unwieldy
8-tirade
9-income
10-compatible

Review #17, page 199
Matching:
1-j
2-f
3-b
4-i
5-e
6-c
7-a
8-h
9-g
10-d

Fill in the Blank:
1-daze
2-ratify
3-timid
4-ideal
5-fret
6-mentor
7-behooves
8-belittle
9-vast
10-gorge

Review #18, page 210
Matching:
1-f
2-j
3-i
4-h
5-g
6-c
7-a
8-b
9-d
10-e

Fill in the Blank:
1-attract
2-ductile
3-vegetates
4-obscure
5-whet
6-toxic
7-dispute
8-senile
9-collided
10-flee

Review #19, page 221
Matching:
1-d
2-f
3-a
4-g
5-i
6-e
7-b
8-j
9-c
10-h

Fill in the Blank:
1-warble
2-capsized
3-neophyte
4-supple
5-jocular
6-feat
7-latitude
8-anguish
9-vocation
10-glowered

Review #20, page 232
Matching:
1-g
2-h
3-a
4-j
5-b
6-f
7-d
8-i
9-c
10-e

Fill in the Blank:
1-salient
2-topics
3-erode
4-strutted
5-trek
6-skimpy
7-rakish
8-fumbled
9-entrap
10-mettle

Review #21, page 243
Matching:
1-i
2-h
3-e
4-b
5-a
6-c
7-f
8-g
9-d
10-j

Fill in the Blank:
1-occupant
2-robust
3-facades
4-summit
5-nimble
6-unruly
7-awed
8-fruitful
9-solitude
10-armada

Index